# WELCOME TO T

MW00627670

New Science Fiction on Climate Change

0/
R

Also edited by Gordon Van Gelder

*The Best from* Fantasy & Science Fiction: *The 50th Anniversary Anthology* (with Edward L. Ferman) (1999)

*One Lamp: Alternate History Stories from* Fantasy & Science Fiction (2003)

*In Lands That Never Were: Swords & Sorcery Stories from* Fantasy & Science Fiction (2004)

*Fourth Planet from the Sun: Tales of Mars from* Fantasy & Science Fiction (2005)

*The Very Best of* Fantasy & Science Fiction (2009)

# WELCOME TO THE GREENHOUSE

## New Science Fiction on Climate Change

Edited by
**Gordon Van Gelder**

O/R

OR Books, New York

First printing 2011.

Library of Congress Cataloging in Publication Data:
A catalog record for this book is available from the Library of Congress

British Library Cataloging in Publication Data:
A catalog record for this book is available from the British Library

Visit our website at www.orbooks.com

Typeset by Wordstop, Chennai, India

Printed by BookMobile, USA

The printed edition of this book comes on Forest Stewardship Council-certified, 30% recycled paper. The printer, BookMobile, is 100% wind-powered

10 9 8 7 6 5 4 3 2 1

Zoe, this book is for you.

# CONTENTS

# FOREWORD

We live at a time when everyone knows—or should know—the future. A crucial, but often misunderstood fact about global warming is that the climate system runs on a time delay. Thus, from the concentration of greenhouse gases in the air today, it is possible to predict, with a fair degree of certainty, what average global temperatures will be like thirty or forty years from now. Ditto for sea levels and ice cover. Climate scientists refer to this as our "commitment to warming." We're committed to warming long before we actually experience it.

How to represent this future that we are already committed to? Climate modelers tend to rely on charts and graphs to get the message across. The contributors to this volume offer something else—stories. The characters in these stories are made up and the situations invented. The events haven't happened and, in a strict sense, never will. But the science behind these tales is all too real. (The true "science fiction" of our time, peddled on talk radio and in the halls of Congress, is that global warming is a myth.)

At the same time, there is a lot about global warming that we don't know. As the planet heats up, almost certainly some regions will experience more intense droughts, but which regions, exactly, and how intense will those droughts be? Monsoon patterns will shift, and produce flooding, but which cities will be submerged? Will new heat-resistant crops be developed, and new technologies invented to transport, like floating highways? The greatest unknown of all is, of course, how people, collectively, will respond. Will they be chastened? Genocidal? Or will they just muddle along, behind growing seawalls and shrinking coasts? Science—even social science—can't answer questions like this, which is why we turn to science fiction. Welcome to the Greenhouse!

—Elizabeth Kolbert

# INTRODUCTION

"This month, negotiators will meet in Cancún for another round of international climate talks, and it's a safe bet that, apart from the usual expressions of despair, nothing will come of them. It may seem that we'll just keep going around and around on climate change forever. Unfortunately, that's not the case: one day, perhaps not very long from now, the situation will spin out of our control."
—Elizabeth Kolbert, *The New Yorker*, 22 November 2010

I am, I readily admit, something of a contrarian. It's probably the result of having had a scientist for a father. Whatever the reason, if you present to me a truth that is universally acknowledged, I'll question it instinctively.

I've largely sat on the sidelines during the global warming controversies that have raged over the past decade. Do I think Earth's climate is warming? Yes. Do I know what the causes are? Can't say for certain that I do. In fact, I don't think anyone can say for certain that they know.

I suspect my position is a fairly common one.

However, as Elizabeth Kolbert points out, that sort of complacent attitude is likely to lead to chaos. Consequently, I asked a number of writers who speculate on the future to consider the subject of climate change. What might life be like in five, fifty, or five hundred years?

The results make for rewarding reading. In assembling the book, I tried to get a wide variety of responses to the issue of climate change, from the comic to the grave (one contributor told me, "I can't find anything optimistic about global warming"), from the hopeful to the despondent, from the realistic to the wildly imaginative. A couple of stories seek answers to the climate change issues that we face, but more of the stories ask questions.

Overall, I wanted stories that make the reader consider what sorts of futures might await us. They might not all be futures we like, but I think they're all worth considering.

—Gordon Van Gelder
Jersey City, December 2010

# BENKOELEN

Brian W. Aldiss

Yes, that's how I knew the place. Whether it or I still exist, it has to be Benkoelen. There it is or was, an isolated stone peg in the middle of the ocean, a round rocky desolation, no beaches, fifty miles from the southwest coast of Sumatra. No place like it anywhere on the planet.

You never heard of Benkoelen? My life has always been linked to it. My father, rather late in life, married a Sumatran-Chinese lady by the name of Trilm Ma. Between them, they devised a helicopter pad here which for some years served as a single physical communication link between the island and the mainland port of Padang. Padang was ruined by recent tsunamis. But my first sight of Benkoelen was in a photograph taken by Stan, my father. The view showed a bleak and steep stairway ascending from a no less bleak quayside. Why this drab depiction could have captured my imagination I cannot say, but so it was.

Benkoelen was deserted in those days, before the heat really struck. Its earliest inhabitants had built monumentally, setting up large windowless buildings. Then it seems they left. Who they were we'll never know. The island was empty again—apart from sparse wildlife.

Oh, I have to tell it. This was before the thronging people of the world could grasp the inescapable fact of global warming. Bainya Hosta de l'Affiche Salle, she, blue of eyelid, red of lip, gold of skin, petulant, prideful, passionate, bought Benkoelen from the Indonesian Republic . . . . But why go over all that again?

As the oceans of the world began to heave their mighty shoulders, so it seemed that a generation of hermits came to inhabit places that had hitherto been regarded as uninhabitable. Many another island sank forever beneath the waves, many a coastline was consumed. Benkoelen remained, seeming to stand proud above the storms like a bundle of fossilized corks.


I was sitting halfway up the west cliff, too out of breath to go further for a while. I had lost all my kit. Since the tsunami, the regular tourist run from Padang had ceased. I hired a flimsy motorized boat from Solingal on the mainland. It had capsized as we approached the bulk of Benkoelen. The waves were steady, relentless; we had been saved by the so-called fish-people, coming out to us in canoes. My briefcase and all my tackle were at the bottom of the ocean by now. But still I lived and breathed. Although I looked like a drowned rat.

This geological monument stood like a sentry box perched on the edge of the Mentawoi Trench. Seabirds screamed with excitement over it. Their cries had puzzled me as a child. My father, teasing, laughing, had said they were the souls of babies waiting to be born. Later, he told me the truth. They were only the cries of birds. He had no wish to mislead me.

In his young days, he had been a priest. But he found he could not improve the ways of people. Being on Benkoelen was a form of self-exile. There were no humans on Benkoelen. Nothing of the greed or the comfort of the West.

At last I got myself on my way, driven by the gloomy news I had to deliver to my sister. I had only myself to blame, had come all the way from Cairo just to speak to Cass.

That bent, barbarous Bainya—how did she get into the picture?

I had been drinking in a Medan hotel bar. Bainya's photo was there, curled around the edges. She was looking for contributions to help establish support for her new Chimp Center. Steep Street, Benkoelen. She looked good, vile, delicious. We became lovers. I lived with her in her palace in Cairo. Although the affair could not last, I still had a stake in the island.

Oh well, so the world was... nothing if not complex.... Greed, money, ambition—we had made it too complex to live in in peace...

The morning over Benkoelen was rough. Great blasts of rain, thunder, lightning. Nothing unusual. The Sumatrans were spooked by such weather; no aircraft were aloft. Soon enough, there that isolated chimney of rock was, Benkoelen, braving the wine-dark Indian Ocean, scene of my childhood and my love life—and my sister's project. Now, without any instruments, I looked for Steep Street, as if there were a street on the island that was not steep.

Rain came thrashing down. I went marching upward, against the stream. Crude edifices on either side gave no sign of life. But wait!—a light showed in a grim window, offering shelter. I pounded on the door. A long wait before it opened.

"It's raining. Come on in."

Although there was no welcome in the voice, the words were welcome enough. A bowed figure stood back to let me pass. We moved into a small room furnished by a table and two wooden chairs. A lantern standing on the table illuminated a muddle of papers there.

"I shall find you a towel. I have precious items here I do not want ruined."

My host was pale and whiskery, a slip of a man, drifting like a leaf toward old age.

"You're soaked. I'll get you something to drink, too," he said.

He left the room, that seedy little room, without an ounce of comfort in it and a window looking out on barren rock. A wicker cage stood on a shelf, a silent and motionless bird within it.

My reluctant host returned with a bottle and two glasses, all the while keeping an eye on me.

He placed the bottle carefully on the table.

"It's Metaxa. The Greeks are selling it off cheap."

As he half-filled the two glasses, he continued to talk, "It's yet another proof of my theory. The human race developed from the apes, with spurts of quality here and there but never enough. Never sufficient real wisdom. Just herd things. The family. . . Take most kinds of sport—soccer, boxing, cricket, baseball, and the rest, all encouraging violence, applauding it—they are children's games. True, intellectuals do crop up, but the ordinary people hate intellectuals."

I was working on the Metaxa.

"And intellectuals have no wish to govern, knowing that the crowd they have to govern are incorrigible. And now this ecological disaster. We saw it coming. We were warned. Scientists warned us. We didn't do anything until it was too late. I doubt we'll live through it."

Both of us drank in silence.

"Patrick White!" the older man burst out suddenly. "A great writer, wouldn't you say? Deep understanding of human folly."

"I don't know the name."

"You don't know the name of Patrick White?" He was astonished or feigned astonishment. "Patrick was a friend, stayed here one time." He stared at me, summing me up. "Well, there you are! Patrick is dead now, of course. Great writer—already forgotten. . . Some men never read. Not properly."

"As a kid, I read a lot," I told him. "I liked the mysteries of Erle Stanley Gardner. As a man—well, I got better things to do."

"Mysteries. . ."

To break a rather strained silence, I said I must be on my way. I was going to the Chimp Center.

My host appeared suddenly alert.

"You look to be in a bad way, if you don't mind my saying so. You can stay here for the night. I can cook some fish. I've got some fish. There's only one bedroom, but you can sleep in with me."

Avoiding his gaze, I said I had to be on my way. I said I had an appointment—in fact, with my sister. He shrugged.

"You must please yourself." Spoken in tones of disgust.

He said he had a map. It was difficult to get to the Chimp Center without one. He looked vexed as he thumbed the cork back into the Metaxa bottle.

There I stood, impatient to be away, running a fingernail down one of the seams of the table. A woodlouse came running from its place of refuge. It was small, sand-colored. I looked more closely. Several of the little insects now emerged, as if in answer to a general alarm.

I had never thought much of the creatures. Now with sudden compassion I realized they would all be swept away when Benkoelen yielded to the onslaught of the high seas.

The Patrick White scholar and I bade each other goodbye.


A hot muggy wind was blowing, dying, blowing again. Although I could not see the ocean from the refuge in a valley, I could hear a kind of cannonade of waves against the tower, and each blow against the tower I felt through the soles of my boots.

Climbing over fallen rock—rock patched by dark mosses—was necessary until I reached a track where the going was easier. There I came across a length of sturdy driftwood to assist me. My climb across piles of boulders became easier.

I gained a wide and open platform, on the far side of which was a glimpse of the green tops of trees. A rare sight on Benkoelen. It was, I thought, my first sight of the Chimp Center. My anxieties awoke again.

In part, memory came back to taunt me. I had a photo back in Cairo of my father standing on this very spot, smiling his lazy friendly smile. The dear old boy had led a more fruitful life than I; if only I could be granted another ten years. . .

Meanwhile, a distraction to one side, where a small cliff was covered by a curtain of what I took to be a kind of ivy—until part of it flew off. Intrigued, I moved closer. The cliff was covered with a kind of bird with wings more resembling a split shell than an ordinary wing of feathers.

The birds were packed so tightly they resembled a curtain. Claws were their thing, being long and thin but powerful. The claws, not the wings; the changing climate had rendered the mainland too distant, too difficult, to reach. One or two birds took flight, flying about me to scare me off.

The claws threatening my head had recently speared a wriggling thing resembling a shelled uncooked shrimp. So that was what the birds were at—bug-hunting, probing the stones, eating the maggots hidden there.

Of course I recognized the bird. It was a so-called Benkoelen bullfinch, such as I had seen caged in the hermit's house.

This one was coming too close. I managed to knock it away. The creature gave a shrill squawk of surprise.

As luck would have it, the turn I made to strike the bird gave me sight of a man, some meters distant, approaching me with every sign of stealth and a cudgel in his left hand. I stood up straight to him, holding my stick ready, but without exhibiting any particular signs of threat.

The stalker stopped stalking. Without lowering his weapon, he stared and shouted something at me.

"I don't understand. Who are you?" I asked. I could see he was one of the type of fisher-folk who had saved me from the ocean.

His answer was incomprehensible.

He made a rush at me, swinging his stick at my skull. Dropping on one knee, I gave a mighty swipe to his shins as he charged past. He fell.

Before he could rise, some bullfinches forsook the wall and flew at my opponent. Their long cruel beaks sought for his eyes. They were old enemies. He hauled himself to his feet. I caught a whiff of fish as he departed. The bullfinches went squawking back to their wall, taking no notice of me.

I headed for where the tops of the green trees showed, while I could not help but meditate on the episode just past. No doubt the Benkoelen bullfinches had suffered the depredations of the fisher-folk and fought to defend themselves; but why two strangers should attack each other was another matter. Overpopulation must take some blame. And if two strangers then why not two nations? And two nations or an alliance against another alliance, why, then, all things necessary for climate change were in preparation: machinery, armament, tanks, missiles, nuclear weapons, huge expenditures of oil and coal. . . I was sickened by my own reasoning.

Yet I still clutched my club. . . It seemed only reasonable.


Where the flat stretch ended was a cliff. I stood there looking down at the crowns of a number of trees: in fact, a small forest. Of course an imported forest. There were creatures in the trees, swinging from bough to bough. I remembered that the orangutan was the only ape which remained arboreal throughout life. How wise they were not to come down. . . And they were safe here: practically extinct on the mainland.

Well, "safe"? I feared that the knowledge I had to deliver meant that they were doomed.


The strange geology of Benkoelen allowed me to find something resembling a stairway down into the forest; soon I was walking among the entangled trunks, where often the branches of one tree embraced the branches of the next.

As I pressed on through the entanglement, the odd nut landed on my head, accompanied by scuttlings from above and sounds resembling human laughter. I came unharmed to a clearing. A notice stood there: ORANGUTAN CONSERVATION CENTRE PROP. CASS PHILLIMORE.

"Salaam Aleikum," came a lazy voice. A young man was sitting by the doorway of a house built in a clearing, to which were attached cages of wire netting.

I returned the youngster's greeting. He sat there unmoving, looking to my mind half in a dream. Passing him, I went into the house, calling Cass' name. She emerged from a kind of office, mopping her eyes.

"Oh, hello, Coyne. Dum Dum has died." She retreated into the room from which she had emerged, and I followed. On the table by the window was a cushion and on the cushion lay the body of a small orang-utan. Cass began to snivel again. "She was just playing and she fell out of a tree. My vet quit last week. I've done what I could. Dum Dum was my special darling, poor little pet."

She began to weep compulsively. I put my arm about her shoulders, but she shook it away, rejecting any attempts to comfort her.

I might have been a stranger. Indeed, I was.


"You'll have to bury her now, Cass. In this heat, she'll soon begin to stink."

She showed her reddened face to me. "Oh, go away! Do you think I don't know that?"

"A typical welcome. I'll be in the next room while you calm down a bit. I'm afraid I have some rather dire news for you."

"Oh god, I don't wish to hear about the outside world. It's so full of misery."

"That's not so." But said wearily, knowing what had to come.

I found a Michelob in the fridge, and sat in a rattan chair to consider that it might not prove so easy to break my news to my sister, as I had imagined; but I had volunteered just for the sake of seeing Benkoelen for what I believed would be the last time.

Switching on an old-fashioned TV, I listened to an announcer, possibly speaking from Jakarta, announcing that China had invaded South Korea. Indonesia had bombed Australia, in return for Australia's strike against the blowing up of terrorists from Surabaja. Cass came into the room and switched the screen off.

She entered the room in a controlled way, still clutching a handkerchief, and with the dead baby orang-utan clutched to her breast. "I'm surprised to see you. Why didn't you call me first?"

She wore a rough overall with an apron over. Her hair was ragged and untended. She had aged—by which token I saw that I had aged myself.

I stood up, to speak to her nonchalantly, gesturing dismissively, as if what I said was of no importance.

"I had to hire a boat to get over. Benkoelen will soon be cut off entirely. The damned boat overturned and sank at once. All my kit is now down on the seabed. I'm lucky not to be there myself."

She made a gesture, simultaneously raising her eyebrows and shaking her head. "And you're still with Bainya Hosta?"

"With her? I work for her, yes."

"She kicked you out?"

"She has serial lovers. Not so many now as once she did. Look, Cass, this is really none of your business. Remember it was through my affair with Bainya you got this job. You've been here a good long while but now it's over. There's some bad news for you. It's not personal, as you may think. It's just the way the world is with this bloody climate change."

"Oh yes? Bainya's coming to live here. One more baboon. . ."

"Never mind the cheap sarcasm, dear. You know Bainya was briefly married to the richest man in the Middle East? Most of that money has gone on good causes. Causes such as this one. That's all over now.

The climate is tearing everything apart. Various funded enterprises are having to close. It has now become necessary to close down the chimp sanctuary. Funding must close last day September next."

I pulled from my pocket the official form, rumpled, still slightly damp.

She took it and dropped it without looking at it. She sat down.

"Where will we all go?" Asked in a small voice.

"You will be permitted to take six orangs of both sexes to captivity in the Jakarta Zoo. Rest of the animals remain here."

"They'll die."

"They'll have to take a chance. Like the rest of us. . ."

She asked me to come and see the creatures. She praised their innocence, their playfulness. I said I did not wish to see them. I just wanted to drink.

She stood by the window, face in shadow, hugging the dead baby. "What chance have they got?"

I said quite calmly, "That's the question we're all asking."

# DAMNED WHEN YOU DO

Jeff Carlson

It was not a virgin birth, I can tell you that much. The boy never could fly or stop bullets with his teeth, and those people who say he was twenty feet tall are full of it. He didn't have God on the phone, either. I guess I'm not the one to say he wasn't Jesus come again, but if he was, the Book's got everything mixed.

There were signs before his birth. We had tremors, then record heat waves and drought and flood and drought again. Margie and me didn't think anything about it. The world was already going to hell in a handbasket. Every disaster was just business as usual—earthquakes in China, nukes in Iran, war, poverty, and hundreds of millions of people pumping carbon whatever into the sky, everybody knowing it was causing global warming but not changing their routines a bit.

I was one of them.

In the documentaries, they always show L.A. freeways and New York taxi jams. My neighbors had a great time complaining how the crops and grazing were hard hit by out-of-season storms and dry spells, which they blamed on pollution caused by the same city people who needed our farms, but no one can say Jack Shofield isn't honest. I accept my share of it. It doesn't matter that all of southern Oklahoma has fewer people in it than downtown Hollywood or that I typically saw no more than five or six other trucks on my way to the feed shop. Poison is poison. Like everyone, I just wanted to get about my business ASAP.

I'm no preacher and I think we've all heard all we need about sin, destruction, and salvation. I just want to set the record straight.

He was my son.

People called him everything from Savior to Satan in every language known to man. We named him Albert Timothy after his grandfathers. Margie and me are old-fashioned enough to believe in things like honor and respect, and we would have taught him so if we'd had the chance. But we only met him twice.

It's true in a literal sense that the world revolved around him. I think the real miracle lies in the fact that *people* revolved around him. From the news at the time, you wouldn't have thought there were twelve decent folk left anywhere, and yet he grew to be strong, caring, and smart despite having every last one of six billion selfish apes as parents.

Margie's a tough girl. That's why I married her. She didn't scream until our baby was all the way out of her. The doctor yelled, too. I thought the boy must have three arms or something, so I shoved a nurse to get a look at him. He was already tumbling toward the door like a little pink log. Then the first quakes knocked the building down. I was thrown to the floor, and I never did catch up.

How did our infant son survive? Utter strangers fed and changed him as he passed. Folks kept him warm with the clothes off their backs. They emptied their wallets to get bottles and formula when store owners didn't put those things in their hands for free. After a few days, entire nations prepared for him even when his projected course was nowhere near, because the projections weren't worth much. He usually rolled east to west, opposite of Earth's natural rotation as if pushing the planet beneath him, but for the first few years he wobbled north and south seemingly at random—and when he learned to walk, he jaunted from pole to pole as he chose.

There's been a lot of talk from scientists, holy men, and politicians. Believe what you want. The truth is nobody can explain him and nobody ever will. The proportion's all wrong. It's flat-out scary, in fact, like a flea spinning a ball the size and weight of Australia.

Clocks and calendars quickly became useless. One day would pass in twenty hours, the next in twenty-eight or seventeen. Seasons changed in a matter of weeks.

There was just no way to ignore him.

Wars stopped as he went by. Starving tribes in West Africa mashed their last handfuls of grain into mush for him.

Why didn't he bruise to death? Microgravitational skins, they said. Angels, they said. Before he was old enough to control it, some instinct or higher power wove him around buildings and cliffs and trees. Later in life, he walked the globe like a man on a spherical treadmill. When he was just four months old he got stuck in a box canyon in Peru and the whole world shuddered for three hours until a brave rancher went in on hands and knees and shoved him in the right direction.

You'd think he would've had trouble keeping food down, rolling, always rolling, but eventually some big brain proved he was actually orbiting the sun as smooth as silk while it was the planet itself that did the shifting up and back and sideways beneath him.

And the oceans? Rivers and lakes? He walked on water. As a baby he returned to shore hungry and stinking, wailing because no one had fed or changed him. Later, as a child, he went hog-wild playing with dolphins and seals—and in the end, his only refuge was the sea.

Of course he had monstrous effects on the weather, tides, fault lines, and volcanoes. It's impossible to guess how many deaths he caused directly. Yesterday I heard a newsman say upward of twenty million. More than a few people tried to kill him right off the bat, but twice as many protected him. He took a razor in the shoulder somewhere in Burma. A man shot him in the guts outside Madrid. Five doctors across Spain saved his life that time, and dozens more around the world contributed to the treatment.

He had an obvious way of pulling people together.


For us, it started badly. Albert broke Margie's heart before she even really saw him. Leaving his mother so fast, well, Margie never did recover.

She spent her days following him on the news. Pretty soon we had a TV and a computer in every room, not that she moved much off the couch. She kept saying she hurt even after Doc Hanley pronounced her fit.

People sent us things—money and things—mostly expecting us to keep these donations but plenty more of them looking for a blessing. We were easier to track down than our boy and easier to reach because the crowd around us was smaller.

Some ladies wanted me. I doubt I had much to do with what made Albert different, and that's a good thing. Can you imagine what the world would have done with two such boys?

Suddenly we were richer than we'd ever expected. I hated it—all the attention that came with it. We gave most of the money to charity, but that only seemed to brighten the media spotlight and triple the contributions coming in.

I had to quit my job at the feed shop. None of the reporters or those so-called holy pilgrims ever bought any feed or tack. They just got in the way and stole small items for souvenirs. By the end of the first week, you couldn't find a pen to save your life. They'd taken every one. We had to calculate weights and costs in our heads. It made the bookkeeper crazy, so I quit before my boss had to ask, which left me with nothing to do but hole up in our trailer with poor Margie as she talked to her TVs and computers. I don't mean she talked to them the way those things are like phones now. I mean she just laughed and chattered to herself as faces and maps flashed on the screens. Sometimes she cried, too, always when there was footage of mothers trying to touch their babies against him or when the Army lost track of him. None of those billion-dollar satellites were much good in the beginning because the cloud cover got too thick.

Our boy never saw the sun or any real kind of sky until he was five. People say he backpedaled like crazy just so he could stare up at the clear patch for an instant.

Nothing else surprised him. He knew everything about the human condition before he took his first step, which didn't happen until he was three and a half. Some folks had the nerve to call him slow, but I'd like to see those full-grown fools stay on their feet if the world spun beneath them. He was fluent in more languages than you've got fingers and toes, comfortable in twice as many cultures and always learning. He personally witnessed more geology and biology and all the other ologies than a football stadium packed with teachers.

Margie and me learned with him on the TV. So did billions of others. And we all saw too much to be ashamed of.

No one could say hate, stupidity, and greed were new. The effects of such things had been in the papers our whole lives, but everybody said this baby made it personal for them.

Hundreds of thousands of people tried to walk with him. Huge migrations rushed from the east side of every continent to the west end, then charged back again to wait for his next arrival. Knowing where he'd come ashore was a challenge in the early days, but crowds formed thirty deep along hundreds of miles of coastline just hoping he'd land near them.

What else did they have to do while they were waiting except talk and make friends? Even during the migrations, most of them never got anywhere near the boy. In fact, sometimes ten thousand people got detached from the rest and paraded off on their own, never knowing and never worried that they were without their messiah. Just walking together was enough.

Maybe I should have been among them. It might have helped Albert and me. For years I puttered around our small trailer feeling like an empty sack because he was so far outside my reach. When he was two, he passed within a mile of our place, but that only hurt more. All of Lincoln County was buried in strangers, helicopters, hot dog vendors, and the whole shebang. The dozens of times he touched through Oklahoma's borders felt almost as bad. I'd never been helpless before.

More than one corporation wanted to fly me into Albert's path, but they wanted me to dress up in logos for corn chips or vacuum cleaners. That didn't seem right. And I was afraid. Taking care of Margie helped fill the hollowness in me, but I was not a well man. Like millions of others, I had the nerve to envy him for being so powerful. Somehow we all forgot he'd never use the lavish homes he'd been given by every government in the world. Roofs and walls were a danger to him. The elaborate playgrounds they built with train tracks and water slides, well, he would never play with any toy he couldn't carry. He never had any friends, either. I guess he had favorites everywhere and constantly tried to reach them, but more often than not he was blocked or distracted by new people with new problems. He was never alone, not even going to the bathroom. People actually fought over his leavings as keepsakes no matter how often he admonished them with a laugh and the promise to generate more.

Times like those, it was easy to remember Albert was just a kid. Eight-year-olds shouldn't rule the world.

That was how old he was when we first met him. We knew he was headed in our direction, of course. There were still some shows on the air that had nothing to do with Albert or the changes he was making, but all of them dedicated at least a small window to his progress so they could keep their viewers from surfing off. Margie was watching her dramas, silly romantic stuff I'd encouraged her to indulge in because it had nothing to do with our boy. I figured that was healthy.

Then she screamed and I burned myself rushing out of the kitchen. "What! What is it?"

She could only point at the TV.

"He's coming straight at us," I said, stupidly, but the thought was too big to keep in my head. "Straight at us."

It wasn't until then that the growing din outside made sense. Margie and me didn't bother much with the outside anymore, and I'd figured the noise for another of the concerts or revivals always going on in town. When I pulled the drapes open, I yanked them shut again like a joker in one of her shows.

There was a stampede of people more than a mile wide bearing down on our trailer. At its head was our son—and the news vans. The dust cloud looked like a cape on a giant worm.

"Get up," I said.

Margie was trying to scream again but couldn't breathe. She seemed like she was trying to look at me, too, but she couldn't pull her eyes away from the TV.

"Honey, please." I took her arm as gently as I could with all that adrenaline in my veins. "Get up. If you want to talk to your son, you'll have to get out there and move. Does this shirt match my good tie?"


Those same small-minded people who'd tut-tutted about how slow he'd been to walk were also free with their opinions about a boy who never visited his parents, but you have to remember, he didn't know us and he wasn't used to thinking of any one place as being more special than the next. Also, the crowd was always in the way.

You couldn't have blamed Albert if Margie disappointed him. She slobbered and screamed and pawed. Embarrassment made my body so heavy I could barely keep up, but his smile was a mystery just like in that Lisa painting.

His smile was patient and knowing. He seemed to understand everything about Margie's pain and he was not afraid. We'd learned all about his empathy and genuine interest in people from the TV, but now that magic was real. It was hypnotizing.

"Walk with me," he said. We were already trudging alongside him, and his followers made sense of his invitation before we did. They backed off to give us some privacy.

Albert was much leaner than he appeared on TV. Up close, his robes couldn't hide the fact that he was all angles and elbows. He was beautiful. He had Margie's black hair and dark eyes. He also had a ridiculous walk like a kangaroo crossed with a drunk, bouncing, skipping, letting the earth zip by in between each step. Otherwise we never would have been able to keep up. Nobody understood yet what it meant that he'd developed this level of control.

"I love you," he said, and Margie screamed some more. His eyes locked with mine. "I'm sorry I haven't visited before."

"It's okay, son."

He smiled again, more of a grin this time like you'd expect on a boy. "I need some fatherly advice," he said.

"From me?"

He just grinned. I remember it perfectly; the gritty taste of the dust and rumbling crowd behind us; sunlight flashing on the camera lenses; his calm, strong words.

For whatever it's worth, so help me, I said his idea sounded mighty fine.


It took Albert most of a year because he started out careful, dodging back and forth across the equator, slowing the planet's rotation in unsteady spurts, forgoing meals and sleep to keep a schedule that only he knew. He riled up a storm unlike anyone had ever seen, a "strato"- something way at the top of the sky. Fortunately, during his first years every landmass in the world had shaken out at least a hundred years' worth of quakes. There were some small tidal waves and one big fault opened up in India, but all in all it wasn't bad.

The scientists lost a lot of weather balloons and robot planes trying to prove that he couldn't be doing what he was doing. For the next eighteen months, we had wicked beautiful sunsets in the States but not much sun. I was surprised at how little panic there was. He'd explained what he was doing and people believed him. People thanked him everywhere.

At that point we'd only had a taste of the future we'd created, damning our grandchildren, but one taste was plenty. For ten years we'd seen scorching summers and short, late winters. Fire ants had spread so far north they'd reached Idaho. New diseases were everywhere. Most of Africa was baked sterile and other rainless hot spots had cropped up across Asia and California. Beachside cities and in some places whole countries were seeping under the rising oceans. . .

Somehow he shook all the gases and carbon whatever out of the atmosphere.

At the same time, he was also talking up a storm. Albert was in a unique position to change things. People loved or feared him, but he always had everyone's attention.

Because he talked with everyone, he knew everything about those few who hid from him. He personally visited the fat cats who'd been sitting on clean technology because their fortunes came from dirty energy. He visited them again and again with the eyes of global television staring over his shoulder. "You've already got more money than you know what to do with," he said. It was practically that simple. Albert started things going and the new economies proved stronger than the old. Hydro-what's-it engines aren't any faster than oil-driven, but they don't pollute, which saved billions of dollars in health and cleanup costs. That didn't happen overnight, but the benefits were as obvious and dizzying as a stack of presents under a Christmas tree.

He visited warlords and dictators, too, especially the Chinese leaders, probably because they controlled so much land and so many people that he couldn't avoid their policies for more than a day at a time. Albert even brought several of these hard men with him around the globe, pushing them in heavy-duty wheelchairs he'd had designed for exactly this purpose. We don't know what they talked about, but he showed them a borderless world. He showed them their real size.

Meanwhile the weather in Oklahoma had become like I remembered it as a boy. It was steady and predictable. We sent our crop surpluses to places where they couldn't shake their trouble, countries where civil war or famine had held sway for generations.

There were some things he couldn't fix. Africa had reached the peak of its AIDS plague and something like seven out of every ten people were dying or seriously ill. Murderers and rapists still walked among us. Several endangered species had dwindled to such small numbers that they were doomed regardless of any new rescue effort, no matter how well funded or stocked with volunteers.

None of that ruined the sense of hope and cooperation sweeping the planet. Some people said he was an incarnation of Earth itself sent to scare us into taking responsibility before it was too late, but Albert didn't want to be worshipped. He just wanted to stop seeing so much pain.

He hadn't quite turned eleven yet when he took on that crazy bastard up north.


Empathy and trust are not universal traits. Albert taught us that we were poorer because of it. He taught us to pity, but he also believed in taking action.

That madman in Korea had ruled his miserable half-frozen hunk of land for twenty years, building nukes, selling nukes, starving his own people so he could put more money into the walls and guns that kept them in and everyone else out.

Albert attempted to meet with this man for years but was rebuffed.

He sent messages and was met with silence. At last he issued commands. More silence.

He stopped the world. Albert put that bastard's territory in eternal darkness even as he managed to bring sunshine to neighboring countries on a regular basis. It must have felt like God himself had cursed them.

Weeks passed and our son exhausted himself, only catnapping, taking a bite or two when folks pleaded with him. It seemed to be working. The TV and the net were abuzz with praise from the leaders of the world, issuing the madman terms, promising relief to his beleaguered people. But that sick bastard had hunkered down in his luxurious shelters more than once before. He must have been used to the dark. I think it was pride that drove him to such extremes.

They call it ABC war: atomic, biological, chemical. The missiles were duds that got no further than Hawaii and often went wide or fell short into Japan, but the madman's agents had spread worldwide with three low-grade fission devices and more vials and test tubes than anyone could count.

Albert tried to keep the airborne diseases from spreading. He ran for days, stumbling, cutting his leg on the Himalayas, twisting an ankle in the Amazon delta.

It just wasn't enough.

Three days of massive retaliation from the U.S. and Britain demanded even more effort from our son or else another hundred million souls might have been killed by fallout.

Revenge was no consolation to Albert or to the billions of wounded survivors. He was stoned in the Philippines and shot at twice in New York, two areas that had taken the brunt of it. Albert renounced his political agenda and every good work he'd done in a terrified, sobbing message that was almost lost in the chorus of outrage.

He retreated to the oceans and the cold night-side of the planet. He denied himself sunshine and human companionship for two years, running whenever planes and ships came after him. There were sightings during this self-exile, some of which must have been real. Many more were surely hoaxes and lies like that woman in South Dakota and those German cults. He wouldn't have visited landlocked areas.

I still have nightmares for my son. The loneliness he must have experienced isn't something I can put into words.

Albert snuck across the narrowest stretches of Central America, picked his way through the densely laid islands of Malaysia, and sprinted across Africa, but the chance of running into people on that broad continent was frequently too much for him. Most days the world shifted wildly as he ran south around Africa's horn.

What he ate, we don't know. Fish, I guess. Bugs and fruit. He needed fresh water, too, like any human being. Maybe he conjured it up from the sea somehow. I think too often he did without.

Hiding for seven hundred days would have been a sad existence for any boy, but it must have been a form of death for someone whose only home had been the crowd. Finally he tried to come back. He was smart enough to pull off the trick of resurrection, but I guess we were too dumb to let him.


Many people had yet to lose hold of their grieving. A hundred million lives was a heavy price to pay to get some sense knocked into us, but in a lot of ways the world was much improved. The big war had put a stop to border conflicts and most ethnic strife. Africa was still suffering its AIDS die-off, and China wasn't having a smooth time with its new Cultural Revolution, but we had clean industry and transportation. The global economy was roaring like crazy. There were also quite a few less people to share this wealth, although we were well into a worldwide baby boom.

Even Margie and me were trying. At least she thought we were. I'd had myself a vasectomy years before, paying thirty times the regular fee to buy the doctor's silence.

Margie was doing better. Her TVs and computers weren't exactly dusty but now she only spent an hour or two following her dramas. After the war, she'd found the chance to mother someone at last. We spent our fortune on an orphanage/soup kitchen and she became a part of more lives than I could count. Somehow she always knew their first names. She often came home humming.

I was doing better, too. I had a job again, good, hard, paying work at a dairy farm on top of helping out around the soup kitchen. The labor shortage was so bad there was even room for Albert's father. The cows didn't care who I was and I pulled overtime without complaining. It even got to a point where my boss would offer me a beer at the end of the day and we'd talk some, no big questions or personal stuff, though he must have been tempted. I was an ordinary joe again and I liked that just fine.

Everything changed when Albert came ashore near Washington.

It's important to know why Margie acted the way she did. The reporters and the crazies ate up our small lives again. Having everything taken from her a second time, having her new life destroyed—they shoved her right off the fine edge she'd been walking. Suddenly we were right back in our cage. She couldn't call her friends because our lines were jammed. Even her TV shows were canceled for Albert Albert Albert. There was nothing to do but worry. A body can only sleep so many hours and it was impossible to go about any kind of business without fighting off fifty shouting maniacs. On the third day she tried baking pies but burst into tears when she spilled a cup of sugar. I put my arms around her and kissed her neck, but she pushed me away like she never wanted to be touched again. She retreated to her couch and stayed there playing old movies.

Albert was wicked pale on TV, taller and skinnier now. He was practically wasted away—but it wasn't food that brought him back.

He begged for an audience with the president as he was swarmed by passersby. A few hugged him, rejoicing that their messiah had returned. Others pelted him with soda bottles and hunks of asphalt.

Amateur video shows him bleeding from his head but never using his awesome powers to knock down the people assaulting him.

He was small for a thirteen-year-old, stunted by malnutrition. He was obviously sick, too, with spots of fever burning through that fish-pale skin. How sick, nobody knew.

The president granted Albert's request. I don't suppose it matters that the boy's attitude was submissive or that he looked so fragile and lost. You can't say no to someone who's stopped the sun dead overhead.

Albert had an idea how he could make amends.


Not every desert can bloom. Albert explained it like this: Energy flows in patterns rather than existing as a blanket. Snow and sand, grassland and jungle, all of these things balance each other, but he thought he could improve on nature's work and turn every inch of the planet into a garden. The politicians agreed. No doubt they hoped to take credit for it.

He tried. Oh, how he tried, leaping valleys, fighting swamps, always running and running and running. He didn't have anything else, you see, and his spectacular plan did seem to be slowly coming true. Maintaining this delicate new balance would have become his life's work.

Unfortunately he'd picked up the HIV virus somewhere and he had scurvy and other vitamin deficiencies. Worse, people kicked at him or threw things as he passed. It was like some awful game of global whipping boy. He was a reminder of the war, an easy scapegoat, plus there were plenty of folks who'd always said he was evil for not fitting into their small religions.

Albert ran and bled and sweated and ran some more until the pneumonia hit.

He was as ugly as a rabid stray when he came home for the last time. I've seen the replays now of Margie and me peeking out as he approached. I wish we hadn't looked so scared.

At first I didn't even think it was him because he'd stopped. I mean, he was walking—stumbling, really—but other than that he was motionless. The world wasn't turning under his feet anymore. He was that far gone.

"Mother," he whispered and Margie screamed, a long high shriek like a horse would make if it broke all four legs. She ran back inside. After that, whatever bit of hope was left in him seemed to fade.

I did my best to say the right things, holding Albert as he died. It was important to him to share everything he'd seen and felt. His words weren't so much a confession as a confiding.

All he'd ever wanted was to be one of us.

If we're lucky, the world will never see anything like him again. We didn't deserve him. We never knew what to do with Albert, and some debts are so great you can only reject what's been given to you.

# THE MIDDLE OF SOMEWHERE

## Judith Moffett

Kaylee is entering data on Jane's clunky old desktop computer, and texting with a few friends while she does it, when the weather alarm goes off for the second time.

Cornell University's NestWatch Citizen Scientist program runs this website where you have a different chart for each nest site you're monitoring. You're supposed to fill in the data after each visit to the site. Jane's got a zillion different kinds of birds nesting on her property, and she knows where a lot of them are doing it, so Kaylee's biology teacher fixed it up with Jane, who's a friend of hers, for Kaylee to do this NestWatch project for class. Twice a week all spring she's been coming out to Jane's place to monitor seven pairs of nesting birds. The place used to be a farm but is all grown up now in trees and bushes except for five or ten acres around the house, which Jane keeps mowed. Bluebirds like short grass and open space.

Jane is nice, but seriously weird. All Kaylee's friends think so, and to be honest Kaylee kind of slants what she tells people to exaggerate that side of Jane, who lives a lot like people did way before Kaylee was born, in this little log house with only three small rooms and no dishwasher or clothes dryer, and solar panels on the roof. She has beehives—well, that's not so weird, though for an old lady maybe it is—but all her water is pumped from a cistern, plus she has two rain barrels out in the garden. Rain barrels! Kaylee knows for a fact that a few years back, when they brought city water out this far from town, Jane just said, Oh well, I can always hook up later if I think I need to. So you have to watch every drop of water you use at Jane's house, like only flushing the toilet every so often, unless they're getting plenty of rain. There's a little sign taped to the bathroom wall that you can't avoid reading when you're sitting on the toilet: IF IT'S YELLOW / LET IT MELLOW / IF IT'S BROWN / FLUSH IT DOWN. Sometimes Kaylee flushes it down even when it isn't brown, out of embarrassment.

The flushing thing is partly about water and partly about the septic tank. Kaylee's friend Morgan's house has a septic tank too, so Kaylee already knows it's best to use them as little as possible, and that there are things you can't put into them or the biology of the tank will get messed up and smell. If you happen to mention anything to Jane about, like, your new SmartBerry, or a hot music group or even the Anderson High basketball team, the Bearcats, when they went to the state finals, she just looks blank, but once when Kaylee asked a simple question about why Jane didn't clean paintbrushes at the sink, like her dad always did, Jane talked animatedly for ten minutes about bacteria and "solids" and drain fields and septic lagoons. Kaylee's friends laughed their heads off when they heard about that ("So she's going on about how the soil in Anderson County is like pure clay, duh, so it doesn't pass the 'perk test,' which is why she's got this *lagoon*, and I'm thinking 'Fine, great, whatever!' and trying to like edge away. . .''). Kaylee's seen the little outhouse in the trees on the other side of the driveway, across from the clothesline (clothesline!), for dry spells when flushing even a few times a day would use more water than Jane wants to waste. That would normally be in late summer. Kaylee's relieved it's spring right now.

The computer Kaylee has to use for data entry here is a million years old and slow as anything. She couldn't believe it when Jane said one day that when and if DSL finally made it this far into rural Kentucky, she planned to sign up.

But the thing that makes all that beside the point for now, is that

Jane has been monitoring certain species of birds here for years and years, and knows just about everything there is to know about them. Anything she doesn't know, she looks up in books, or on the Birds of North America website, and then she knows that too.

On the Garden Box page Kaylee fills in blanks. Species: Tree swallow. Date of visit: 05/04/2014. Time of visit: 4:00 PM. Number of eggs: 0. Number of live young: 6. Number of dead young: 0. Nest status: Completed nest. Adult activity: Feeding young at nest. (Both parents dive-bombed Kaylee today for the entire ninety seconds she had the front of the nest box swung open, swooping down like fighter pilots, aiming for her eyes, pulling up just before they would have hit her head (she happened to have forgotten her hat). When she was done they chased her all the way back to the house. Tree swallows are beautiful, sleekly graceful little birds, white and glossy dark blue, but Kaylee is *so* not crazy about the dive-bombing part.) Young status: Naked young. (The babies—"hatchlings" she should remember to say—hatched out only two days ago, and resemble squirming wads of pink bubble gum with huge dark eyeballs bulging under transparent lids still sealed shut, and little stumpy wings.) Management: No. Everything's fine. Comment: Leave blank. The only thing not ordinary about this nest is how early it is, the earliest first-egg date for tree swallows ever recorded on Jane's farm. Everybody on NestWatch is posting early nesting dates. Climate change, is the general assumption. Kaylee's parents think climate change is a hoax. Kaylee doesn't care whether it is or not, but saying so makes her project feel more dramatic, like, more cutting-edge. Submit.

Next site: Barn. Species: Black vulture. Date of visit: 05/04/2014. Time of visit: 4:00 PM. Number of eggs: 2. Number of live young: 0. Number of dead young: 0. Nest status—and right then Jane's NOAA Weather Radio emits its long piercing shriek.

Jane comes in off the porch, where she's been putting Revolution on the dogs to kill the ticks they pick up in the hay that grows wherever there aren't any trees or blackberries. "What now? They only announced the watch twenty minutes ago." The shrieking goes on and on, you can't hear yourself think. Finally it stops and the radio buzzes three times, and then a robot voice declares, *The National Weather Service in Louisville has issued a severe thunderstorm warning for the following counties in Kentucky: Anderson, Franklin, Henry, Nelson, Mercer, Scott, Shelby, Spencer.* . . Kaylee stops listening and goes back to her data entering and her texting. Nest status: No constructed nest. Adult activity: At/on, then flushed from nest. (When Kaylee squeezed through the crack between the barn doors an hour ago, the mother vulture, as always, got up and hesitantly stalked, like a huge black chicken, away from her two gigantic eggs lying on the bare dirt floor. The father didn't show up this afternoon, which suits Kaylee just fine. Jane says he's all bluster, but he threatens her as if he means it, hissing and spreading his enormous white-tipped black wings like an eagle on a banner, and she's scared of him. Scared he'll barf on her, too; they do that, to drive predators away.)

"I'm going out to the garden," Jane says now. She's wearing her big straw hat, so she'll be safe from dive-bombing tree swallows. "If you hear thunder, get off the computer fast, okay?"

"Okay." Though right now the sky through the study window looks just flat gray, not stormy at all. Young status: (Leave that blank. The eggs should be hatching in ten days or so. Jane's hoping for two live babies this time. Most often one of the eggs is infertile.) Number of dead young: 0. And so on. Submit.

She's worked her way through Patio (eastern phoebe) and Pond Box (Carolina chickadee) while keeping up on Lady Bearcats practice with Morgan, and Macy's cat's hairball with Macy, who's at the vet's, and checking Facebook every few minutes, and is just starting on Path Box (bluebird, her favorite) when the radio emits its blood-curdling screech once again. Jane is still in the garden. When the robot comes on again, Kaylee is the only one in the house to hear it say, *The National Weather Service in Louisville has issued a tornado warning for the following counties in Kentucky: Anderson, Franklin,*

*Grant, Marion, Owen, and Washington until 6:30 pm. The National Weather Service has identified rotation in a storm located fifteen miles southwest of Lebanon and heading north-northeast at 40 mph. Cities in the path of this storm include Lebanon; Springfield; Harrodsburg; Lawrenceburg; Alton. . .* Kaylee shoves back her chair, grabbing her SmartBerry, and runs to the door. "Jane! Hey Jane!" she yells, "They just said it's a tornado warning!" Behind her the robot says sternly *This is a dangerous storm. If you are in the path of this storm, take shelter immediately. Go to the lowest level of a sturdy building. . .* "They said take shelter immediately!" she shouts.

Jane drops her shovel and starts trotting toward the house, calling "Fleece and Roscoe! Come!" She doesn't trot too fast, she's got arthritis in her knees like Kaylee's grandma, but Jane is much, much thinner than Mammaw; think of Mammaw trotting anywhere! The dogs race up the steps onto the deck, followed by Jane holding on to the handrail. "Are you sure they said *warning*?" she puffs. "I wouldn't have thought it looked that threatening," and just then they hear the heavy rumble of thunder. Fleece, the white poodle, trembles violently and slinks through the doggy door into the house; she *hates* thunderstorms. The sky is starting to churn. As the rest of them come in, the radio is repeating its announcement, including the part about taking shelter immediately. Jane says, "Well *that* blew up out of nowhere! Okay, I guess we get to go sit in the basement for a while. Did you turn off the computer?" Kaylee shakes her head. "Get your data submitted?"

She nods. "Almost all of it."

"Good. Go on down, I'll be there in a sec."

Kaylee snatches up her backpack and runs down the basement stairs, then isn't sure what to do. Jane's house is set into a slope, so half the basement is underground and the other half isn't; you can walk straight out the patio doors, climb a ladder kept out there for the purpose, and check on the phoebe's nest perched like a pillbox hat on the light fixture. It's pretty crowded down here; the basement is the size of the house, tiny, and piled with boxes containing mostly books. But now Jane's hurrying down with Roscoe the beagle behind her, leading the way into what looks like a closet under the stairs, but turns out to be a kind of wedge-shaped storm shelter. Fleece is already in there, lying on a mat and panting. Roscoe flops down beside Fleece; they must be used to this drill. There's a folding canvas chair in the shelter too. Jane says, "I guess you'll have to squeeze in with the dogs. Or maybe just sit here on the mat next to them. I have to take the chair or in five minutes my back will be screaming worse than the radio." Which, Kaylee sees, she's brought down with her, and which she now switches back on.

But the robot voice is only repeating what it said already. Jane turns down the volume. Kaylee sits cross-legged on the edge of the mat and consults her SmartBerry.

When she first started working on the nesting project with Jane, she'd kept the SmartBerry in her jacket pocket or in her hand all the time; but when Jane noticed, she'd made her put it away. "You can't do science like that, hon, texting seven of your friends while checking out a nest. Good observation requires all your attention, not just some of it." Kaylee doesn't see why; she's always doing half a dozen things at once, everybody does. It's actually hard to do only one thing. She tried to argue that she could record the data directly onto the NestWatch site from her SmartBerry, skipping the note-taking and data entry phases completely, *and* take pictures. But Jane doesn't trust her not to spend the travel time between nest sites chatting, instead of listening and looking around, which is smart of Jane, Kaylee grudgingly admits. They've compromised: she can use her smartphone during data entry time, but not while actually monitoring nests. It makes Kaylee feel twitchy, all that time hiking between sites and trying to identify bird songs, not knowing what's going on everywhere else.

Now she says, "I should probably call my mom so she doesn't worry."

"Good idea."

Nobody answers at home. Kaylee's brother Tyler always drops her off at Jane's on his way to work his shift, so he's at work, and her dad picks her up on his way home, but her mom must be out. When the answering machine comes on, Kaylee says, "Mom, did the siren go off? There's a tornado warning, I hope you're someplace safe. I'm down in Jane's basement till it's over, so don't worry. See you later." Then she rapidly texts *safe in basement @ janes dont worry* and sends that to her mom and dad, then sends *im in janes basement where r u?* to all her best friends at once, Hannah, Tabby, Andrew, Shannon, Jacob, Morgan, Macy, and waits for somebody to text back. It takes her mind off being scared, not that she's all that scared really. There are tornado watches and a few warnings every spring—more and more of them in the last few years, her mom is always complaining—but they've never actually come to anything around Lawrenceburg, though she's seen the TV shots of other places, even in Kentucky, where whole houses got turned into piles of rubble in a few seconds. The worst watches are the night ones, when you can't see what the sky looks like.

While she waits—in the circumstances Jane can hardly object— she gets on Facebook and posts, "I'm in a tornado warning in Jane's basement!"

She's reading Tabby's text—*me + my mom + the twins r in the city hall shelter*— when Jane puts her hand on Kaylee's arm, "Listen. Do you hear that—like a freight train?" Something *does* sound like a freight train, getting louder and louder. She feels a thrill of serious fear, which spikes into panic when Jane says urgently, "Better get down low."

At that instant three more buzzing beeps interrupt the droning radio robot. *A tornado has been sighted on the ground near Glensboro, heading north-northeast at forty miles per hour. If you are in the path of this storm, move to the lowest level of a building or interior room and protect yourself from flying glass.* Kaylee and Jane look at each other; Glensboro is only a couple of miles west of here. *If it stays organized this tornado should pass near Lawrenceburg at 5:45 pm, near Birdie at 5:50 pm, near Alton at 6 o'clock pm, and near Frankfort at 6:15 pm*, the flat voice states.

"Kaylee, get down. Get under the blanket and hold that pillow over your head." Fleece and Roscoe are both whining now; Jane slides out of the low chair onto her knees and stretches herself out on top of Fleece, with her arm tight around Roscoe and terrified Kaylee; she pulls the blanket up over all of them.

The roar becomes deafening. There's pressure in Kaylee's ears, she can feel the floor vibrating. The house blows up.


After the shaking and roaring have stopped, and they've thrown off the blanket, Kaylee can't see anything through the cracked but miraculously unbroken patio doors but a tangle of branches full of new green leaves. The basement has held together, though light is coming through some new cracks in the aboveground foundation block. "Kaylee, let me look at you. Are you okay?" Jane says worriedly.

"I think so." She feels lightheaded with relief that the tornado is over, but nothing hurts when she moves her arms and legs. She automatically checks her SmartBerry, still in her hand, but there are no bars at all. Dismayed, she reports to Jane, "I'm not getting a signal. We can't call anybody."

"I expect the tornado took out the cell tower. Phone line too. Keep the dogs in here with you—I want to check things out, all right?" Holding to the shelter's doorframe, Jane hauls herself up, grimacing, steps carefully out into the basement and looks around. "Looks like we were lucky. The ceiling's still in one piece, far as I can tell." She moves a few cautious steps farther and stops. "The stairs look solid but they're full of junk, I don't think we better try to get out that way. Let's see if the patio doors will open." She goes over and tugs at the sliding door, but it won't budge. "Frame's bent. The window frame may be bent too, but I'll check before we start breaking glass."

Startled, Kaylee says, "You're bleeding! Jane, you're bleeding!" There's a big spreading bloodstain on Jane's shirt and jeans on one side.

"I am? Where?" Jane looks down, sees the blood on her clothes, sees it dripping onto her right boot. "Hunh. Now how the dickens did that happen? I must have cut my arm on something." She comes back toward Kaylee. "There's a plastic tub with a lid, see it? Way inside, back where the stairs almost come down to the floor? That's the first-aid stuff; can you pull that out here? Fleece, Roscoe, come. Down. Stay. Get out of Kaylee's way." The dogs, both panting now, slink out of the shelter, very subdued, and slump down on the basement floor by Jane's feet without an argument. Fleece has some blood on her woolly white back but seems unhurt. Apparently the blood is Jane's.

There are three or four plastic tubs with lids back there, all blue. "Which one?"

"The closest one, nearest the door. Just drag it out here." Suddenly Jane leans against the wall, then reaches into the shelter, pulls out the camp chair and sits in it.

Kaylee backs out with a tub. "This one?"

Jane snaps off the lid and looks in. "Yep. Thanks." She rummages around inside, gets out a packet of gauze pads and a pressure bandage, and rips the seal off the packet. She starts unbuttoning her flannel shirt. "Do you faint at the sight of blood? If you don't, maybe you can help me find the cut. The back of my arm is numb, I guess I cut a nerve."

Kaylee isn't crazy about the sight of blood, but this is no time to wimp out. But the cut makes her feel a little sick. It's high up on the back of Jane's left arm, deep and triangular, and thick-looking blood is welling out of it. She can't help sort of gasping through her teeth. "I see it. It's pretty bad. What should I do?"

"Put the pads right on it and apply pressure, don't worry about hurting me. The important thing is to stop the bleeding."

Gingerly, Kaylee presses the pads against the wound, but they're saturated in seconds; the cut is really bleeding. "Do you have anything bigger? These aren't really big enough."

"Use my shirt while I look." She paws through the box. "There's this sling thing, but that's not very absorbent, or very big, come to that. And some cotton balls. I guess we could pack the cut with these."

Kaylee suddenly says "Oh! I know!" and lets go of the shirt, which Jane grabs and tightens with her other hand. "Sorry," says Kaylee, "only I just remembered, I've got some, well, some maxipads in my backpack, because you know, just in case. . . anyway—" she fishes in her pack and pulls out a plastic bag triumphantly.

"Perfect!" Jane says. "Brilliant!"

Kaylee flushes, embarrassed but gratified. She snatches away the shirt and slaps a pad onto Jane's wound, wrapping it around her arm. Then, showing further initiative, she says, "Hold that like that," and puts another pad on top of the first, and binds them both to Jane's arm with the pressure bandage. "There! Just hold that really tight. If you bleed through the first one there's another one all ready to go"

"I will," Jane says. "Thanks." She looks around. "I need to sit still while this clots. Do you want to see if the window will open? I don't like to have you walking around down here till we know for sure the house isn't going to cave in on that side"—her voice catches and Kaylee thinks for the first time, *Her house is totally wrecked, her perfect little house!*—"but it should be okay. Just pry up the levers and try turning the crank. It kind of sticks. If anything shifts or falls, jump back."


What felt like an explosion turns out to have been a humongous old hickory tree smashing down right on top of the house. The tornado only clipped one corner, peeling back part of the roof and tearing the screened porch off, but it dumped that hickory right in the middle of the crushed roof, where it's hanging with its branches on one side and its roots on top of Jane's car on the other. The car is crushed and plainly undrivable, but even if it could be driven there would be no way to get it down to the road; Jane's steep quarter-mile driveway is completely blocked with downed trees.

In fact, the world has become a half-moonscape. Everything on one side of the house just looks about the way it might look after a really violent windstorm, but everything on the other has been toppled and ripped and broken to pieces. "We must have been right on the very edge," Jane says, holding her wounded arm with her other hand. "And this must have been one hell of a big tornado." There are no trees standing in the creek valley below Jane's house: none. They're all laid down in the same direction, pointing uphill on this side and downhill on the other. The road that follows the creek, the only way there is to get to Jane's house, has completely vanished under a pile of trunks and branches, broken and jagged, piled many feet deep on top of each other.

The sight of this world of leafy destruction has obliterated Kaylee's spurt of competence. She's shaking and crying in little sobs, arms wrapped about herself. "I need to talk to my mom," is all she can think of to say, "I need to find out if she's okay."

Jane says soothingly, "The best thing you can do for your mom and dad right now is just take care of yourself and stay calm. They know where you are, and they know you're with me. Eventually somebody will come looking for us. It might take them a few days—if that twister hit any population centers, all the emergency equipment and personnel are going to be very, very busy for a while. We have to give people time to get things up and running again. But they'll be along."

"But the road's covered with *trees!*"

"I'm betting on a helicopter ride long before they get the road open. The good news is, lots of people know where you are. We just have to hunker down and wait."

Kaylee pictures KY 44 as it looked before the tornado, two lanes, no shoulders, a steep wooded bluff on one side and Indian Creek on the other, with another wooded bluff across the creek. The road follows the creek. If all the trees on both sides of the valley went down the whole way to town, like they did here, she can't imagine how they'll *ever* get the road open again. Worst of all in a way, her wonderful new SmartBerry, her Christmas and birthday presents combined, that keeps her continually connected her to everything that matters, is useless. She's worried to death about her family and friends, and there's no way to find out if they're okay. From being in constant touch with everybody, suddenly she's out of touch with everybody! It makes her feel lonely and frantic, and furious with Jane, because of whom she's stranded in this war zone. "How can you stand living out here all by yourself?" she yells. "Something like this happens and you're stuck, you're just stuck!" When Jane reaches toward her she jerks away and takes off running, crying hard, down the mowed path to the garden where things still look almost normal, away from the wrecked house and jagged devastation in the other direction.

She'd changed out of her sneakers into flip-flops after visiting the nests. Running in flip-flops on a path grown up thick in clover and scattered with broken branches doesn't work, so she's walking and crying when she gets to the path box, which is down on its side, metal post bent and half uprooted. It's empty, the baby bluebirds fledged over the weekend, thank goodness. The box in the garden has been knocked over too—but that one's not empty, Kaylee remembers now, there were six new hatchlings in that one this morning. She shakes off the flip-flops and runs to the gate, left open in Jane's haste. The latch on the box popped open when it hit the ground; the nest has fallen out, scattering tiny pink bodies and loose feathers on the grass. Quick as she can, Kaylee stands the nest box up and steps on the base with her bare foot, to jam it back into the ground. She picks up the nest, built entirely out of Jane's straw garden mulch—square outside like the square nest box, a soft lined cup inside—and fits it back in. Then, one by one, with extreme delicacy, she picks up the fragile, weightless baby birds, puts them back in their cradle, and latches the front. She can't tell whether the tiniest are even alive, but a couple of others twitch a little bit when she's handling them. It's a warm day. Now, if the parents come fast, most of them ought to make it.

But then Kaylee thinks, Where *are* the parents? She's never once checked this nest, not while it was being built and not while the eggs were being incubated and not this afternoon, when the parents weren't carrying on something terrible. There's been no sign of them. With a sinking feeling she faces the truth: They were almost certainly killed in the tornado.

She hears footsteps swishing through the clover and starts to explain before Jane even gets to the gate: "The garden box was down and the nest fell out, and I was trying to put everything back together, but the parents haven't come back—what should we do?"

Jane comes in carrying Kaylee's flip-flops, looks into the box, then scans the sky, then shakes her head. "I doubt the parents survived. These babies won't either unless we hand-raise them, which is a big job under ideal conditions and right now—nature can be ruthless, Kaylee. You did the right thing, and if the parents had come through, they could take over now. But as it is—"

"You said we could hand-raise them? How?"

Jane makes a pained face. "I've never tried it with swallows. With robins or bluebirds you make a nest, using an old bowl or something lined with paper towels. Then you soak dry dog food in water and feed them pinches of that *every forty-five minutes*, for a week or ten days. You have to change the paper towel every time you feed them, because they'll poop on it. When they get bigger—"

"Do we have dog food?" Kaylee says. "I want to try! I'm sorry I behaved like such a creep," she adds contritely. All at once she desperately wants to try to save these morsels of life, helpless and blameless, from the wreckage of the world. How badly she wants this amazes her. She can see Jane thinking about it, wanting to refuse. "*Please!*" Kaylee says. "I'll do everything myself, well, I will as soon as you teach me how. Do we have paper towels? Please, Jane, I just have to try this, I just *have* to."

With a rush of relief she sees Jane make up her mind. "Well—we do have dog food. Very expensive, low-fat dog food. No paper towels, but toilet paper and tissues. We can manage. But Kaylee, listen to me now: even experienced rehabbers commonly lose about half the baby birds they try to rear, more than half when the babies are so young. You can see why, when they've been stressed and banged around, and gotten chilled—I don't want you to set your heart on this without understanding how hard it is to be successful."

Kaylee nods as hard as she can. "I understand! Really, I really do, I won't go to pieces if it doesn't work. Oh, thanks, Jane, thank you, I don't know what I'd have done if you'd said no."

"But if we're going to do this we need to act fast. We'll take the whole nest," she says. "Back to the house. It takes a little while for kibble to soften up, so we'll start with canned; these babies need to get warmed up and fed ASAP."


"How come you've got all this stuff stashed under the stairs?" Kaylee asks Jane, when the little swallows are safely tucked into their artificial nest (Roscoe's bowl, lined with Kleenex).

First she and Jane had to hold the hatchlings in their hands, three apiece, to warm them up enough so they could eat; Jane said little birds can't warm up by themselves when they first hatch out, which is why the mother has to brood them. "Normally we do this with a heating pad or a microwaved towel or something." Then she opened a can of Hill's Prescription Diet w/d, under the intense scrutiny of Roscoe and Fleece. "Watch this time, then next time you can help. Their gape response isn't working, but it should come back once we can get a bite or two down the hatch," Jane said. And sure enough, when Jane carefully pried a tiny beak open and pushed a bit of canned food as far back as she could with her little finger, and closed the beak to help the baby swallow, the beak opened again by itself.

Now they had all been fed. (They hadn't pooped, which probably just meant they hadn't eaten since before the tornado.) And Kaylee, yearning over their bowl, thought to ask Jane about the supplies.

Jane sits back in her chair, then stiffens. "Oh!" she says, "*That's* what I cut myself on, that bracket on the shelf there. Wedged between paint cans. Can you push it back out of the way?" Kaylee gets up, holding the bowl carefully, and tucks the bracket out of sight; she is helpfulness itself. "Last summer," Jane says when Kaylee sits back down on the mat, "after I'd been down here with the dogs three times in about three weeks, I started thinking, What if this was the real deal? All I've got in the way of emergency supplies is six jugs of water!" So I took a weekend and made a list and went shopping. Good thing I did."

"Are we getting more tornadoes than we used to? My mom keeps saying that, but my dad thinks she just doesn't remember."

"I don't think anybody knows for sure. But a lot of information about climate change passes through this house," Jane says, and pauses, and Kaylee can tell she's thinking, *used to pass*, so she hitches forward and looks very interested, and Jane catches herself and goes on: ". . .and I've seen several articles about the effect of climate change on weather lately, and quite a few climate scientists seem to be leaning that way. The argument goes that warmer ocean temperatures mean more storms. Heat is just energy, and heat affects how much moisture there is in the atmosphere."

"So more heat and more moisture in the atmosphere means more tornadoes?"

"It means more frequent and more violent storms in general, apparently. There are computer models that say so, not that that proves anything necessarily. Tornadoes are complex, lots of things affect their formation—but it *is* true that they've been occurring earlier and farther north than they used to. Unusually high temperatures, unusually frequent tornadoes, so the thinking goes, and it does make sense. Though actually," she adds, "there've always been more tornadoes in Kentucky than people think."

"We had something last year in science about Hoosier Alley,"

Kaylee chimes in. "It was something about a new definition of Tornado Alley—if my SmartBerry was working I could look it up! But anyway, there's still Tornado Alley but now they're talking about Dixie Alley and Hoosier Alley and something else."

"I hadn't heard that." Jane winces and shifts in her chair.

Pleased to think there was anything she knew that Jane didn't, Kaylee says, "Hoosier Alley, that's Indiana and the western two-thirds of Kentucky, and pieces of a couple other states too. So what all do you have here?"

"Besides what you see?" Jane considers. "Mostly food. Cans and PowerBars. Dishes. Spare clothes. Tools. Stuff to clean up with. Also cans and kibble for the dogs—birds too, as it turns out." Kaylee grins happily. "And speaking of birds, before it's time to feed them again, would you mind helping me with this cut? I can't see the darn thing, and I want to pour some peroxide in there to clean it out and bandage it with something less, ah, bulky. It's going to need stitches but we'll let a professional handle that part."

Kaylee *does* mind, quite a lot really, but she takes herself in hand and acts like she doesn't. They climb back out the window—Jane's set a little step stool just outside, to make it easier to come and go—and then Jane takes off the bloody shirt, and the tee shirt too this time, and holds the arm out from her side while Kaylee pours most of a bottle of peroxide into the jagged mouth of the wound, struggling to keep from gagging while pink bubbles froth and fizz there. In nothing but a bra, Jane's back and arm look scrawny and old. She *is* old, Kaylee thinks uncomfortably; and while she's helping apply the clean bandage and wash dried blood off the arm, and helping Jane into a clean shirt from one of the plastic tubs, she's hoping she won't have to do this again. She's not proud of it, but that's how she feels.

When the arm has been dealt with, Jane becomes managerial. Feed the baby swallows. When that's done, get the dogs out by lifting them through the window (Kaylee lifts, Jane directs, protecting her arm). Bring the boxes of supplies outside. The porch above the patio is gone, but they clear the pink insulation batts, tumbled firewood, broken branches, and nameless debris away, and have a firm, level surface to work on. It's also enclosed by fencing which has survived the tornado, making it a good place for the dogs to sleep if it doesn't rain tonight, and in fact the sky has cleared completely and the radio robot says it will stay clear. Roscoe and Fleece can look through the patio doors straight into the shelter.

Amazingly, the outhouse has withstood the storm. A tree right next to it is down, but the little structure is still sitting there a trifle cattywompus on its foundation. "Praise the Lord," Jane says, "at least that's one problem we haven't got." She also says, "It might be a good thing these patio doors won't open. They may be reinforcing the wall. We can stay in here and keep dry till they come to get us, unless there's another storm." Kaylee doesn't want to think about another storm. "Let's make a fire," Jane says. "It'll cheer us up to have something hot. Want to build it, Kaylee?" Kaylee admits she has no earthly idea how to go about building a fire. "Watch and learn, then," Jane says. "Next time it'll be your turn."


The evening has turned chilly; the fire feels good. Kaylee puts down her empty plate and holds her mug of instant hot cider in both hands. She's sitting on a log of firewood, but Jane's chair has been handed through the window and Jane is sitting in that, cleaning up her plate of beans with the shambles of her house around her, as if nothing could be more natural. The dogs, stomachs full and bladders empty, lie peacefully on either side of Jane. There's almost a campfire feeling to the moment, except when Kaylee accidentally looks at the light fixture from which the phoebe nest with its five babies has disappeared without a trace. She looks away quickly, and thinks instead about how deftly Jane built the fire. How she assembled the big sticks, smaller sticks, really tiny twigs, and dry grass Kaylee collected for her—combining them like following a sort of recipe—then lit one match, and hey presto! magicked forth the coals that heated the pots of water and beans. She says, "Where did you learn to build a fire like that? Without even any newspaper? My dad always uses lots of newspaper."

Jane hands her a granola bar and unpeels one for herself. "I usually use paper too, when I'm firing up the wood stove," she says, and then there's another one of those pauses when Kaylee knows she's thinking *But I'll never do that again*. Jane takes a deep breath. "But I always make fires for grilling or whatever without paper. One match, no paper, that's the rule. I can't do the 'one match' thing every single time, especially not if there's any wind, but it seems like a good skill to keep up."

"But *where*? Did your parents teach you?" She bites off the end of the bar.

"I learned in Scouts," Jane says. "I was a Girl Scout from Brownies clear through high school. We did a lot of camping. Then later I was a counselor at different Scout camps for several summers. Primitive camps, these were, with latrines and cold water from a hydrant, and lots of campfire cooking. Plenty of fire-building practice, all in all." In a moment she adds, "I never had any kids, but I always assumed I would, and I always thought that when I did I would teach them certain basic skills. How to swim, was one. How to build a fire with one match and no paper, that was another."

"I wish somebody'd taught *me*."

Jane laughs. "The last time I looked, somebody *was* teaching you! By the time you get home you'll have something to show your dad. But the skills kids need nowadays are so different than they were when I was your age, it's hard to believe. What are you, fourteen, fifteen?"

Kaylee swallows her bite. "Fifteen last month." She takes another.

"You've got so many skills already, at fifteen, that I don't have and never will have. I wouldn't have the faintest idea what to do with that SmartBerry, for instance; I've seen your thumb going lickety-split on that thing and wondered how the dickens you do it!"

Kaylee grins, feeling proud. Then the grin fades. She says slowly, "Right now those skills aren't too useful, are they?"

"We're in a sort of time warp here, just for a couple of days. A natural disaster. When things get back to normal—"

"But you were saying before," Kaylee says, feeling funny, "that there's going to be more and more natural disasters. Because of climate change."

Jane looks at her sharply. "*I* didn't actually say that, you know. What I said was, some scientists think there will be, but we don't know for sure."

It was obvious she was trying to avoid saying anything that would offend Kaylee's parents if it got back to them, but Kaylee wanted to know what she really thought. "We're pretty sure though, right?"

After a moment Jane nods. "Yes, we are. We're pretty damn sure. But it's good to know how to manage whenever a crisis *does* come, nobody could argue with that."

"Right, but what I'm thinking now," Kaylee says, refusing to be deflected from her line of thought, "is that there's something wrong with getting so far away from knowing *how* to manage. I mean, if you weren't here, what would I do? I don't know anything, nobody I know knows anything! My mom would *die* if she had to use an outhouse! Let alone go in the bushes! I mean," she said more quietly, "it's not about outhouses, that's dumb, but it seems like there's just something *wrong*. About everybody getting so far away from, like, the basics."

Now Jane is looking at Kaylee in a new way, more serious, almost more respectful. "It could be argued," she says finally, "that getting so far from the basics is one way of thinking about climate change. Why it's happening. Why people don't want to believe in it, so they won't have to stop doing the things that make it worse."

"My parents sure don't believe in it: they think it's hogwash," Kaylee admitted. "Nobody in my church believes in it. But," she says, "*you* do, you live like this on purpose. Is that why? To stop making things worse?"

Jane stands up carefully and stretches. "Time to feed the babies. When we're done, if you really want to know, I'll tell you about that."

Kaylee lies in the dark, thinking. She and Jane are sleeping in their clothes on the basement floor, in beds put together from a hodge-podge of old porch cushions and blankets. Kaylee has insisted that Jane take the only pillow; her own head rests on a bundle of Jane's spare clothes stuffed in a bag. The dogs are sharing a blanket on the patio. A funky lamp in what looks like a pickle jar, that burns olive oil, is a comforting source of light in the otherwise total darkness.

It turns out you don't have to feed hatchlings every forty-five minutes all night, only during the daytime. The six babies are asleep too on the work bench, their dog bowl nestled in the hollow of a hot-water bottle, covered by a towel.

Kaylee's thinking about Jane's story. It turns out that living like this—conserving water, composting, recyling everything, compost-ing, driving as little as possible, generating some of her own electric-ity, growing most of her own food, buying most of the rest locally ("Except tea. I could give up tea only if there were none to be had.")—is *consistent* with trying to reduce the impact of people on climate change. But Jane had been living like this long before anyone had thought to worry about global warming. The reason is that when Jane was in college she had met an old couple who were living completely off the grid, except they had an old car they used to go to cultural events sometimes. They had no electricity, no phone or indoor toilet. *Their* cistern was higher than the house, so they didn't need a pump. They would never have even noticed a power outage. "They would have noticed a tornado," Kaylee had said darkly, and Jane had nodded ruefully. "They were lucky. A huge tornado came quite close to their place about forty years ago, but it missed them."

The term for that sort of life was *homesteading*. "They did things I could only dream about—grew and put up *all* their own food, for instance, plus picked berries and nuts and wild greens. And they kept goats for milk and cheese, meat too."

Kaylee is intrigued. "Why don't *you* have goats? You've got plenty of room."

Jane sighs. "I always meant to have some. Tennessee fainting goats—they're a cashmere type. But before I could get that far I broke my wrist, and that's when I found out that you can't have livestock if you live by yourself. Somebody has to be able to take over if you get injured or sick. Orrin had Hannah, you see, that's why it worked for them—plus Orrin was tough as nails. But even he got snakebit once, and Hannah had to go for help."

Their names were Hubbell, Orrin and Hannah Hubbell. Orrin was a landscape painter. He had built the house they were living in, on the Ohio River, and all the furniture. Hannah cooked and put up food on a wood-burning cookstove, Orrin fished and gardened and milked. Jane was nineteen when she met them, five years older than Kaylee, and she had fallen utterly in love with their homestead on the river. "I thought their place was magical, and the life they were living there was magical. I could see it was a lot of work, but the work seemed to keep them, well, you said it yourself: in touch with fundamental things, things they got enormous satisfaction out of. They were old by then, and got tired and cranky sometimes, but underneath there was always this—this deep serenity. It was like—well, as if what they did all day every day was a religious calling, as if they were monks or something, living every moment in the consciousness of a higher purpose."

And *that* was why Jane had chosen to live as she did. "Oh, I compromise in ways they never would have. I've got electricity, though I make as much of it as I can myself, and conserve what I make. I've got gadgets: a washer, a TV, a computer, a landline phone. *Had* gadgets," she corrected herself, and paused again. But then she went on without

Kaylee having to prompt her. "The purity of *their* life came at the cost of ignoring society—though society didn't ignore them, people heard about them and were always dropping by. I didn't aspire to go as *far* as they did—they paid no attention to current events, never voted, they basically chose not to be citizens of the world. But if there had been another person or two who wanted the life I wanted, we would have been able to come much closer to the Hubbell's self-sufficiency than I have. Sustainability, that's the word for that."

"But nobody did."

"Nobody did. Not really. Not after they'd tried it for a while, experimentally."

"So you finally just went ahead and did it by yourself."

"Mm-hm. Compromises and all."

"Are you glad?"

Jane thinks a bit. "On the whole," she says finally, "Yes, very glad."


By the third day Jane and Kaylee have developed a routine. They've run out of bottled water for washing and cooking, so Kaylee hauls it a bucket at a time from the cistern—the pump house is gone but the cistern is below grade and is still there, still full—and Jane purifies it with tablets from the first-aid box. They take turns feeding and changing the hatchlings, all six of whom are eating and pooping up a storm, and have grown amazingly on bites of low-fat kibble; they're all-over gray fuzz now, with open eyes and big yellow mouths. Jane and Kaylee don't bother with a fire except at night, when they wash up all the dishes and then themselves with minimal amounts of water from the kettle. (Kaylee washes out her underwear, the only pair she's got, and dries it by the embers.) They take naps after lunch. Kaylee's period starts: no big deal, she's got pads and cramp pills. Kaylee changes the bandage on Jane's arm, which doesn't seem infected and has started to heal, though if it doesn't get stitched up soon she'll have one humongous scar. They've shoved all the loose junk in the basement against the walls, so they have more room in there, and a clear path from the shelter to the window.

On the third afternoon it rains. Their ceiling, which is the upstairs floor, leaks in a few places, so they retreat to the shelter with their bedding and Jane's chair, and bring the dogs back inside. "No fire tonight," Jane prophesies, though they've anticipated rain, and brought some firewood inside to keep it dry. "We'll have one in the morning if it's still raining at dinnertime." Jane breaks out an old board game, Clue, which they play by solar lantern light.

In the middle of the second game the dogs leap up and dash to the open window, barking wildly. A moment later they can both hear it: the deep nasal roar of a helicopter, flying low. Kaylee skins out of shelter, basement, and window in a flash, and jumps up and down in the rain, waving a blanket, yelling, "We're here! We're down here!" They couldn't have actually heard her over the racket, but an amplified voice from heaven thunders, "We see you! Stand by!"

Jane comes carefully through the window too now, wearing a rain jacket, and waves too, and tells the dogs to be quiet. The chopper hovers, then gradually settles in the hayfield next to the garden, and a guy in a yellow rain slicker jumps out and hurries toward them. "Jane Goodman? Kaylee Perry? You ladies all right—any injuries?"

"Jane's got a bad cut," Kaylee says, dancing around in the rain, excited by the suddenness of rescue, "but I'm fine! Are my mom and dad okay?"

"They're just dandy, and they sure do want to see you!" To Jane he says, "The tornado passed west of Lawrenceburg but Frankfort got clobbered. An EF3, they're saying. We been busy." He looks Jane over critically, sees she's not too badly hurt. "Okay, let's get going then," the guy says, turning to head back to the chopper.

Kaylee starts to hurry after him, but stops abruptly. "The hatchlings! Wait, I have to get. . ." she doubles back and pops through the window.

While she's stuffing a few things into her backpack, and putting the bowl of tree swallows into a rainproof plastic bag, she can hear them talking. "Baby birds," Jane's explaining. She'll just be a second. But I've got two dogs here, I can't leave them. I'll stay till we can all be lifted out together. Or till the road's open." Kaylee's mouth falls open; Jane's not coming?

"What about the cut?" says the guy in the slicker, and Jane's voice says, "It'll keep."

"Supplies?"

"Running low, but enough for another day or so."

"We'll drop you a bag of stuff on the next trip out. Should be able to pick you all up tomorrow."

Jane's not coming! Kaylee pops through the window between the dogs, who are barking again because of all the commotion, without the bowl of hatchlings or her backpack. "Jane, listen, if you're not leaving, I'm not either. You need me to change your bandage."

She's the only one not wearing rain gear and she's standing in the rain getting soaked. The adults look at her with surprise and consternation. "Honey, your parents need to see you, I'll be fine here for another day or so."

"We'll be back tomorrow to pick up this lady and the dogs," says the EMS guy. "You need to get on home."

"No," Kaylee says. She backs away from them. "I won't go so don't try to make me. Not till Jane does. As long as my parents know I'm fine, I'm staying here with her."

"I appreciate it, hon, I really do," Jane starts to say, "but—"

"*No!*" She stamps her foot; why won't they take her seriously? "I'm not leaving you here by yourself!"


The rain stops after all in time for them to have a hot supper, consisting of some of the food the chopper dropped off an hour before. Hot soup. Bacon and cheese sandwiches on fresh bread, mm. Apples.

Bananas. Even Ding Dongs. Kaylee got the fire going herself, though not with one match. More like fifteen. "How long do you think it'll take to get your new house built?" she asks now, licking Ding Dong off her lips. She feeds each dog a piece of banana.

Jane is staring into Kaylee's fire. She looks up. "Hm?"

"To replace this one," Kaylee says. "How long?"

"Oh—" Jane sighs heavily. "I don't think. . . it doesn't make much sense, does it? Everybody says I'm nuts anyway, living out here alone in the middle of nowhere. I'm almost seventy, Kaylee. I'd been hoping to hang on a while longer, but maybe the tornado just forced a decision I've been putting off."

Kaylee sits up straight on the log. Her heart starts pounding. "What do you mean?"

"There's a retirement community in Indiana I've been looking at. Maybe it's time."

Stricken, Kaylee says, "But—you have to build a new house *here!* What about the birds, what are they supposed to do if you're not here? What would the *hatchlings* have done?"

Jane smiles. "The birds got along without me before I came. They'll be okay. I gave them a nice boost for a while, that's worth something; and as for the hatchlings, they have you to thank more than me."

Abruptly Kaylee bursts into tears, startling herself and making Jane jump. "What about *me* then? How am *I* gonna learn everything if you go away? What if the *Hubbells* went somewhere, just when you found out you wanted to live like them and be like them, and come see them all the time and help out, and—and feed the goats when they cut their arms or whatever, how would *you* feel?" She wipes her face on her sleeve, but the tears won't stop coming.

"Mercy," Jane says mildly after a minute. "I apologize, Kaylee. I had no idea you felt like that."

"Well, I do," she says, sniffling.

"Well, in that case, I guess I might have to think again. No promises, mind, but I won't decide anything just yet." She smiles. "You came at me out of left field with that one."

Kaylee wipes her sleeve across her eyes and smiles back shakily. "We'll get you a cell phone. Then if something happens, you won't be out here alone in the middle of nowhere 'cause you can call *me*. You wouldn't have to text message or anything."

# NOT A PROBLEM

Matthew Hughes

Bunky Sansom was the kind of man who knew that the time to say yes was when all around him were saying no. Or vice versa. That's how he got to be a multibillionaire.

When he heard the United Nations Secretary-General say, "Climate change is now a reality. Nothing we can do in our lifetimes can reverse it," Bunky's answer was, "I don't buy it, lady. Something can always be done."

The Secretary-General's image was superimposed on video of the last dike failing on the last of Kiribati's storm-swept chain of islands. Bunky watched the remaining few thousand of the now drowned nation's population forming forlorn lines and wading out to the U.N. flotilla that would take them to join the rest of their compatriots huddled in Australian and New Zealand refugee camps.

He told the hi-def to turn itself off and stepped out onto the balcony of his mountainside eyrie, with its grand-scale view of Vancouver's golden towers, crowded together within the confines of the massive seawall that had been one of Canada's bicentennial projects. But instead of looking down at the place where he had made his wealth, he looked up and saw the stars.

That's when he got the idea. "We need help," he said. "It's gotta be out there, somewhere."

Bunker Hill Sansom—though he told everyone to call him Bunky, and God help any who didn't—had made his billions by finding new ways to do old things. Inarguably, his ways were better ways, provided your definition of "better" was "more fashionable." He had pioneered the genetic redesign of key elements of the human genome—well, not the actual redesign, but the marketing of the application, through a worldwide string of franchise clinics that sold the fruits of other people's genius to the eager masses.

So while others were eliminating hereditary disease or enhancing intelligence, Sansom was making it possible for parents to bear children with huge, dark eyes the size of silver dollars—you couldn't look at them without saying, "Aw,"—or with the silky blue hair that, this year, was all the rage in Japan. He was already taking preorders for next year's sensation: feathers!

As soon as he received his inspiration about help from the stars, Bunky put some people on it. They reported back that scientists had been scanning the stars for intelligent signals for about a century.

"And what have they got?" he said.

"Well, nothing," said his number-one baby-strangler. Actually, Bunky had never happened to need a baby strangled, but if he ever did, Number-One was there to take care of it.

"Nothing? A hundred years and they've got nothing?"

"They don't have much money."

"How much is not much?" Bunky said. He didn't believe the number his people gave him. It was less than he'd spent on media alone when he'd launched the modification that let people have babies that produced excrement in about the same quantity and conformation as a rabbit's. "Chicken feed," he said. "Put a coupla billion into it."

His people went away and put a couple of billion into the search for extraterrestrial intelligence. Every month, he got reports; every month, progress was skimpy. Like the time his team reported that they'd overheard signals from deeper in the galaxy that were definitely coherent, but the scientists decoding the transmissions concluded that the senders were insectoids.

"Insectoids?" Bunky said. "You mean, like, bugs?"

"Yes, sir," said Number-One.

"Big bugs?"

"Yes, sir."

Bunky shivered. "Give 'em another billion but tell 'em they gotta look somewhere else. Bugs ain't gonna help us."

More months went by. The sea barriers protecting lower Manhattan cracked then collapsed under the continuous battering from Atlantic waves. "I told 'em they shouldn'ta let the mob finesse those construction contracts," Bunky said. He called Number-One and said, "Whatta we hear from space?"

The man had just been about to call the boss. "Something good," he said.

"Not bugs?"

"Not bugs. More like slugs, but smart slugs."

"What's good about smart slugs?" Bunky said.

"They sent through the schematics for a different kind of communicator. We can talk to them in real time, no more waiting years for messages to go out and come back."

"That sounds good."

A week went by. Number-One called back. "We made contact."

"Excellent. Can they help us?"

"There's a problem."

"What problem?"

"Well, we established communication, but the only thing they wanted to know is did we have any *fafashertzz* we wanted to get rid of?"

"*Fafashertzz*?" Bunky said. "What's *fafashertzz*?"

"They sent another schematic. It appears to be what our scientists call a transuranic element, but way heavier than anything we've ever conceived of. You'd need a cyclotron the size of the moon to make it."

"So our guys told these slugs we were all out of *fafashertzz*?"

"They did."

"And?"

"Dial tone. No answer. Nada. Mukwoy."

"Buncha jerks!" Bunky said. "Still, whatta ya expect from slugs?"

"But there's good news," said Number-One.

"Tell me."

"The communicator works on other frequencies. Our brainiacs say it looks like we can start calling around, see if we can find someone not so single-minded."

Bunky had built his business partly on an aggressive telemarketing campaign. "Put another billion into it," he said, "build a few million of those things and hire India to make the calls."

To himself, he said, *This works out, I could rule the world.* And when Bunky Sansom talked to himself, he never indulged in hyperbole.


"It's looking good, boss."

"It better," Bunky said. For the umpteenth time, the worst-case global warming scenarios had proved to be too optimistic: now the U.N. climatologists were predicting that everything from the Gulf of Mexico to the Black Hills was going to end up as a warm, shallow sea. "So whatta we got?"

"We're talking to about twenty civilizations, maybe half of them within *bluberiskint* distance."

"What's this *bluberiskint*?"

"Seems to be the main purpose of *fafashertzz*—some kind of interstellar faster-than-light drive."

"So, we're talking to ten or a dozen kindsa space aliens," Bunky said. A thought occurred to him. "How many of them are bugs?"

"Big bugs?"

"Size don't matter."

"Three."

"And the rest? Can they help us?"

Number-One made an *it-ain't-good-news* face. "Most of them first want to know if we've got any *fafashertzz*."

Bunky looked at the ceiling, which was painted with scenes of triumph from his long, contrarian career. "Give me somethin' here," he said, "'fore I drown."

Number-One said, "There's one good prospect." He caught his boss's sideways look and added, "And they're not bugs or slugs. They look like big birds, although they've got teeth."

Bunky tried it out in his head. "Birds aren't so bad. How big?"

"Pretty big. Hard to tell. Maybe twenty feet high."

"That's some bird," Bunky said. "And with teeth yet."

"The thing is," Number-One said, "they said they were glad we got in touch. They're familiar with our world. When we told them it was heating up, the answer came back: 'Not a problem.'"

"Not a problem?" Bunky said the words again, slowly. "I like their attitude. And they're within whatsit distance?"

"They can be here in a month."

Bunky didn't get where he was by procrastinating. He slapped one plump hand down onto the marble top of his decision desk. "Sign 'em to an exclusive contract. Give 'em whatever they want."

"Already done," said Number-One. "Everything we proposed, they said, 'Not a problem.'"

"I like these birds," Bunky said. "Get the PR and media people in here. We gotta plan the announcement."


The world took Bunky Sansom to its bosom like never before. He had more honorary citizenships, keys to cities, and propositions from hot celebrity babes than he knew what to do with. Not only did "Not a problem" become his signature phrase, but three countries and seven states adopted it as their official mottoes. Privately, he was already negotiating the protocols that would see him become *de facto* ruler of the world.

Three weeks after he made the big announcement, the first of the expected spaceships were detected decelerating out beyond the orbits of the gas giants. Two days later, the lead ship eased itself into orbit and then, after circling Earth a few times, descended gently into the atmosphere and came to hover over the coordinates Bunky's people had sent. For his convenience, the contact site was the roof of the Sansom Enterprises head office, a vast, truncated pyramid overlooking the sea-girt island that was all that now remained of Vancouver.

The roof was huge, but even so, the ship was too large to land on it. It was too large to land on the shrunken city. Instead it hovered a few yards above where Bunky waited with the Secretary-General, a flock of presidents and prime ministers, a few kings and queens, and one ayatollah.

From the ship's flat base, a long, wide ramp uncurled itself. There was a pregnant pause, then the first of the arrivals came down the sloping gangway.

"That's some bird," Bunky said to Number-One. "Twenty-feet, nothin'—that thing goes thirty."

"I don't think it's a bird," Number-One said. "It's got feathers, all right, but those are arms, not wings. And those teeth—"

The Secretary-General was speaking. She offered a welcome from all the people of Earth, and thanked the newcomers for their kindness in coming to help with the problem of global warming. Bunky stepped up proudly beside her, carefully prepared speech in hand.

The huge feathered being opened its mouth in a kind of smile, revealing dozens of teeth shaped like curved daggers. Its voice was a series of hisses and squawks, but Bunky heard a translation from an earpiece that connected to a device that was also the result of the communicator schematic the slugs had sent through. He had already made a fresh billion from manufacturing it.

"We keep telling you," the creature said, "it's not a problem—it's a solution." It cast its plate-sized, yellow-irised eyes across the crowd of dignitaries, then focused on the king of Tonga. A clawed hand as wide as an armchair scooped up the portly monarch. Then, almost before the king could scream, the foot-long teeth bit off his top half. The jaws crunched. A spray of blood, bone flakes, and meat scraps speckled the heads and shoulders of the dignitaries as they turned and fought each other to reach the roof's single exit. Bunky heard the voice in his ear say, "Hey, didn't I tell you they'd taste just like *sheeshrak*? Come on, try one!"

Then the claws closed around Bunky's torso—he was the plumpest specimen still uncaught—and he was carried to the edge of the roof. He saw the big three-toed feet sink deep into the tar-and-gravel surface with each step. From behind his captor he heard a cacophony of screams and feeding sounds, while the translator conveyed the squabbles over the choicer morsels.

Soon it grew quiet. He twisted in the thing's scaly grip and saw it looking out over the warm sea, its nostrils distending as it breathed in the thick and sultry air. Above it, the sky was now full of immense ships.

The great voice hissed and clacked, the translation duly fed into the billionaire's ear: "It's so good to be back. It'll be like we never left."

"Listen," Bunky gasped, as he was lifted and the bloodstained jaws opened wide.

A moment later, the translator said, sliding down the dinosaur's gullet, "Or maybe not *sheeshrak*. Maybe *chikkichuk*."

# EAGLE

Gregory Benford

The long, fat freighter glided into the harbor at late morning— not the best time for a woman who had to keep out of sight.

The sun slowly slid up the sky as tugboats drew them into Anchorage. The tank ship, a big, sectioned VLCC, was like an elephant ballerina on the stage of a slate-blue sea, attended by tiny, dancing tugs.

Now off duty, Elinor watched the pilot bring them in past the Nikiski Narrows and slip into a long pier with gantries like skeletal arms snaking down, the big pump pipes attached. They were ready for the hydrogen sulfide to flow. The ground crew looked anxious, scurrying around, hooting and shouting. They were behind schedule.

Inside, she felt steady, ready to destroy all this evil stupidity.

She picked up her duffel bag, banged a hatch shut, and walked down to the shore desk. Pier teams in gasworkers' masks were hooking up pumps to offload and even the faint rotten egg stink of the hydrogen sulfide made her hold her breath. The Bursar checked her out, reminding her to be back within twenty-eight hours. She nodded respectfully, and her maritime ID worked at the gangplank checkpoint without a second glance. The burly guy there said something about hitting the bars and she wrinkled her nose. "For breakfast?"

"I seen it, ma'am," he said, and winked.

She ignored the other crew, solid merchant marine types. She had only used her old engineer's rating to get on this freighter, not to strike up the chords of the Seamen's Association song.

She hit the pier and boarded the shuttle to town, jostling onto the bus, anonymous among boat crews eager to use every second of shore time. Just as she'd thought, this was proving the best way to get in under the security perimeter. No airline manifest, no Homeland Security ID checks. In the unloading, nobody noticed her, with her watch cap pulled down and baggy jeans. No easy way to even tell she was a woman.

Now to find a suitably dingy hotel. She avoided Anchorage center and kept to the shoreline where small hotels from the TwenCen still did business. At a likely one on Sixth Avenue the desk clerk told her there were no rooms left.

"With all the commotion at Elmendorf, ever' damn billet in town's packed," the grizzled guy behind the counter said.

She looked out the dirty window, pointed. "What's that?"

"Aw, that bus? Well, we're gettin' that ready to rent, but—"

"How about half price?"

"You don't want to be sleeping in that—"

"Let me have it," she said, slapping down a fifty dollar bill.

"Uh, well." He peered at her. "The owner said—"

"Show it to me."

She got him down to twenty-five when she saw that it really was a "retired bus." Something about it she liked, and no cops would think of looking in the faded yellow wreck. It had obviously fallen on hard times after it had served the school system.

It held a jumble of furniture, apparently to give it a vaguely home-like air. The driver's seat and all else was gone, leaving holes in the floor. The rest was an odd mix of haste and taste. A walnut Victorian love seat with a medallion backrest held the center, along with a lumpy bed. Sagging upholstery and frayed cloth, cracked leather, worn wood, chipped veneer, a radio with the knobs askew, a patched-in shower closet and an enamel basin toilet illuminated with a warped lamp completed the sad tableau. A generator chugged outside as a clunky gas heater wheezed. Authentic, in its way. Restful, too. She pulled on latex gloves the moment the clerk left, and took a nap, knowing she would not soon sleep again. No tension, no doubts. She was asleep in minutes.

Time for the reconn. At the rental place she'd booked, she picked up the wastefully big Ford SUV. A hybrid, though. No problem with the credit card, which looked fine at first use, then erased its traces with a virus that would propagate in the rental system, snipping away all records.

The drive north took her past the air base but she didn't slow down, just blended in with late afternoon traffic. Signs along the highway warned about polar bears—even more dangerous than the massive local browns—coming down this far now. The terrain was just as she had memorized it on Google Earth, the likely shooting spots isolated, thickly wooded. The internet maps got the seacoast wrong, though. Two Inuit villages had recently sprung up along the shore within Elmendorf, as one of their people, posing as a fisherman, had observed and photographed. Studying the pictures, she'd thought they looked slightly ramshackle, temporary, hastily thrown up in the exodus from the tundra regions. No need to last, as the Inuit planned to return north as soon as the Arctic cooled. The makeshift living arrangements had been part of the deal with the Arctic Council for the experiments to make that possible. But access to post schools, hospitals and the PX couldn't make this *home* to the Inuit, couldn't replace their "beautiful land," as the word used by the Labrador peoples named it.

So, too many potential witnesses there. The easy shoot from the coast was out. She drove on. The enterprising Inuit had a brand new diner set up along Glenn Highway, offering breakfast anytime to draw odd-houred Elmendorf workers, and she stopped for coffee.

Dark men in jackets and jeans ate solemnly in the booths, not saying much. A young family sat across from her, the father trying to eat while bouncing his small, wiggly daughter on one knee, the mother spooning eggs into a gleefully uncooperative toddler while fielding endless questions from her bespectacled, school-aged son. The little girl said something to make her father laugh, and he dropped a quick kiss on her shining hair. She cuddled in, pleased with herself, clinging tight as a limpet.

They looked harried but happy, close-knit and complete. Elinor flashed her smile, tried striking up conversations with the tired, taciturn workers, but learned nothing useful from any of them.

Going back into town, she studied the crews working on planes lined up at Elmendorf. Security was heavy on roads leading into the base so she stayed on Glenn. She parked the Ford as near the railroad as she could and left it. Nobody seemed to notice.


At seven, the sun still high overhead, she came down the school bus steps, a new creature. She swayed away in a long-skirted yellow dress with orange Mondrian lines, her shoes casual flats, carrying a small orange handbag. Brushed auburn hair, artful makeup, even long, artificial eyelashes. Bait.

She walked through the scruffy district off K Street, observing as carefully as on her morning reconnaissance. The second bar was the right one. She looked over her competition, reflecting that for some women, there should be a weight limit for the purchase of spandex. Three guys with gray hair were trading lies in a booth, and checking her out. The noisiest of them, Ted, got up to ask her if she wanted a drink. Of course she did, though she was thrown off by his genial warning, "Lady, you don't look like you're carryin.'"

Rattled—had her mask of harmless approachability slipped?—she made herself smile, and ask, "Should I be?"

"Last week a brown bear got shot not two blocks from here, goin' through trash. The polars are bigger, meat-eaters, chase the young males out of their usual areas, so they're gettin' hungry, and mean. Came at a cop, so the guy had to shoot it. It sent him to the ICU, even after he put four rounds in it."

Not the usual pickup line, but she had them talking about themselves. Soon, she had most of what she needed to know about SkyShield.

"We were all retired refuel jockeys," Ted said. "Spent most of thirty years flyin' up big tankers full of jet fuel, so fighters and B-52s could keep flyin', not have to touch down."

Elinor probed, "So now you fly—"

"Same aircraft, most of 'em forty years old—KC Stratotankers, or Extenders—they extend flight times, y'see."

His buddy added, "The latest replacements were delivered just last year, so the crates we'll take up are obsolete. Still plenty good enough to spray this new stuff, though."

"I heard it was poison," she said.

"So's jet fuel," the quietest one said. "But it's cheap, and they needed something ready to go now, not that dust-scatter idea that's still on the drawing board."

Ted snorted. "I wish they'd gone with dustin'—even the traces you smell when they tank up stink like rottin' eggs. More than a whiff, though, and you're already dead. God, I'm sure glad I'm not a tank tech."

"It all starts tomorrow?" Elinor asked brightly.

"Right, ten KCs takin' off per day, returnin' the next from Russia. Lots of big-ticket work for retired duffers like us."

"Who're they?" she asked, gesturing to the next table. She had overheard people discussing nozzles and spray rates. "Expert crew," Ted said. "They'll ride along to do the measurements of cloud formation behind us, check local conditions like humidity and such."

She eyed them. All very earnest, some a tad professorial. They were about to go out on an exciting experiment, ready to save the planet, and the talk was fast, eyes shining, drinks all around.

"Got to freshen up, boys." She got up and walked by the tables, taking three quick shots in passing of the whole lot of them, under cover of rummaging through her purse. Then she walked around a corner toward the rest rooms, and her dress snagged on a nail in the wooden wall. She tried to tug it loose, but if she turned to reach the snag, it would rip the dress further. As she fished back for it with her right hand, a voice said, "Let me get that for you."

Not a guy, but one of the women from the tech table. She wore a flattering blouse with comfortable, well-fitted jeans, and knelt to unhook the dress from the nail head.

"Thanks," Elinor said, and the woman just shrugged, with a lopsided grin.

"Girls should stick together here," the woman said. "The guys can be a little rough."

"Seem so."

"Been here long? You could join our group—always room for another woman, up here! I can give you some tips, introduce you to some sweet, if geeky, guys."

"No, I... I don't need your help." Elinor ducked into the women's room.

She thought on this unexpected, unwanted friendliness while sitting in the stall, and put it behind her. Then she went back into the game, fishing for information in a way she hoped wasn't too obvious. Everybody likes to talk about their work, and when she got back to the pilots' table, the booze worked in her favor. She found out some incidental information, probably not vital, but it was always good to know as much as you could. They already called the redesigned planes "Scatter Ships" and their affection for the lumbering, ungainly aircraft was reflected in banter about unimportant engineering details and tales of long-ago combat support missions.

One of the big guys with a wide grin sliding toward a leer was buying her a second martini when her cell rang.

"Albatross okay. Our party starts in thirty minutes," said a rough voice. "You bring the beer."

She didn't answer, just muttered, "Damned salesbots. . .," and disconnected.

She told the guy she had to "tinkle," which made him laugh. He was a pilot just out of the Air Force, and she would have gone for him in some other world than this one. She found the back exit—bars like this always had one—and was blocks away before he would even begin to wonder.

Anchorage slid past unnoticed as she hurried through the broad, deserted streets, planning. Back to the bus, out of costume, into all-weather gear, boots, grab some trail mix and an already-filled back-pack. Her thermos of coffee she wore on her hip.

She cut across Elderberry Park, hurrying to the spot where her briefing said the trains paused before running into the depot. The port and rail lines snugged up against Elmendorf Air Force Base, convenient for them, and for her.

The freight train was a long, clanking string and she stood in the chill gathering darkness, wondering how she would know where they were. The passing autorack cars had heavy shutters, like big steel Venetian blinds, and she could not see how anybody got into them.

But as the line clanked and squealed and slowed, a quick laser flash caught her, winked three times. She ran toward it, hauling up onto a slim platform at the foot of a steel sheet.

It tilted outward as she scrambled aboard, thudding into her thigh, nearly knocking her off. She ducked in and saw by the distant streetlights vague outlines of luxury cars. A Lincoln sedan door swung open. Its interior light came on and she saw two men in the front seats. She got in the back and closed the door. Utter dark.

"It clear out there?" the cell phone voice asked from the driver's seat.

"Yeah. What—"

"Let's unload. You got the SUV?"

"Waiting on the nearest street."

"How far?"

"Hundred meters."

The man jigged his door open, glanced back at her. "We can make it in one trip if you can carry twenty kilos."

"Sure," though she had to pause to quickly do the arithmetic, forty-four pounds. She had backpacked about that much for weeks in the Sierras. "Yeah, sure."

The missile gear was in the trunks of three other sedans, at the far end of the autorack. As she climbed out of the car the men had inhabited, she saw the debris of their trip—food containers in the back seats, assorted junk, the waste from days spent coming up from Seattle. With a few gallons of gas in each car, so they could be driven on and off, these two had kept warm running the heater. If that ran dry, they could switch to another.

As she understood it, this degree of mess was acceptable to the railroads and car dealers. If the railroad tried to wrap up the autoracked cars to keep them out, the bums who rode the rails would smash windshields to get in, then shit in the cars, knife the upholstery. So they had struck an equilibrium. That compromise inadvertently produced a good way to ship weapons right by Homeland Security. She wondered what Homeland types would make of a Dart, anyway. Could they even tell what it was?

The rough-voiced man turned and clicked on a helmet lamp. "I'm Bruckner. This is Gene."

Nods. "I'm Elinor." Nods, smiles. Cut to the chase. "I know their flight schedule."

Bruckner smiled thinly. "Let's get this done."

Transporting the parts in via autoracked cars was her idea. Bringing them in by small plane was the original plan, but Homeland might nab them at the airport. She was proud of this slick work-around.

"Did railroad inspectors get any of you?" Elinor asked.

Gene said, "Nope. Our two extras dropped off south of here. They'll fly back out."

With the auto freights, the railroad police looked for tramps sleeping in the seats. No one searched in the trunks. So they had put a man on each autorack, and if some got caught, they could distract from the gear. The men would get a fine, be hauled off for a night in jail, and the shipment would go on.

"Luck is with us," Elinor said. Bruckner looked at her, looked more closely, opened his mouth, but said nothing.

They both seemed jumpy by the helmet light. "How'd you guys live this way?" she asked, to get them relaxed.

"Pretty poorly," Gene said. "We had to shit in bags."

She could faintly smell the stench. "And those are . . . ?"

"In the trunk of another gas guzzler," Gene said, chuckling. "Nice surprise for the eco-fuckin', money-hungry bastards who sell these."

She said nothing, just nodded. Everybody had their point of view.

Using Bruckner's helmet light they hauled the assemblies out, neatly secured in backpacks. Bruckner moved with strong, graceless efficiency. Gene too. She hoisted hers on, grunting.

The freight started up, lurching forward. "Damn!" Gene said.

They hurried. When they opened the steel flap, she hesitated, jumped, stumbled on the gravel, but caught herself. Nobody within view in the velvet cloaking dusk.

They walked quietly, keeping steady through the shadows. It got cold fast, even in late May. At the Ford they put the gear in the back and got in. She drove them to the old school bus. Nobody talked.

She stopped them at the steps to the bus. "Here, put these gloves on."

They grumbled but they did it. Inside, heater turned to high, Bruckner asked if she had anything to drink. She offered bottles of vitamin water but he waved it away. "Any booze?"

Gene said, "Cut that out."

The two men eyed each other and Elinor thought about how they'd been days in those cars and decided to let it go. Not that she had any liquor, anyway.

Bruckner was lean, rawboned and self-contained, with minimal movements and a constant, steady gaze in his expressionless face. "I called the pickup boat. They'll be waiting offshore near Eagle Bay by eight."

Elinor nodded. "First flight is 9:00 AM. It'll head due north so we'll see it from the hills above Eagle Bay."

Gene said, "So we get into position. . . when?"

"Tonight, just after dawn."

Bruckner said, "I do the shoot."

"And we handle perimeter and setup, yes.

"How much trouble will we have with the Indians?"

Elinor blinked. "The Inuit settlement is down by the seashore. They shouldn't know what's up."

Bruckner frowned. "You sure?"

"That's what it looks like. Can't exactly go there and ask, can we?"

Bruckner sniffed, scowled, looked around the bus. "That's the trouble with this nickel-and-dime operation. No real security."

Elinor said, "You want security, buy a bond."

Bruckner's head jerked around. "Whassat mean?"

She sat back, took her time. "We can't be sure the DARPA people haven't done some serious public relations work with the Natives. They're probably all in favor of SkyShield—their entire way of life is melting away with the sea ice, along with any chance of holding on to their traditions for the next generation. And by the way, they're not "Indians", they're "Inuit". Used to be called Eskimos, but the Inupiat and Yup'ik councils finally agreed to one name that didn't offend the Canadian peoples."

"You seem pretty damn sure of yourself."

"People say it's one of my best features."

Bruckner squinted and said, "You're—"

"A maritime engineering officer. That's how I got here and that's how I'm going out."

"You're not going with us?"

"Nope, I go back out on my ship. I have first engineering watch tomorrow, oh-one-hundred hours." She gave him a hard flat look. "We go up the inlet, past Birchwood Airport. I get dropped off, steal a car, head south to Anchorage, while you get on the fishing boat, they work you out to the headlands. The bigger ship comes in, picks you up. You're clear and away."

Bruckner shook his head. "I thought we'd—"

"Look, there's a budget and—"

"We've been holed up in those damn cars for—"

"A week, I know. Plans change."

"I don't like changes."

"Things change," Elinor said, trying to make it mild.

But Bruckner bristled. "I don't like you cutting out, leaving us—"

"I'm in charge, remember." She thought, *He travels the fastest who travels alone.*

"I thought we were all in this together."

She nodded. "We are. But Command made me responsible, since this was my idea."

His mouth twisted. "I'm the shooter, I—"

"Because I got you into the Ecuador training. Me and Gene, we depend on you." Calm, level voice. No need to provoke guys like this; they did it enough on their own.

Silence. She could see him take out his pride, look at it, and decide to wait a while to even the score.

Bruckner said, "I gotta stretch my legs," and clumped down the steps and out of the bus.

Elinor didn't like the team splitting and thought of going after him. But she knew why Bruckner was antsy - too much energy with no outlet. She decided just to let him go.

To Gene she said, "You've known him longer. He's been in charge of operations like this before?"

Gene thought. "There've *been* no operations like this."

"Smaller jobs than this?"

"Plenty."

She raised her eyebrows. "Surprising."

"Why?"

"He walks around using that mouth, while he's working?"

Gene chuckled. " 'Fraid so. He gets the work done though."

"Still surprising."

"That he's the shooter, or—"

"That he still has all his teeth."


While Gene showered, she considered. Elinor figured Bruckner for an injustice collector, the passive-aggressive loser type. But he had risen quickly in The LifeWorkers, as they called themselves, brought into the inner cadre that had formulated this plan. Probably because he was willing to cross the line, use violence in the cause of justice. Logically, she should sympathize with him, because he was a lot like her.

But sympathy and liking didn't work that way.

There were people who soon would surely yearn to read her obituary, and Bruckner's too, no doubt. He and she were the cutting edge of environmental activism, and these were desperate times indeed. Sometimes you had to cross the line, and be sure about it.

Most of the blithely unaware LifeWorkers had plenty of complaints about the state of the world, loved hikes in the open, belonged to the Sierra Club, recycled, turned vegetarian, owned a Prius. Many were as neurotic as a cadre of waltzing mice. But in her experience, they also thought life had dealt them a bad hand, and reality was hard to locate. So they sought big causes to wash away those conflicted feelings. *Serenity now!* seemed their cry. *And the way we want it.* Without having to make hard choices, of course.

Elinor had made a lot of hard choices. She knew she wouldn't last long on the scalpel's edge of active environmental justice, and that was fine by her. Her role would soon be to speak for the true cause. Her looks, her brains, her photogenic presence and charm—she knew she'd been chosen for this mission, and the public one afterwards, for these attributes, as much as for the plan she had devised. A fortunate confluence of genetics and nurture. People listen, even to ugly messages, when the face of the messenger is pretty. And once they finished here, she would have to be heard.

She and Gene carefully unpacked the gear and started to assemble the Dart. The parts connected with a minimum of wiring and socket clasps, as foolproof as possible. They worked steadily, assembling the tube, the small recoil-less charge, snapping and clicking the connections. She admired the recoil-less ejection motor that hurled the projectile out of the barrel and to a distance where they wouldn't get hurt by the next stage's back blast. On the training range in Ecuador she had been impressed with how the solid fuel sustainer rocket ignited at a safe distance, accelerating away like a mad hornet.

Gene said, "The targeting antenna has a rechargeable battery, they tend to drain. I'll top it up."

She nodded, distracted by the intricacies of a process she had trained for a month ago. She set the guidance, the smart- proportional navigation that controlled the missile's sequential sensor modes. Tracking would first be Infrared only, zeroing in on the target's exhaust, but once in the air and nearing its goal, it would use multiple targeting modes—laser, IR, advanced visual recognition—to get maximal impact on the main body of the aircraft.

They got it assembled and stood back to regard the linear elegance of the Dart. It had a deadly, snakelike beauty, its shiny white skin tapered to a snub point.

"Pretty, yeah," Gene said. "And way better than any Stinger. Next generation, smarter, near four times the range."

She knew guys liked anything that could shoot, but to her it was just a tool. She nodded.

"Y'know, Stingers—the first really good surface to air missiles, shoulder launched like the Dart—went into use against the Soviets in the late eighties. Even then, with less than five K of effective punch, they made it hell for gunship choppers, supply planes. Inside two years, the Russians were pushed out of Afghanistan and the Berlin Wall came down and then the whole damn Soviet Union fell, too."

"Not just because of Stingers," Elinor couldn't resist saying.

Gene sniffed, caressed the lean body of the Dart, and smiled.

Bruckner came clumping up the bus stairs with a fixed smile on his face that looked like it had been delivered to the wrong address. He waved a lit cigarette. Elinor got up, forced herself to smile. "Glad you're back, we—"

"Got some 'freshments," he said, dangling some beers in their six-pack plastic cradle, and she realized he was drunk.

The smile fell from her face like a picture off a wall.

She had to get along with these two but this was too much. She stepped forward, snatched the beer bottles and tossed them onto the Victorian love seat. "No more."

Bruckner tensed and Gene sucked in a breath. Bruckner made a move to grab the beers and Elinor snatched his hand, twisted the thumb back, turned hard to ward off a blow from his other hand—and they froze, looking into each other's eyes from a few centimeters away.

Silence.

Gene said, "She's right, y'know."

More silence.

Bruckner sniffed, backed away. "You don't have to be rough."

"I wasn't."

They looked at each other, let it go.

She figured each of them harbored a dim fantasy of coming to her in the brief hours of darkness. She slept in the lumpy bed and they made do with the furniture. Bruckner got the love seat—ironic victory—and Gene sprawled on a threadbare comforter.

Bruckner talked some but dozed off fast under booze, so she didn't have to endure his testosterone-fueled eine kleine crocked-musik. But he snored, which was worse.

The men napped and tossed and worried. No one came to her, just as she wanted it. She kept a small knife in her hand, in case. For her, though, sleep came easily.

After eating a cold breakfast, they set out before dawn, 2:30 AM, Elinor driving. She had decided to wait till then because they could mingle with early morning Air Force workers driving toward the base. This far north, it started brightening by 3:30, and they'd be in full light before 5:00. Best not to stand out as they did their last reconnaissance. It was so cold she had to run the heater for five minutes to clear the windshield of ice. Scraping with her gloved hands did nothing.

The men had grumbled about leaving absolutely nothing behind. "No traces," she said. She wiped down every surface, even though they'd worn medical gloves the whole time in the bus.

Gene didn't ask why she stopped and got a gas can filled with gasoline, and she didn't say. Tech guys loved their gadgets as mothers did their children.

She noticed the wind was fairly strong and from the north, and smiled. "Good weather. Prediction's holding up."

Bruckner said sullenly, "Goddamn *cold*."

"The KC Extenders will take off into the wind, head north." Elinor judged the nearly cloud-free sky. "Just where we want them to be."

They drove up a side street in Mountain View, and parked overlooking the fish hatchery and golf course, so she could observe the big tank refuelers lined up at the loading site. She counted five KC-10 Extenders, freshly surplussed by the Air Force. Their big bellies reminded her of pregnant whales.

From their vantage point, they could see down to the temporarily expanded checkpoint, set up just outside the base. As foreseen, security was stringently tight this near the airfield—all drivers and passengers had to get out, be scanned, IDs checked by portable comp against global records, briefcases and purses searched. K-9 units inspected car interiors and trunks. Explosives-detecting robots rolled under the vehicles.

She fished out binoculars and focused on the people waiting to be cleared. Some carried laptops and backpacks and she guessed they were the scientists flying with the dispersal teams. Their body language was clear. Even this early, they were jazzed, eager to go, excited as kids on a field trip. One of the pilots had mentioned there would be some sort of pre-flight ceremony, honoring the teams that had put all this together. The flight crews were studiedly nonchalant—this was an important, high-profile job, sure, but they couldn't let their cool down in front of so many science nerds. She couldn't see well enough to pick out Ted, or the friendly woman from the bar.

In a special treaty deal with the Arctic Council, they would fly from Elmendorf and arc over the North Pole, spreading hydrogen sulfide in their wakes. The tiny molecules of it would mate with water vapor in the stratospheric air, making sulfurics. Those larger, wobbly molecules reflected sunlight well—a fact learned from volcano eruptions back in the TwenCen. Spray megatons of hydrogen sulfide into the stratosphere, let water turn it into a sunlight-bouncing sheet—SkyShield—and they could cool the entire Arctic.

Or so the theory went. The Arctic Council had agreed to this series of large-scale experiments, run by the USA since they had the in-flight refuelers that could spread the tiny molecules to form the SkyShield. Small-scale experiments—opposed, of course, by many enviros—had seemed to work. Now came the big push, trying to reverse the retreat of sea ice and warming of the tundra.

Anchorage lay slightly farther north than Oslo, Helsinki, and Stockholm, but not as far north as Reykjavik or Murmansk. Flights from Anchorage to Murmansk would let them refuel and reload hydrogen sulfide at each end, then follow their paths back over the pole. Deploying hydrogen sulfide along their flight paths at 45,000 feet, they would spread a protective layer to reflect summer sunlight. In a few months, the sulfuric droplets would ease down into the lower atmosphere, mix with moist clouds, and come down as rain or snow, a minute, undetectable addition to the acidity already added by industrial pollutants. Experiment over.

The total mass delivered was far less than that from volcanoes like Pinatubo, which had cooled the whole planet in 1991-92. But volcanoes do messy work, belching most of their vomit into the lower atmosphere. This was to be a designer volcano, a thin skin of aerosols skating high across the stratosphere.

It might stop the loss of the remaining sea ice, the habitat of the polar bear. Only ten percent of the vast original cooling sheets remained. Temperature increases were now so high that crops were failing in tropical regions and billions of people were threatened with starvation.

But many felt such geoengineered tinkerings would also slow cutbacks in carbon dioxide emissions. People loved convenience, their air-conditioning and winter heating and big lumbering cars. So fossil fuel reductions were still barely getting started. Humanity had already driven the air's $CO_2$ content to twice that before 1800, and with every developing country burning fossil fuels—oil and coal—as fast as they could extract them, only immediate, dire emergency could drive them to abstain. To do what was right.

The greatest threat to humanity arose not from terror, but error. Time to take the gloves off.

She put the binocs away and headed north. The city's seacoast was mostly rimmed by treacherous mudflats, even after the sea kept rising. Still, there were coves and sandbars of great beauty. Elinor drove off Glenn Highway to the west, onto progressively smaller, rougher roads, working their way backcountry by Bureau of Land Management roads to a sagging, long-unused access gate for loggers. Bolt cutters made quick work of the lock securing its rusty chain closure. After she pulled through, Gene carefully replaced the chain and linked it with an equally rusty padlock, brought for this purpose. Not even a thorough check would show it had been opened, till the next time BLM tried to unlock it. They were now on Elmendorf, miles north of the airfield, far from the main base's bustle and security precautions. Thousands of acres of mudflats, woods, lakes, and inlet shoreline lay almost untouched, used for military exercises and not much else. Nobody came here except for infrequent hardy bands of off-duty soldiers or pilots, hiking with maps red-marked UXO for "Unexploded Ordnance." Lost live explosives, remnant of past field maneuvers, tended to discourage casual sightseers and trespassers, and the Inuit villagers wouldn't be berry-picking till July and August. She consulted her satellite map, then took them on a side road, running up the coast. They passed above a cove of dark blue waters.

Beauty. Pure and serene.

The sea level rise had inundated many of the mudflats and islands, but a small rocky platform lay near shore, thick with trees. Driving by, she spotted a bald eagle perched at the top of a towering spruce tree. She had started birdwatching as a Girl Scout and they had time; she stopped.

She left the men in the Ford and took out her long-range binocs. The eagle was grooming its feathers and eyeing the fish rippling the waters offshore. Gulls wheeled and squawked, and she could see sea lions knifing through fleeing shoals of herring, transient dark islands breaking the sheen of waves. Crows joined in onshore, hopping on the rocks and pecking at the predators' leftovers.

She inhaled the vibrant scent of ripe wet salty air, alive with what she had always loved more than any mere human. This might be the last time she would see such abundant, glowing life, and she sucked it in, trying to lodge it in her heart for times to come.

She was something of an eagle herself, she saw now, as she stood looking at the elegant predator. She kept to herself, loved the vibrant natural world around her, and lived by making others pay the price of their own foolishness. An eagle caught hapless fish. She struck down those who would do evil to the important world, the natural one.

Beyond politics and ideals, this was her reality.

Then she remembered what else she had stopped for. She took out the comm and pinged the call number.

A buzz, then a blurred woman's voice. "Able Baker."

"Confirmed. Get a GPS fix on us now. We'll be here, same spot, for pickup in two to three hours. Assume two hours."

Buzz buzz. "Got you fixed. Timing's okay. Need a Zodiac?"

"Yes, definite, and we'll be moving fast."

"You bet. Out."

Back in the cab, Bruckner said, "What was that for?"

"Making the pickup contact. It's solid."

"Good. But I meant, what took so long."

She eyed him levelly. "A moment spent with what we're fighting for."

Bruckner snorted. "Let's get on with it."

Elinor looked at Bruckner and wondered if he wanted to turn this into a spitting contest just before the shoot.

"Great place," Gene said diplomatically.

That broke the tension and she started the Ford.

They rose further up the hills northeast of Anchorage, and at a small clearing, she pulled off to look over the landscape. To the east, mountains towered in lofty gray majesty, flanks thick with snow. They all got out and surveyed the terrain and sight angles toward Anchorage. The lowlands were already thick with summer grasses, and the winds sighed southward through the tall evergreens.

Gene said, "Boy, the warming's brought a lot of growth."

Bruckner was fidgeting, but said, "Sure, 'cause nobody'll stop burning fossil fuels. Unless we force them to."

"Look there." Elinor pointed, walking down to a pond.

They stopped at the edge, where bubbles popped on the scummy surface. "Damn," Gene said. "The land's warming, so—"

"Gas's released," Bruckner said. "Read about that. Coming out of the tundra and all."

Bruckner knelt and popped open a cigarette lighter. He flicked it and blue flames flared above the water, pale flickers in the sunlight. "Better it turns into carbon dioxide than staying methane," he said. "Worse greenhouse gas there is, methane."

They watched the flames die out, and turned away.

Elinor glanced at her watch and pointed. "The KCs will come from that direction, into the wind. Let's set up on that hillside."

They worked around to a heavily wooded hillside with a commanding view toward Elmendorf Air Force Base. "This looks good," Bruckner said, and Elinor agreed.

"Damn—a bear!" Gene cried.

They looked down into a narrow canyon with tall spruce. A large brown bear was wandering along a stream about a hundred meters away.

Elinor saw Bruckner haul out a .45 automatic. He cocked it.

When she looked back the bear was looking toward them. It turned and started up the hill with lumbering energy.

"Back to the car," she said.

The bear broke into a lope.

Bruckner said, "Hell, I could just shoot it. This is a good place to see the takeoff and—"

"No. We move to the next hill."

Bruckner said, "I want—"

"Go!"

They ran.

One hill farther south, Elinor braced herself against a tree for stability and scanned the Elmendorf landing strips. The image wobbled as the air warmed across hills and marshes.

Lots of activity. Three KC-10 Extenders ready to go. One tanker was lined up on the center lane and the other two were moving into position.

"Hurry!" she called to Gene, who was checking the final setup menu and settings on the Dart launcher.

He carefully inserted the missile itself in the launcher. He checked, nodded and lifted it to Bruckner. They fitted the shoulder straps to Bruckner, secured it, and Gene turned on the full arming function. "Set!" he called.

Elinor saw a slight stirring of the center Extender and it began to accelerate. She checked: right on time, oh-nine-hundred hours. Hard-core military like Bruckner, who had been a Marine in the Middle East, called Air Force the "saluting Civil Service," but they did hit their markers. The Extenders were not military now, just surplus, but flying giant tanks of sloshing liquid around the stratosphere demands tight standards.

"I make the range maybe twenty kilometers," she said. "Let it pass over us, hit it close as it goes away."

Bruckner grunted, hefted the launcher. Gene helped him hold it steady, taking some of the weight. Loaded, it weighed nearly fifty pounds. The Extender lifted off, with a hollow, distant roar that reached them a few seconds later, and Elinor could see media coverage was high. Two choppers paralleled the takeoff for footage, then got left behind.

The Extender was a full extension DC-10 airframe and it came nearly straight toward them, growling through the chilly air. She wondered if the chatty guy from the bar, Ted, was one of the pilots. Certainly, on a maiden flight the scientists who ran this experiment would be on board, monitoring performance. Very well.

"Let it get past us," she called to Bruckner.

He took his head from the eyepiece to look at her. "Huh? Why—"

"Do it. I'll call the shot."

"But I'm—"

"Do it."

The airplane was rising slowly and flew by them a few kilometers away.

"Hold, hold. . ." she called. "Fire."

Bruckner squeezed the trigger and the missile popped out—*whuff!*—seemed to pause, then lit. It roared away, startling in its speed—straight for the exhausts of the engines, then correcting its vectors, turning, and rushing for the main body. Darting.

It hit with a flash and the blast came rolling over them. A plume erupted from the airplane, dirty black.

"Bruckner! Resight—the second plane is taking off."

She pointed. Gene had the second missile and he chunked it into the Dart tube. Bruckner swiveled with Gene's help. The second Extender was moving much too fast, and far too heavy, to abort takeoff.

The first airplane was coming apart, rupturing. A dark cloud belched across the sky.

Elinor said clearly, calmly, "The Dart's got a max range about right so. . . *shoot.*"

Bruckner let fly and the Dart rushed off into the sky, turned slightly as it sighted, accelerated so they could hardly follow it. The sky was full of noise.

"Drop the launcher!" she cried.

"What?" Bruckner said, eyes on the sky.

She yanked it off him. He backed away and she opened the gas can as the men watched the Dart slashing toward the airplane. She did not watch the sky as she doused the launcher and splashed gas on the surrounding brush.

"Got that lighter?" she asked Bruckner.

He could not take his eyes off the sky. She reached into his right pocket and took out the lighter. Shooters had to watch, she knew, and Bruckner did not seem to notice her hands.

She lit the gasoline and it went up with a *whump.*

"Hey! Let's go!" She dragged the men toward the car.

They saw the second hit as they ran for the Ford. The sound got buried in the thunder that rolled over them as the first Extender hit the ground kilometers away, across the inlet. The hard clap shook the air, made Gene trip then stagger forward.

She started the Ford and turned away from the thick column of smoke rising from the launcher. It might erase any fingerprints or DNA they'd left, but it had another purpose too.

She took the run back toward the coast at top speed. The men were excited, already reliving the experience, full of words. She said nothing, focused on the road that led them down to the shore. To the north, a spreading dark pall showed where the first plane went down.

One glance back at the hill told her the gasoline had served as a lure. A chopper was hammering toward the column of oily smoke, buying them some time.

The men were hooting with joy, telling each other how great it had been. She said nothing.

She was happy in a jangling way. Glad she'd gotten through without the friction with Bruckner coming to a point, too. Once she'd been dropped off, well up the inlet, she would hike around a bit, spend some time birdwatching with the binocs, exchange horrified words with anyone she met about that awful plane crash—No, I didn't actually *see* it, did you?—and work her way back to the freighter after noon, slipping by Elmendorf in the chaos that would be at crescendo by then. Get some sleep, if she could.

They stopped above the inlet, leaving the Ford parked under the thickest cover they could find. She looked for the eagle, but didn't see it. Frightened skyward by the bewildering explosions and noises, no doubt. They ran down the incline. She thumbed on her comm, got a crackle of talk, handed it to Bruckner. He barked their code phrase, got confirmation.

A Zodiac was cutting a V of white, homing in on the shore. The air rumbled with the distant beat and roar of choppers and jets, the search still concentrated around the airfield. She sniffed the rotten egg smell, already here from the first Extender. It would kill everything near the crash, but this far off should be safe, she thought, unless the wind shifted. The second Extender had gone down closer to Anchorage, so it would be worse there.

Elinor and the men hurried down toward the shore to meet the Zodiac. Bruckner and Gene emerged ahead of her as they pushed through a stand of evergreens, running hard. If they got out to the pickup craft, suitably disguised among the fishing boats, they might well get away.

But on the path down, a stocky Inuit man stood. Elinor stopped, dodged behind a tree.

Ahead of her, Bruckner shouted, "Out of the way!"

The man stepped forward, raised a shotgun. She saw something compressed and dark in his face.

"You shot down the planes?" he demanded.

A tall Inuk, racing in from the side, shouted, "I saw their car, coming from there!"

Bruckner slammed to a stop, reached down for his .45 automatic—and the man shot Bruckner, pumped his shotgun. Gene yelled, and without pause, the man shot him, too. The two seemed to jump backward, then sprawled, lifeless. All in the time it took her to blink.

Elinor stood rigid, staring. She felt the world collapsing around her. She shook her head, stepped quietly back. Her pulse came fast as she started working her way back to the Ford, slipping among the trees. The soft loam kept her footsteps silent.

A third man, face congested with rage, tears pouring down his face, stepped out from a tree ahead of her. She recognized him as the young Inuit father from the diner, and he cradled a black hunting rifle. "Stop!"

She stood still, lifted her binocs. "I'm birdwatching, what—"

"I saw you drive up with them."

A deep, brooding voice behind her said, "Those planes were going to stop the warming, save our land, save our people."

She turned to the man pointing the shotgun, hands spread. "The only true way to do that is by stopping the oil companies, the corporations, the burning of fossil—"

The shotgun man barked, "That will not save us. Not save the Arctic. Our beautiful home." He had a knotted face and burning eyes beneath heavy brows.

She talked fast, hands up, open palms toward him. "All that SkyShield nonsense won't stop the oceans from turning acid. Only fossil—"

"Do what you can, when you can. We learn that up here." This came from the tall man. They all had their guns trained on her now. Faces twitched, fingers trembled, fury pumped through them, but the bores pointing at her stayed as steady and implacable as their eyes.

"Okay, really, I'm on your side. And what are you doing? I was just—"

"Not birdwatching. You dropped those airplanes on our village. Our homes. Our families! We were out here getting rid of a bear that mauled a fisherman yesterday."

"I didn't mean, I, those guys you killed—they didn't mean, they were just trying to stop the corporate—"

"You killed our families!" the big man said. The young father stood frozen, staring at her, full growing realization striking him mute.

She froze. What he said was true, but he could not see the big picture. What words could she use, what words could make them see why this had been necessary? "I, I—" and there she stalled, looking in the agonized eyes of the young father, windows upon a hell she could not imagine.

*"Why?"* he asked, his voice a choked whisper. "I, I... need to know, for them..."

"I, we, we had to... We had to stop them. People won't give up fossil fuels... until, until it gets... worse, until it hurts them where they live... and SkyShield would've slowed that down, made things too, too... easy for them. I saw that—we saw that—and this was, was the only way to make the world see that. People don't do what's right unless... they... have to..." Her words ran out, facing a man whose world had already ended. Her heartbeat thundered in her ears, her knees felt unsteady. She wondered if she might faint. What to say, what words, what words could get her out of this...?

He finally spoke, hoarse, but clear.

"Principles over people. That's what you chose, wasn't it? You've never seen people as anything but objects to be moved... I learned about that at college—the word was 'sociopathy,' or 'megalomania'—when I studied history... And not *one* of your '*principles*' is worth a hair on my little Pitka's head..."

He turned to the man with the shotgun, clearly their leader, an Elder, and said, "I know enough, now. A diseased mind, and a diseased heart. Her madness should not be allowed to spread, or to infect others."

He stopped, gathered himself, and almost whispered,

"I speak for my family."

The man with the shotgun glanced at the tall man with the rifle. They exchanged nods, quick words in a complex, guttural language she could not understand. The rifleman seemed to dissolve into the brush, steps fast and flowing, as he headed at a crouching dead run down to the shoreline and the waiting Zodiac.

She sucked in the clean sea air and thought about the eagle. She looked up for it in the sky but it was not there. Not there when she needed it.

It was the last thing she thought, yet it was only a mild regret.

# COME AGAIN SOME OTHER DAY

Michael Alexander

I was watching a political news channel over coffee. The United Nations was debating in the General Assembly whether somebody should do something about restarting the Gulf Stream.

Sorry about that.

There were the usual paid ads denouncing Israel, the United States of America, Tsarstvo Russkoye, the Caliphate, and the North Pacific Gyre Republic. The last one bugged me; any country founded on the recovery of floating ocean garbage should get a chance, even if it feeds illegal immigrants to sharks. I mean, they *are* warned.

The representative from Eurocorp was arguing that people there were finally getting acclimated to the changes and that viewing the annual polar bear migration across the Baltic through Gdansk was becoming a significant part of the winter tourist trade. Then the representative from Brazil got up to complain that that was all well and good for Europe, but his country didn't appreciate losing its rainforests in return. The Eurocorp rep bought rebuttal time to note that Brazil had done a fine job destroying the forests on its own. Brazil replied his government was considering formally calling the situation an Act of Aggression and Eurocorp called Brazil an Arse (he was English). Mutual threats of preemptive defensive aggression were tossed around freely. Sounded like 1914 all over again; just shoot the fat guy and get it over with.

The representative from Oz noted that the floods in the Murray-Darling Basin were more than offset by increased rainfall in northwestern New South Wales, and he was perfectly happy to let things continue as they were. The Eurocorp and Brazil reps huddled for a minute and then bought time to mutually condemn the Aussie for showing indifference to the rest of the world's problems, to which the 'roo said how does it feel to be on the receiving end for a change (he actually said they were a couple of poofters and should shut their gobs)?

The Central African Conglomeration formally joined Brazil in protest. The North African Conglomeration joined Australia, noting that the Sahara was shrinking with the increased rainfall and wondered idly if Europe still wanted to import grain from the Sahel? Europe objected to the veiled use of food as a weapon.

Watching the U.N. is more fun than watching your dog after you give him a mouthful of peanut butter. Like the General Assembly he just stands there and smacks his lips a lot, then makes a mess on the floor a while later. Insane, but another datum.

I turned off the box and ran up the periscope for a quick look around. Everything was calm, so I went back to the kitchen, put the tuna casserole in a stay-warm bag, and went upstairs. Pushed the door up and stepped out into a gorgeous summer Wyoming afternoon. The sky was clear and the breeze carried a scent of sagebrush and sulfur as I walked over to Gladys' place.

I stepped on the buzzer. "That you, Hap?" she asked over the intercom.

"Last time I looked. Mind if I come in? Brought some hot dish for dinner."

There was a click and Gladys said, "Come on, the door's open." I lifted the hatch and went down the stairs.

Gladys's place was a duplicate of mine, so I wandered through the den/office to the kitchen, set the bag down and walked over to give her a friendly peck on the cheek. "Do you want to eat right away?"

she asked. "Or should we look over the odd stuff first? I just finished brewing a pot of herbed tea."

Gladys is about my age, tall and lean with short hair the color of freshly cracked iron. "Tea sounds nice," I said, so she poured two big mugs, handed me one and walked out to the consoles in the office, me trailing. We usually take turns, one day her place, one day mine.

The folks at Langley have created some really nice software to help us sort things out, but a big part of the job is just sitting back and letting the information river flow over you while you keep your eyes open. Gladys is better at looking down from above, seeing bigger trends. I'm better at spotting the individual outliers. It works out well.

"Hm. Hap, have you been noticing the stock markets?"

"I've been watching commodities." Pork bellies had been acting strangely lately, varying with pirate activity in the Malaccan Straits and groundwater levels in Arizona, $p < 0.0005$. "And did you catch the U.N. coverage this morning?"

"Getting crazy." She sipped her tea. "The way the Footsie and Hang Seng are going I think maybe we should do something about those dust storms in central Asia." She flicked the data over; I took a long look and agreed. Then we talked about where to grab or put and the probable consequences.

I guess people finally began to take the whole climate thing seriously when the north Asian tundra began rapidly thawing *en masse*, releasing enough methane to make it dangerous to strike a match anywhere between Vladivostok and the Ural Mountains. After the Great Siberian Fart, the Clathrate Catastrophe, melting Greenland and other interesting occurrences the world's leaders finally decided to stop talking about studying the situation some more and start talking about doing something. At least the ones who still had countries above water.

When my father was a kid everything had to be studied some more. But after a while you'd better stop studying that mole on your nose and do something about it. Unless you have a vested interest in metastatic cancer - metastatic cancer is highly successful from the cancer's point of view, after all. So we went from climate change to climate crisis to climate catastrophe, with the blame levels rising in a sort of log-normal fashion.

But in fairness to everyone, the real problem was the maddening lack of strong correlations between causes and effects. Carbon dioxide in the atmosphere went up, temperatures went up. Sometimes. And then they'd stop going up. Scientists could point to irrefutable mechanistic proof that $CO_2$ trapped heat. Skeptics would point out, like some anti-Galileos, that nevertheless, the temperature, she don't a-move. So there were clouds, and water vapor, and El Camino, and North Atlantic Decadal Oscillations, and a million other things, until everyone tripped on their own models.

It seemed to take forever for some genius to finally figure out that the real problem wasn't an incomplete understanding of cause and effect, but a weakening of cause and effect itself. The climate change couldn't be properly modeled because a lot of it wasn't our own doing. A big chunk of it was coming from somewhere else.

Someone was sending batches of bad climate back to us from the future.

That took a while to sink in. There was no basis in scientific thought for such a silly hypothesis, but that didn't stop the government. DARPA set up a black study, convinced itself, then began looking for anyone with an ability to affect the weather. Remember, they also looked at remote viewing a while back. "When I was a little girl I would always say 'Rain, rain, go away' when I wanted to go out and play," Gladys had told me. "And apparently it would go away. Wonder where I sent it." Me, I had never really made the connection between undone homework and snow days. So while the scientists and engineers were working on adding sulfate particulates to the atmosphere or designing improbable mirrors for the Lagrange point, a few of us were learning how to export climate to the past or import it to the present.

People like Gladys and I move climate around. Somewhere uptime people like us are shoving their unwanted climate back and we're trying to get some kind of balance while shoving it even farther back. So all that stuff about orbital eccentricity and Milankovich cycles aside, you might get a tweak about why the last Ice Age ended so quickly; glaciers are a good heat sink.

The biggest problem with moving anything through time is, as I said, that it messes up causality. This wasn't obvious at first. Well, there were a few canaries who had done their Monte Casino simulations, but the point was that temporal swapping let people do something right away about a rapidly deteriorating situation ("Swap, Baby, Swap!" was the slogan early in the program). People who pointed to what appeared to be increasingly weird side effects were told the matter needed "more study."

(It's possible to spot periods where lots of climate swiping and swapping were going on by the increase in strange or inexplicable occurrences. You can only move so much climate to or from any given time before the probability side effects get bad, and then you end up with unbelievable stuff like frogs raining out of the sky or the First World War.)

It turned out that the work was much more intuitive than analytical. Modifying the climate is more conducting an orchestra than solving differential equations. No offense to the mathematicians, but most of them don't have a sense of rhythm. You have to look around and shuffle a lot of relatively minor changes instead of going for the brass ring in one big grab.

So they found us and teamed me and Gladys up and put us in the middle of nowhere in central Wyoming to work on it. We convinced them we had to be isolated from other humans for our amazing powers to work without interference. That was bull, of course. We both just liked the place and were a couple of loners who didn't appreciate the thought of officious types hovering over our shoulders.

"I still feel bad about screwing up the deep ocean currents," Gladys had remarked near the beginning.

"How could we know? To be fair, all we're trying to do is unscrew a bigger mess someone else is laying on us."

"Trouble is, it's like trying to unscrew a virgin. The improbabilities are really starting to pile up."

"And the ones uptime are unscrewing what we screw back in. We're really getting into a positive feedback loop here."

We were importing cool climate from the Maunder Minimum that month. It's best to keep a balance between exporting heat and importing cold. (Too much net heat causes a spike in gasoline prices, among other things. Too much cold brings a rise in dissatisfied employees shooting their bosses. Don't ask, I just work here.) It's also less perturbing to move smaller amounts of climate over shorter intervals. We don't use the Ice Ages anymore. Gulf Stream, cessation of, *vide supra*. Not to mention the mammoths.

What's that hand up over there? Thermodynamics? Fine, smarty pants; try integrating over discontinuous time when t=0 changes partway through. Show your work. Dirac delta functions not allowed.

But in truth things were starting to get out of hand. The Indian monsoon had unexpectedly shifted three hundred miles west last year, and while we managed to more or less move it back, such a big swap meant three Category Five hurricanes hitting the southeast United States, Argentina declaring war on South Africa and the simultaneous introduction by six different fast food chains of deep-fried butter sticks ("Try 'em with BACON!"). You had to wonder just what was going so wrong uptime.

A few hours later I leaned back and switched the console off. "I think we missed dinner," I said.

Gladys was still looking at her box. "Would you mind putting it in the oven to warm up? I'd like to finish something here."

"Sure." I walked back to the kitchen, slid the casserole in the oven, and set it for fifteen minutes at three hundred. Then I picked up a cookbook and sat down, looking for some interesting new recipes.

Gladys eventually followed the scent of food into the kitchen. "You like tofu?" I asked.

"Only if it's free-range."

"Ah, well, too bad. How about banana-nut bread?"

"With candied cherries I can eat a whole loaf."

"Excellent. Tomorrow." I spooned casserole onto two plates and slid one over to her.

She took a bite and nodded. "Good." We ate in silence for a while, which was unusual. Something was bothering her. "Hap. . ."

I looked at her and raised an eyebrow.

"We're running out of wiggle room."

I nodded. Causality was beginning to have kittens and we were rapidly being painted into a corner.

"There was a bulletin just before I came in. The tsar announced he's converting to Judaism."

"*What*? Reform?"

"No, Orthodox."

"Oy." Some things are improbable, but now we were rapidly sliding over to the impossible. I looked around. "You know, we can probably hold out here for quite a while if we have to."

She nodded. "Unless the Yellowstone caldera blows."

"And what are the odds of *that*?" I asked without thinking. Then we both laughed.

I ladled out seconds and we ate some more. "I have an idea," Gladys finally said.

"Excellent. That makes one of us." I was thinking about defense. One of the things I had insisted on was having guns, and I had kept up my marksmanship by plinking cans and the occasional varmint.

"Seriously. It's a little out there—okay, it's way out there."

"Given what we do for a living, I find it hard to think of *anything* truly way out there."

"Good point. The problem is that we keep shuffling improbability around along with climate through time. The whole thing is just getting harder and harder to balance."

"Agreed." I let Gladys talk; she's the smart one.

"So what if we could uncouple the improbability from time?"

I sat there. Nothing happened. "Explain, please."

So she did, and suddenly this great big clue-by-four came down and whapped me in the head. "Beautiful!" I laughed. "Just beautiful!" I leaned over and gave her a kiss. A real one. Ooooh, it suddenly hit me that we had some spooning to do when everything was done.

"Okay, let's get Goddard and Langley on a three-way."

"It could backfire, you know."

"Sure. But we're going to try it anyway, aren't we?"

"Yes. So I guess it's only polite to tell them first."


Goddard was intrigued. Langley was cautious. Needed "more study."

Gladys was adamant and I backed her up. "Look," she finally said, "We'll try a small test and see if there is any measurable result." Goddard agreed that their instruments would probably be able to detect any transfer. Langley finally conceded there was no additional harm in trying, given how things were going. "Okay," Gladys finished, "Leave us alone for a while. Then we'll give it a go at twenty-hundred hours." She flicked off the box. "Dessert?" she asked me.

"There's cherry ice cream in the freezer. I'll scoop some out if you'll make a pot of herbed tea."


It went off without a hitch.

Goddard reported the probe registered a change in response three standard deviations above background. We looked at each other, raised our mugs, and clicked rims. "To the future," I said.

"*Screw* the future," she replied, giggling. Quite girlish for Gladys.

Like all elegant solutions, this one was a headslapper in retrospect. Instead of moving climate through time, we found it was just as easy to move it through space. Easier, really, once you got the feel for it. And the obvious place to put extra warm climate was Mars.

If we work it right, Mars will be well on the way to being terraformed in a century or so. Maybe sooner, if the people uptime figure out what's going on and stop dumping on us and use Mars instead. The causality of that could get interesting.

"Of course, in addition to the warmer climate, we're also adding all that improbability to Mars," I noted as I paused at the foot of the stairs. "It's a smaller place. I wonder if that will have any effect."

Gladys shrugged. "If in a couple of decades something wanders up to one of our probes and waves we might have to rethink things. But for now we're just riding the tiger. As usual." She looked at me. "Would you like to stay a bit longer, Hap?"

"Let's get everyone else's cause and effect worked out first." I winked and headed up the stairs, going home.

# THE MASTER OF THE AVIARY

Bruce Sterling

Every Sunday, Mellow Julian went to the city market to search for birds. Commonly a crowd of his adoring students made his modest outing into a public spectacle.

The timeless questions of youth tortured the cultured young men of the town. "What is a gentleman's proper relationship to his civic duty, and how can he weasel out of it?" Or: "Who is more miserable, the young man whose girl has died, or the young man whose girl will never love him?"

Although Julian had been rude to men in power, he was never rude to his students. He saw each of these young men as something like a book: a hazardous, long-term, difficult project that might never find a proper ending. Julian understood their bumbling need to intrude on his private life. A philosopher didn't have one.

On this particular market Sunday, Julian was being much pestered by Bili, a pale, delicate, round-headed eccentric whose wealthy father owned a glass smelter. The bolder academy students were repelled by Bili's mannerisms, so they hadn't come along. Mellow Julian tolerated Bili's youthful awkwardness. Julian had once been youthful and awkward himself.

Under their maze of parasols, cranes, aqueducts, and archery towers, the finer merchants of Selder sold their fabrics, scissors, fine glass baubles, medications, oils, and herbal liquors. The stony city square held a further maze of humble little shacks, the temporary stalls of the barkers. The barkers were howling about vegetables.

"Asparagus! Red lettuce! Celery! Baby bok choy!" Each shouted name had the tang of romance. Selder's greenhouses close-packed the slope of the mountain like so many shining warts. It was for these rare and precious vegetables that foreigners braved the windy mountain passes and the burning plains.

Mellow Julian bought watercress and spinach, because their bright-green spiritual vibrations clarified his liver.

"Maestro, why do you always buy the cheapest, ugliest food in this city?" Bili piped up. "Spinach is awful."

"It's all that I know how to cook," Julian quipped.

"Maestro, why don't you marry? Then your wife could cook."

"That's a rather intrusive question," Julian pointed out. "Nevertheless, I will enlighten you. I don't care to indulge in any marriage ritual. I will never indulge in any bureaucratic ritual in this city, ever again."

"Why don't you just hire a cook?" persisted Bili.

"I'd have to give him all his orders! I might as well simply cook for myself."

"I know that I'm not very bright," said Bili humbly. "But a profound thinker like you, a man of such exemplary virtue. . . Everybody knows you're the finest scribe in our city. Which is to say, the whole world! Yet you live alone in that little house, fussing with your diet and putting on plays in your backyard."

"I know people talk about me," shrugged Julian. "People chatter and cackle like chickens."

Bili said nothing for a while. He knew he had revealed a sore spot.

Mellow Julian examined the sprawling straw mat of a foreign vendor. All the women of Selder adored seashells, because seashells were delicate, pretty, and exotic. Mellow Julian shared that interest, so he had a close look at the wares.

The shell vendor was a scarred, bristle-bearded sea pirate. His so-called rare seashells were painted plaster fakes.

Julian put away his magnifying lens. He nodded shortly and retreated. "Since you were born almost yesterday, Bili," he said, glancing over his shoulder, "I would urge you to have a good look at that wild, hard-bitten character. This marketplace has never lacked for crooks, but this brute may be a spy."

Bili pointed. "There's even worse to be seen there, maestro."

Huddled under a torn cotton tarp were five dirty refugees: black-haired, yellow-skinned people in travel-torn rags. One of the refugees was not starving. He was the owner or boss of the other four, who visibly were.

"They shouldn't let wretches like those through the gates," said Bili. "My father says they carry disease."

"Every mortal being carries *some* disease," Julian allowed. He edged nearer to the unwholesome scene. The exhausted refugees couldn't even glance up from the cobblestones. "Well," said Julian, "no need to flee these wild invaders. My guess would be that somebody invaded them."

"They're some 'curious specimens,' as you always put it, maestro."

"Indeed, they most certainly are."

"They must have come from very far away."

"You are staring at them, Bili, but you are not observing them," said Julian. "This man is in the ruins of a uniform, and he has a military bearing. This younger brute must be his son. This boy and girl are a brother and sister. And this older woman, whom he has dragged along from the wreck of their fortunes. . . Look at her hands. Those hands still have the marks of rings."

The ruined soldier rose in his tattered boots and stuck out his cal-lused mitt. *"Money, water, food, house! Shelter! Fish! Vegetable!"*

*"I understand you,"* Julian told him, in a fluent Old Proper English. *"I'm touched that you've taken the trouble to learn so many nouns. So. What is your name, sir? My friends call me Mellow Julian Nebraska."*

"*You give me money for her,*" the soldier demanded, pointing. "*You take her away, I buy shelter, water, food, fish, vegetable!*"

"I have some money," offered Bili.

"Don't get hasty, Bili."

"But I think I understand what this foreigner is saying!" said Bili. "Listen! I want to try out my Old Proper English on him. *I buy this woman. You take my money. You eat your fish and vegetables.*" Bili pointed at the boy and girl. "*You feed these children. You wash your clothes. You comb your hair.*" He glanced at Julian. "That's the right English word, isn't it? *Comb?*"

"It is," Julian allowed.

"*You wash yourself in the public bath,*" Bili persisted. "*You stink lesser!*" He turned to Julian triumphantly. "Just look at him! Look at his eyes! He really does understand me! My lessons in the Academy of Selder. . . That dead language is practical! I can't wait to tell my dad!"

"You should no longer call this city 'Selder,' Bili. The true name of your city is 'Shelter.' 'The Resilient, Survivable, Sustainable Shelter,' to list all her antique titles. If your ancestors could see you speaking like this—in their own streets, in their own language—they'd say you were a civilized man."

"Thank you, maestro," said Bili, with a blush to his pale, beardless cheeks. "From you, that means everything."

"We must never forget that we descend from a great people. They made their mistakes—we all do—but someday, we'll surpass them."

"I'm going to buy this woman," Bili decided. "I can afford her. The Selder Academy doesn't cost all *that* much."

"You can't just buy some woman here in the public street!" said Julian. "Not sight unseen, for heaven's sake!"

Julian untied the mouth of his scholar's bag and rustled through the dense jumble within it—his watercress, spinach, scarf, pipe, scissors, string, keys, wax tablet, and magnifying glass. He pulled out one ancient silver dime.

Julian crouched beside the cowering woman and placed the time-worn coin into her blistered hand. "Here," he said, "this coin is for you. Now, stay still, for I'm going to examine you. I won't hurt you. Stick out your tongue."

She gripped the coin feverishly, but she understood not one word.

"Stick out your tongue," commanded Julian, suiting action to words.

He examined her teeth with the magnifying glass.

Then he plucked back the slanted folds of her eyelids. He touched both her ears—pierced, but no jewels left there, not anymore. He thumped at her chest until she coughed. He smelled her breath. He closely examined her hands and feet.

"She's well over forty years old," he said. "She's lost three teeth, she's starving, and she's been walking barefoot for a month. These two youngsters are not her children. I dare say a woman of her years had children once, but these are not them. This brute here with the leather belt, which he used on her legs. . . He's not her husband. She was a lady once. A civilized woman. Before whatever happened, happened."

"How much should I pay for her?" said Bili.

"I have no idea. This is no regular auction. The Godfather is a decent man, he prohibited all that slave-auction mischief years ago. You'd better ask your father how much he thinks a house-servant like her is worth. Not very much, I'd be guessing."

"I'm not buying her for my house," said Bili. "I'm buying her for *your* house."

A moment passed.

"Bili—," Julian said severely, "have I taught you nothing with my lectures, or from the example of my life? I devote myself to sustainable simplicity! Our ancestors never had slaves! Or rather, yes they did, strictly speaking—but they rid themselves of that vice, and built machines instead. We all know how *that* ugly habit turned out! Why would I burden myself with her?"

Bili smiled sheepishly. "Because she is so much like a pet bird?"

"She is rather like a bird," Julian admitted. "More like a bird than a woman. Because she is starving, poor thing."

"Maestro, please accept this woman into your house. Please. People talk about you all the time, they gossip about you. You don't mind that, because you are a philosopher. But maestro, they talk about *me!* They gossip about *me,* because I follow you everywhere, and I adore you! I'd rather kneel at your feet than drill with the men-at-arms! Can't you do me this one favor, and accept a gift from me? You know I have no other gifts. I have no other gifts that even interest you."

After Mellow Julian accepted Bili's gift, Bili became even more of the obnoxious class pet. Bili insisted on being addressed by his antique pseudonym Dandy William Idaho, and sashayed around Selder in a ludicrous antique costume he had faked up, involving "blue jeans." Bili asked impertinent, look-at-me questions during the lectures. He hammed it up after class in amateur theatricals.

However, Bili also applied himself to his language studies. Bili had suddenly come to understand that Old Proper English was the language of the world. Old Proper English was the language of laws, rituals, boundary treaties, water rights, finance arrangements, and marriage dowries. The language of civilization.

That was why a wise and caring Godfather took good care to see that his secretaries wrote an elegant and refined Old Proper English. A scribe with such abilities could risk some personal eccentricities.

Julian named his new servant House Sparrow Oregon. Enquiries around the court made it clear that she was likely from Oregon. War and plague—they were commonly the same event—had expelled many of her kind from their distant homeland.

Deprived of food and shelter, they had dwindled quickly in the cruelties of the weather.

Sometimes, when spared by the storms, refugees found the old grassy highways, and traveled incredible distances. Vagrants came from the West Coast, and savages from the East Coast. Pirates came from the North Coast, where there had once been nothing but ice. The South was a vast baking desert that nobody dared to explore.

Once a teenage boy named Juli had left a village in Nebraska. Julian had suffered the frightening, dangerous trip to Selder, because the people in Selder still knew about the old things. And they did know them—some of them. They knew that the world was round, and that it went around the sun. They knew that the universe was thirteen thousand, seven hundreds of millions of years old. They knew that men were descended from apes, although apes were probably mythical.

They had also built the only city in the known world that was not patched-up from the scraps of a fallen city. Created at the sunset of a more enlightened age, Selder was a thousand years old. Yet it was the only city that had grown during the long dark ages.

The court of the Godfather was a place of sustainable order. The council-of-forty, the Men in Red, were its educated, literate officials. They held the authority to record facts of state. They knew what was meet and proper to write, and what was of advantage to teach, and what should be censored. They had taught Julian, and he had worked for them. He had come to know everything about what they did with language. He was no longer overly fond of what they did.

House Sparrow Oregon had no language that Julian understood. To test her, Julian inscribed the classic letters of antiquity into his wax tablet: THE QUICK BROWN FOX JUMPS OVER THE LAZY DOG. PACK MY BOX WITH FIVE DOZEN LIQUOR JUGS.

In response, Sparrow timidly made a few little scrapes with the stylus. Crooked little symbols, with tops and bottoms. They were very odd, but she knew only ten of them. Sparrow was nobody's scholar.

Julian was patient. Every child who ever entered a school was a small barbarian. To beat them, to shout at them, to point out their obvious shortcomings. . . what did that ever avail? What new students needed were clear and simple rules.

This aging, frightened, wounded woman was heartsick. She had lost all roles, all rules, and all meaning. She was terrified of almost everything in Selder, including him.

So: it was about a small demonstration, and then a patient silence: the wait for her response. So that Sparrow's dark eyes lost their cast of horror and bewilderment. So that she observed the world, no longer mutely gazing on it.

So: This is the water. Here, drink it from this cup. It's good, isn't it? Yes, fresh water is good! The good life is all about simple things like clear water.

Now, this is our bucket in which we bring the water home. Come with me, to observe this. There is nothing to fear in this street. Yes, come along. They respect me, they will not harm you.

You see this? Every stranger living in Selder must learn this right away. This is our most basic civic duty, performed by every able-bodied adult, from the Godfather himself to the girl of twelve. These waterworks look complex and frightening, but you can see how I do this myself. This is a water-lever. It holds that great leather bucket at one end, and this stone weight here at our end.

We dip the great bucket so as to lift the dirty water, so that it slowly flows in many locks and channels, high back up the hillside. We recycle all the water of this city. We never spill it, or lose its rich, fertile, and rather malodorous nutrients. We can spill our own blood in full measure here, but we will never break our water cycle. This is why we have sustained ourselves.

After we heave this great bucket of the dirty civic water—and not before!—then we are allowed to tap one small bucket of clean water, over here, for our private selves.

Now you can try.

Don't let those stupid housewives hurt your feelings. We all look comical at first, before we learn. Yes, you are a foreigner, and you are a curious specimen. That is all right. In the House of Mellow Julian Nebraska, we embrace curiosity. Our door is always open to those who make honest inquiries. We house many things that are strange, as well as you.

Now for the important moral lesson of the birds. Yes, I own many birds. I own too many. Some are oddly shaped, and special, and inbred, and rather sickly. Quite often they die for mysterious reasons. I cannot help that: It is my fate to be the master of an aviary.

Yes, the name I gave you is Sparrow, just like that smallest bird hopping there. These are my pigeons, these are my chickens, these are my ducks. In antiquity there were many other birds, but these are the surviving species.

One can see that to care for these birds suits your proclivities. When you chirp at them in your native language, they hear you and respond to you. As Sparrow the bird-keeper, you have found new purpose in the world. We will have one small drink to celebrate that. It's pretty good, isn't it? It isn't pure clean water, but a moderate amount of sophistication has its place in life.

Now that you have become the trusted mistress of the aviary, it is time for you to learn about this cabinet of curiosities. Being a scholar of advanced and thoughtful habits, I own a large number of these inexplicable objects. Old drawings, fossil bones, seashells, coins and medals, and, especially, many arcane bits of antique machinery. Some are rare. Most are quite horribly old. They all need to be cleaned and dusted. They break easily. Be tender, cautious, and respectful. Above all, do not peel off the labels.

My curiosities are not mere treasures. Instead, they are wonders. Watch with the students, and you will see.

Students, dear friends of learning and the academy: Tonight we study the justly famous "external combustion engine." Tonight we will make one small venture in applied philosophy, revive this engine from its ancient slumbers, and cause it to work before your very eyes.

And what does it do? you may well ask me. What is its just and useful purpose? Nobody knows. No one will ever know. No one has known that for three thousand years.

Now my trusted assistant Sparrow will light the fire beneath the engine's cauldron. Nothing sinister about that, a child could do it, an illiterate, a helpless alien, yes, her. Please give her a round of applause, for she is shy. That was good, Sparrow. You may sit and watch with the others now.

Now see what marvels the world has, to show to a patient observer. Steam is boiling. Steam travels up these pipes. Angry steam flows out of these bent nozzles. This round metal bulb with the nozzles begins to spin. Slowly at first, as you observe. Then more rapidly. At greater speed, greater speed yet: tremendous, headlong, urgent, whizzing speed!

This item from my cabinet, which seemed so humble and obscure: This is the fastest object in the whole world!

Why does it spin so fast? Nobody knows.

It is sufficient to know, young gentlemen, that our ancestors built fire-powered steaming devices of this kind, and they wrecked everything. *They utterly wrecked the entire world.* They wrecked the world so completely that we, their heirs so long after, can scarcely guess at the colossal shape of the world that they wrecked.

You see as well, little Sparrow? Now you know what a wonder can do. When it spins and flashes, in its rapid, senseless, glittering way, you smile and clap your hands.


In the summer, a long and severe heat came. The wisdom of the founders of Selder was proven once again.

Every generation, some venturesome fool would state the obvious—why don't we grow our crops outside of these glass houses? Without those pergolas, sunshades, reflectors, straw blankets, pipes, drips, pumps, filters, cranes, aqueducts, and the Cistern. That would be a hundred times cheaper and easier!

So that error might well be attempted, and then disaster would strike. The exposed crops were shriveled by heat waves, leveled by storm gusts, eaten by airborne hordes of locusts and vast brown crawling waves of teeming mice. In endless drenching rains, the tilled soil would wash straight down the mountainside.

In the long run, all that was not sustainable was not sustained.

Brown dust-lightning split the angry summer sky. Roiling gray clouds blew in from the southern deserts and their dust gently settled on the shining glass of Selder. There were no more pleasant, boozy, poetic star-viewing parties. People retreated into the stony cool of the seed vaults. When they ventured out, they wore hats and goggles and wet, clinging, towel-like robes. They grumbled a great deal about this.

Mellow Julian Nebraska made no such complaint. In times of civic adversity, it pleased him to appear serene. Despite this unwholesome heat and filth, we dwell in a city of shining glass! We may well sweat, but there is no real risk that we will starve! Let us take pride in our community's unique character! We are the only city of the world not perched like a ghost within the sprawling ruin of some city of antiquity! Fortitude and a smiling countenance shall be the watchwords of our day!

Julian sheltered his tender birds from the exigencies of the sky. He made much use of parasols, misting-drips, and clepsydra. The professor's villa was modest, but its features were well considered.

Dirt fell lavishly from the stricken sky, but Sparrow had learned the secret of soap, that mystic potion of lye, lard, ashes, and bleach. Sparrow spoke a little now, but not one word of the vulgar tongue: only comical scraps of the finest Old Proper English. Sparrow wore the clean and simple white robes that her master wore, with a sash around her waist to show that she was a woman, and a scarf around her hair to show that she was a servant. Sparrow would never look normal, but she had come to look neat and dainty.

Julian's enemies—and he had made some—said dark things about the controversial philosopher and his mute exotic concubine. Julian's friends—and he had made many—affected a cosmopolitan tolerance about the whole arrangement. It was not entirely decent, they agreed, but it was, they opined, very like him.

Julian was not a wealthy man, but he could reward his friends. His small garden was cool in the stifling heat, and Sparrow had learned to cook. Sparrow cooked highly alarming meals, with vegetables cut in fragments, and fried in a metal bowl. This was the only Selder food that Sparrow could eat without obvious pangs of disgust.

His students ate these weird concoctions cheerily, because healthy young men ate anything. Then they ran home in darkness to boast that they had devoured marvels.

The wicked summer heat roiled on. It was the policy of the finer folk of the court to dine on meat: mostly rabbit, guinea pig, and mice. Meat spoiled quickly.

When he fell ill, there were rumors that the Godfather had been poisoned. No autocrat ever died without such claims. But no autocrat could live forever, either. So the old Godfather perished.

On the very day of the old man's death, the dusty heat wave broke. Vast torrential rains scoured the mountains. Everyone remarked on this fatal omen.

It was time for the Godfather's cabal to retire into the secret seed vaults, don their robes and masks, and elect the successor.

Julian's students had never seen a succession ritual. It was a sad and sobering time. Men who had never sought out a philosopher asked for some moral guidance.

What on earth are we to do now? Console the grieving, feed the living, and lower the dead man into the Cistern.

What will history say of Godfather Jimi the Seventh? That the warlike spirit of his youth had matured into a wise custodianship of the arts and crafts of peace.

Then there were others with a darker question: What about the power?

There Mellow Julian held his peace. He could guess well enough what would happen. There would be some jostling confusion among the forty masked Men in Red, but realistically, there were only two candidates for the Godfather's palace. First, there was the Favorite. He was the much-preened and beloved nephew of the former Godfather, a well-meaning idiot never tested by adversity.

There was the Other Man, who had known nothing but adversity. He had spent his career in uniform, repressing the city's barbarian enemies. His supporters were hungry and ambitious and vulgar. He would not hesitate to grasp power by any means fair or foul. His own wife and children feared him. He was stubborn and bold, as Julian knew, because he had once been Julian's classmate.

Who would complain if a professor, in a time of trouble, retired into his private life? No rude brawling for the thinking man, no street marches, no shouted threats and vulgar slogans. No intrigues: instead, civility. The cleanly example of the good life. Food, drink, friends, and study. Simplicity and clarity. Humanity.

Humanity.


"Tonight," said Mellow Julian, in his finest Old Proper English, "as scholars assembled in civil society, we shall study together. The general theme of our seminars is remote from all earthly strife. Because she is shining, she is gorgeous, she is lovely, she is the planet Venus. In all her many attributes."

Hoots and cheers and claps.

"Young men," said Julian, "I do not merely speak to you of the carnal Venus. You will recall that your ancestors sent *flying machines* to Venus. *Electrical* machines, gentleman, and they had *virtual* qualities. The people of antiquity *observed* Venus. And Mercury. And Mars. And Jupiter, Saturn, and Neptune. It is written that they sent their machines to observe moons and planets that we can no longer see."

Respectful silence.

"We do not deny that Venus has her venereal aspects," said Julian. "What we want to assert—as civic philosophers—is a solid framework for systematic understanding! What is a man, what is his role in the universe, under the planets and stars?

"Consider this. If a man has a soul, then Venus must touch that soul. We all know that. But how, why? It is not enough to meander dully through our lives, vaguely thinking: 'Venus is the brightest planet in the heavens, so surely she must have something to do with me.' Of course the vibrations of Venus affect a man! Can any man among you deny that we live through the vibrations of the sun? Raise your hand."

Being used to rhetorical questions, they knew better than to raise their hands.

"Certain students of our Academy," said Julian, "have chosen not to attend this course of Venusian seminars. They felt that they needed to be together with their families in this difficult season... In this perilous moment in the long life of our city. Yet when we, as scholars, by deliberate policy... when we remove ourselves from the unseemly dust and mud of our civil strife... from all that hurly-burly..."

A hand shot up in the audience.

"Yes, Practical Jeffrey of Colorado? You have a question?"

"Maestro, what is *hurly-burly*? Is that even a word? *Hurly-burly* doesn't sound very Old Proper English."

"You make a good point as usual, Practical Jeffrey. *Hurly-burly* is an onomatopoeic term. That word directly arises from the sonic vibrations of the natural universe. Are there other questions about *onomatopoeia*, or the general persistence of some few words of Truly Ancient Greek within the structure of Old Proper English?"

There were no such questions.

Julian gestured beyond the row of chairs. Sparrow rose at once from her cross-legged seat on her mat.

"You gentlemen have never witnessed a device remotely like this one," said Julian, "for very few have. So let me frame this awful business within its rhetorical context. How did our ancestors observe Venus? As is well known to everyone, our ancestors tamed the lightning.

On top of the wires in which they confined that lightning, they built yet another mystic structure, fantastic, occult, and exceedingly powerful. Their electrical wires, we can dig up in any ruin. No traces of that virtual structure remain: only certain mystical hints.

"So we know, we must admit, very little about antique virtuality. But we do know that virtuality moved vibrations: It moved images, and light, and sound, and numbers. Tonight, for the first time in your lives, you will be seeing a projected image. Tomorrow night—if you see fit to return here—you will see that image *moving. With sounds*."

Sparrow bent her attention to the magic lantern. Julian arranged the makeshift stage. It was a taut sheet of white cotton, behind a flooring of bricks.

Then Julian ventured through the small crowd to the aviary, where he had seen an ominous figure lurking.

This unsought guest wore a red robe, with a faceless red hood. Everyone was cordially pretending to ignore the Man in Red. Even the youngest students knew that this was how things were done.

"Thank you for gracing us with your presence tonight," murmured Julian.

"I haven't seen that magic lantern in forty years," said the Man in Red.

"It consumes a very special oil, with a bright limestone powder. . . rare and difficult," said Julian.

"Are you willing," said the Man in Red, "to pay the rare and difficult price for your failure to engage with the world?"

"If you're referring to the cogent matter of the succession," said Julian cordially, "I've made it the policy at these civil seminars to discuss that not at all."

"If the Other Man takes command of the Palace," said the Man in Red, "he will attack you. Yes, you academics. Not that you have done anything subversive or decadent! No, I wouldn't allege that! But because your weakness invites attack. Since you are so weak, he can make an example of you."

Julian now had a quite good idea who the Man in Red was, but Julian gave no sign to show that. "I refuse to despair," he said, smiling. "This is merely a change of regime. The world is not ending, sir. The world already ended a thousand years ago."

"Our world," said the Man in Red, "this world we both enjoyed under the bounty of the previous Godfather, does not have to end. It's true that the Other Man has the force of numbers on his side—because he's forged an ignoble alliance of the greedy and the stupid. But it's not too late for a small, bold group to preempt him."

"If there is trouble," said Julian, "my students will come to harm. Because my students are brave. And bold. And idealistic. And exceedingly violent. You can start a brawl like that. Do you think you can end it?"

"You could rally your students. These young men of fine families. . . Many about to lose their sinecures from the old man's court. . . They trust your counsel. They adore you. Some of them more than they should, perhaps."

"Oh," said Julian, "I don't doubt I could find you one bold, bright, expendable young fool with a cloak and a dagger! But may I tell you something? Quite honestly? I spit on your cynical palace intrigues. I do. I despise them. They repel me."

"You quarreled with the old regime, Julian. The next regime might be kinder to you."

"I live simply. You have nothing that I want."

"I can tolerate a man of integrity," said the Man in Red, "because the innocent men are all fools. But a man who reasserts his integrity—after what you did?—that is a bit more difficult to tolerate."

"Don't let me be difficult," said Julian. "You must have many pressing errands elsewhere."

"To tell the truth, I envy you," admitted the Man in Red, with a muffled note of sadness behind his red fabric mouth-hole. "All of us envy you. We all tell each other that we would love to do just as you did: put aside the pen, take off the robes, and retire to a life of the mind. Oh yes, you do make that sound mild and humble, but this private dreamworld of yours, with these sweet little birdcages. . . It's much more exciting and pleasurable than our grim, sworn duties. Your life merely seems lighthearted and self-indulgent. You have found a genuinely different way of life."

"My friend, yes I have, and I believe. . . I know that all of life could be different. Despite the darkness of world it ruined, humanity could still transform itself. Yes, humanity could."

"You even have found yourself some creature comforts, lately. One of your minions bought you a mistress. I'm not sure I understand the appeal of that—for you."

"I rather doubt I'd understand the appeal of your mistress, either."

"I don't understand that myself," sighed the Man in Red. "A man imagines he's cavorting like a rooster, while all the time he's merely bleeding wealth. A mistress who cares nothing for you is an enemy in your bed. A mistress who does care for you is your hostage to fortune. A pity that my warnings were so useless. Good evening, sir."

The Man in Red left, with serene and measured step. The crowd parted silently before him as he approached, and it surged behind him as he left.

Julian filtered through the crowd to Sparrow, where she knelt by the lantern, cautiously unwrapping fragile slides of painted glass.

He gripped her by the arm and dragged her to her feet. "Sparrow will sing tonight!" he announced, pulling her toward the stage. "Sparrow will sing her very best song for you! It's very curious and unusual and antique! I believe it may be the oldest song in the whole world." He lowered his trembling voice. "Go on, Sparrow. Sing it, sing. . ."

Sparrow was in an agony of reluctance and stage fright.

Julian could not urge her to be brave, because he was very afraid. "This is the oldest song in the whole world!" he repeated. "Gentlemen, please try to encourage her. . ."

In her thready, nasal voice, Sparrow began to choke out her

mournful little wail. Although her words meant nothing to anyone who listened, it was clearly and simply a very sad song. It was something like a sad lover's song, but much worse. It was a cosmic sadness that came from a cold grave in the basement of the place where lovers were sad.

The lament of a mother who had lost her child. Of a child who could find no mother. A heartbreaking chasm in the natural order of being. A collapse, a break, a fall, a decay, a loss, and a lasting darkness. It was that sad.

Sparrow could not complete her song. She panicked, hid her face in her wrinkled hands and fled into a corner of the house.

Julian set to work on the magic lantern.

His student Practical Jeffrey came to his side. Jef spoke casually, in the local vulgar tongue. "Maestro, what was that little episode about? That was the worst stage performance that I've ever seen."

"That was the oldest song in the whole world, Jef. And now, you have heard it."

"I couldn't understand one line of that lousy dirge! She's a terrible singer, too. She's not even pretty. If she were young and pretty, that might have been tolerable."

"Don't let me interfere with your pressing quest for a young and pretty girl, Jef."

"I know that I didn't understand all that," Jef persisted, "but I know that something has changed. Not just that the old man is finally dead, or that the antique world is so rotten. We have to force the world to rise again in some other shape... For me, this was enough of that. I'm leaving you, maestro. I'm leaving your academy for good. I've had enough of all your teaching and your preaching, sir. Thank you for your efforts to improve me. I have to get to work now."

Julian glanced up. He was not much surprised by Jef's news. "You should stay to see this magic lantern, Jef. Projected images are extremely dramatic. They are very compelling. Really, if you've never seen one, they are absolutely wondrous. People have been known to faint."

"I'm sure your phantoms are marvelous," said Jef, pretending to yawn. "I'm going back to the Palace now, I have a family meeting. . . You stay well."


Jef did not appear for the next night of the Venus seminar. Julian's house and yard were densely packed, because word had gotten out about the magic lantern and its stunning effects. The little house roiled and surged with metalsmiths, sculptors, mural painters, orators, men of medicine, men of the law. . . Even a few women had dared to show up, with their brothers or husbands as escorts.

Practical Jeffrey had sent his apology for leaving the school, written in his sturdy, workmanlike calligraphy. He'd also shipped along a handsome banquet, and, as a topper, a wooden keg of the finest long-aged corn liquor. All the other students were hugely impressed by Jef's farewell gesture. Everyone toasted him and agreed that, despite his singular absence from the proceedings, Practical Jeffrey was a gentleman of high style.

So the second night started lively and, lavishly lubricated by Jef's magnanimity, it got livelier yet.

This night, the students put on a series of dramatic skits, performed in Old Proper English. These episodes involved the myths and heroes of remote antiquity: the Man who walked on the Moon, the Man who flew alone across the ocean, the Man who flew around without any machines at all, and was made of steel, and fought crime (he was always popular).

These theatricals were an unprecedented success, because the crowd was so dense, and so drunk, and because the graceless Dandy William Idaho was not there to overact and spoil anything.

Three of the masked Men in Red graced the scene with their presence, which made life three times more dangerous than life had been the night before. Julian watched them, smiling in his best mellow fashion, to hide his pride and his dread.

All his glamorous, shining young men, striking their poses on the tiny stage, with their young, strong, beautiful bodies. . . Maybe it could be said that Julian had saved them from deadly danger. It might also be said that he was fiddling as the city burned.

Julian knew that a settling of accounts was near. A time of such tension needed only one provocation. An obscure clash by night, a sudden insult offered, an insult stingingly returned, and Dandy William Idaho had been beaten senseless in the street. Bili was crushed, spurned, trampled on, and spat upon. Bili had never been the kind of kid you could hit just once.

Then the troubles started. Bitter quarrels, flung stones near glass houses. . . The police restored order through the simple pretext of attacking the foreigners. Everybody knew that the foreigners in the city were thieves, because so many had been forced to be thieves. No one of good sense and property was going to defend any thieves.

The police richly enjoyed the luscious irony of the police robbing thieves. So the police kicked in the doors of some of the wealthier foreigners, and seized everything they had.

Julian spent the night of that seminar activating an electrical generator. Electrical generators had been true fetish objects for the remote founders of Selder. Periodically, as a gesture of respect to antiquity, some scholar would disinter an old generator and rebuild another new generator in the same shape. So Julian owned a generator, packed in its moldering, filthy grease. It had elaborate, hand-etched schematics to explain how to work it.

This electrical night was not nearly so successful as the earlier seminar nights. After much cursing and honest puzzlement, the students managed to get the generator assembled. They even managed to crank it. It featured some spots of bare metal that stung the bare hand with a serpent's bite. Other than that, it was merely an ugly curio. The generator did not create any visible mystical powers or spiritual transcendence. Society did not advance to a higher plane of being.

Next day, the emboldened police repressed some of the darker elements of the old regime. These arrogant time-servers were notorious for their corruption. So the police beat the fancy crooks like dogs and kicked them out the door, and the crowd cheered that action, too.

People spoke quite openly of who would be serving in the Other Man's new regime, and what kind of posts they would hold.

The Favorite for the post of Godfather acted the fine gentleman: He urged calm, made dignified noises, and temporized. In the meantime, the gate guards had been bribed. Exiles poured into the city. The sentence of exile had been the merciful punishment of the late Godfather's later years. Now it became clear that the Godfather had merely exported resentments to a future date. These exiles—those among them who survived—had become hard, weathered men. They knew what they had lost. They also knew what they had to regain.

So there were more clashes, this time with gangs of hardened cutthroats. The Favorite pulled up his stakes and fled in terror.

Julian spent that night explaining how to use electricity and virtuality to connect the soul of Man with the planet Venus.

There was a large crowd for his last hermetic ceremony, and not because it was such an interesting topic. People had fled to Julian's refuge because the city was convulsed with fear.

It had always been said of the people of Selder that they would shed their own blood rather than lose one drop of water. Like many clichés, that was true. The smothered resentments of a long, peaceful reign were all exposed to the open air. That meant beatings, break-ins, and back-alley backstabbings.

The elections were held in conditions of desperate haste, because only one man was fit to restore order.

To his credit, the new Godfather took prompt action. He averted anarchy through the simple tactic of purging all his opponents.

Julian surrendered peaceably. He had rather imagined that he might have to. The grass that bent before the wind would stand upright again, he reasoned. The world was still scarred with the windblown wrecks of long-dead forests.

Prison was dark, damp, and dirty. The time in prison weighed heavily on a man's soul. Julian had nothing to write with, nothing to read. He never felt the sun, or breathed any fresh air.

Julian's best friends in the underground cell were small insects. Over a passage of ten centuries, cave insects had somehow found the many wet passages beneath the city. Most of these wild denizens were smaller than lice, pale, long-legged, and eyeless. Julian had never realized there were so many different breeds of them. The humble life sheltered within the earth had suffered much less than the life exposed to mankind on its surface.

At length—at great length—Julian had a prison visitor.

"You will forgive Us," stated the Godfather, "for trying a philosopher's well-known patience. There were certain disorders consequent on Our accession, and a great press of necessary public business. Word has reached Our ears, however, that you have been shouting and pleading with your jailers. Weeping and begging like a hysterical woman, they tell Us."

"I'm not a well man now, your eminence. I cannot thrive without the vibrations of the sun, the stars, and planets."

"Surely you didn't imagine that We would ever forget a classmate."

"No, sir."

"They tell Us you have been requesting—no, sobbing and pleading—for some literary material," said the Godfather. He nodded at his silent bodyguard, who passed a sheaf of manuscripts through the carved stone pillars of the cell. "You will find these documents of interest. These are the signed confessions of your fellow conspirators."

Julian leafed through the warrants. "It's good to see that my friends kept up their skills in calligraphy."

"We took the liberty of paging through the archives of our

predecessor, as well," said the Godfather. He produced a set of older documents. "You will recognize the striking eloquence of these death sentences. You were in top form back then. These documents of state are so grandiloquent, so closely argued, and in such exquisite English. They killed certain members of my own family—but as legal court documents, they were second to none."

Julian sighed. "I just couldn't do that any longer."

"You won't have to do it," the Godfather allowed. "You wrote such sustainable classics here that We won't need any new death sentences. We can simply reuse your fine, sturdy documents, over and over."

"It was my duty to write sentences," said Julian. "Sentences are a necessity of statecraft. Let me formally express my remorse."

"You express your remorse now," remarked the Godfather. "At the time, you were taking great pride in your superb ability to compose a sentence."

"I admit my misdeeds, sir. I am contrite."

"More recently, you and your friends were plotting against Our election," said the Godfather patiently. "As a further patent insult to Our dignity, you had yourself crowned as the 'President of the United States.' There are witnesses to that event."

"That was a diversion," said Julian. "That was part of a magic ceremony. To help me electrically reach the virtual image of the planet Venus."

"Juli, have you become a heretic, or just a maniac? You should read the allegations in these confessions! They are fantastic. Your fellow conspirators say that you believe that men can still fly. That you conjured living phantoms in public. We don't know whether to laugh or cry."

"People talk," said Julian. "In a cage, people will sing."

"You dressed your slave as a golden goddess and you made people worship her."

"That was her costume," said Julian. "She enjoyed that. I think it was the only time I've ever seen her happy."

"Juli, We are not your classmate any more. We have become your Godfather. It is unclear to Us what you thought you were gaining by this charade. In any case, that will go on no longer. Your cabal has been arrested. Your house, and all that eerie rubbish inside it, has been seized. In times this dark and troubled, We have no need for epicene displays. Is that understood?"

"Yes, sir."

"Now tell Us what We are supposed to do with you."

"Let me go," said Julian, sweating in the stony chill. "Release me, and I will sing your praises. Some day history will speak of you. You will want history to say something noble and decent about you."

"That is a tempting offer," mused the Godfather. "I would like history to say this of me: that I was an iron disciplinarian who scourged corruption, and struck his enemies with hammer blows. Can you arrange that?"

"I can teach rhetoric. Someone will say that for you, and they'll need great skill."

"I hate a subtle insult," said the Godfather. "I can forgive an enemy soldier who flings a spear straight at me, but a thing like that is just vile."

"I don't want to die here in this stone cage!" screeched Julian. "I can write a much better groveling confession than these other wretches! A man of your insight knows that confessions are nothing but rhetoric! Of course they all chose to indict me! How could they not? They are men with families to consider, while I am foreign-born and I have no one! We're all intelligent men! We all know that if someone must die, then I'm the best to die. I'm one against four! But surely you must know better!"

"Of course I know better," said the Godfather. "You imagined that, as men of letters, you were free of the healthy atmosphere of general fear so fit for everyone else. That is not true. Men of letters have to obey Us, they have to serve Us loyally, and they have to know that their lives are forfeit. Just like everyone else."

"'Uneasy lies the head that wears the hood,'" said Julian.

"You always had a fertile mind for an apposite quote. We are inclined to spare you."

Light bloomed in the dampest corner of Julian's mind. "Yes, of course, of course I should be spared! Why should I die? I never raised my hand against you. I never even raised my voice."

"Like the others, you must write your full and complete confession. It will be read aloud to the assembled court. Then, a year in the field with the army will toughen you up. You're much too timid to fight, but Our army needs its political observers. We need clearly written reports from the field. And the better my officers, the worse they seem to write!"

"Is there a war? Who has attacked us?"

"There is no war just as yet," said the Godfather. "But of course they will attack Us, unless We prove to them that they dare not attack. So, we plan a small campaign to commence Our reign. One insolent village, leveled. You'll be in no great danger."

"I'm not a coward."

"Yes, in fact, you are a coward, Julian. You happened to live in a time when you could play-act otherwise. Those decadent times have passed. You're a coward, and you always were. So, make a clean breast of your many failings. We pledge that you too will be spared. You might as well write your own confessions, for your sins are many and you know them better than anyone."

"Once I do that for you, you'll spare my friends."

"We will. We don't say they will suck the blood of the taxpayer anymore, but yes, they will be spared."

"You'll spare my students."

"Fine young men. They were led astray. Young men of good family are natural officer material."

"You'll give me back my house and my servant."

"Oh, you won't need any house, and as for your wicked witch. . . You should read the thunderation that rings around her little head!

Your friends denounced you—but in their wisdom, they denounced her much, much more violently. They all tell Us that this lamentable situation is not your fault at all. They proclaim that she seduced you to it, that she turned your head. She drove you mad, she drugged you. She used all the wicked wiles of a foreign courtesan. She descended to female depths of evil that no mere man can plumb."

Julian sat on his stony bench for a moment. Then he rose again and put his hands around the bars. "Permit me to beg for her life."

"To spare her is not possible. We can't publish these many eloquent confessions without having her drowned in the Cistern right away. It would be madness to let a malignant creature like that walk in daylight for even an hour."

"She did nothing except what I trained her to do! She's completely harmless and timid. She's the meekest creature alive. You are sacrificing an innocent for political expediency. It's a shame."

"Should We spare this meek creature and execute you, and four friends? She was a lost whore, and the lowest of the low, as soon as her own soldiers failed to protect her from the world. You want to blame someone for the cold facts? Blame yourself, professor. Let this be a good lesson to you."

"You are breaking a bird on an anvil here. That's easy for you to do, but it's a cruelty. You'll be remembered for that. It will weigh on your conscience."

"It will not," said the Godfather. "Because We will kindly offer to spare the witch's life. Then We will watch your friends in a yapping frenzy to have her killed. Your noble scholars will do everything they can to have her vilified, lynched, dumped into the Cistern, and forgotten forever. They will blame her lavishly in order to absolve themselves. Then, when you meet each other again, you men with a cause, you literati—that's when the conscience will sting."

"So," said Julian, "it's not enough that we're fools, or that we're cowards, or that we failed to defend ourselves. We also have to be evil."

"You are evil. Truly, you are fraudulent and wicked men. We

should wash you from the fabric of society in a cleansing bath of blood. But We won't do that. Do you know why? Because We understand necessity. We are responsible. We know what the state requires. We think these things through."

"You could still spare us. You could forgive us for the things we wrote and thought. You could be courageous and generous. That is within your great power."

The Godfather sighed. "That is so easy for a meager creature like you to say, and so difficult for Us to do. We will tell you a little parable about that. Soon, this cell door will open. Now: When this door is opened, place your right hand in this doorframe. We will have this husky bodyguard slam this iron door on your fingers. You will never scribble one mischievous word again. If you do that, Julian, that would be 'courageous and generous.' That would be the bravest act of your life. We will spare the life of your mystic witch for that noble act."

Julian said nothing.

"You're not volunteering to be so courageous and generous? You can marry her: You have Our blessing. We will perform that ceremony Ourselves."

"You are right. I don't want her," said Julian. "I have no further need for her. Let her be strangled in all due haste and thrown down the well. Let the hungry fish nibble her flesh, let her body be turned into soup and poured through the greenhouses. She came to me half-dead, and every day I gave to her was some day she would never have seen! Let me see that sunlight she will never see again. I hate this cage. Let me out of here."


After his release from darkness, very little happened to Julian that he found of any interest. After two years of service, Julian managed to desert the army of Selder. There had been no chance of that at first, because the army was so eager, bold, and well disciplined.

However, after two years of unalloyed successes, the army suffered a sharp reverse at the walls of Buena Vista. The hardscrabble villagers there were too stubborn, or perhaps too stupid, to be cowed by such a fine army. To the last man, woman, and child, they put up a lethal resistance. So the village was left in ruins, but so was the shining reputation of the Godfather and his troops.

Julian fled that fiery scene by night, losing any pursuers in the vast wild thickets of cactus and casuarina. Soon afterward, he was captured by the peasants of Denver. There was little enough left of that haunted place. However, the Denver peasants sold him to a regional court with a stony stronghold in the heights of Vale.

Julian was able to convince the scowling peers of that realm that they would manage better with tax records and literate official proclamations. That was true: They did improve with a gloss of civility. They never let him leave, but they let him live.

After a course of further indifferent years, word arrived in Vale that the Godfather of Selder had perished in his own turn. He had died of sickness in a war camp, plague and war being much the same thing. There were certain claims that he had been poisoned.

After some further tiresome passage of years, the reviving realm of Selder began to distribute traders, bankers, and ambassadors. They were a newer and younger-spirited people. They were better dressed and brighter-eyed. They wrote everything down. They observed new opportunities in places where nothing had happened for ages. They had grand plans for those places, and the ability to carry them out.

These new men of Selder seemed to revel in being a hundred things at once. Not just poets, but also architects. Not just artists, but also engineers. Not just bankers, but gourmands and art collectors. Even their women were astonishing.

Julian had no desire to return to the damp glassy shadows of Selder. He had come to realize that a Sustainable City that could never forget its past could become an object of terror to simpler people. Also, he had grown white-haired and old.

But he was not allowed to ignore a velvet invitation—a polite command, really—from Godfather Magnanimous Jef the First. Practical Jeffrey had outlasted his city's woes with the stolid grace that was his trademark. Jef's shrewd rise to power had cost him a brother and two bodyguards, but once in command, he never set his neatly shod foot wrong.

In his reign, men and women breathed a new air of magnificence, refinement, and vivacity. Troubles that would have crushed a lesser folk were made jest of, simply taken in stride.

Men even claimed that the climate was improving. This was delusional, for nothing would ever make the climate any better. But the climate within the hearts of men was better. Men were clearly and simply a better kind of man.

Julian had never written a book, for he had always said that his students were his books. And with the passage of years, Julian's students had indeed become his books. They were erudite like books, complex like books, long-lasting like books. His students had become great men. Their generation was accomplishing feats that the ancients themselves had never dreamt of. Air wells, ice-ponds and aqueducts. Glass palaces of colored light. Peak-flashing heliographs and giant projection machines. Carnivals and pageants. Among these men, greatness was common as dirt.

It was required, somehow, that the teacher of such men should himself be a great man. So the great men delighted in honoring Julian. He was housed in a room in one of their palaces, and stuffed with creature comforts like a fattened capon. His only duty was to play the sage for his successors, to cackle wise inanities for them. To sing the praises of the golden present, and make the darkest secrets of a dark age more tenaciously obscure.

Futurity could never allow the past to betray it again.

# TURTLE LOVE

Joseph Green

"The refusal of Amos and Stephanie Byers to accept voluntary buyout for their place of legal residence is hereby entered into the record. Your appeal of my ruling for disallowance will be forwarded to the local Joint Resolution Board for final disposition. By law, that decision must be rendered within ten working days, and is final. No further appeals are allowable, or will be accepted in any court of law."

Administrative Law Judge Sebastian Carver leaned back from the recorder on his desk, glancing at the clock on the left wall. Amos followed his gaze; they had six minutes remaining of their allotted fifteen. They could spend that time pleading, crying, or threatening suicide, and it wouldn't really matter. Appealing to the Joint Board was a pro forma excuse for a genuine legal appeal. This was a new process, but so far, throughout the entire country, the Fed-State-County Boards had very rarely overruled a decision by an Interior administrative judge.

Looking past Carver, Amos saw a small banner pasted on the rear wall of this borrowed office, the unofficial motto of those assigned the thankless but necessary task of forcing millions of people to abandon their homes.

## SAVE AMERICA!

Saving the community as a whole outweighs the loss of homes by the few Sebastian Carver pulled his worn swivel chair forward, placed both elbows on his desktop pad, and focused his gaze on Stephanie. Watching, Amos realized this perceptive man had understood from the beginning that she was the fragile one here.

"Mrs. Byers, I saw in your petition that you've spent almost your entire life in your present home; that you grew up there, and later inherited it from your parents." Carver had a deep, soft voice, with no noticeable accent. Somehow he managed to sound sincerely sympathetic. "You even gave it a name. . ." he picked up and scanned the one-page form. "'Merry Weather.' But your home and three neighbors are on Hurricane Point, which extends out into the Banana River lagoon. According to our engineers, a regular dike won't protect you. They would have to extend a very high reinforced seawall all the way around the Point, which would cost over three million dollars. The four houses have been evaluated at 1.4 million, minus the land. I'm very sorry, but I don't think there's much chance the Joint Resolution Board will authorize such an added expense."

Instead of answering, Stephanie abruptly got to her feet and walked out the door. Amos hastily followed, nodding at Carver as he exited. The gray-haired judge gave him a sad smile and nodded back.

Amos caught up with Stephanie as she hurried down the long hallway of the district courthouse. He saw tears in her eyes, but her expression was more angry and frustrated than sad. When he tried to take her hand, she turned her head and glared at him.

"I didn't hear you saying very much in there, Amos!"

Taken aback, he fell in behind Stephanie as she pushed through the door to the parking lot. He had said earlier that this appeal was a waste of time. He had not shared his hope that fighting back would make her feel better. It didn't seem to have worked.

"Sweetheart, I have to be a little careful in what I say. I work for

Interior too now. But at least we can stay on Merritt Island. Think of the poor people in Cocoa Beach, Satellite, Indian Harbor, the rest of the barrier islands. Their whole *communities* are being abandoned!"

"I know, and that doesn't make me feel any better." They had reached their electric four-seater, and Stephanie walked around to the passenger side. She had driven on the way here, but was clearly too upset to drive safely now. Amos got behind the wheel and turned on the power.

Stephanie was silent on the way home. Amos had not yet told her about the letter received yesterday at work—a printed letter, delivered by the U.S. Mail—and now decided to wait. It was probably nothing anyway. But unlike most similar threats from cranks, this one had been specifically addressed to him, at his place of work; mailed from the downtown post office in Orlando. Someone within easy driving range had selected him as the face of the enemy, and threatened his life.

*Amos Byers. You have set yourself to oppose God's work. For this I will strike you down, as God struck down the Canaanites. Your day of doom approaches.*

In their driveway, at the third of the four homes extending to the east on Hurricane Point, Stephanie asked Amos to stop. She got out and crossed the access road to the seawall on the north side. Amos followed, to find her staring down at the water. "It's up five inches," she said, voice low. "Just five inches. It rises that much after a few heavy rains."

Amos tried to think of something comforting to say, and could not. He also loved their home of the past fourteen years, though not with Stephanie's passion. An only child, as was Amos, she had inherited Merry Weather when her parents died in a high-speed train crash in 2018. The twin girls they had adopted as babies three years earlier needed more room. Selling their small condo and moving to Merry Weather had been an easy choice, helped by the fact her parents' mortgage insurance had cleared the house of debt. That also meant Interior would reimburse them for the full value of the house. Displaced homeowners typically received their equity share of the house, minus the value of the condemned land.

They walked back to the car and Amos drove it inside the garage. Stephanie went past him to the unlocked utility room access door. He was getting out of the car when he heard her scream.

Amos ran for the open door and charged inside to find Stephanie standing at the opposite end of the utility room, staring into the kitchen. He hurried to her. With a shaking hand she pointed across the room to the door that opened into the yard on the south side. It stood open.

"There was a man in here! Well, maybe a teenager. He was standing in front of the junction box when I opened the door."

Amos hurried across the kitchen and out onto the lawn. He was in time to see someone running across the backyard of the first house on the point, the Wilkersons'. The figure vanished around the building. Seconds later he heard the sound of an old gasoline engine starting, and a vehicle driving away.

No point trying to catch him. Amos walked back inside, to find Stephanie in the utility room, staring at the junction box. Its little metal door hung open. He checked, and all switches were on. He closed and latched it, then turned to see Stephanie staring at him.

"That—that was a gutter, wasn't it? My God! Word gets around fast!"

Amos reached for his wife and took her in his arms. He held her trim body—only three inches shorter than his five-foot-eleven—to his chest, and gently patted her back. The open junction box was the clue. Gutters were salvage crews who operated in a legal gray area, stripping a house during the interval between the time the owner moved out and the demolition crew arrived. They would pull out the junction box itself, the copper wires from the walls, the bathroom and kitchen fixtures, the big AC unit in the yard—anything of value that could be resold. They justified their actions under the rationale that the house was going to be demolished anyway. The authorities were not willing to crack down on them, or get into the reclamation business themselves; not enough money recovered to justify the time and manpower.

Stephanie put her arms around his waist and began crying. Amos let her sob, face against his neck, her short, curly chestnut hair tickling his ear. The teenage appraiser for some local gutter crew—they were springing up everywhere along the coastlines—had forced her to see their home as it would be when they finished; a roof over a concrete block shell, a skeleton with the body gone. Everything that made the house a comfortable home, with lovely views north and south along the Banana River lagoon—gone. Merry Weather had been at the upper limit in price for a middle-class working couple like Stephanie's parents. They had sacrificed many of life's other pleasures to afford this place. And the same twist of fate that had cost them their planned retirement here had given the house to Stephanie, free and clear.

When her sobbing eased, Amos led Stephanie into the kitchen and seated her at the breakfast table. A large picture window in the wall looked south over the water, to the causeway and bridge connecting Merritt Island with Cocoa Beach. He could see Cape Canaveral Hospital, on its man-made island abutting the Highway 520 causeway, and beyond that the tops of the tallest buildings in Cocoa Beach. The launch facilities on Cape Canaveral to the north, built at a cost of billions of dollars, had been adjudged worth saving. So was most of Merritt Island, including the main part west of Hurricane Point. A case of lucky location would save the city of Cape Canaveral, just below the Cape itself, but half of Cocoa Beach to its south would be lost. Private homes and giant condominiums, office towers and supermarkets, all would be torn down, the concrete block walls and pillars salvaged and cut up into manageable pieces, becoming part of the riprap covering the sloping surfaces of twenty-foot-high dikes.

Climatologists had firmly stated that the maximum possible rise in sea level would be thirteen feet. Congress had decreed that all dikes must protect for twenty.

Amos had earned a degree in mechanical engineering, then specialized in hydraulics. He hadn't said so aloud to Stephanie, but he agreed with the dike route planners. Hurricane Point was simply too expensive to save. So were the homes near the ends of the two long, narrow southern extensions of Merritt Island. The dike would run from about three miles below the Highway 520 Causeway and bridge, across Sykes Creek and the shallow Indian River lagoon, to the mainland. All homesites east and south of that line would be lost to the rising Atlantic.

And that was just the local area, admittedly one of the most vulnerable in Florida. All the islands off the west coast—Sanibel, Long Boat Key, Santa Rosa—had been condemned, their inhabitants among the first to be told they must move. The Florida Keys were being sacrificed in their entirety. There were no winners here, only some losing less than others. The largest civil works and relocation project in history was well under way, and would last for forty years.

Amos felt the warm air as the front door opened and Jada and Janine hurried across the living room and into the kitchen. The fraternal twins, now seventeen, had grown into pretty, brown-skinned young women. Stephanie had wanted to adopt, not bring more children into a crowded world. They had found the twin babies in an orphanage in Guatemala. Now they were juniors, with only a week to go before the end of the school year.

Jada seated herself opposite her parents while Janine opened the refrigerator and got out their afternoon maintenance snacks. "Dad, Mom—how did the appeal go?"

"Your father was right," said Stephanie. She seemed to be holding herself under tight control. "It was basically a waste of time."

"So now what?" asked Janine, seating herself in the vacant chair and handing Jada a diet power drink.

"Our appeal will be denied within ten days," said Amos. "Interior will credit our account with the appraised equity value, house minus land, within sixty days. And we have sixty days after the money arrives to move out."

"We'll try to find an apartment in your school district," said Stephanie. The girls had hated the idea of changing schools for their senior year.

The girls left for their rooms. "Are you going to work tomorrow?" asked Amos.

Stephanie nodded. "I want to keep busy."

"Me too, then." It was Thursday, and Amos had asked for two days off. But it was too early to start packing, and he wanted to save what little leave he had. Last year he had left his job as a facilities engineer for Boeing at the Launch Pad 17 complex and joined the Holland Corps, the new Interior Department group formed to dam the nation's rivers. The Corps of Engineers had the largest single job, building the dikes, but even that storied old organization had been transferred from the U.S. Army to Interior.

In bed later that night Stephanie became unusually demanding, reaching for Amos as soon as he joined her after a late shower. She made love to him with an intensity that left him breathing heavily, and ready for sleep. But Stephanie cuddled close and kept him awake, their foreheads almost touching on the firm pillow, her body shaking with muffled sobs. He held her, petting and soothing, until she finally drifted off into a troubled sleep.

Early next morning Amos drove their hybrid the twelve miles to his new office in the old Kennedy Space Center complex. Stephanie kept the electric for the much longer drive to the Florida Tech campus in Melbourne. She had been teaching at the College of Marine Sciences for the past nine years. The sea turtle nesting season began in May, and the local beaches had been heavily used by loggerheads for centuries. Stephanie had told Amos that she and her three marine biology summer classes were working on a coordinated effort to tag and rope off each new nest in the county. The rubbery, ping-pong-ball-size eggs would later be removed and transferred, under carefully controlled conditions, to higher beaches throughout Florida; one of a million such efforts to preserve threatened sea life.

Amos parked in the large lot behind what had been the huge Kennedy Space Center Headquarters, a six-wing office building, lightly occupied since the demise of the Manned Space Flight Program. Interior had recently claimed the building and it now served as regional headquarters. They had also taken over most of the other KSC office and support buildings. All launches were now from the pads on Cape Canaveral.

In his shared office Amos said hello to the group coordinator at her central desk, got a cup of coffee, and settled in at his cubicle. His group of three engineers had been assigned the task of designing and installing the pumps that would lift the largely fresh water of Sykes Creek, the island's primary south-flowing drainage system, over the southern dike. The pumps not only had to be reliable beyond the possibility of failure, they had to be supported by independent backup power systems of equal reliability.

But this work wouldn't save Merry Weather, his own home. Before Amos had finished his first cup of coffee, he was again thinking of Stephanie and her heartbreak over the coming loss. And this was not something they could put off. In many ways Interior had become horribly efficient, especially for a government agency growing in size and responsibility each month. The seizure and demolition of condemned buildings was moving rapidly ahead. The first dikes were going up in Florida and California. Buildings were coming down along the Manhattan shoreline, while the owners complained bitterly about inadequate compensation. A withhold-your-taxes movement was growing, led by people living safely away from the coasts. In short, the federal government was for once acting decisively, and the country was in turmoil.

All Interior employees were working ten-hour days, often six days a week. Not surprisingly, Amos received his reward for coming in that afternoon (after getting the day off). The branch supervisor asked him to report again on Saturday—though only for an eight-hour day.

Just before leaving Amos pulled out the threatening letter and read it again. He considered turning it over to Interior security, but decided against it. Whoever had sent it was smart enough not to leave fingerprints. The typeface was Times New Roman, probably impossible to identify as from a specific printer. He started a new paper file, labeled "Odd," and put it away.

At 5:30 Amos followed a crowd of other vehicles to the south entrance gate, exiting the controlled access area onto Florida Road 3—and into chaos. A long flatbed truck stood parked across both lanes of the southbound road, a few hundred yards from the gate. Forced to stop, Amos got out of his car and looked ahead, over two rows of shiny car tops. A man holding a microphone, dressed all in green, paced back and forth on the truck bed, haranguing the few people who had gotten out of their cars to listen. A powerful sound system amplified his voice. A three-piece band sat by the truck cab, occasionally emphasizing his words with drumbeats and fanfares, or playing short riffs. A sheriff's car had pulled up behind the truck, but a wall of people, also dressed in green, refused to move aside for the two deputies. Amos could see over the low truck body, and watched as the officers gave up on trying to force their way through, instead starting to arrest the people passively resisting them. But they quickly ran out of plastic restraints, and the backseat of their vehicle held only three.

The deputies had still not reached the truck when two more sheriff's cars arrived, followed a few minutes later by a large prisoner transport van. As they began arresting the protesters en masse, someone in a lead car in front of the truck managed to back up slightly, and turned his vehicle to the east. He crossed the soft dirt median to the northbound lanes without getting stuck and triumphantly fled, continually blowing his horn. But it was a thin, weak sound, immediately drowned out by the small band.

Other cars jockeyed to follow the leader across the median. Some of the green-clad men and women left their defense of the truck and tried to put their bodies across the escape route, but the deputies shifted their focus and arrested them first. One deputy took up traffic control duties, urging the Interior workers on their way. After only a short distance Amos followed the car ahead back across the median into the southbound lanes, and was home in another fifteen minutes.

"The Greenies? That's the group that says the ocean rise is natural, and we shouldn't have built houses near the beaches in the first place?" said Janine at dinner, after Amos told them about the incident.

"Officially 'Green Earth.' One of the largest and best-organized protest groups," said Stephanie. "There are others."

"But don't they have a point?" asked Jada. "Didn't we do this to ourselves?"

"A lot of climatologists don't think so," said Amos. "We know sea levels fluctuated long before humans started putting man-made gases into the atmosphere. But we probably caused the extreme speed-up in melting the ice packs, and this really fast rise in ocean levels."

Both girls gave Amos a look that told him they thought this well-worn topic boring, so he stopped and listened to accounts of their day instead. After dinner the girls went to their rooms to study for two remaining finals, and Amos and Stephanie watched an old movie. He looked over at her frequently and realized that her eyes were on the screen, but she wasn't seeing or hearing the movie at all.

The first loggerheads were arriving. Stephanie spent seven evenings over the next two weeks rescuing turtle eggs. At home she remained quiet and withdrawn as they waited for the inevitable final rejection of their appeal. It came, with the two official deadlines. Now it was time to start looking for an apartment. Neither wanted to buy another house on the island, even if one could be found.

Three weeks after the first threatening letter, Amos received a second; physically identical, again mailed from Orlando. Only the message had changed.

> *Amos Byers. You disregarded my first warning. Repent of doing the devil's work, or God will soon strike you down, and you will burn in hell forever.*

Whoever this was, he—and Amos felt almost certain this was a man—knew Amos had not quit his job. Someone was watching him, or at least checking his job status; not hard to do with a government employee. But the threat of death had grown more immediate. He would be struck down "soon."

Amos placed the letter in his "Odd" file, and again did not tell anyone of the threat.

Over the next eight weeks Amos watched Stephanie slowly but steadily deteriorate, as ferment seethed in the world around them. Under hastily passed legislation, the nation's prison population was cut by more than half, when inmates serving terms for minor offenses received paroles for agreeing to work ten years in the Save America program. The crime rate fell to its lowest point since national records were kept. Factories sometimes quiet for decades roared back to life, to produce the needed machinery. The most massive mobilization of national resources since the end of that war was well under way, with labor shortages everywhere. The unemployment rate fell close to zero, because the Labor Department counted as employed the millions receiving government stipends for returning to school, to learn the skills needed for Save America jobs. The country had not been so unified or busy since World War II, a hundred years ago. Congress had just passed a series of new taxes and surcharges to pay the huge bill, with little protest from anyone.

On his Sunday morning Newsreader one day in July, Amos saw a notice that the Green Earth organization had dissolved. With considerable amusement, he read that the national president had somehow appropriated most of the available funds for himself, and absconded with them. The board of directors had given up their charter as a charitable organization and issued a statement that it had become too difficult to get members to rallies because everyone was working such long hours.

Amos received a third note. It said judgment had been passed; since he had not repented, his life was forfeit. He finally took all three to the Interior security officer, who admonished Amos for not bringing them to him sooner. After comparing it with letters that other employees had received and finding no matches, he promised an immediate investigation and said Amos shouldn't worry too much. The air of national crisis gripping the country had brought squirrels down out of the trees everywhere.

"How tired are you?" Stephanie asked after dinner the next Saturday. They had spent the day packing.

"Not too bad," said Amos. "Why?"

"Our monitors indicate the first nest we moved will break out tonight. Two of my students will be there, to keep away the predators. I'd like to see it too."

Stephanie's tone was wistful, but she seemed to have more life and animation than Amos had seen recently. He realized this hatching of the baby turtles was very important to her. She had told him of growing up in Cocoa Beach, and visits with her parents to turtle nests when the eggs were due to hatch. This was always at night, when the sand had cooled and the fragile baby turtles could avoid the heat of the sun. This early exposure had been one of the drivers causing her to select marine biology as a career.

Jada and Janine were spending the night at a friend's house. "Sure. Let's go," said Amos.

Stephanie made coffee and sandwiches, and they left at ten for the beach. She had called one of her students, already there, and learned the sound monitor indicated the breakout would be within two hours. All hundred or so eggs always hatched at the same time. The baby turtles scrambled toward the water in a crowd, increasing the number who would survive to reach it.

They drove south, east over the 520 causeway, and south again on State Road A1A along the beaches. Stephanie pulled into a small local park, where wooden walkways over the fragile, grass-covered sand dunes provided access to the beach. One other vehicle sat in the parking area. Stephanie carried the hamper of sandwiches, Amos the large thermos jug of coffee. A three-quarter moon provided enough light for safe walking as they crossed over the dunes to the beach. Stephanie headed south for another hundred yards, to where the dunes, well east of the almost flat beach, gradually reared up to become more than ten feet high. The two students, one male and one female, were waiting for them.

Stephanie made hasty introductions. "Sasha and Tamburu, my husband Amos. What's the activity level?"

"Point eight on our scale," said Tamburu, a short, sturdy, round-faced young woman with close-cropped black hair and very dark skin. Sasha was tall and thin, with lank blonde hair hanging to his shoulders. Florida Tech enjoyed a high percentage of foreign students working for engineering degrees. "They should be out in thirty minutes."

Amos poured coffee into plastic cups and handed them to the students. Stephanie opened the hamper and gave them sandwiches. As the two ate, Stephanie led Amos to the nest, near the top of the gently rising slope of the dune. Voice very low, she said, "We moved the eggs from the original lower site to this elevation. The experts pretty much agree the ocean level will rise no more than seven feet over the next twenty years, and that will leave this nest still well above the waves. This is one of the few areas where we didn't have to transport the eggs to a new beach."

"I know the adult female always returns to her hatching beach to build a new nest, but I didn't think the elevation mattered," said Amos.

Stephanie hesitated, then said, "There's still a lot we don't know. The exact chemical markers that separate one beach from another, for example. But the adult female can find her birthplace, unerringly. We think it's safest to have these babies born in a nest where that sand will still be above water when she returns."

Sasha and Tamburu had spread a wide blanket on the flatter sand, about thirty feet below and north of the nest. It became a little crowded with four people, but they managed to sit without rubbing shoulders. Stephanie suggested they wait in silence. Some of her research indicated the baby turtles, somehow aware of the external environment through the thin layer of sand that hid them, would not emerge on the first possible day if it was noisy above them.

Now it was past midnight. Amos could hear the gentle sound of waves washing up on the sand and retreating, the engine of an occasional hybrid passing on the road a hundred yards to the west. There were no lights in the park, and the communities north and south of them had passed laws restricting the use of lights along the beaches during turtle hatching season. The tiny crawlers were easily disoriented, heading toward the brightest lights when they emerged instead of moonlight reflecting off the water.

Tamburu wore the earphones monitoring the sound sensors adjacent to the nest. She took off the phones and gestured. Amos heard the sound without amplification, a low, hissing susurration, as almost a hundred small bodies simultaneously struggled up through the thin layer of sand. All four got to their feet and hurried to the nest, staying well away from the slope leading to the flat beach. They were in time to see a mass of small black bodies, struggling and clutching for support in the heaving sand, push themselves up and out, onto the firmer surface below the round nest.

"They're beautiful," said Sasha softly. Noise no longer mattered to the tiny travelers, now that they had begun their long and dangerous journey.

Tamburu wore thin plastic gloves. She dropped to her knees and assisted a last few stragglers out of the soft sand, then swept both hands slowly through the nest area, searching for any still buried. She found none.

"Hey! Raccoon!" Sasha suddenly yelled. Amos turned, to see a small dark animal darting toward the stream of babies struggling across the sand to the water. "Hey!" Sasha yelled again, and took off at a run toward the animal. Startled, the raccoon stopped. In the moonlight Amos saw it turn to face this intruder, unexpectedly interfering with the easy dinner this predator and its kin had long enjoyed on these beaches. But the human rushing toward him, yelling and waving his arms, seemed about to attack. The raccoon turned and fled.

Tamburu, satisfied the nest was clear of babies, joined the other three as they stood a couple of yards away from the direct path to the water. She suddenly darted forward, picking up a large crab that had emerged from nowhere and was scuttling toward the last few babies. She held it carefully in her gloved hand as it tried in vain to reach back with its single large pincer. Still carrying the crab, she paced along with the other three as they followed the last of the hatchlings toward the water. It took several minutes for the newborns to cross the forty feet of flat beach, but eventually the last slow one made it, and disappeared into the water. Tamburu gently lowered the crab to the sand and watched it scurry away in frustration.

"We counted ninety-eight eggs," said Stephanie. "I think they all made it into the water. Every single one!"

"One of our best," said Sasha. "I wish we could be at every nest breaking this season."

"We know we can't save them all," said Stephanie. "But this was a darn good start."

They returned to the blanket, where Stephanie handed the coffee jug to Amos and picked up the hamper. When they turned to leave, Stephanie saw that Sasha and Tamburu had made no move to go. She took out the remaining sandwiches, handed them to Sasha, and said goodnight. The use the two young adults would make of the blanket, for the remainder of this lovely, moonlit night, was not a concern of their teacher.

Stephanie led the way back up the beach, across the wooden walkway over the dunes, and into the small parking area. As they neared their car, walking side by side, a dark figure suddenly stepped out from concealment behind it. The moonlight provided enough illumination for Amos to see what appeared to be a pistol in his hand. And then Amos saw that in their absence, a third car had parked near the end of the lot.

"Hold it!" said a man's voice. Amos and Stephanie came to an abrupt halt. The man, dressed dramatically all in black and wearing a ski mask over his face, stepped closer, the pistol pointed at Amos. "I warned you. Three times I told you to stop doing the devil's work. And now God says you must pay."

Stephanie turned toward Amos, fear and shock on her face; and the dawning realization that Amos had been threatened, and not told her. Then she took a short step toward the man with the pistol pointed at her husband's stomach. "Greg? Is that you? Have you gone completely batty?"

Stephanie had recognized the voice. Gregory Hentson. And now Amos understood the threats, and why he had been singled out. They had never been friends, but he had known Greg since they were teenagers; attended the same high school in Orlando, and UCF in overlapping years. Stephanie had dated Greg for two months, breaking it off when she learned he was an avid hunter; she would not be involved with someone who got a thrill from killing wild animals. Greg had taken it badly, blaming Amos, though in fact he hadn't even met Stephanie until weeks later. She had told Amos back then that she thought Greg Hentson a little offbeat; extremely religious, but handsome, polite, and less pushy for sex than most. And no, their relationship hadn't gotten that far in two months.

Amos knew that Greg Hentson had been taught hunting and fishing by his father. In one of their few conversations in high school, Greg had earnestly explained that God placed man in dominion over the animals, and they were expressly put here to serve his needs. For his part, Amos had tried fishing but found it too slow a sport, and never gone hunting at all. He had heard from mutual friends that Greg, still single, worked for a local charity in Orlando. And apparently Stephanie's rejection, and the supposed theft of her affections by Amos, had festered like an infected boil, growing steadily over the years and turning into blind, unreasoning hate.

"Greg?" Stephanie's voice was tremulous. "You've been threatening Amos?" Her voice steadied, became firm. "But it isn't really him you hate. No, it's me, because I tossed you, twenty years ago. All this time. . . And you're getting back at me now, by killing the man I love? While claiming you're doing *God's* work?"

"No! Amos is evil! These are the end times, and he's trying to thwart the expressed will of God!"

Greg had let the pistol barrel fall, but raised it again and aimed at Amos. Stephanie screamed and jumped in front of her husband, arms waving wildly. The gun fired, a bright streak of red fire in the night. Stephanie's momentum kept her moving past Amos, before she lost her balance and fell to the sandy ground.

Greg stared at Stephanie, uncertain of what he had done. Amos still held the empty coffee jug. He hurled the large container at Greg, then charged after it. The jug hit the gun in Greg's extended hand and he involuntarily pulled the trigger, a second bright flash, directed toward the ground. Then Amos reached him, grabbing for the gun with his left hand and pushing it back as he hit Greg with a hard right to the nose. He hadn't been in a fight since junior high, but had the satisfaction of feeling the nose flatten under his fist. The pistol went off a third time. Greg fell backward, dropping the weapon and clutching his stomach as he lay on the ground, moaning in pain. Blood from his nose soaked the black ski mask.

Amos grabbed the weapon first, then turned to Stephanie. She was scrambling to her feet, unhurt. "He pointed it away from me," she said breathlessly. Stephanie hurried to kneel by Greg. She forced his hands away from his abdomen and examined him. "Through the left side and out again. Maybe got a kidney. Call 911! He should be okay if they get here fast enough."

Amos pulled out his communicator and pressed 9.


Amos awoke late on Sunday morning, to find Stephanie already up and dressed. "About time, sleepyhead. Grab some cereal, and then we have to finish packing."

The success with the baby turtles seemed to have lifted Stephanie out of her depression. She had shaken off the trauma of having Gregory Hentson appear like a ghost from the past and threaten their lives.

"I just called the hospital. They had to repair two holes in his intestines, but Greg is out of danger. He's under arrest, of course, with a sheriff's deputy at the door."

"I wish I could feel sorry for him," said Amos, "but I don't."


"Thank you all for coming." Interior Admin Judge Sebastian Carver rose from a chair near the front of the meeting room in the Merritt Island Park recreation building and walked to the podium. About ten people were seated in the closest chairs. He spoke without using a microphone, the deep, soft voice easily heard. "First, every one of you is someone for whom I had the sad duty of deciding your home couldn't be saved. I invited you here in the hope of possibly relieving some of the emotional pain you've suffered. Second, this is an informal meeting. I'm a member of an unofficial association of admin judges that tries to help people making difficult career moves. Interior cooperates by giving us early word on upcoming projects. I want to show you one of those tonight."

Carver lifted a remote control off the podium and pointed it at the screen on the wall behind him. It flickered to life, the Interior logo large on the bottom right. The camera hovered far above a snow-covered mountain peak, wooded slopes spread around it on all sides. A narrator came on and explained that they were seeing the Mt. Hood Wilderness area, a federal park over sixty thousand acres in size, with several small rivers supplied by the glaciers on Mt. Hood. The camera view moved down and focused on one large wooded valley. And the narrator briefly detailed one of the largest, most ambitious plans in the Save America program.

Amos listened and watched, fascinated, for thirty minutes. This high-level valley in Oregon was to be diked at its three lowest points, creating a new lake fed by several of Mt. Hood's rivers. When full it would exceed 200 square miles in surface area. But in effect it was nothing more than a huge reservoir. Giant pumps would be installed a few miles to the north at the Columbia River; fourth largest in vol ume in the United States. They would feed two large concrete pipes climbing up to the new lake. The dam that would protect the Columbia River gorge from the rising water of the Pacific was to be located near Astoria, saving the much larger city of Portland to the southeast. In addition, as much as possible of the 150 inches of rainfall a year, for which the area was famous, would be diverted to the new reservoir.

That much water would overflow even this huge high-level lake in just a few years. But two wide new covered aqueducts were to be built south and east of Mt. Hood, carrying two rivers' worth of water south. The eventual users were the drier parts of Oregon east of the Cascades, and the states of California, Nevada, and Arizona. According to the narrator this huge and dependable new supply of water would turn the dry areas of those states into gardens, providing vast new areas of farmland. As a side benefit, the Colorado River would be much less used, and should once again provide a supply of freshwater to Mexico.

When the program ended, Carver returned to the podium. "This project is going to be one of the biggest of Save America. It was proposed decades ago, but the country wasn't willing then to spend the money. Now we are, because we must be. The first thousand or so jobs are about to be posted, and each of you here have some of the required skill needs." He picked up a printed list off the podium. "First, Amos Byers. How would you like to work on the pumps that will lift Columbia River water all the way to the new reservoir? And Stephanie Byers; there are jobs for biologists at the Pacific Coast Wildlife Rescue Center in Portland. You'll be working to save the Pacific sea lions, finding higher level breeding beaches for them. Now Arturo and Juanita Delgado. . ." but Amos stopped listening when Stephanie rose, grabbed his hand, and led him to the door.

The area outside was brightly lit. Amos stared at Stephanie when she stopped and turned to face him, still holding his hand. "Amos—I want to go. I don't want to move into that dreadful apartment, I want a whole new life! Becoming a part of something that will change our country for the better, not just save overpriced real estate. . . I want this, Amos."

He stared at her, unable to believe the change in Stephanie. Her eyes were almost sparkling, her face more animated than he had seen in months. He had the awful feeling that if he refused to move and said no, she would leave him and go anyway.

"But the girls! Their senior year. . ."

"Amos, I talked to Judge Carver when he called and invited us to this meeting. I've had time to think about it, and talk with the girls. They say Florida with a dike around it won't be the same, and they love the idea of moving to a cooler climate."

"It was the turtles," Amos said softly, his gaze still on Stephanie's face. "You and your students saved *all* of them. . ."

Stephanie turned to look at him, surprised. "Yes, we did. But I've worked with turtles for decades. I'm ready for something new, and saving the Pacific sea lions will be fascinating work. They aren't like turtles; they can be taught to change their habits."

"And so can we," said Amos. He pulled Stephanie into his arms and kissed her, thoroughly and warmly. Neither had ever lived outside Florida; it was time for a change.

But twenty years from now, he planned to bring Stephanie back here for a vacation. The first of the adult female loggerheads from the nest Stephanie and her students had saved should be coming ashore to lay their eggs. He wanted to watch the awkward, lumbering, indomitable females struggling to perpetuate their species, no matter the odds against the survival of their offspring. Someone would be waiting there, to move those eggs to higher ground.

# THE *CALIFORNIA QUEEN* COMES A-CALLING

Pat MacEwen

The first sign of trouble was nothing more than a shadowy glint, and Taiesha missed it, being too busy arguing with the judge. The *California Queen*'s paddlewheel threshed the dark water at half speed as they edged their way past another half-drowned town full of skeletal trees and rotted rooftops. It should have been safe enough, this far offshore. There was no source of fresh water out here, so no people either.

*A used-to-be someplace,* Taiesha thought, *without even a name nowadays.*

No, that wasn't entirely true. A hundred yards starboard, she caught a glimpse of an old water tower, its rusted remains still graced by dark lettering. Hilmar-something. Irving? Irwin? She couldn't tell. The rest of it had been stolen by time, water, weather, and weariness. Some little farm town, then, swallowed up by the Inland Sea the same as so many larger cities—Sacramento, Stockton, Tracy. . . Half of California was gone, seemed like.

"Why me?" she demanded.

"Look, you're a public defender," Judge Hebert insisted. "It's your job."

"Are you kidding me?"

"No," he replied, with no hint of a smile. On his long pale deep-graven face, it would look out of place anyway, she thought, like a grim reaper's grin.

Taiesha snorted at that notion, which cut a little too close to the bone. She turned away from her boss, but as the deck yawed underfoot, she veered to the right and the morning sunlight cutting across the Texas deck caught her full in the face. It blinded her for a critical moment, so bright that tears soon threatened to slide down her cheeks.

Oh, Lord. She couldn't let Hebert see *that*. She grabbed hold of the railing in front of her and tried to get a grip of another kind. The blistered paint bit at the scars across her palms, but she ignored the lesser pain. She stared instead at the skeins of silvery water flying off the great paddlewheel as it churned away at the *Queen's* stern, two decks below.

"Well, Chavez is sick, and there's nobody else aboard anywhere near as qualified," Judge Hebert said.

"It's a child murder," Taiesha ground out, unable to keep her voice totally level.

"Yes. A capital crime," the judge agreed. "And I know how much you hate kid cases. Even so, there's no help for it. Somebody has to defend this man. He's a pre-Rise landowner. His case is getting a lot of attention."

Taiesha shook her head hard enough to arouse a faint jingle from the tiny metallic beads at the ends of her cornrows. The sound, as always, reminded her of the wind chimes her daughter brought home from the fair that last summer, before everything went to hell. Pretty things, those chimes, adorned with little butterflies of anodized aluminum, flashing blue and green in the sun as they spun about. How many years had it been since. . .

Somewhere below, a gun went off and someone screamed. A splash was followed by several men shouting, then more gunshots.

Only then did Taiesha notice the boats that had pulled up alongside the *Queen*—a kayak, a dinghy, and what looked like one of those fiberglass paddleboats she used to rent at Lodi Lake in the summer. The ungainly things were propelled by one or both of the passengers working bicycle pedals set under the seats. Her little girl had loved the silly contraptions.

Where the hell had this one come from?

The shadows, she realized. They'd been hiding behind what remained of the houses of Hilmar-Ir-whatever, counting on the glare of the morning sun to keep the *Queen*'s crew from spotting them too early on.

"Pirates!" somebody finally cried down below. The pilothouse bell began clanging like mad.

"Ah, shit!" muttered the judge.

Taiesha moved toward the portside stairway leading down to the boiler deck. Her hand found its way to the small of her back without her guidance, and then she had the comforting weight of blued steel in her grip. The judge did not follow. His post was right there, at the top of the stairs, where he could keep boarders from reaching the pilot, from taking control of the *Queen*.

Her own lay two flights down, on the main deck, but already one of the pirates had swarmed up a column amidships. The barefoot bastard scrambled over the railing just as she reached the boiler deck. For a fleeting second, Taiesha gaped. He looked like a friggin' cartoon of a buccaneer. White or Hispanic mixed with black, he wore brown dreadlocks and torn denim cut-offs and some sort of gun belt, but most of the rest was earrings and tattoos and beard stubble. Jesus! The scrawny little mutt even had a naked knife's blade clenched in between what was left of his teeth.

All this news her eyes gathered in while her hands acted on their own. She heard a loud bang. Instantly, a small black hole appeared beside the blue spider tattooed above his left eyebrow. There wasn't much blood. Just wide brown eyes full of dull surprise. Then he was falling back over the railing again, all before she'd even realized those two slender dark-skinned hands in front of her and the smoking pistol they held were her own.

"Good shot, lass."

The voice was male and deep as the pit, but softened by a Scottish burr. Iain MacClure. Had to be, she thought, whirling around. The gun, by necessity, followed her line of sight, and she fired again but on the fly. A spurt of blood flew from the side of the Scotsman's head as he threw himself at the deck but that didn't deflect the bullet much. It still found its target—another boarder swinging an ax at MacClure's broad back. The next man ducked and she missed him. Worse yet, the shell casing stove-piped, jamming her pistol.

Poxy thing. But there was no time to think about it. The third guy had already reached for the ax.

In two long strides, she delivered a place kicker's boot to the third man's gonads. It sent a shockwave of pain up her spine and lifted him up off the deck by a full three inches, but didn't kill him. It did drop him onto his hands and knees when he came back down again, though, and thereafter he spent his time trying to vomit and scream simultaneously. She had to bring the gun's butt down like a club and bash the man at the base of his skull to shut him up. Only then did she have time to worry about MacClure and his condition.

Had she killed him?

No.

Damn the luck!


Three hours later, they pulled into Atwater. Four dead pirates hung from the rails on the starboard side. The two they'd captured were chained to the same rails, spread-eagle, one of them wailing about it. The rest of them had either escaped or their bodies had been too much work to recover.

Right now, the crewmen were lined up along both sides of the boat, a show of force for the locals that took up entirely too much room on the cargo-laden main deck. Worse yet, Taiesha had to sidle past MacClure as she made her way forward. She braced herself for the too-close encounter, not least because of her still-aching back, but the auditor merely nodded her way and said nothing at all.

What was up with *that* anyway? Most men would have said: (a) "Hey, girl! Thanks for saving my ugly ass!" or (b) "You damn near blew my head off, bitch! What up!"

Not MacClure. He was too busy fluffing his gray-blond curls, still damp from having the blood clots washed out. His right ear had been bandaged, and that made his round ruddy face look a little misshapen, but when it healed up he would probably be more symmetrical rather than less, since his left ear had a chunk missing too.

Hunh. There were more scars that she'd never noticed before, underneath the long hair and the sideburns.

*Where did he get those,* she wondered, next easing her way past a long row of steel water barrels. *And who saved his hairy ass last time around?*

On reaching the capstan, she was none too pleased to discover the man had fallen in right behind her. What? Was he planning to follow her all day long? What on Earth had she done to deserve a six-foot-tall Scottish thorn in her ass?

There was no time to ask him. She had her own role to play right now, one that called for a navy blue pinstriped business suit, a lawyerly bearing, and her smallest hide-away holster. That was the part she disliked the most. The form-fitting suit made it nearly impossible to conceal any serious weapons. But as Hebert kept on telling her, appearances would, sooner or later, start making a real difference.

"Ah, there you are, my dear." The judge looked as sober as. . . well, himself. He was wearing his black robes in spite of the heat, and carrying his symbol of office—the gavel he'd use when his clerk called court into session. "Look sharp," he told everyone else.

The *Queen's* white gangplank hung from her nose like an anteater's long snout, not yet in actual contact with the docks. As soon as she reached him, however, Hebert nodded to the boat's captain.

"Showtime!" the captain replied with a sardonic smile, and gave the order to lower the plank.

Judge Hebert was, as always, the first to disembark. He moved with a priestly air of deliberation and the crowd ashore parted like the Red Sea before Moses. Well, John Alton Hebert was also a lawgiver, right?

She'd just have to hope no one here realized how vulnerable they really were, how easily the man, the show, and the *Queen* herself could be blown apart.

Dry land felt odd underfoot, as if she were still aboard ship. Her feet kept expecting a rhythmic rise and fall that wasn't there anymore. *Must make me look like a drunk*, Taiesha thought, trying to keep herself in hand.

It didn't help, having to push her way through the crowd. They'd made way for the judge, but not for her, not until the detail assigned to her caught up and formed a flying wedge around her. She didn't care for that either, though. Relying on somebody else for your safety made you careless. That's how you wound up facing death all alone, with your family's blood on the walls.

Then again, there were only the three of them. Well, four, counting MacClure. Most of the others were assigned to Bobby Rishwain's detail. Already, she could hear pulses of radio code on her earbug as his squad spread out and began their half of the hunt. Her own team had been put ashore quietly almost a mile north of town, and an hour ahead of their reaching the landing. If all went well, they'd be showing up here any minute and then she could link up with Rishwain and finish the job. Meanwhile, Judge Hebert was joining a man on a plank platform up ahead. Who the hell was that? The mayor?

*I'll be damned*, Taiesha thought. The man was actually wearing a waistcoat over a short-sleeve dress shirt. The rest of his three-piece suit was missing (he had jeans on, not slacks), but it did lend the fellow an air of decorum. He needed it. He had to shout to make himself heard above all the general uproar.

"Welcome to Atwater!" he bellowed over the heads of his fellow townsmen. "We are delighted to have you here, Judge, and we hope this will be only the first of many official visits to our little town. I see you've already run into our biggest problem." At which point, he waved at the pirates, living and dead, adorning the *Queen*.

"Indeed," answered Hebert. "And that will be our first order of business on the morrow." He didn't shout. He was wearing a lapel mike, and his somber voice boomed out across the dock with a startling volume thanks to loudspeakers mounted on the *Queen*. Several small children clutched at their mothers and cried. They were all young enough, they'd probably never heard the like. Hebert ignored them, aiming his words at their parents, who largely fell silent, more out of surprise than respect.

"Now, then. Ladies and Gentlemen," said the judge. "It is my pleasure to be here, and I can assure you all, on behalf of the sovereign state of California, that Atwater will be a regular stop for the circuit court."

That met with applause. Taiesha used it to cover a radio query. "Little Bo Peep, calling all her lost sheep. . . Buzz? Where are we?"

"Already aboard," Bustamente reported.

"What?!" Taiesha forced herself to maintain her direction. She would *not* turn and stare at the *Queen*, or get anyone else intrigued by doings on the boat, not right now. "Did you get all three?"

"Sure did."

She wanted to smile. Instead, she asked him, "How did you manage it?"

Buzz chuckled. "Easy. I told 'em there was too such a thing as free lunch, and it's part of the witness fee. Never had to show 'em the warrant."

"Outstanding," she told him. To the rest of the team, she said,

"Okay, we have our material witnesses. Now, all we need is the defendant."

She'd made it to the end of the platform by then, but she paid no attention to the two men presently treading the boards. Her attention was centered instead on a burly cocoa-colored brute with broad *indio* cheek bones. An ancient M-16 hung from his shoulder on a rawhide strap, much as a woman would carry a purse. While his stance was calm and his hands were still, his eyes danced over the crowd with professional speed, skipping over the kids and most of the women, zeroing in on a few of the townsmen and more than a few of the raggedy teenagers on the crowd's outer fringes. He's picking targets, she realized. Just in case.

Using hand signals, she split up her escorts, two and two, so they could set up a crossfire, should support in force be needed. "Look sharp," she told them. "This could turn ugly in a heartbeat."

MacClure nodded, grinning as if the fool didn't know what ugly was, which might be all too true.

As she came closer to M-16, he turned his gaze her way, so, rolling her hips a bit, Taiesha smiled at him. "You the sheriff?" she inquired.

"Not exactly," he replied.

"Hunh. Well, I don't see a badge, but I do see. . . authority."

That went over as she'd intended, allowing her to sidle closer.

Meanwhile, up on the platform, Judge Hebert was just hitting his oratorical stride. "As you know, the state is striving with all its might to suppress the kind of lawlessness represented by these sorry specimens." He waved at the two surviving raiders, still hanging in chains. One screamed an obscenity in response.

The crowd roared even more graphic crudities back at the pirate.

Hebert allowed that to peter out. Then he announced, "The survivors will be tried this very afternoon, and their sentences. . ." Here he paused, to whet their interest. ". . .will most likely be carried out first thing in the morning."

"Are you gonna hang 'em?" somebody shouted.

Judge Hebert smiled. "I cannot say, since they have been neither convicted nor sentenced as yet. But if I were a betting man. . ."

That got a rise out of everyone present. It wasn't a happy noise, she thought. It reminded her of the old Westerns she used to watch with her Gramps on a Sunday afternoon. A herd of cattle about to stampede sounded like that—a low, uneven, grumbling that kicked at her heart with a cowboy's spurs. She wondered which way they were leaning. Pro or con on executions?

Maybe both. There was a clear divide, she noticed, between the folks actually standing around on the dock and those lurking on the periphery. The former were much better dressed, and cleaner too. Most of them even had shoes, while the latter wore rags and perched in trees or atop wooden fences and crates and such—all positions with both a good view and a handy escape route.

Townies and refugees, Taiesha told herself. The heart of her personal problem.

Waistcoat chuckled. "Well, judge, somebody here might be willing to lay odds for you, but of course, by California law. . . *that* would be illegal too!"

Laughter gusted among the townies, and was met with unease on the part of the refugees. Three guesses who thought the laws now being revived would be mostly applied to them, she thought. She was close enough now to touch M-16, and did, tracing out the flowing form of a lion tattooed on his arm.

"We look forward to seeing justice done," said the mayor.

"I'm glad to hear you say that," Judge Hebert replied, donning his grim reaper's grin.

The mayor eyed him, hesitating.

"Oh," said the judge. "Please forgive me. We haven't actually been introduced as yet, have we? I am John Alton Hebert, Judge of the First Circuit Court of the Central Valley. And you, sir?"

Waistcoat seemed reassured by this, by a formal brand of courtesy not often seen in the Valley even before the sea reclaimed so much of it. "I'm Eric Moreland," he replied, "and pleased to meet ya!"

He thrust a hand out, intending to shake the judge's mitt.

"Well met, indeed," Hebert replied, and struck like a snake.

*Snick!*

Moreland blinked, staring down at the steel around his wrist in utter astonishment.

To his left, on the ground, M-16 got it instantly. By the time he made his move, though, Taiesha was pressing the muzzle of her injection gun into his arm, right into the lion's mouth. When she fired, the gun spat scores of nano-needles into him. He jumped like a cat and swung the M-16 at her head, but MacClure was there and grabbed the rifle. Two seconds later, its owner went cross-eyed and slid to the ground in a boneless heap. He wasn't the only one. Between her team and Bobby's, they'd knocked out half a dozen men, all of them heavily armed and strategically located.

"Jesse, where are you?!" Moreland cried, panicking, trying to yank his hand free of the judge. Then Bobby's men pressed inward, ringing the man as he was pulled down off the planks and spun about and the other handcuff applied. He kicked at them but it was already too late, especially if M-16 was the 'Jesse' he wanted to come to his aid.

"Eric Alvin Moreland," the judge intoned, "you are under arrest for the murder of Ramon Izquierdo, following your indictment on the same charge pursuant to testimony heard by the Modesto Grand Jury on April 14th of this year."

"What the hell are you talking about?" Moreland shrieked at him. "No one in *this* town would *ever* take *me* on! They all damn well *know* better!"

Some of them, maybe. As people caught on, pandemonium broke out here and there. Most appeared to be taking Moreland's side, but more than a few were cheering his arrest. Some of the townies suddenly surged toward the platform. The rescue attempt, if that's what it was, petered out just as quickly, however, when the bailiffs turned and took aim at them. Meanwhile, aboard the *Queen*, somebody fired a burst from the 50-mm machine gun mounted on the Texas deck.

While the crowd took that in, Rishwain ordered, "Go!"

Moving as one, the bailiffs hustled Moreland across the dock and onto the gangplank before anybody could quite figure out what to do.

As soon as they had him aboard, Judge Hebert addressed the crowd with an uncharacteristic note of good cheer. "You wanted to see justice done! And you will! Mr. Moreland will have a bail hearing this afternoon. Then we'll proceed to trial, most likely right after sentence is carried out on those two pirates."

An angry growling arose, but Hebert only shook his head. "Now, now, good people! You haven't seen the long arm of the law hereabouts for a very long time. I understand that, but I assure you, the wheels of justice are still turning. In the meantime, Mr. Moreland will be our guest, and *you* will all behave yourselves."

In the resulting silence, the judge climbed down off the platform. Taiesha joined him as he made his way back to the California *Queen*, with her detail now acting as his bodyguards.

As soon as they reboarded, Judge Hebert turned to Taiesha. "Tag. You're it."


*Atwater. Rhymes with Backwater,* Taiesha told herself, taking a seat in the interview room. She couldn't help but sigh. There being no facilities in town that could be secured against the town itself, the accused had been locked up below decks and she, perforce, also had to put up with the overheated stuffiness down there.

"All right, Jerome. Bring him in," she told the bailiff on duty, a beefy black man who looked a little too much like her husband, Tremaine, for her personal comfort, but was also a solid reliable type, just like Tremaine.

Damn it. Why was she thinking of him right now?

*Get your mind on the case,* she told herself, *and quit mooning around like an idiot. Tremaine is dead. Jerome is not him, and you've got a job to do, like it or not. So get your head wrapped around this thing.*

At which point, a niggling voice in the back of her mind spoke up, asking, "Why?"

*Why what?*

"Why worry about it?"

She frowned, and the voice continued. "Why bother defending this clown? Wave your hands in the air, and let him hang too."

*The man has a right to a decent defense,* she told herself. *And I'm a professional.*

Self merely snorted. "Yeah, right." Then the door slammed open, propelled by a shoulder. Eric Moreland's. He was still wearing his cuffs, and the cuffs were chained to his waist. His feet were chained to each other.

"Hey, get these damn things off me!" he snapped at her, flapping his hands around.

Taiesha frowned at the man. "Excuse me?"

"*I said*, get 'em off me!"

"I'm not a bailiff, Mr. Moreland. I don't have the keys."

"Then get someone in here that does!"

Clearly, he was used to giving orders. Could he take one?

"*Sit down*," she told him, using what Tremaine used to call her none-of-your-nonsense voice.

It didn't go over well. He leaned forward, planted his knuckles on the table and glared at her with an intensity that sent a little spike of adrenaline through her veins. It brought Jerome a step nearer too, but she shook her head and that stopped his advance on the suspect.

Apparently, Moreland thought that was due to his importance. He developed a nasty grin. "I don't know who you think you are. . ." he began.

"Taiesha Daniels. I'm your attorney."

That stopped him. In silence, he gave her the hairy eyeball. She returned the favor.

Pretty well fed for a farmer. Most of them hereabouts had lost all their water rights early on. When the snowpack up in the mountains subsided to one-fifth of "normal" the cities and big corporations got first dibs. Now most of the rivers were dry by July. Worse yet, when the Inland Sea swallowed the valley, it took out the Aqueduct too, and the wells soon after, thanks to saltwater intrusion. No water to drink from above or below, let alone irrigate anything, for at least half the year. So just how had this redneck hung on to his land, and how was he maintaining that minor league beer belly?

"You? A lawyer?" said Moreland. He straightened, then pointedly ran his gaze over her corn rows. "Where'd *you* go to school, huh? Ghetto Tech?"

"UCLA," she replied.

That got a dry sneer of a laugh. "Another south state water-sucker, and a shining example of the equal-opportunity program, I bet. State scholarship, right? Or a grant. Anything but your own dime."

"G.I. Bill."

The correction derailed him for a moment, but didn't convince him. That, she thought, came from his spotting the long twisted scars on her left hand and wrist. They had nothing to do with her tours of duty, but he didn't know that. Moreland brought his head back an inch or so. Something darkened in his eyes. Then, with a skeptical grunt, he finally settled into the chair on his side of the table. After a moment, he inquired, "*My* lawyer?"

"Yes. I'm the public defender for the First Circuit Court of the Central Valley," Taiesha told him. "I've been assigned to your case, and now. . ."

"Don't need one."

Taiesha frowned. "Mr. Moreland, you've been charged with murder."

"Yeah, right." Moreland shrugged that off as if it were dandruff. "I killed me a thief. A sea rat. That ain't murder. That's me, exercising my right to defend me and mine."

"Really? Why don't you tell me about it."

Suspicion glittered in those eyes. On more than one front, she thought, but he'd either get over the skin color thing or he wouldn't. She didn't much care about that. She could only address the more patent problem.

Taiesha nodded to Jerome et al. "Gentlemen?"

When they'd stepped out, she assured Moreland, "Whatever you say to me is protected by attorney-client privilege. It can't be used against you. It can't even be shared with anyone else, not unless you agree to it."

Moreland was, what? Forty-one? Old enough to remember what life was like, back before Second Rise. Back when sea level had only gone up by a couple dozen feet, back when we all thought we could simply *adjust*, when everyone in the country had power and cable and working wall screens, and every other TV series was a cop show. Back when everybody knew their Miranda rights by heart and could tell you the best way to use Luminol at a crime scene. Did he remember the rules about privilege? She could only hope so.

Once more, she gently urged him on. "Tell me what happened."

He licked his lips, and she pushed a ration bladder his way, but Moreland didn't take it. "I, uh, I have a warehouse," he told her. "Not far from here. Me and my brother, we built it. The roads wasn't comin' back, right? So there wasn't no good way to get things to market. At first, it was no big deal 'cause we weren't even growing enough to feed our own selves. But once we got the de-sal plant started up, well, *then* we come up with a surplus. The town got together and put in a dock, and boats started coming. . . and we were a port town, just like that.

"Nothing big, see? But we did a lot better'n some."

Taiesha nodded. She'd seen the towns he was talking about—the ones that did not come together and pull themselves back from the brink. Towns that made Hilmar-whatever look damn good and pirates were really the least of it, where people wound up eating each other. But that thought brought up other things she would rather not remember clearly—the sound of their screams and the smell of their blood. . .

Not now.

She rubbed at the scars on her wrist, and shifted her hips in a vain attempt to ease the pain still enfolding her spine, thanks to her early morning encounter with Hilmar's unlucky buccaneers.

*Hey! Come on, focus!*

Her client, thank God, didn't notice the lapse. He said, "Next thing you know, the whole damn town was overrun with sea rats."

A term Taiesha found distasteful, to say the least.

"All over the place, we got squatters," said Moreland. "They tear the hell out of whatever place they get into. They steal everything, and there's more of 'em every damn day! When they start taking the food out of *our* kids' mouths, well, a man has to *do* something."

Taiesha nodded.

"That deputy they sent out here from Merced is the first one we've seen in ten years, so the rule is the same as in L.A. You see a looter, you shoot him. And that's what I did."

Taiesha peered at the case file. "It says here the victim, Ramon Izquierdo, was nine years old."

Moreland nodded.

"I don't see any property listed, except for his clothes and a home-made slingshot. That and a pair of real rats, both dead. Did you see him steal something?"

"That little bastard was inside the fence, and about to get into the warehouse. He would've stole something, sure as shit."

"Did he attack you in any way? With the slingshot, perhaps?"

"Hell, no." Moreland scoffed at the very idea. "Didn't give him the chance."

Taiesha frowned. "It says here he was shot in the back."

"That's right. That's how we do it around here. Ain't no such thing

as a warning shot. Not with a sea rat. You take your shot when you see
'em. You don't, they'll either get away or they'll get you first."

A rational attitude, five or six years ago. Now?

Taiesha swallowed a bad taste and pressed on. "Did you get a look
at him first? Were you aware that he was a child?"

A movement of the man's shoulders might've been either a twitch
or a shrug. "Ain't about size," he said. "My Daddy taught me that
much. All guns are loaded. All dogs bite. And a rat is a rat."

*Great*, she thought. *Just great.* That little tidbit was likely to be the
centerpiece of her closing argument, come the trial, when she'd have
to act as this man's mouthpiece and do her best to justify his killing
this kid.

*Why me?* she asked the Universe At Large.

Nobody answered, not even Self.


Her next stop was the galley, where she could look at her witnesses
through the service window without being spied upon herself. The
three of them were seated in the Mess, at the captain's table. All three
were stuffing their faces, surrounded by ration pack wrappers and
soup bowls.

"Been eating their heads off," the cook told her. "Them kids'll finish a pack and get up and go run laps around the boiler deck. They're
trying to make room for more, I guess. 'Specially when they found
out they was gettin' dessert."

Taiesha nodded. "How long do you think it's been since any of
them got to eat their fill?"

"No tellin', honey. I reckon that boy been hungry his whole life.
The little one ain't quite so fixated on it, but she sure ain't picky! And
Momma's already got three or four picnics' worth tucked into her
underwear."

Taiesha could see a certain lumpiness in regions that ought to
have curved a bit more, but some of that was the sheer lack of meat

on her bones. The woman looked to be in her late twenties—a skinny brownette with long tapering fingers and ragged nails. She might have been pretty once, when she was still a kid. Now, mostly, she looked worn out.

Small wonder. The boy seemed to be in perpetual motion. Keeping up with him would wipe out a Marine. And the girl. . .

Oh my God.

The little girl had Kayla's snub nose. She turned her head toward the window, presenting a backlit profile, and just at that moment, the woman reached out and tapped the tip of that upturned nose. The move transferred a dollop of cream from the pie she'd been eating.

"Tia Trina!" the child protested. She promptly went cross-eyed, trying to look at her new decoration. Then she tried to lick it off, only her tongue wouldn't reach. The two of them burst into giggles, and Taiesha's heart did a belly flop as she remembered the barbecue, that final Fourth of July before her own daughter was killed.

Something crashed to the floor—a stack of pie tins. She'd knocked them off as she staggered back.

"Hey! You all right, honey?" Large warm floury hands took hold of her. They held her up when Taiesha's legs didn't want to. She clung to the counter and closed her eyes and turned away, from the view and the memory.

"Here," said another deeper voice, and she felt herself pressed into a chair. At the sound of that second voice, though, her eyes flew wide open again, and she found that while two of the helping hands were the cook's, the other two were MacClure's. Where in hell had *he* come from?

She pulled free of both sets, and growled out a low, "No, don't!"

To the Scotsman, she said, "*You* get the fuck away from me."

To her relief, and without a word, he did. But the trio pigging out in the Mess must have heard all the noise, and been spooked by it. When she looked back through the service window, all three were gone. There was nothing left but wrappers and crumbs, and damn few of those.

Taiesha sighed. She hauled herself upright again. "It's. . . I'm okay," she told the cook when the latter moved in again, ready to grab her. "It's just the heat." And since the kitchen was indeed overly warm, that gave her a semi-graceful exit.

She made it by way of the Mess, where she pulled on gloves and carefully gathered up lunch's remains. There just might be a little bit more she could do for these people.

Moreland's hearing took all of ten minutes. The bailiffs allowed thirty townsmen aboard, but also insisted on disarming everyone. Taiesha had Jerome make sure at least five were refugees, too. Some townies weren't happy about that, but justice, as Jerome loudly informed them all, either applied to everyone or nobody. That, plus the big guns the bailiffs all carried around on their belts, served as a convincing argument and the protest subsided, at least until the judge ordered remand for the mayor.

*What do they expect on a charge like this?* Taiesha wondered. There weren't any bail bondsmen left, for God's sake, not around here.

Then, after her client was hauled back to lock-up, the judge's clerk called out the traditional Oyez announcement, and they proceeded directly to trial for the two surviving pirates. She was saved from having to mount the witness stand herself by MacClure's testimony about what took place on the boiler deck that morning when they were boarded, but realized now why she'd won that round so easily. The "man" she'd kicked and cold-cocked was nowhere near full grown. He was a teenager, half starved to death, and so striped with scars as well as tattoos, there was hardly a square inch of him unmarked by one or the other. Fifteen, sixteen, maybe? Scared, for sure.

His compadre was older by a decade or so, but missing an eye and still more of his teeth. The second man wasn't frightened at all.

He was grinning at one of the local women and smacking his lips as he grabbed his crotch. One of the bailiffs cracked a baton across his elbow, hoping to improve his manners, but mostly it just made him noisier.

To her surprise, the Scot's account of the morning's encounter was both concise and accurate. Unemotional, too. His brevity let her concentrate on her clients' defense, which mainly amounted to a plea for mercy on account of the younger buc's age.

In the end, however, the judge's ruling surprised no one. Rishwain made his closing argument, she made hers, and the clerk handed up a neat sheaf of the paperwork involved to His Honor. Judge Hebert nodded his thanks, and glanced at the forms, but what he saw there deepened the lines engraved in his long face. He turned toward the pirates again with a grave air better suited to funeral parlors.

"Michael Dysart, and James Alan Wilson," he intoned. "You have both been found guilty of attempted piracy on a public waterway. The penalty for attempted piracy is the same as for actual piracy—it is not the policy of this state, after all, to reward you for failing."

He paused, and got a nervous laugh from the townies. Was that intentional? Hebert had an improv actor's sense of timing, Taiesha thought, but she hoped he wasn't going to play up this crowd, not when one of their own was about to be tried here.

"In addition," the judge announced, "the two of you were tested while in custody. Your, ah, bodily by-products, that is." Again he paused, letting that one sink into a growing silence. Taiesha, who'd run the tests, knew where he was going with this, but the locals didn't. "James Alan Wilson, you tested positive. Human myoglobin from muscle tissue was found in your feces. You, sir, are a cannibal."

The courtroom erupted and the bailiffs were hard pressed to keep the townsmen away from the two defendants. A clamor arose and became a chant, and the chant was soon loud enough to be heard ashore, where still more voices joined in. Moments later, the whole town of Atwater seemed to saying the same thing: "Hang 'em! Hang 'em!"

It didn't subside until Judge Hebert used all of the *Queen's* many loudspeakers. Over and over again, His Honor shouted, "Order in the Court!" and banged his gavel with such a will that it sounded like gunshots. That was what finally shut them all up—the fear that it might be.

Hebert waited until everyone had sat down again, too, before he banged the gavel once more and announced his decision. "Michael Dysart and James Alan Wilson, you have both been convicted of a capital crime. In accordance with the laws of the sovereign State of California, I do hereby sentence the pair of you to be hanged by the neck until you are dead."

Again, the crowd in the courtroom roared, and drowned out the rest of it. This time, though, Hebert let them go at it until they were tired of shouting. Then he told them, "Said sentence will be carried out immediately."

That's when Dysart, the younger one, shot to his feet and cried, "No fair! *He* ate the meat, *not me*! That bastard wouldn't even give me a *taste*! Hang *him*, not *me*!"


Half an hour later, Taiesha found herself back on the Texas deck. Alongside Judge Hebert, she watched while the bailiffs erected the collapsible gallows behind the pilot house. "Why hang them today?" she asked the judge.

"Why not?" said Hebert.

"Well. . ."

"We'd have to feed them again, for one thing," His Honor went on, not waiting for her reply. "And they'd both have to suffer through a long sleepless night, knowing there was no hope. I think that would be cruel."

"But. . ."

"What?"

Taiesha shook her head. "I'm just wondering how long it'll be before we can afford *not* to kill everyone we convict."

The judge sighed as he turned to face her. "You know we don't have the resources to keep anybody in prison. We don't have the space, or the guards, or the money for that, much less the food."

"But a kid that young. . ." Here she pointed at Dysart. ". . .if he ever had even half a chance. . ."

"He's a cannibal." Hebert put his hand on her forearm. "You heard him. The boy was mad at his compadre. Why? Because he *didn't* get his fair share of their last victim. Besides, you know there must have been others."

"I realize that," she retorted. "It just doesn't feel right, that's all."

"Tell me, then. Why are we here?" the judge asked her.

Taiesha shrugged.

"*Why?*" he demanded.

When she still didn't answer, he moved closer and took hold of both shoulders, so that she had to look up at him. "We *are* the law," Hebert reminded her. "This circuit court, these robes?" he said, waving a hand at his wind-fluttered expanse of black muslin. "This whole damn ridiculous floating courthouse? *This* is the heart of the law, and we must bring it back to life. Because if we don't, there's no hope for any of us."

The urge to argue that point must have shown in her face.

"You know it's true," Hebert told her. "We made it through First Rise, but Second has damn near done in the entire world. How many people have died already, of flooding and droughts and famine and war? Of murder, disease, and cannibalism? Three billion? Four? Hell, we don't even know. But we do know this. We've only got one more chance at it. We've *got* to get things back under control. Because if we don't, then sure as hell, Third Rise is coming. If that happens, civilization is over with. Probably, so is what's left of humanity."

She knew he was right, knew it down in her bones, but that didn't do much for the queasiness rumbling through her gut, or the aching pain in her lower back, where things had healed up, but would never be totally right again.

There was so damn much that wouldn't, Taiesha reminded herself. Why *are* we here?

For Ramon Izquierdo. For my daughter, too, and Tremaine. And for that little girl with the snub nose, and for all the rest of them that are still breathing, so they'll have a ghost of a chance.

She pulled in a deep breath. This time around, when she glanced at her clients, she saw them for what they were—bits of anomie, ready to murder again and again. The two pirates stood at the foot of the gallows, now nearly erect, but the bailiffs hadn't covered their heads yet. Michael Dysart, the teenager, looked like he might be sick any minute. The other one, Wilson, grinned at Taiesha. Licking his lips, he said, "You look yummy."

"Shut your mouth," the judge instructed. "I'll tell you when it's your turn to talk."

"You go to hell," the pirate snarled back.

"Gag him," Hebert ordered.

That took a couple of minutes and three of their burliest bailiffs, but that was because the condemned man kept trying to bite them. Then both buccaneers were dragged on up the thirteen steps and positioned on top of the trapdoor, with nooses around their scrawny necks. When the bailiffs had finished, the judge got up on the platform too. He took a theatrical tour of the gallows, circling both men. The teenager nearly fell over, just trying to keep him in sight, but the older man was much too busy caterwauling around the muzzle they'd strapped to his face. He nearly drowned out the rowdy crowd on the dock, where it looked like the whole damn town had turned out to watch the proceedings.

They hadn't allowed any locals to stay aboard ship, not for this. Moreland and their three witnesses had been sequestered below decks, and everyone else had been herded ashore.

So far, none had admitted to knowing the two raiders. Still, they might either one have some unknown connection to Atwater's residents. That's why the *Queen*'s captain stood ready to cut the big riverboat loose from the landing. They could always continue the hangings offshore, once they'd gained a safe distance from anyone trying to interfere.

"Ladies and Gentlemen," said the judge, using the *Queen's* PA system. The sound of his voice boomed out, eliciting howls from dogs and small children, and still more excitement among the adults, who were treating the whole thing like some kind of holiday. Maybe it was. No one seemed to be working today.

"Your attention, please!" the judge went on. "These proceedings are serious business. I must ask for your forbearance while we complete the legal niceties."

That got a laugh out of some of the onlookers. Townies, not sea rats. However, the general noise level did drop dramatically, if not the tension Taiesha felt.

*Oh, God*, she thought, panic rising. *God, help me*, she pleaded. Her hands knotted up on their own as she fought for control, and her heart turned into a giant-size fist. It knocked at her ribs again and again while Hebert once more pronounced the death sentence for each man.

*Sweet Jesus, why was he taking so long?*

Next, Hebert solemnly asked each man if he wanted a priest or a preacher of some kind.

The kid merely shook his head.

Wilson, unmuzzled, proceeded to spit at the three nearest bailiffs. His Honor, however, stayed well out of range as he inquired of the boy, "Michael Dysart, do you have anything you'd like to say?"

The teenager squeaked out: "I never ate nobody!"

"You lyin' sack o' shit!" Wilson spat his way as well. And at that point, without waiting till both their heads were bagged, or giving Wilson his chance to speak, Judge Hebert nodded. Jerome hit the big black release lever. The trap door crashed downward. Both men dropped, and a loud double crack echoed over the water.

Taiesha shuddered, hit hard by the sound of their neck bones snapping. That was how Kayla finally died, she remembered. A broken neck was what ended it. How in hell could her own heart have kept on beating after *that*?

She turned away from the gallows, only to find herself facing MacClure. When he smiled, she lashed out without thinking, catching the Scotsman across the face.

*Crack!*

But he never said a word. He simply stepped back and let her sweep past him and on down the stairs to her own tiny stateroom, the one place where she could be truly alone.


That's where Bobby Rishwain found her. A rangy balding man with a tiny Vandyke beard, he wore a black eye patch and looked like a pirate himself, only cleaner and with better teeth. He wore black cargo pants and a genuine Izod shirt sporting their green lizard logo—the kind of thing no one had seen in a store in a decade or more. *God knows where he got it*, Taiesha thought as she let him in. It was a lovely light teal green in color too, something she envied. Her own wardrobe didn't have much in the way of pastels.

"How you doin'?" he inquired, folding up into the only chair she could offer him while she herself took a seat on the folded-out bunk.

"I'm okay," she replied.

"Hurt your hand?"

A heat wave swept across her face as she flexed the appendage in question. Scar tissue resisted the movement, but otherwise everything worked. "Didn't hit the guy *that* hard," she argued.

He gave her a skeptical look that needed no words to say, "Bullshit."

She scowled at him. "Why is he dogging *my* heels like that? He's supposed to be auditing *everyone*, not just me."

"Maybe MacClure likes you."

Taiesha groaned and rolled her eyes heavenward. "Oh, please."

Rishwain laughed. He'd made his own offer months back, but he had a wife and two children in Fresno as well as an aggressive nature that made him a good prosecutor but a poor prospect otherwise. Taiesha much preferred men who felt no special need to demonstrate their manliness, who simply had no doubts about it, though Bobby at least could take no for an answer.

He glanced at the case file laid out on her fold-out desk. "Ah, yes. Our dear Mr. Moreland. A prince of a man. It won't bother me much to hang *him.*"

"Me, neither," Taiesha replied. "But I'm stuck with him. And I think we might have a hard time with the locals in his case. He's got this town organized, and his guys have some hardware to work with." Meaning assault rifles—even antiques like the M-16 from this morning could still produce real firepower. Who knew what else they had?

Rishwain nodded. "You ever hear how he got to be mayor?"

She shook her head.

"Well, a few years back, when the Carquinez Dam failed, and seawater started to flood the whole valley? A few places figured out where things were going. They put in desalinization plants. It was mostly to make sure they'd have drinking water, but the sea kept on coming, and the snowfall didn't. Pretty soon, anyplace without de-sal was dying."

Taiesha kept silent, but tipped her head forward to indicate she understood, so Rishwain continued. "Willets was one of 'em. Danville and Mountain House. Atwater, though, didn't do it. They thought it was too damn expensive."

"But. . . I thought they had one."

"They do," Bobby said. "But it ain't *theirs.* They stole it."

"What?" *Surely he's kidding,* she told herself. *You can't lift a whole water plant, for God's sake, any more than you can shoplift a bridge.* She got up and began to pace the full length of the bunk, just to use up some of that agitation.

"You said it. They're organized," he went on, watching her turn about in the narrow space. "They found out this new charter community north of Merced had one. Stony Creek, I think they called it. A yuppie commuter town—all gated neighborhoods, everything painted the same color, that sort of thing. So one night about eight years ago, Moreland takes his guys up there, and they raid the place. But they don't hit and run. No, they stay there a week. They load up all their food and their livestock, and they take the whole damn desalinization plant apart, and they haul it all home again. Anyone gets in the way gets a bullet."

Taiesha turned once again. "How did they manage *that*? Nobody had any gas back then. There weren't any riverboats, either. Well, not big enough to haul freight."

"Horses," said Rishwain. "And wagons, if you can believe it, made out of old pickups. The yuppies were ready for refugees on foot, with maybe a handgun or two and a half dozen bullets between 'em. They weren't prepared for an army of thirty or forty men on horseback, armed with assault rifles, shotguns, and dynamite."

"An army."

He nodded.

She sank down again on the bunk, trying hard not to bite a hole right through her lip. "And these Stony Creek guys let 'em keep all that?"

"*Let them*?" He sighed. "I don't know what all happened, but Stony Creek just isn't there anymore. More than half the town burned down, and what didn't, drowned. So I don't think *let* is the word for it."

"How about piracy, then?" she demanded. "Shit! Why do I have to defend this guy on the murder charge if we can get him on that?"

Bobby shrugged. "Apparently, San Francisco thinks we need farmers way more than yuppies. Besides, there's no witnesses left, and no paper trail. There's no physical evidence either, so, really, what *can* we do?"

Taiesha had no idea what to tell him. She did have to get her case

ready, however, and shooed Bobby out of her stateroom before heading into the *Queen*'s tiny closet-size lab. There were no chairs at all
in there, and no room for them either, so she braced herself on the
bulkhead, leaned over the DNA sequencer's keyboard, and called up
results on her last set of samples—the swabs she'd used on the ration
wrappers her witnesses handled while eating their lunch.

No, not hers, she thought. Bobby's. As assistant D.A., it was his job
to prosecute, his right to bring in the victim's kin, and his responsibility to question them about the dead boy. It was her job to minimize,
undercut, or disprove what they told him, especially if it could hurt
her client.

Taiesha truly hated that.

The other three Izquierdos were victims too, and in this particular case, they had their half-starved backs to the wall. Well, maybe
she could change that. The new Population Control laws required
registration for everyone, including their DNA profiles. A lot of the
refugees hadn't been able to, though, or else ducked it to stay out of
trouble. The problem was, unregistered kids had no access to health
care. They couldn't go to school, either. But if she herself did the fil-
ing, if she paid the fees, the surviving cousins would at least get a fair
shot at a future.

She laid her results out on the counter, side by side.

Good, she thought. All three profiles were clean. *I can fill out the
paperwork, get Mom to answer a couple of questions about the girl's
parents. . .* but then her eye traveled a bit, and she realized what she
was seeing there.

"Oh, shit!"


There was no way around it. Taiesha thought hard about throwing
the whole goddamn thing out, and maybe the DNA sequencer too,
but she couldn't quite make herself do that. Instead, she requested a
conference in chambers, and waited while Judge Hebert, Rishwain,

the three Izquierdos, and Eric Moreland were all rounded up. Iain MacClure sauntered in too, but played statue thereafter. Still, his presence, all by itself, made her nervous.

The two Izquierdo kids looked just about scared to death, and they wouldn't come near Moreland. He kept on griping about his restraints until Hebert told him that he'd either shut up or he'd get muzzled too.

Rishwain, mostly, was puzzled by all this, and she couldn't tell what the judge thought. She focused instead on Catrina Izquierdo, pale and silent and yet defiant. She sat and glared at Moreland as if she thought she might be able to bore a hole right through his forehead by means of sheer willpower.

"What's this about?" said His Honor, once everyone settled down.

Nausea coiled through her gut, but Taiesha stood up and presented the judge with fresh copies of her DNA results. Her own, she handed to Rishwain. Then, turning to Mrs. Izquierdo, she said, "You haven't registered, have you?"

"What?" Mama pretended to misunderstand, but Taiesha had seen it, the way her narrow nostrils flared and the way her eyes squinched when she spotted the bar codes on those papers. She knew what they were, and she knew what they meant.

"The Global Population Control laws have been in force for more than eight years," said Taiesha. "The law says that you have to register with the state, you and the children. You're refugees, so you may not have realized that. But the fact is, you all have to register. And provide a DNA sample."

"But. . . we don't do nothing wrong!"

"Yes, I'm afraid you did," Taiesha told her. She glanced at Rishwain, who still hadn't figured it out, and said, "You know what the law says about having kids?"

Mama shrugged, her dark eyes bright with tears.

"You can only have one, if you clone yourself. Two, if you have them the natural way. You can pass on a hundred percent of your own genome, or you're allowed to give half of your genes to each of your natural children. Do you understand that?"

"I. . . no. No, I don't. Having children is what mothers do!"

*Probably Catholic,* Taiesha thought. They'd fought the Pop Control laws tooth and nail. So had the Mormons, and Muslims, and practically everyone else. *But the root of the problem is too many people, and Third Rise is coming. If we blow it, Third Rise will kill us all.*

"You can only have two kids," Taiesha insisted. "Any more than that aren't citizens, or even legally persons. They can't go to a public school. They can't go to a doctor. And if something happens to them, they're not protected by the law."

To one side, Hebert nodded. Then Rishwain sat up and said, "Fuck!"

Moreland's gaze bounced back and forth like a ping-pong ball.

Taiesha licked cotton dry lips, hating all of this. She told the woman, "I took DNA samples on all three of you, and we also have one from the body of your son, Ramon. You had three children, didn't you?"

Now Moreland got it, but still didn't understand what it meant.

"NO!" Mama cried. "I have two sons. That's all. Lupe, she is my niece. My sister's child."

"No, she's not." Taiesha pointed at Mama. "She's your daughter. You may have taught her to call you Aunt Trina, but she's yours. The DNA proves it."

"But. . ."

"Hey." That was Moreland. "What's this all about? What do I care if she has two kids or three?"

"We'll get to that," Taiesha told him. "Sit tight."

Then she turned to the judge. "Only two of her kids can be legal. But she's still within the grace period, due to her refugee status. So she can simply go ahead and register two of them right now."

"I can?" said Mama. She wrapped her arms around the girl, who wriggled in protest. The boy swallowed hard but sat tight.

"Yes, you can," Taiesha said, "but only those two will come under the law's umbrella. So if you decided to register both of your sons, then we can prosecute Mr. Moreland for killing Ramon. But your daughter's illegal. And if Mr. Moreland decided to shoot her too, well, we couldn't do a damn thing to him."

That gave the mayor a happy thought, so much so that she longed to kick the man. Not in the shins, either.

Dame Izquierdo looked like she might fall through the floor. "Is that true?" she demanded, staring at Hebert.

"It is," His Honor assured her. "I'm sorry to say so, but Ms. Daniels has it right."

"If, on the other hand," Taiesha went on, "you register your two surviving kids, then it's Ramon who's illegal. We wouldn't be able to try Mr. Moreland for shooting *him*. But if he were to do any harm to *these* children, *then* he'd have to face the full force of the law."

"We could hang him," said Rishwain. He sounded almost as unhappy as Taiesha felt, and she suffered a twinge of guilt as he shot a hard glance her way. *I should have given the man a heads-up*, she thought.

"But. . . I don't know what to do," Mama cried to the judge. "Tell me, what do I do? *¡Dios!* Do I have no right to justice for my boy? That man killed him!"

"Sure did," said Moreland, enjoying himself.

Mama snarled at him. "He didn't break into nothing. And he didn't steal nothing. He was just there hunting rats! For our supper. Your warehouse got plenty of rats. What you kill him for, you stinking bastard?" Then, spouting Spanish invective, she leaped at him. So did the boy, and it took all of them and a couple of bailiffs to pull them apart while Taiesha snatched the girl out of the line of fire. Finally, Mama subsided, but only because of Jerome, who now stood right in back of her chair and kept one of his oversize hands on her shoulder. The boy had retreated into the corner already occupied by MacClure, and stayed there, so everyone left him alone.

Moreland's face was bleeding where Mama had scratched him, but Taiesha made no move toward getting that treated. She rather hoped he'd get a flesh-eating infection and die of it.

Releasing the girl to her mother, she told the woman as gently as possible, "You have to make a decision, and you have to make it right now. You can either get justice for the son you've lost, or protect the two kids you have left."

In the end, there was really no question. What else could any mother do but try to protect her living children?

Moreland, of course, was a total asshole about the whole thing. He laughed at the poor woman and the two kids in between his insistent demands that they take off his shackles and cut him loose. When Jerome finally did so, the mayor promptly spun about. Seizing Taiesha, he whirled her around in a dizzying circle and damn nearly took out the judge with her feet.

"That will be quite *enough!*" Hebert bellowed, backed up by Jerome.

Moreland set her back down again, quite unrepentant. He told Taiesha, "Y'know, you're a hell of a lawyer! I tell you what! We're gonna throw us a party tonight. Gonna celebrate, big time! You're invited, too. Whaddya say?"

Taiesha wanted to hurl her breakfast into his face, but restrained herself, saying only, "We'll see."

Then, thank God, he was gone.

"Nice," Bobby hissed as he left.

"Yes. An interesting tactic," MacClure noted on *his* way out.

"Fuck you," Taiesha told him.


The town of Atwater looked far more attractive after dark.

Walking the streets by the light of the moon, Taiesha could no longer see all the peeling paint, or the mismatches where some repairs had been made, using whatever was handy and not what was actually needed. She could, however, still smell the miasma born of mud and rotting wood and broken sewer lines. She could hear random gunshots, and live music—amateur stuff, but lively, involving a fiddle, at least two guitars, and a number of drums.

They were holding a dance in the torch-lit parking lot of a minimall. At least thirty couples were stomping away in a reeling line dance. Where was Moreland?

There. He fired a six-shooter into the sky, and then tipped a bottle back, draining it while other men crowded in to congratulate him.

The sight of him burned her. She felt it most in her gut, where a tight knot of anger still nestled below her heart. With every indrawn breath, too, she felt red hot slivers of pain in her chest, as if she'd been hit by invisible shrapnel. "*Damn* you!" she whispered and fingered the butterfly knife in her pocket.

Then, because no one had seen her as yet, she slid into the lengthy shadow cast by an abandoned Greyhound bus. She hunkered down beside a tire that reeked of old urine. About twenty minutes went by before she got her first chance at Moreland. He fired four more rounds and drank three more beers in the meantime, then snagged a fresh bottle and staggered away from his buddies. As he neared the shadows, he holstered the hog leg and started to fumble with his fly.

Taiesha rose in a single smooth movement and placed herself in his path.

"Hey!" Moreland exclaimed. "It's my Ghetto Tech lawyer!" He grinned broadly. "How the hell are ya?"

Taiesha smiled at him. "I'm just fine. I was wondering how *you* are." Then, pointedly, she checked out the package he was still attempting to lay bare.

The mayor's surprise didn't keep him from lurching a few inches closer. The stink of beer-breath enveloped her as Moreland leered. "I could show ya," he offered.

"Why not?" she replied. But when he tried to press her against the bus, Taiesha slipped out of his grasp and took his hand. "Come on," she said. "Let's go somewhere a little more private."

With little urging, he followed her back toward the waterfront and a dirt towpath running alongside the water. Two and a half blocks was all, and he just barely made it that far before he dropped his beer bottle. "I gotta water m'lily," he mumbled, and pawed at his crotch. He paid no attention at all to Taiesha.

She stood there, staring at his sweaty neck while her fingers traced out the long sleek steely shape of the knife's handle. *Come on,* she said to herself. *The man is a kid-killer. He's a thief whose stealing doomed an entire town. Even if he saved his own in the process, he did in hundreds of other people. Give him a power base here he can build on, and who knows what kind of a monster he'll be?*

But if she cut his throat, they would know it was murder—the whole town of Atwater. At best, they'd blame the surviving Izquierdos. What little good she'd done for them would be undone again, and they probably wouldn't survive that. The townies might very well blame the *Queen's* crew for it too, and they'd come after everyone.

*Damn it all!* She let the knife slide back into her pocket. This had to look like an accident, and it had to happen while the Izquierdos were still in protective custody.

She reached for her injection gun, but then hesitated. In cold blood, it felt different. It felt wrong. In his drunken confusion, the mayor was nearly as helpless as Kayla, that day of the raid on her suburb. He wasn't a child, but he wasn't much of a man either.

Then Moreland grabbed her and pulled her in close. "Come on," he mumbled. "Help me out, honey. M'zipper's shtuck." And the smell of him did it. The combined effluvia, B.O., rotgut, gunpowder, and manly testosterone rolled off his unwashed expanses and brought back too much of that godawful day. She couldn't breathe, couldn't get any air past red splinters of agony lining her ribs.

Gasping, she stuck the gun's barrel into his armpit and fired twice.

The hair there would keep anybody from noticing the needles' reddish entry points.

He didn't seem to even feel it. Moreland just jerked back a bit. Then, all of a sudden, he lost his grip on her, slid to the ground, and rolled onto his back.

*First things first*, Taiesha told herself, wheezing a bit. *Disarm the clown.*

She undid his gun belt's buckle, letting the ends fall away on either side. The second belt, the one holding his pants up, she left alone. Then she found and pulled down the zipper on his Levi's. She fished out his limp dick and clucked at it. *Sizewise, not very impressive*, she thought. Then again, it would certainly serve her present purpose.

Once his clothing was rearranged, she tipped Moreland over the edge of the tow path and watched his ass slide down the muddy bank, into the water. A white froth of bubbles erupted as soon as his fat head went under, and once his lungs had emptied out, the man doubled over. He vomited some of the swill he'd been drinking when his body tried for that next breath but got only water. He opened his eyes too, and scared the hell out of her just for a second. Then it was too late. He was sinking down into the inky depths, his face as pale as the moon above. It got smaller and smaller, and then simply vanished.

For four long minutes, she stood there and watched, but he didn't come up again. *Later,* she thought. *He'll turn into a floater and wash up along the bank. Whether he does or not, someone will find him, and that'll be that.*

Taiesha nodded, satisfied that Moreland would shoot no more children, would steal no more lifelines from other small towns, and would get no leg up to positions of real power.

Down inside her, a tightness had eased up. She carefully pulled in a deeper breath, experimental and somewhat tainted by the warm fishy waterfront smell of the place, but the knot underneath her heart was gone, and the pain in her chest along with it. She pulled in two more. Then she bent down and used her scarf to erase her own foot-prints along the path, leaving only his and the bottle he'd dropped. She arranged the gun belt she'd taken off him beside it before standing back to inspect the results.

Okay. Hopefully, the locals would stumble across all this first thing in the morning, and then go looking. When they located Moreland's corpse, they'd also find his fly open and figure it out. Clearly, he'd gotten totally smashed and developed a powerful need to pee. He'd dropped his stuff in the course of relieving that need, and somewhere along the way, he'd fallen into the water and drowned, too damn drunk to crawl out again.

Taiesha started to turn away from the little scene, taking care not to step off the grass, but she froze when a voice rumbled out of the darkness behind her.

"Nicely done," said MacClure.

The words hit her amidships, like ice bullets. *Oh, God.*

"In fact," he continued, stepping into the moonlight, "I don't think I could have done any better."

Say what? She made herself finish the turn so that she wound up facing him.

"What are you *doing* here?" she demanded, as if that part mattered somehow when he'd seen her do murder.

The Scotsman smiled. "Completing my evaluation."

She stared at him with a certain dreadful fascination, waiting for the snake to strike. "And what," she finally had to ask, "are you going to tell the attorney general?"

"Nothing," he answered affably. "I don't work for him, or for the state."

"You're a *fed*?"

This evoked outright laughter. "I'm with the U.N." he explained, "not the U.S."

So. . . did that mean she *wasn't* dead? Or was this whole thing about to become "international"?

"I'm not really an auditor," said MacClure, "as you've probably guessed."

"Then what *do* you want?"

"You."

Hunh?

Taiesha couldn't make sense out of that. Did he mean to arrest her? All by himself? Or was this about blackmail, about using her? For what?

He shook his head just as if he knew what she was thinking and said, "I'm a headhunter. I heard about you and needed a closer look."

More nonsense.

He lost the grin. "Look, I have a position I'm trying to fill. A job that needs a very specific type of person."

She peered at him, half-minded to run. "And that would be?"

"Someone who can handle herself and keep a cool head under fire. Somebody who understands the law, but also knows what's truly at stake. Who's not in it just for the rush or the money. I need people who can put on a show, but who can also think. . . and act. . . outside the box. Who can and will see justice done, whatever it takes."

If by that he meant what he'd just seen. . .

"I am *not* an assassin," Taiesha told him, although her right hand had already reclaimed her injection gun.

"If I thought you were, you'd already be dead."

Her hand paused, the gun still mostly holstered. She thought about those extra scars of his, hidden by hair on his neck and his jawline, the way he'd snuck up on her here in dead silence, and his current air of complete self-assurance.

He watched her make that reassessment, and then the decision to hold off. He smiled again. "If you like, you can go on this way, one case at a time, one killer at a time. Or. . ."

She waited him out, determined not to take the bait, and he finally gave in, saying, ". . .you can expand the scope of your work to a somewhat larger scale."

Meaning. . . what?

"I'm starting a new agency at the U.N.," MacClure told her. "It's going to handle mass-casualty situations. The things that are too large for cops to take on and too small to need armies. Its focus will be on the larger pirate bands and the cannibal cults, which are mostly run by people much worse than our poor Mr. Moreland." He nodded toward the dark waters beside her, gently lapping at the bank, where there was no longer a single sign of the mayor's passing. "We're going after the men and women who run the meat markets."

Who slaughtered whole families, Taiesha thought. Men mowing their lawns on a Saturday. Little girls who tried to hide under their beds. Women washing the dishes.

Her left hand contracted to make a fist, remembering the water glass that she'd been rinsing out when they struck, how the shards had sliced into her own flesh as well as the man she'd decapitated that day. Would she now have a chance at the ones who'd sent him?

She let the injection gun settle back into its holster. She took a tentative step toward MacClure, then another three around him. The Scotsman didn't even try it, despite the big fat opportunity she'd offered him. Instead, he fell in beside her, keeping pace in perfect silence. As they began the long walk back to the *California Queen*, Taiesha told him, "All right, let's talk."

# THAT CREEPING SENSATION

Alan Dean Foster

"Code four, code four!"

Sergeant Lissa-Marie nodded to her partner and Corporal Gustafson acknowledged the alarm. It was the fourth code four of what had long since turned into a long hot one—both temperature-wise and professionally. She checked a floating readout: It declared that the temperature outside the sealed, climate-controlled truck cab was ninety-six degrees Fahrenheit at two in the afternoon. Happily the humidity was unusually low, floating right around the eighty-percent mark.

"Gun it," she snapped. From behind the wheel Gustafson nodded and floored the accelerator. Supplying instant torque, the electric motors mounted above each of the panel truck's four wheels sent it leaping forward. As the sharp acceleration shoved her back into her seat she directed her attention to the omnidirectional pickup mounted in the roof. "What is it this time?" she asked.

"Bees." The human dispatcher's reply was as terse as it was meaningful. "Nobody dead, but two teens on their way to Metro Emergency."

"They're getting smarter." Gustafson chewed his lower lip as he concentrated on his driving.

"Manure," she shot back. "You're anthropomorphizing. That's dangerous in a business like ours."

Her younger subordinate shook his head as much as his contoured seat would allow. "It's true." He refused to drop the contention. "They're getting smarter. You can sense it. You can see it. They don't just crawl around and wait to be smoked anymore. They react earlier. They're. . ." He glanced over at her. "They're anticipating."

She shrugged and returned her gaze forward, out the armored windshield. "Just drive. If you insist, we can continue with your insane speculations after we've finished the job."

The streets of Atlanta's outer ring were nearly deserted. Few people chose to spend money on an expensive personal vehicle anymore. Not when public transportation was so much cheaper and a steady stream of workers kept the rails and tunnels free of the insects that obscured windshields and clogged wheel wells after barely twenty minutes of driving. The lack of traffic certainly made things easier for the exterminator branch of the military to which the two people in the truck belonged. Lissa was musing on the vilm she had been reading when a sudden swerve by Gustafson caused her to lurch and curse. Her partner was apologetic.

"Sorry. Roaches," he explained.

She nodded her understanding and relaxed anew. One three-foot roach wouldn't damage the specially armored truck, but if they'd hit it full on they would have had to explain their carelessness to the cleanup crew back at base.

As they neared their destination she lifted her reducer off its hook and made sure it fit snuggly over her nose and mouth. Like everyone else she hated having to wear the damn things. No matter how much they improved and miniaturized the integrated cooling system, you still sweated twice as much behind the device. But it was necessary. It wouldn't do to consistently suck air that was nearly forty percent oxygen and still rising. That might have been tolerable if the runaway atmosphere hadn't also grown hotter and distinctly more humid.

At least she'd never been in a fire, she told herself. Like most people she shuddered at the thought. Given the current concentration of oxygen in the atmosphere, the smallest fire tended to erupt into an inferno in no time. *Leave those worries to the fire brigades,* she told herself. The multinational she worked for had enough to do trying to keep ahead of the bugs.

As studies of the Carboniferous Era, the climate in Earth's history nearest to that of the present day, had shown, the higher the oxygen content of the air, the bigger bugs could grow. Mankind's loathing of the arthropods with whom he was compelled to share the planet had grown proportionately.

"We're here." Gustafson brought the truck to a halt outside the single-family home.

They didn't have to look for the bees. They were all over the one-story residence they intended to appropriate. A cluster of civilian emergency vehicles was drawn up nearby. Occasionally a crack would sound from one of the tightly sealed police cruisers and a six-inch bee would go down, obliterated by a blast of micro bugshot. Operating in such piecemeal fashion the cops could deal with the bees, but only by expending a lot of expensive ammunition and at the cost of causing serious collateral damage to the immediate neighborhood. Buttoned up in their cruisers and guarding the perimeter they had established around the home, they had hunkered down to await the arrival of military specialists.

*That would be me and Gustafson,* she knew.

Already half dressed for the extirpation, she wiggled around in the truck cab as she donned the rest of her suit. An ancient apiarist would have looked on in amazement as she zipped up the one-piece reinforced Kevlar suit, armorglass helmet, and metalized boots. Once dressed, individual cooling systems were double-checked. Ten minutes trapped inside one of the sealed suits in the current heat and humidity would bring even a fit person down. The coolers were absolutely necessary, as were the tanks of poison spray the two exterminators affixed to their back plates. When both had concluded preparations they took care to check the seals of each other's suits. A few stings from the six-inch long bees contained more than enough venom to kill.

"Let's go," she murmured. Gustafson shot her a look, nodded, and cracked the driver's-side door.

The bees pounced on them immediately. Exhibiting a determination and aggression unknown to their smaller ancestors, several dozen of them assailed the two bipedal figures that had started toward the house. The swarm covered that edifice entirely. From decorative chimney to broken windows it was blanketed by a heaving, throbbing, humming scrum of giant bees. Lissa grunted as one bee after another dove to fruitlessly slam its stinger into her impenetrable suit. Walking toward the house through such a persistent swarm was like stumbling around the ring with a boxer allowed to hit you from any and every angle.

As they reached the front of the overrun house a nervous voice sounded on an open police channel on Lissa's helmet communicator.

"We think the queen's around back, near the swimming pool."

"Thanks." She didn't have to relay the information to Gustafson. The corporal had picked up the same transmission.

Working their way around to the back they found the swarm there even thicker than what they had encountered out front. Surrounded by increasingly agitated workers, the queen had settled herself into a corner of the house where workers were already preparing hexagonal wax tubes to receive the first eggs. She never got the chance to lay them.

"You know the routine," she muttered into her helmet pickup. "Start with the queen, work back to front."

Holding his sprayer, her partner nodded even as he opened fire.

The killing mist that would render the house uninhabitable began to send bees tumbling off the walls, roof, and one another. Most staggered drunkenly for a few seconds before collapsing in small black and orange heaps. Lissa kicked accumulating piles of plump, boldly striped bodies aside as she and Gustafson finished up in the back yard and started working their way around to the front.

"Ware ten o'clock!" she yelled as she raised the muzzle of her sprayer.

The trio of foot-long yellow jackets, however, were only interested in taking a few of the now panicky live bees. Natural predators of such hives, they were the human's allies in extirpation. Though even more formidable than the giant honeybees, they had no interest in the two suited humans. Which was a good thing, Lissa knew. A yellowjacket's stinger could punch into an unprotected human like a stiletto.

As she and the corporal worked their way through the swarm she reflected on the unexpected turn of history. When the greenhouse effect had begun to set in, scientists had worried about the presumed surplus of carbon dioxide that was expected to result. They had failed to account for Earth's astonishing ability to adapt to even fast-changing circumstances.

With the increased heat and humidity, plant life had gone berserk. Rainforests like those of the Amazon and Congo that had once been under threat expanded outward. Loggers intent on cutting down the big, old trees paid no attention to the fecund explosion of ferns, cycads, and soft-bodied plants that flourished in their wake. A serious problem in temperate times, vines and creepers like the ubiquitous kudzu experienced rates of growth approaching the exponential.

The great sucking sound which resulted was that of new vegetation taking carbon dioxide out of the atmosphere and dumping oxygen in its wake. Their size restricted for eons by the inability of their primitive respiratory systems to extract enough oxygen from the atmosphere, arthropods responded to the new oxy-rich air by growing to sizes not seen since similar conditions existed more than 300 million years ago. Short-lived species were the first to adapt, with each new generation growing a little larger than its predecessor as it feasted on the increasingly oxygen-rich atmosphere.

There had been no bees in the Carboniferous, she knew, because there had been no flowers. But modern plants had adapted to the radical climate change as eagerly as their more primitive ancestors. The result was fewer and increasingly less workable beehives as bigger bees crowded out smaller competitors. Changes occurred with such startling rapidity that in little over a hundred years insects, spiders, and their relatives had not only matched but in some cases surpassed the dimensions attained by their ancient relatives. This made for an increasingly uncomfortable coexistence with the supposedly still dominant species on the planet, but a very good living for Lissa and her hastily constituted branch of the military. Nearing fifty, she could remember when her company, one of many that had appeared in the wake of the Runaway, had been able to offer its enlisted personnel predictable hours and regular furloughs. Such downtime still existed, of course, but she was making so much combat pay that she felt unable to turn down the assignments that came her way.

Sure enough, scarcely moments after they had finished their work and a pair of city front-loaders had begun the odious task of scooping up the thousands of dead bee bodies, the truck's com whistled for attention.

"We got a 42B." Gustafson had removed his reducer and was leaning out the open door. The oxygen-dense air might be dangerous for steady breathing, but it was great for making a quick recovery after a bit of heavy physical exertion. One just had to be careful not to rely on it too long. "Boy stepping on scorpion."

She shook her head as she approached the truck. "That's 42A. 42B is scorpion stepping on boy."

Fortunately, the yard-long arthropod they trapped and killed half an hour later in the public playground hadn't stung anyone. Nocturnal by nature, it had been disturbed by children who had been building a fort. They stood around and watched wide-eyed as the two exterminators hauled the chelatinous carcass away. The scorpion wasn't such a big stretch, Lissa knew. Nine-inch long predecessors had thrived in equatorial rainforests as recently as the twenty-first century. It hadn't taken much of an oxygen boost to grow them to their present frightening size.

They were finishing coffee when the code two red call came in. Looks were exchanged in lieu of words. It was one call neither of them wanted to answer. As senior operative, it fell to Lissa.

"Why us?" she spoke tersely into her tiny mouth pickup. "We've been hot on it all morning."

"Everyone's been hot on it all morning." The dispatcher on duty at the Atlanta Metropolitan Command Center sounded tired. He would not be moved, Lissa knew. "You're the best, Sergeant Sweetheart. Take care of this one and I'll let you break for the rest of the day."

She looked over at Corporal Gustafson, who was hearing the same broadcast. Inside the sealed restaurant equipped with its own industrial-strength reducers they had no need for their face masks. She checked her chronometer. If they wrapped up the call early they would each gain a couple of hours of paid free time.

"All right." She was grumbling as she rose from the table. Other patrons regarded the two uniformed specialists with the respect due their unpleasant and dangerous calling. "But not because you called me the best, Lieutenant. Because you called me Sweetheart."

"Don't let it go to your head," the officer finished. "Take care on this one."

A single descendant of *Meganeura* shadowed their truck as they sped through the city streets and out into the suburbs. Since this was an emergency call they had their lights and sirens on, but they didn't dissuade the dragonfly. Its four-foot wingspan flashed iridescent in the heavy, humid air until, finally bored with riding in the truck's airflow, it flashed off toward a nearby office building. Going after a goliath fly, Lissa mused as she let Gustafson focus on his driving. Or one of the city's rapidly shrinking and badly overmatched population of pigeons. Unable to compete with the increasingly large and powerful insects, birds had suffered more than any other group under the Runaway.

The family that had put in the emergency call were grateful for the arrival of the exterminator team, but refused to emerge from the house's safe room where they had taken refuge.

"It's in the basement." On the small heads-up display that floated in front of Lissa's face, the mother looked utterly terrified. So did the two children huddled behind her. "We've had break-ins before. Ants mostly, when they can get across the electrical barrier, and roaches my son can handle with his baseball bat. But this is a first for us."

"Take it easy, ma'am. We're on it."

Looking none too reassured, the woman nodded as the transmission ended. Lissa checked her gear and made sure her reducer was tight on her face before nodding at Gustafson.

"This'll be your first time dealing with a chilopoda, won't it?" Her partner nodded slowly. "Watch your chest. They always go for the chest."

Donning helmets, they exited the car and headed for the single-family home. No sprays this time. Not for this afternoon's quarry. Both of them hefted pump guns.

The front door had been left open, not to greet the arriving exterminators but in the forlorn hope that the invader might depart of its own volition. Not much chance of that, Lissa knew. Chilopoda favored surroundings that were dark and damp. Eying the family compound and the looming, nearby trees, she sighed. If people were going to live in the woods in this day and age. . .

As they entered the basement the house's proximity lights flicked on. A good sign. It meant that their quarry wasn't moving. Gun barrel held parallel to the floor, she was first down the stairs. The basement was filled with the usual inconsequential detritus of single-family living: crates of goods meant to be given away that would remain in place forever, a couple of old electric bikes, lawn furniture, the home $O_2$ reducer that allowed residents to move freely about the sealed building without having to don face masks, heavy-duty gardening gear, and more.

A sound made her raise her left hand sharply in warning.

Whispering into her mask, she pointed toward a far, unilluminated corner. Gustafson nodded and, without waiting, started toward it.

"I'll take care of it, Lissa. You just. . ."

"No! Flanking movement or. . .!"

Too late.

The six-foot long centipede burst from its hiding place to leap straight at her startled companion. Its modern Amazonian ancestors had jumped into the air to catch and feed on bats. This oxygen-charged contemporary monster had no difficulty getting high enough off the ground to go straight for Gustafson's throat. If it got its powerful mandibles into his neck above his shirt and below his helmet and started probing with the poison claws that protruded from its back end. . .

She raised her gun and fired without thinking.

Guts and goo sprayed everywhere as the pumper blew the monster in two. Still it wasn't finished. As both halves twitched and jerked independently, she approached them with care. Two more shots shattered first the dangerous anterior claws and then the head containing the powerful, snapping mandibles.

Turning, she found her partner on the ground, seated against a trunk still holding his weapon and staring. Walking over to him, she bent slightly as she extended a hand to help him up.

"I. . .," he didn't look at her, "I'm sorry, Lissa. It came out so fast that I. . ."

She cut him off curtly. "Forget it. First encounter with a chilopoda, no need for excuses."

He stared at her. "You warned me. You said they were fast. The class manual talks about their quickness. But I didn't. . ." His voice trailed away.

She gave him a reassuring pat on the back. "Like I said, forget it. Visuals and words in a manual are one thing. Having it jump you in a basement is a little different. They make a tiger seem slow and an insurgent unarmed. Next time you'll be ready."

He nodded somberly, and they climbed the stairs. The basement was a mess, but that was a job for a city or private cleanup crew. Back in the truck she kept expecting to be assigned another job as soon as they reported in that they had successfully completed this one. Surprisingly, the officer on duty seemed inclined to keep his word. The bugband stayed silent.

As a chastened Gustafson headed the truck back toward the military base on the outskirts of the city she leaned forward to have a look at the sky through the windshield. Overcast, as always. The usual tepid rain on tap for the evening. Other than that the weather report was promising. Temperatures in the low nineties and humidity down to seventy-five percent. Things were a lot worse the closer one got to the now nearly uninhabitable tropics, she knew. The tech journals were full of reports of new threats emerging from the depths of the impenetrable Amazon. Ten-foot carnivorous beetles. Deadlier scorpions. Six-inch long fire ants. . .

Home and business owners might fret over giant centipedes and spiders with three-foot leg spans, but as a military-trained specialist she worried far more about the ants. All ants. Not because they were prolific and not because they could bite and sting, but because they cooperated. Cooperation could lead to bigger problems than any sting. In terms of sheer numbers, the ants had always been the most successful species on the planet. Let them acquire a little of the always paranoid Gustafson's hypothetical intelligence to go with their new size and. . .

She checked the weather a last time. Atmospheric oxygen was up to forty-one percent give or take a few decimals. It was continuing its steady rise, as it had over the preceding decades. How big would the bugs get if it reached forty-five percent? Or fifty? How would the fire brigades cope with the increasingly ferocious firestorms that had made wooden building construction a relic of the past?

Rolling down her window she removed her mask and stuck her head outside, into the lugubrious wind. Gustafson gave her a look but said nothing and stayed with his driving. Overhead and unseen, another giant dragonfly dropped lower, sized up the potential prey, and shot away. A human was still too big for it to take down. But if its kind kept growing...

Lissa inhaled deeply of the thick, moist air. It filled her lungs, the oxygen boost reinvigorating her after the confrontation in the basement. Drink of it too much and she would start feeling giddy. There were benefits to the increased oxygen concentration. Athletes, at least while performing in air-conditioned venues, had accomplished remarkable feats. Humanity was adapting to the changed climate. It had always done so. It would continue to do so. And in a radically changed North America, at least, the military would ensure that it would be able to do so.

As an exterminator non-com charged with keeping her city safe, her only fear was that something else just might be adapting a little faster.

# THE MEN OF SUMMER

David Prill

*I know I am but summer to your heart,*
*And not the full four seasons of the year*
—Edna St. Vincent Millay

Unfortunately, it was another spectacular summer day.

Marion woke early, sensing the heat trying to elbow its way past the drawn shades. She didn't bother checking the forecast; she could already feel the sweat of the coming day on the back of her neck. Her clock was keeping time, so that must mean the air conditioner was on the fritz again. At least it wasn't another greenout.

She lifted a corner of the shade and peered out. The sun was besieging the neighborhood. On the sidewalk outside her house stood a young man. What was his name again? Marion wondered, her mind still wrapped in post-dawn murk. Mark? Jim? Fernando? None of those names seemed to fit. Bob? Stan? Sigfried? No. It certainly wasn't Andre. Doug? Maybe. Shoot. Perhaps after she drained her first cup of coffee the name would find its way into the daylight side of her mind.

Problem was, not only was there a maybe Doug outside, there was no joe inside. Marion wasn't in the mood to spoon, not before her first coffee anyway, so she snuck out the back way. The alley was free of summer loves, hallelujah. She cut through backyards and scaled a fence, grabbing as much shade as possible, and made it the three blocks to Bunny's Java Den without incident.

She paid for her iced coffee, slapping it against her forehead even before she sat down at a table in the far corner. The Den smelled worse than a high school locker room, all pent-up sweat beneath rigid, unlaundered clothes. It always took a minute for the stink to fade into the furniture.

Just as Marion took her first long swig of the frosty brew, she noticed a young man, stranger, watching her.

He was standing by the bulletin board, coffee in hand... watching.

A familiar smile, but unique in its own way. It made Marion excited, sad, and just plain tired. She smiled back in that order, but he came over anyway.

"Mind if I join you? There aren't any empty tables."

It wasn't true, so she said, "Please do."

"My name's Alan."

Arthur. Andrew. Anthony... She thought hard... No Alan.

Alan the First.

Well that was something.

He was attractive, naturally. Dark curly hair, boyish dimples, decent build. The usual setup. She never grew tired of that first surge of energy, even if the energy was at a lower wattage than it used to be. It was still special. It was still spine-tingling. The thought that they would have a summer of romance and fun, of freedom, before reality took over again. Only it never did. Not anymore. It was always drop-dead hot, day in, day out, no matter if there was a beach umbrella or ski scene on the calendar. These days, the boys of summer were always underfoot.

"I'm Marion," she said dreamily, determined to enjoy the ride before the tires went flat.

"Maid Marion!"

She laughed at the joke, as she always did. They always said it with such joy, such innocence.

"You have a nice smile," he said. "Your eyes sort of dance around."

"Thanks."

"Do you like to dance?"

What a transition. "Sure, I like to dance."

"Maybe we should go dancing some time then."

"Awful hot for hoofing. I work up a lather just tapping my foot to the music."

"Let's go somewhere and cool off then. How about the beach?"

"I like to go swimming, especially since the global mean temperature has been so historically above average."

"I'll pick you up. Can I have your number?"

"Here you go." A couple of years ago Marion had cards printed up with her name and phone number on them. She got a discount when she ordered a box of five hundred. A real time-saver.

Alan the First studied the card, beaming, then tucked it into his shirt pocket, patting it with pride.

They kept chatting as they downed their coffees, Marion fading out as the words automatically tumbled from her. She tried to focus on Alan, wanting to relish these first moments of hormonal discovery, but the intensity of the initial attraction was leavened by an equally acute feeling of déjà vu. A disconnect. Like she was watching a movie. A date movie. A quirky love story, about a girl and her summer love.


That afternoon, Marion climbed into her air-cooled, hydromatic swimming suit with the viewing window where it counted and met Alan as he pulled up in his streamlined rust bucket. He was just dressed in trunks and a white muscle T-shirt.

"Nice suit," said Alan, nodding approvingly.

"It's air-cooled, and hydromatic."

"Where did you buy it?"

"Over at the mall."

"I like the scenery in your viewing port," he said playfully.

"Thanks," she replied, blushing.

They drove to Lake Failin, surf music shaking their top-down ride as they wove around the buckled asphalt on the highway. Marion felt happy and young and free again. It was summertime. Livin' was easy. Dyin' wasn't as hard as it used to be. When they reached the beach, Marion noticed that the parking lot didn't appear to be as close to the water as it used to be either.

Alan spotted it, too. "I wonder why they decided to move the parking lot so far back?"

Marion didn't say anything as they walked hand in hand onto the beach.

"Where exactly is the water?" Alan asked, looking for it, hand cupped above his eyes.

"I dunno. It was here the last time I went for a dip."

In the distance, dissolute half-dressed figures shuffled around in uncertain groups.

"I bet that's where the water is," said Marion. "Let's go see."

On the lifeguard stand, a blond, burned teen was screaming into a bullhorn. "Riptide! Riptide! Everyone out of the water! Everyone out!"

Marion and Alan ignored the warnings and strolled together across the sand, sidestepping floundering fish and seaweed salads. The fish that no longer flopped put up a stench. Marion could feel the broken snail shells and jagged rocks even through her flip-flops.

It was a long hike, but finally they reached the water's edge. Nobody was actually swimming, since the water was only ankle-deep, but a few members of the small fry set were splashing around in the brine. The water smelled like a musty basement.

"I didn't really feel much like swimming anyway," said Marion as her hydromatic suit clicked into overdrive, cool water rushing over her shoulders.

"Let's get some ice cream instead," Alan said cheerily.

Marion liked his attitude. Anecdotally speaking, swimming was one of the most dangerous activities on the summertime hit parade, right behind Jarts. Marion realized it didn't matter if the lake was drying up or not. It was summer and there was love in the air. A love that would never wither, as long as the weather stayed torrid anyway.

At the snack shack, another smiling boy of summer was stationed at the counter with a slushee. Ken? Ben?

"Friend of yours?" Alan asked.

"Oh, just someone I know from work," Marion lied. Stan? Can't swing a dead fish without hitting one of them, she thought.

They sat on a bench and attacked their ice cream, she peppermint bon bon, he Neapolitan. She wondered what that said about his character. Only good things. He was flexible and willing to look at other people's points of view. He wasn't stuck in a rut. He was adventurous.

"The only thing sweeter than this cone is you," said Alan, offering her a lick.

"Oh, you're a dear."

"Prettiest girl on the beach."

"Oh my."

"I can't believe we found each other."

"I certainly never expected it."

But Marion expected it all, including, at date's end:

"Will I see you again?"

Talk about a no-brainer.

So they did, and after their third date, Marion dropped a pair of ice cubes down her shirt and called it a day. The fall issue of *Flair* magazine had just arrived, and she hopped into bed and began to browse through its stylish pages.

"Fifteen Top Makeup Tips for Hiding Skin Cancer Scars"

"Heat Stroke CAN Make You Look Younger"

"Summer Fling or the Real Thing?"

That last one was a quiz. Maybe it was too early, but Marion wanted to see where Alan stood, clinging to the possibility that he might be more than he appeared to be.

Q: *Do you know your summer love's last name AND how to spell it?*
   *Yes*
   *Yes, but I'm not sure how to spell it.*
X  *No*

Q: *Do you know your summer love's birth date?*
   *Yes*
   *I know the month and day but not year.*
   *I know the month but nothing else.*
X  *No*

Q: *Do you and your summer love have any hobbies in common?*
   *Yes*
   *No*
X  *Not sure*

Q: *Can you name your summer love's three favorite things?*
   *Yes*
X  *No*
   *I think so, but I'm not 100% sure.*

And about thirty more head-scratchers.

Marion tried to give herself the benefit of the doubt, but couldn't imagine many of those negatives flipping to affirmatives anytime soon. She expected the sweet-as-ice-cream phase to plod on for some time.

Her score of twenty put her firmly in the Major Fling category. She wasn't surprised, although she always fostered hopes that her latest summer love, the airy confection of the world of romance, would turn out to be something more filling.

How many dates were left in this fling? It was hard to tell. You couldn't judge anything by the weather. The summer swelters were a life sentence.

Their next date, at the municipal go-kart track, was romantic as hell. As they took a break from the races and shared a Yoo-hoo, she quizzed him.

"What's your last name, Alan?"

"I like it when you say my first name."

Birth date?

"Younger than you think, old enough to know better!"

Hobbies.

"Seeing you, babe."

Three favorite things.

"Marion, Marion, Marion."

Around and around and around they went.

Can't beat a twenty with those answers, Marion thought, leaning into a turn. Major Fling confirmed.

After they had a post-racing snack at Bunny's, Marion asked her summer love to turn down a side street, which took them past the camp, not far from her house.

"Stop here," she said.

"What's wrong?"

"Thank you for a lovely day." She kissed him quick as she opened her door.

"I don't understand."

"I can walk home from here. It's just around the corner."

"But why didn't you let me drop you off there? It's getting dark out."

"Because you need to be here."

He looked like he didn't know his last name.

"*Here*," she said, pointing at the grouping of tents in the vacant lot. She touched his cheek, trying to wash the confusion from his face. "Just walk over there and see what you find. Talk to the people."

"Are you dumping me?"

"Trust me."

"Can I see you again?"

"I don't think there's any doubt about that."

She left him then, glancing over her shoulder as he exited his heap and cautiously approached the camp.

Soon, he would understand.


Back home, the guilts got Marion even before she kicked off her Vans. She didn't enjoy tommy-gunning a summer love at the knees, but in the long run, for her sanity's sake, it was the only way to fly.

More remorse as she headed upstairs, wondering what Alan would find, knowing that she had only visited the camp that one time. Which was one time more than she could handle. Which was why she had never gone back. Nobody could blame her for not going back, after what she saw. What she saw nobody should have to see, even someone who had seen it all.

Up in the guest room window, Marion regarded the night. She could see the lights of the camp from here, hurricane lamps on poles. A few shadows moved about, too far to make out any details. The details didn't matter; it was the big picture that told the real story. Safer just to look at the big picture, too. Didn't get your hands dirty that way. Didn't get your heart mussed up.

In the distance, a sign of lightning. Not a bolt, just a flash on the bellies of dark clouds. Marion grew hopeful at the prospect of a cool front strong enough to break summer's back. Could it really be possible? Marion could scarcely remember the last time it rained. It was during Craig; on their first date they had taken a walk in the wet stuff. But that was eons ago.

All night Marion kept a vigil as the storm moved in. It began to sprinkle, then when the rain went steady she rushed outside and danced the Frug in her front yard. A boom of thunder sent her scurrying back inside. She followed the rest of the action from her bed, watching in wonder as the storm rolled through town. When the worst had passed, she slept, feeling a cool, rain-soaked breeze wash over her.

In the morning, though, the heat was on her again like a tiger. It crawled in her open window and was at her throat before she could react. Groggy, she fought her way to the window and slammed it down to the sill. She shut her eyes, the heat trying to get at her through the pane. Was the rain just a dream? she wondered.

Marion thought about the boys of summer, in the camp. They were still in her heart, every one of them. She wondered if they survived the storm, if their love saw them through. Those tents couldn't hold their own against a gale.

It's not a dumping ground, she kept telling herself as she bravely went to the front door, pushing her way into the stifling air. It's a camp. A convention. A Happening.

Marion expected to find a boy of summer on her stoop, and was oddly disappointed when not only the stoop but the street was unoccupied.

When she arrived at the camp, she felt relieved at the sight of an intact collection of multicolored tents of all sizes and configurations arranged like the streets of a town. The camp had rode out the storm, but there didn't seem to be anybody around.

Maybe they've had enough of me, she fretted. Maybe I've been taking them for granted for too long. Maybe they decided to get another girl. Wiping the sweat from her upper lip, she was chilled by the thought. An endless summer without a summer love. What kind of life would that be? But maybe, she thought, if I no longer had a summer love, I would find a love that would last forever. But the boys of summer had been part of her life so long that it was hard to imagine loving any other way.

Maybe they got arrested. For loitering. Or littering. Or loving her too much.

It was strange being here again. So much happened since her last fiasco of a visit. So much had happened, but nothing had really changed. She drew near one of the tents, a smaller Aztec-blue model, took a deep breath, and poked her head in. At first she felt funny about it, almost like she was intruding into someone's private domain. Until she realized it was probably their most common fantasy.

Nobody home. A red sleeping bag, and a metal coffee cup on a small folding table.

She didn't try her luck again. She roamed through the camp, looking for loves.

There was a bulletin board on a pole outside one of the tents. A handwritten chart, with a series of names, all close to her heart, on the horizontal plane, and a string of numbers and month abbreviations in vertical columns. Check marks where the two values intersected. Marion mulled, trying to decipher them. It was a schedule, she decided. They didn't want to overwhelm her, make her feel hemmed in. So one or two boys of summer at a time, in shifts, while the others worshipped her from afar, until it was their turn.

As she took a corner, stepping around a picnic table, Marion stopped, listening. Voices were coming from a large military-style tent across the way. The screened front entrance was open, but she ducked around the side instead. There she found a window and peeked in.

It was a mess hall tent, with long tables and folding chairs. A counter on the far end featured a coffee urn and cups, plates of pastries and fruit on the side.

The tables were arranged so that the group of perhaps twenty-five men were sitting in a circle. She recognized the faces, every last one.

They stirred up memories, moments caught in time. They were part of her life, even if they were just summer flings.

In the middle of the circle stood Marion's very first boy of summer, Chip. Chip. She smiled at the sight of his face. Blond hair, decent build, dimples, etc. She had run into him occasionally since she let him loose, although not for a couple of years or so. He looked older, some silver in his sideburns, crinkles in the corners of his eyes, his stomach battling with his belt for supremacy.

". . .she doesn't like daisies," said Chip, holding a sheet of paper in his hand. "Perhaps change it to violets."

"But what rhymes with violets?" someone in the circle said. It was Dwayne, a summer love from earlier this year.

"'Regrets' might work here, although it's not really clear. But I think the larger problem with the piece is the form you chose. I would recommend rewriting it as a heroic couplet, and see how that goes." He shuffled papers. "Next up? Anybody? Ah, the newcomer. What was your name again, my friend?"

"Alan."

"Alan. You are so close to her yet. Your feelings for her must be very strong; she's not someone you will soon forget."

"That's why I needed to put my feelings for her into words."

"You're halfway to success in the poetry game, so go right ahead, we're all the same."

"It's sort of a haiku."

"Whatever works for you works for us, too."

"It doesn't rhyme."

"Oh. . ."

Alan shut his eyes and began:

"I call this poem simply, 'Marion.'"

Chip picked up something from a table. Something on a stick. Marion had seen it before. It was a head shot of herself affixed to the end of a wooden dowel. He held it up to his face like a mask. On her only visit to the camp there had been a dozen mock Marions running around, maybe more. Like a funhouse mirror, only the faces in the mirror didn't stay where they belonged. Like the images had stepped out of the mirror and demanded to be recognized. It would have been sweet if one stopped to think about it, which she didn't, because she ran away like she was on fire.

Sweet, she thought sourly. And how did I react? Like a Grade A government-inspected ratfink.

"Don't close your eyes," said Chip. "Open them and speak to me from your heart."

Alan cleared his throat. . .

"Who moved the parking lot

"Flopping fish fail

"To dampen my love for you."

Silence gripped the room, then Chip said, "Shit, Alan, that's deep."

The other boys of summer applauded mightily.

Marion moved away from the window, to the front of the tent.

"Now this demonstrates an important point," said Chip. "Technique is important, but you have to pour your soul into your writing. You have to really mean it. You can just go the moon, June, croon route, but that doesn't make your poem come to life. The quality of your writing is a reflection of what you feel inside. Don't be content with trodding where others have trod before. Do you know why? In spite of the fact that we are all crazy about Marion, each of us has had his own unique and special experience with her. Each of us has a secret Marion place inside himself, a place that nobody else knows about, and that's what you have to bring out in an interesting and meaningful way. Now, let's go on to the next poem, this one's by Jim. . ."

The bard got to his feet.

"Marion, Oh Light of My World,

"Every Time I See You,

"The Flags of My Heart Unfurl. . ."

"Stop it! Just stop it!" Marion cried, bursting into the big tent.

As one, the boys of summer turned to her.

As one, their faces lit up with delight.

As one, they rose and came to her.

She held up a definitive hand. "Stop."

They obeyed.

"We need to have a talk," she said quietly.

Their eyes dropped, their chins hung low.

"This is all very flattering, of course. What girl wouldn't want to be thought of so highly. . . by so many of you? But I think it's time we found someone else. It's time we got back to living our own lives. Summer's over, you know?"

"Then why are you sweating?" Chip asked.

The boys of summer perked up, hope in their eyes.

"Chip. . ."

"Marion, oh light of my life," Jim began reciting, and at once, as if a switch had been thrown, all the boys of summer spoke with deep sincerity the words they had written.

It was cacophony. A poetry fusillade. Marion jammed her hands against her ears and insisted that they cease, but her voice was lost in the waves of ear-piercing adoration.

Marion ran.

She ran like she did the first time she visited Camp Marion. Panicked, embarrassed, frightened.

She ran home, the boys of summer giving chase. When she reached the safety of her house, she slammed the door shut, flipping over the security lock. Then pulled shades and drew curtains. Turned off the phone and punched on the TV. Only then did she dare nudge the edge of the heavy red drapes shielding her front window.

The boys of summer were everywhere—in the driveway, on the lawn, at the door. They looked happy, but in a strange, frenzied way. They were all reciting their verses using their outdoor voices. It must have been the heat. It must have been something she said.

Marion didn't know what to do, so she powered up her phone and made a call.

"Nine-one-one. What's your emergency?"

"Uh, there are people outside my house."

"Prowlers?"

"Not exactly."

"You know these people?"

"Well, yes."

"Who are they?"

"They're all sort of boyfriends, I guess."

"Are they threatening you?"

"They're reading me poems."

"I'm sorry, ma'am. Could you repeat that?"

"Poetry! They wrote love poems to me and now they're standing outside my house reciting them, all at once!"

"I wish my boyfriend would write me a love poem."

"You don't understand! I don't want them here!"

"No, I understand. But do you? Listen to me: You need to cherish these fellas. True love is so scarce in this world that you have to nurture it when you find it. Don't throw it away. Don't shut the door. And most of all, don't call nine-one-one."

"I'll get a restraining order!"

"Cherish them, as they cherish you."

"I'll write my congresswoman!"

"There's no excuse not to love. . ."

Marion hung up, royally steamed.

And then she fell to her knees, sobbing. Deep, heart-shuddering sobs. She felt ashamed for calling the cops. She didn't what else to do. She didn't want to hurt her boys of summer, but she couldn't go on like this. The only thing more unbearable than the heat was the love. She had to escape, get away. . .

The boys of summer swarmed her car as Marion backed out of the driveway. On the roof, the trunk, the windshield. Leaving lip marks and teardrops. They scattered helter-skelter as she hit the curb at the bottom of the blacktop. She sped off without looking in her rearview mirror.

The miles burned away. The other cars were just props. She was flying. Soaring far above her troubles, her life.

When the sky took a determined step toward darkness, Marion stopped. She didn't know what town she had landed in. It looked like any other town. It was as hot as any other town. Maybe hotter.

Marion hadn't hydrated since she left, so she found a local java shop called Bloomer's Beans and went in for an iced coffee. A musician in a bolero hat and sunglasses was strumming a guitar, flamenco-style, on a squat stage in the far corner of the bistro. The joint was solid hipsters. After Marion got her beverage, she glanced at the bulletin board. A new town, but the notices were pretty much old news. Used ski equipment for sale, air conditioner repair services, midnight garage sales.

As she turned to find a seat, she noticed a young man sitting by himself at an orange table by the flyer-covered front windows. Nice-looking. No, very nice-looking! Marion kept staring at him, and when he finally noticed and their eyes met, she smiled.

He flashed her a quick, knowing grin, which she took as a green light and headed over. "It's pretty packed in here. Mind if I join you?"

"Sure," he replied easily, moving his drink to his side of the table.

"My name's Marion," she said, settling in.

"Rey."

"That's a nice name. Hoo-Rey!"

"You make me laugh."

"You have a nice smile," she told him. "Your eyes light up in a real wild way."

"Thank you."

"I like the music."

"So do I. That's Nabetse. He plays here often."

"Do you want to dance?"

"There is not much space, but yes, let's dance."

There was a narrow aisle in front of the guitar player, and this is where Marion and Rey cut a rug, sort of a combination flamenco/mashed-potato, sans castanets. It was fun, she was able to keep pace with him and when the song wrapped up the hipsters howled their approval. Best of all, they held hands on the way back to their table.

Marion felt giddy. "I'm not from around here," she said, knocking back the rest of her coffee.

"No?"

"I'm from out of town. Like way out of town. Like I needed to get away, so I just started driving. . . and here I am!"

"Well I'm glad you found Bloomer's Beans. . . What are your plans then?"

"I don't know. I thought I did, but now I'm not so sure." She looked at him dreamily. "Can I see you tomorrow?"

"That would be very nice. What do you like to do?"

"What do people do for fun in. . . ha, I don't even know the name of this burg."

"Bloomer."

"Like the coffee shop!"

"We have an amusement park, Bloomerwood. Are you a roller coaster fan?"

"Haven't done that since I was a kid. It would be a kick to try again. To be young and carefree again, nothing could beat that."

"Let's meet here tomorrow morning, say nine sharp? We'll have a little breakfast, then head on out to Bloomerwood."

"Maybe not too much breakfast if we're going to ride the roller coaster!"

"Good one."

"I can't wait, Rey."

Marion found a cozy motor inn to spend the night, her head spinning with her good fortune at having stumbled upon someone as wonderful as Rey. As she showered and got ready for bed, she was in disbelief at her own daring. *What a thing to do!* she thought. *Why did I wait so long?*

First thing in the morning she made a return trip to Bloomer's Beans. She was afraid Rey wouldn't show, but there he was, already in line, ordering breakfast for both of them.

"Good morning," she said, squeezing his arm.

"Good morning yourself. Sleep well?"

"Like a dream."

Breakfast, açai-blueberry organic whole-grain waffles and a bowl of Count Chocula, was divine, and the roller coaster was a scream. The whole day was serious ecstasy. Rey seemed so different, so laid-back, not like the other boys. She could tell he dug her, but it wasn't in an overbearing, off-the-rails way. It felt normal. It felt right. Everything about him felt right. It made her wonder what she had been missing all these years.

Their second date was a movie, *Battlefield: Hoboken,* one of those summer science fiction disaster blockbusters that seemed to be in the theaters year 'round these days. Their third rendezvous was an old-fashioned picnic in the park.

As they polished off the last of the cupcakes and kumquats, Marion stretched out on the ground, pretending the dead grass was cool and green. I love the clouds, she thought. I love the birds singing. I love it all so much.

"I wish today would never end," she said.

"As do I, but we should be getting back," said Rey.

"Can't we stay awhile longer?"

He offered her his hands, helping her up. "We'll go for a nice drive. You'll enjoy it."

As they motored along the byways of Bloomer, Marion said, in a contented voice, "What should we do tomorrow?"

"Not sure."

"I'll think of something this time."

"What I mean to say is that I'm not sure tomorrow will work for me."

"I'm sorry," Marion said. "I know I sort of skipped out on my life. I can't expect you to do the same. I'm sure you have to work and stuff."

"Yes, that too."

They were silent for a few blocks, then Marion sat up straight. "Wait a minute, this isn't the way to the motor inn."

Rey didn't respond to her concern.

Marion got scared. She reached for the door handle.

"Don't, Marion. It's not like that at all. I live nearby."

"Are we going back to your place, then?"

"Not exactly."

"I don't understand."

"It's hard to explain," he said, pulling the car over to the curb. "I'm very fond of you, Marion. You're pretty and you're fun to be around."

"But. . ."

"You need to be here."

Puzzled, Marion looked out the window.

They were parked at a vacant lot, a grouping of tents hugging the central space.

He touched her cheek, offered her a caring smile. "Just take a look around. Talk to the folks you find here."

Marion saved her tears for later. "Rey. . ."

"Trust me," he said.

"Will I see you again?"

"I think that's very, very possible."

She left him then, watching forlornly as he drove off, then walked over to the camp.

As she neared the perimeter, women, young and old, emerged

from the tents, encircling her, embracing her without hesitation, accepting her without reservation, bringing her into their hearts.

Marion understood, now more than ever.

It was going to be a long summer.

"Rey, oh light of my world. . .," they began reciting as one, and disappeared into the tents, where they waited for their turn to love.

# THE BRIDGE

George Guthridge

Now that you understand more than your father and brother taught you, you watch the teenager on the middle of the bridge that connects the continents. She looks east, then west. She has never been more than a couple miles in either direction. She knows she never will.

Though told not to smoke, warned of its dangers, she lights a cigarette, cupping it in the hood of her parka to shield it from the Bering Sea wind, uncertain if she should enjoy the taste and wondering whom she should ask about that, now that her father and brother are gone.

It is noon. Dawn and dusk are united in midwinter in the Arctic, the sky ribbed pink and orange. Work to do. She flips the cigarette away half-finished, down into the sea below and, after watching for traffic that never comes, crosses the lanes to check for ice that is never there.

She slips a hand from a mitten, which now dangles from a clip attached to her parka sleeve, and with a pencil X's boxes on the paper on her clipboard. Left box, right box. Makeshift work, you are both painfully aware, for the mentally challenged.

You are sure she has forgotten which box means what side of the bridge. Not that it matters. You have seen the stacks of papers she has submitted, all sitting in the station house, no one bothering to file them anymore.

She sets down the clipboard and with great effort climbs onto the bridge's waist-high wall. Knees first, then rising slowly. After a moment, she lets the toes of her mukluks stick over the edge. The sea is cobalt blue and white-capped. A warm, delightful shiver seizes her. She has never done this before.

She looks back toward the village. People move like phantoms among buildings that, aproned with snow, hug the island's mountain. The ancient shacks of dunnage and tin roofs now line the shore, the government houses that HUD sent having been disassembled and moved up near the school, because of the rising waters. No one sees her or, if they do, seems concerned.

She is seven months pregnant with her second child.

It's her seventeenth birthday.

She will do what she wants.

I remember the day Daddy's glow disappeared. I remember because I still attended high school. I cannot forget no matter how hard I try. It was seventy-two hours and six minutes after Daddy unboxed our telescope.

I found him in the sea. He was staring at the sky as if remembering the Woman from Ambler. Only his face showed above the water, the waves washing over him. I ran into the water. The current slammed me against him as I called "Daddy, Daddy!" and I tried to drag him ashore. But he was too full of whatever weight holds dead people down, and his glow was gone. There was only blackness. It was like the hole in the center of the spiral of stars the telescope showed me, the place where numbers go to die. Seabirds cried and cawed—calling his name, people said later. But I don't believe that. The birds were startled, was all. Nothing called his name except me and the Woman from Ambler. She had come in his dreams from Anchorage to seduce him with sorrow, as he said she used to.

Daddy and I bought the telescope with our Permanent Fund. It is oil money we Alaskans get each year because everyone in the state is a Special Needs child. That's what Daddy says. Gwimaq, my twin brother, wanted a new .22 with a Leupold scope. The telescope was a present from me and Daddy to Daddy and me. But then Gwimaq had money left over from the gun, so he helped too. I said not to, but he helped anyway.

Daddy opened the box one hundred and ninety-seven minutes—eleven thousand eight hundred and twenty seconds—after the Twin Otter brought it. We don't get many planes here. Since the bridge closed, there are only some helicopters, plus barges four times a year and once in a while a government pickup truck.

I checked my watches the moment the plane touched down on the ice runway between Little Diomede Island, where our village is, and Big Diomede, two-point-four miles west. You can't go there. Daddy said that when the bridge was open, big trucks traveling through would drop off things from America, to the east, where the sun rises, and also from Russia. But I hardly remember. I was very little the last time I saw one of the eighteen-wheelers.

I have three watches on each forearm, and I had them set to stopwatch. The instant the plane's skis touched down it had been one million, six hundred and eighty-three thousand, three hundred and sixty-two minutes since Preston Robert walked away and I pulled my jeans back up that day beneath the monkey bars.

When Daddy set up the telescope in his classroom he said it was like bringing a family member home. It had come on what turned out to be the last plane on the last year that there was ice enough for a landing. I thought the telescope would be long and skinny, like on television, but it was fat as a stovepipe and you looked in from a little tube on the side. He turned off the lights, only his weak desk lamp showing, and adjusted some knobs.

Gwimaq said he wanted to see, and he shoved me aside because boys are like that, but Daddy said that he wanted me to go first because he had something special to show me. "It's for you, Andromeda," he said. "It's the galaxy named after you."

At first I said no because I was afraid of it, afraid I might break something. But Daddy insisted, and you can trust him. I put my eye on the rubber eyepiece and blinked several times, my hand over my other eye but Daddy said don't do that and then I could see the stars. They were in a spiral. It is like when Daddy and I walk in the snow and carefully back out so people will think we've disappeared.

I think my eye became blurry because after a few moments, the stars began to move. It made me want to shiver, like when Preston Robert did that to me. The stars spiraled down into blackness, like numbers do that often come into my mind. "Some scientists call it a vampire galaxy," Daddy said, "because it eats smaller ones. But now they say that our galaxy, the Milky Way, does that too."

Maybe Daddy should not have said that, because then Gwimaq did shove me away. He wanted to see, Daddy frowning at him but as usual giving in. Gwimaq looked into the telescope and played with the knobs. Daddy and I sat at the desks. Outside, the aurora was ribbons of green and gold streaming in the darkness. The clock ticked on the wall. I thought about what the Woman from Ambler, the Woman Gone to Anchorage, as Daddy often called her, would tell me when I was little and still thought of her as my mother as she would tuck me into bed.

*You are descended from Maniilaq, our greatest shaman. He lived two hundred years ago and predicted the coming of the whites. He said that boats would fly in the air or be propelled by fire. He also said that Ambler would become an enormous city, but I have seen his vision a thousand times, and it is not a city on the tundra, it is a city in the sky. So sleep, my precious, because a city of stars is watching over you.*

Then the lights snapped on, and my cousin Preston Robert and his two friends came in. They were high school boys back then though they usually only came to school for lunch or open gym. Or they just walked into Daddy's classroom when they felt like it, to link with their clients Outside, not even asking Daddy for permission.

They sat down at the computers that line one wall, watching Daddy as though daring him to stop them. Then they put on their headsets and leaned back, eyes closing, feet up on the desks. Gwimaq left the telescope and stood over them, arms folded.

But there was nothing he could do. The village council had ruled. The bowhead and the walrus are gone, the council members said; there is no more baleen to work or ivory to carve. Some people sat with their heads in their hands when they said that. The troubles Outside have dried up the bridge traffic, the council members said. And so the clients of people like Preston Robert and his friends were the only industry left to the village. Daddy was not allowed to kick them out of class. They were Untouchables, he said.

I have never emotion-linked, using the software that lets you send your emotions over the Internet. Daddy says not to because it's dangerous and addictive. That's why the government tries to shut down websites that allow it. It disgusted him—people here selling the feeling of being Ingalikmiut, the First People, to wannabes Outside. Besides, he said, it is animals that make Native peoples who they are, and except for the birds the animals are gone. So what is Preston Robert selling? Daddy would ask.

Preston Robert said that Daddy was jealous because he's white and cannot sell what he doesn't own. I would hug myself and shake my head whenever Preston Robert teased me about refusing to emotion-link. I think Gwimaq tried it a couple of times back then, but I can't be sure. He knew I'd tell Daddy.

After the Untouchables checked their PayPals they went to work, signaling for Daddy once again to dim the lights, as though he were there to serve them. Gwimaq shook his head, but Daddy did as the boys wished. He didn't want trouble. Gwimaq and I are half Native. Daddy's just half crazy—for teaching here, he sometimes likes to say.

Soon the boys' bodies were limp, their arms at their sides. Gwimaq nodded for us to leave, but Daddy kept watching the boys. Maybe getting angry, maybe not wanting to leave them alone in his classroom, I couldn't be sure. Gwimaq was walking out the door when Mukta, the youngest, tipped over and lay shaking, his eyes rolled back in his head. Daddy sent Gwimaq running for the health aide and started first aid like he tried to show me sometimes.

Put his feet up. Cover him with a blanket. Put a stick in his mouth so he won't swallow his tongue. But then Mukta stopped breathing and Daddy went pale and started to work on him, the glow around him flickering and sparking like the aurora. He pushed on Mukta's chest and breathed into his mouth. By the time Gwimaq and the health aide arrived, Mutka was conscious. Daddy yanked the headphones off Preston Robert and threw them against the wall, Preston Robert blinking open his eyes and suddenly rising to thrust his chest against Daddy, hands fisted, glaring, his glow red and bubbling. Only when he saw that the health aide was there did Preston Robert leave.

Later that night, Daddy returned to school and put a padlock on his classroom door.

The next day he announced to our class that no one would use the computers except for schoolwork, and then only with his permission.

Two days later he was dead. He had slipped and fallen into the sea, smashing his skull against a rock. That's what everyone said.

Despite understanding even more than what your father and brother taught you, it comes as a surprise when you realize that Andromeda, the girl on the bridge, does not intend to jump. You had supposed she would be serious about ending it all.

She is moving along the bridge's ledge with a certainty akin to that of a gymnast on a balance beam, moving away from the village, the toes of her mukluks seeking where the next step should be. She appears to be dancing to a drumbeat—knees bent, mittens dangling, arms out and palms turned up, shoulders rising and falling with each step, face lifted to the sky, eyes open. With a shake of her head her hood falls back, revealing braids. As if in appreciation of the girl, the world suddenly is without wind. She moves beneath one of the mercury lights that have winked on at intervals along the bridge. They herald a path toward the far horizon, where the mainland is, a destination that she has never visited nor, until recently, wanted to.

Night is upon the sea, a red aurora spilling in a curtain of light so thick it appears viscous. Though science insists the northern lights are silent, there are groanings and screechings, the sound of a metal door being pushed shut.

"The mind," her mother, the Woman from Ambler, once said as she sat on the girl's bed and told her stories of the way life is supposed to be, "is not in the brain," touching her temple and then the girl's, the girl giggling. "The brain is merely a conduit, like a DVD player showing us signals that are created elsewhere." She would then draw the life's lesson on the big pad with its spiral binding along the top. The woman was artistic: baking, beading, sketching, scrimshaw. She drew a picture for the girl with an effortlessness that, the girl sensed, belied the pain that her mother kept bottled up. "The mind," her mother continued to draw, "is in the aura, the halo of electromagnetism that surrounds all living things. It's like the aurora for the earth, what for us northern peoples is the singing of the spiritual. That's where the mind is, in the aura. A glow that, it's said, some people can see."

"You mean," the girl sat up and cocked her head in disbelief, "other people can't see it?"


I could not see the glow after Daddy died. We buried him on the North Side, a stranger beside people that, he said, he could not teach or reach no matter how much he loved his students.

Buried him aboveground, because as the Woman from Ambler often said, the earth in the North is too frozen to accept the body and too sullen to want the soul. After the others left, Gwimaq and I piled rocks around and upon the coffin. People used to do that to keep bears from devouring the dead, but the bears are gone now, so now the rocks are for decoration.

Gwimaq was holding a rock and looking down toward the village. Below us the bridge came out of light slitted at the east, the mainland twenty-five miles away. Then at our island it doglegged, as Gwimaq liked to say, and went northwest to Big Diomede, where we weren't allowed. I felt we were at the bottom of forever, like rocks dropped into a deep, dark sea.

"Just you and me now," I heard Gwimaq say. He set the rock atop the coffin and wandered down toward the village without another word.

And then the birds came.

They rose into the dawn from beneath the bridge, where they nested by the thousands. They came from off the cliffs where Gwimaq hunted them despite being a poor shot compared to the other boys. The birds were like a black aurora spiraling up from the earth. Not here to celebrate the soul, but to gorge themselves on the wealth of insects the warmer winters have brought.

I wanted to go with them. I wanted them to stop haunting me. When they reached the darkness they winked out like the numbers that spiral out of my math book and from out of my watches, numbers that flit in my aura like flies I cannot kill. Sometimes I have to sit with my head in my hands, whimpering, other kids peeking at me and then away, pretending I don't exist. I am not retarded, only slow, I tell myself; I am not retarded, only slow. Because of the numbers.

If only I could shut them out, go back before I hung upside-down from the monkey bars Daddy had bought and set up amid the rocks we have for a playground. He bolted the ends of the monkey bar dome into boulders. He spent hours drilling, no one there to help except Gwimaq, always whining and asking to go home, and me rocking back and forth, watching and worrying that Daddy would hurt himself.

When he finished he spread gravel he hauled up to school in a backpack, over three dozen trips, each rock about the size of your thumb. He spread the gravel smooth with the rake he ordered from Home Depot. When he was done, there were just the two of us. He stood holding the rake, his eyes full of pride. He put an arm around my shoulders and kissed my hair. "They'll think I did it for the school," he whispered. "But I did it for you. I built it only for you."

And I ruined it.

A year later, I was hanging upside-down from a lower bar, rocking, the numbers going away whenever I did that. The world is at peace, or should be, when you see it that way.

Then someone pinned my legs. When my eyes jerked open I was looking at a belt buckle, a hand, massive in my sight, clawing at it. Preston Robert, I knew it without peering up. Though only a ninth grader, he had a man's body, a thick, cruel body, the type once useful to row after whales and now here to hurt me. With his free hand he pulled down my kuspuk, tore at my jeans, and ripped at my panties, trying to make me naked up to my knees. He let me drop.

I fell on my head, only the jacket I earlier left on the ground cushioning my fall. I lay there on my stomach, dazed, gripping Daddy's gravel while Preston Robert ripped off my jeans, let his own pants fall to his ankles, took a moment while he did something to himself and then collapsed on top of me.

The numbers came in waves, like hands slapping skin, like insects stinging me before moving on and the next wave of insects coming like a cloud. Between them, except for his grunting, there only was silence and the whispering of wind. I clenched my eyes shut. I would not cry out or cry, I never cried, not even that night when the Woman from Ambler walked out on us, telling Daddy he was boring because he refused to party with her, he with tears in his eyes and

Gwimaq bawling, clinging to her legs, and me sitting in the corner like a stone.

When Preston Robert was done he stood, pulled up his pants and, zippering, said, "If you tell, my friends and I will kill your father."

"If I tell, the troopers will come. They'll haul you away in handcuffs."

I said it into my jacket, just loud enough for him to hear.

Because suddenly I knew what the bridge was for. The bridge few used anymore. "Finally an Alaskan Bridge to Somewhere," the news clipping that Daddy kept called it, but then things had fallen apart, he said, so now it went from there to here, and from here to nowhere.

But now I saw its usefulness.

"They'll take you to Nome," I said. "They'll lock you up and leave you there."

"No one will believe you. I'm not eighteen—not even close to it. I'll say you wanted it."

I looked up at him, and for a moment, between the swirling numbers, I thought I saw the Woman from Ambler standing behind him. Not there to help me or to kill him. Just watching. And for that maybe I hated her. Or maybe I felt nothing at all.

"They'll have to believe me," I said. "It's the law. Because I'm the crazy girl."

Despite his dark skin, I could see the blood leave his face, and I saw his aura whiten. Not white the color of a white man, but white like the bellies of dead salmon that used to wash ashore when the sea still had fish.

But I never told. Maybe I was afraid. Maybe there's something wrong with me. I never told the troopers, I never told Daddy, I only told myself—that it never happened. Once Preston Robert left and I had pulled on my jeans and stuffed my torn-apart panties in my jacket, I set my watches to stopwatch, time ticking until I had courage to turn him in, but I never did. When the telescope arrived that day I started time all over again, setting the watches to zero.

Now Daddy was dead because of me.

I should have told someone. Preston Robert would have gone to jail or wherever they put people his age, and maybe Daddy would still be alive and he would understand why I never used the monkey bars again. All my fault. All. My. Fault.

The dawn was growing as I stood over the coffin. Light came flooding up the mountain. I could not hold anything back any longer, not the numbers, not the pain. I collapsed to my knees and, crying "Daddy, Daddy," beat on the coffin with my rock, demanding that he come back to me, forgive me, hold me, and tell me he understood. The tears came then, I could not control them, and somewhere beyond the dawn, there in Anchorage, the Woman from Ambler became a blurry memory I wanted to forget.

*You are descended from Maniilaq, our greatest shaman*, she said. *He lived two hundred years ago and predicted the coming of the whites. He said that boats would fly in the air or be propelled by fire. He also said that Ambler would become an enormous city, but I have seen his vision a thousand times, and it is not a city on the tundra, it is a city in the sky. So sleep, my precious, because a city of stars is watching over you.*

Despite understanding even more than what your father and brother tried to teach you, you only now feel affinity toward the girl on the bridge. You've been watching without emotion, but now you're leaned closer, increasingly intrigued, as if you're in a theater balcony.

She has climbed down from the ledge and walked farther from the village, not hurried, sauntering, running a mittened hand along the wall as though for emotional support.

Emergency stations are set exactly every two miles from the island's station house. For aesthetics each is shaped like a tower perhaps eight feet in diameter, with a conical top, the effect so squat it appears comical. She looks back toward the village. Lit only by bridge lights that punctuate the darkness, the headland is so imposing that the village's few lighted windows seem like tiny hatches to a netherworld.

Reaching into her ski pants, she takes a wallet from a hip pocket, removes an ID card and after a contemptuous glance sends it sailing into the night. Next she lifts out bills and lets each flutter away. All ones except a five. In a gesture that would seem posed had she an audience, she extends an arm over the wall, opens her hand, and lets the wallet fall. Removing a beaded barrette, she shakes her hair free. It is long and luxurious, the product of a hundred strokes with a hairbrush each night. She drops the barrette over the side.

She enters the emergency station and comes out cradling a telescope. It is white, with silver bands at each end and in the middle. She opens its tripod and, after making sure the telescope is secure, points it toward the northeast, where Ambler is. She looks into the eyepiece and expertly adjusts the knobs.

She reenters the emergency station and emerges with three small padlocks, a length of chain, a collar, and three keys. After padlocking the door, she sets its key on the wall and tests the chain for strength. It is thin, but will do. She threads it between the hasp and the door, locks it to itself and places the second key on the wall, beside the first.

She walks several feet away and, after looking into the darkness as though summoning resolve, removes her parka and mukluks and places them on the wall. Then she takes off the rest of her clothing, folds the pieces neatly and puts them on the wall as well. She stands naked beneath the light, belly protruding, arms folded over her breasts, chin down: a look of shame.

She exhales and lifts her head. Seemingly unmindful of the cold concrete under her feet, she pads back to the telescope and takes the collar she left looped around the eyepiece. It is studded with spikes, sparkling with false diamonds. She places it around her neck, locks it to the chain with the last padlock, puts its key beside the others, walks to the end of the chain and reaches out. Her clothing, as she apparently planned, is a foot too far. She returns to the keys.

With middle finger and thumb she flicks each key into the darkness and steps behind the telescope. Adjusting the knobs, she looks past the stars above Ambler, searching for her galaxy. She wonders if Maniilaq, were he alive, would forgive her for her death.

There were things Daddy witnessed when he was young, he said, that drove him to the end of the earth. His father had been a biologist, and Daddy often had accompanied him on trips. Three grizzlies killed outside Yakutat and left to rot, only the gall bladders taken so rich men in Asia could dine upon them with chopsticks of jade and think themselves virile. A wolf near Tok left to suffer for two days in a trap and his father not allowed to shoot it, so environmentalists could capture its agony on film. Bering Sea Eskimos slaughtering walrus only for the ivory. Killer whales coming into coves so shallow an orca seemingly could never swim there, to devour sea otters because the sea lions were gone, victims of the overharvesting of pollack. The only polar bear he ever saw outside a zoo, drowned in the Beaufort Sea because it was swimming futilely in search of ice broad enough to force seals to seek breathing holes. His father, Daddy said, brought the plane in close, recorded the dead animal's location, then flew away without a word.

The day after he received his college diploma and teaching certificate, Daddy left for Siberia, only to be forced back. Environmental disasters had dried up U.S.-Russian relations. The bridge linking the continents had closed. He settled in Little Diomede to be as far away from the rest of Alaska as possible. The village was dysfunctional, loss of wildlife and rising oil prices having forced those people with any skills to Anchorage or Outside. He loved his students—most of them—but kept his focus on the stars.

Six months after his death we learned how little attention he had paid to *this* world.

Gwimaq and I were in the living room, he cleaning his .22 and me cooking dinner. He had gotten a cormorant. As usual I'd had to clean it, boys even these days not expected to do such things. He sat on the floor, the rifle pointed up, while he held a letter with his free hand, the opened envelope in his lap.

"We're fucked," he said. "That bitch isn't sending us a dime."

The letter was from an Anchorage attorney. Daddy had forgotten to change the beneficiary of the life insurance policy Bering Strait School District gave its teachers. We had tried to fight, but the Woman from Ambler had gotten it all.

With his thumb he clicked the rifle off safety and, his face hard with anger, fired six shots into the ceiling, emptying the clip, so startling me that I dropped the cormorant into hot grease, burning my arm. What gives males the right, I wondered, digging into a cupboard for the salve, that brothers can shoot holes in the ceiling and fathers can burn holes in the human heart?

The next day the terror started. We had no money. You cannot live only on cormorant, a few murre eggs gathered from the cliffs, an occasional brown-tipped gull shot far enough away that it had not feasted on village garbage. Was Jesus going to arrive and turn the rocks beneath the monkey bars into small, gray potatoes? Can you make gravy out of spit?

Gwimaq went to work at the school, sharing his Eskimo soul, as the website proclaimed. *Don't do it,* I begged him when we were at school the day he got his PayPal account. *We can sell everything. Your gun, the couch, the beds, everything in the kitchen. We'll have enough for two tickets to Anchorage, enough to live on for a month.*

"And then what? Become wards of the state? Or live with *her*? I'd rather be dead."

He put on the headphones, slapped my hands away when I tried to tear off the phones. I went to the far side of the room and sat facing the corner, my head on the wall, as Daddy used to make me do when I was a little girl and was bad.

Soon I could hear him grunting. It was like the time Preston

Robert was on top of me. I covered my ears but could not help seeing Gwimaq out of the corner of my eye. He was holding the headphones with both hands, rocking back and forth, his eyes closed and lips parted, sounds coming from deep in his throat.

The door opened. We had locked it from the inside, but there was the rasping of a key, and then Preston Robert and his friends came in. He held up a key and grinned like an animal, then nodded toward Gwimaq. I tried to get to Gwimaq, protect him, but Cray, the largest boy, grabbed me. I clawed at his cheeks and screamed Gwimaq's name, but he was beyond hearing—and then Preston Robert punched me in the face, and Cray let me fall to the floor.

Mukta grabbed my brother's arms, pinning them behind his back, he twisting his body but too far lost in computer dreams to put up a fight. Preston Robert wrapped Gwimaq's head with duct tape, binding the headphones to his ears. Even Gwimaq's eyes did not show. Then Mukta wrapped Gwimaq to the chair. Preston Robert dialed up the intensity on the computer, the bars on the screen dancing in the red zone. He put a foot on Gwimaq's shoulder and toppled him to the floor. Gwimaq lay tremoring, each spasm more powerful than the last.

I did not beg or cry out when Preston Robert pulled me back to my feet, by my hair. There was no use begging; there no one else in the building. His friends pulled off my jeans and forced me facedown over Daddy's desk. They tied me spread-eagled, the duct tape like rope.

"No condom this time," Preston Robert said as he unbuckled his belt and moved behind me. "You'll get welfare, you'll get the Permanent Fund. We'll leave you enough to live on. The rest you'll turn over to us."

"Like your daddy told us in school," Mukta said. "Develop a cottage industry."

"So we did," Cray said. "Computers and cunt."

"Call the troopers," Preston Robert said. "I won't stop you, and I won't hurt you. You're too valuable a commodity. But your brother's dead the minute they haul me away."

He had Cray turn off the lights, for what Preston Robert called ambiance but which, I knew, was so people walking by could not see in.

Now that you understand more than your father and brother tried to teach you, you feel empathy for the death upon the bridge. You see her intent. A woman frozen to death by chaining herself so she cannot reach her clothes truly wants to die. The death will bring troopers and paternity tests, one for the fetus, the other that she left tightly bundled in a sleeping bag: two children by two men, one of who will know the financial rigors of fatherhood, or else will know lockup.

Except, as you now realize, the troopers will not find her body. Only bones.

Out of the last rays of sun, birds come by the hundreds. Except for the rushing of wings, there is no sound, no squawking as they land to tug out her hair and tear at the newly frozen skin, each bit of flesh aglow with her aura. A raven tears off a lip, its head pulled back and claws fighting for purchase on the asphalt. A tufted puffin pokes at an eye. A cormorant takes the other eye, its long throat lifted as it swallows.

A month after we lost the insurance case, two social workers arrived in goose-down jackets, their eyes full of sad smiles. Your father was a good man, they said. And you're such good kids. Smiling sadly, they told us that the Woman from Ambler thought it best that we stay in familiar surroundings instead of in Anchorage or in foster care. Until we were old enough to make our own choices, our uncle, Preston Robert's father, would be our legal guardian.

I never said a word in protest. Daddy was dead. I wouldn't do the same to Gwimaq.

We lost the teacher housing because we no longer had a parent employed by the school. Gwimaq and I took an empty, two-room, low-ceilinged shack by the sea, near where Daddy died. We covered the tiny windows with cardboard to help keep out the cold and ran the potbelly stove when we could afford it. The end of the main room had collapsed. Water sloshed up between the planks and crept into a corner of the ancient linoleum when the tide was high. I left school. I couldn't be in Daddy's classroom anymore. There were too many memories.

I let numbers numb me, and I learned to close my eyes a lot.

After I had my first baby I would whisper to him whenever I tucked him into the sleeping bag on the highest and driest part of the floor. *You are descended from Maniilaq, a great shaman. He lived two hundred years ago and predicted the coming of the whites. He said that boats would fly in the air or be propelled by fire. He also said that Ambler would become an enormous city, but I have seen his vision a thousand times, and it is not a city on the tundra, it is a city in the sky. So sleep, my precious, because a city of stars is watching over you.*

It was Gwimaq who suffered the most, I told myself. Like me with my job, he never saw the money for selling his Eskimo soul. He would stagger home exhausted every morning and babysit my son while I checked the bridge. Otherwise he usually sat in the corner, staring at the wall where he had hidden his .22, and waiting to hook up to the computer again. It was a habit, he said, that he despised but could not deny himself.

I was seven months into my second pregnancy—two hundred and twenty-two thousand, three hundred and twenty minutes after the home pregnancy test told me I was having another baby—when Gwimaq returned one morning so haggard that I thought he had aged a dozen years. He could not hold himself up. He sagged down, his back against the wall, knees up, forehead in his hands, elbows on his knees. Nothing I could do or say could make him budge. In the candlelight his eyes looked sunken, his cheeks like leather.

Finally he said, "Preston Robert plans to open a new market."

Preston Robert and his friends already had entered the Russian market, helped by Gwimaq's fluency, a gift Daddy tried to give me and, failing, insisted Gwimaq learn.

"Porn," he said.

For starters they intended to rape a woman with an oosik, the penis bone of the walrus, which people of our island used to hunt a generation ago. They would capture the act on camera as the computer captured her emotions—to be fed to perverts throughout the world, he told me.

"Preston Robert said you'll be wearing this."

From his pocket he took out a collar studded with spikes, sparkling with false diamonds.

So it was not a question of who. But of when. Would they wait for the baby to be born?

That evening Gwimaq left for work without a word, only to return a few minutes later. From his jacket he took a cat's claw pry-bar that, he said, he had lifted from the custodian closet. He started pulling out the nails of the boards behind which his rifle stood wrapped in plastic. The clip was beside it, in a Ziploc. He inserted the clip, checked the action and wiped the barrel, scope, and stock with a rag.

Then he kissed my forehead. He had to bend down over me, like a dark, gaunt angel as he placed his hands upon my cheeks. "Wait half an hour," he said. "Then slide the boat into the water, put most of our things in it and start the kicker." Daddy's twelve-foot aluminum Lund, one of the few possessions Preston Robert had not taken, mainly because he used it all the time without asking anyway, was among the rocks beside the house.

I was to send the boat into the sea. The current would do the rest, even if the motor quit. Hopefully, everyone would think we had drowned. In the meantime, we would cross the bridge—not to the American mainland, but to Big Diomede. He said he knew a way to climb down the bridge and sneak across the border without the Russian guards spotting us. He had friends on the island.

"When Daddy was alive I wasn't always out hunting cormorant," he said, and headed toward the door, rifle in hand.

I stepped in front of him. "You don't need to do this."

But we both knew he did. For Daddy. And so Preston Robert and his friends would never touch anyone again.

"Russia no longer honors U.S. extradition requests," Gwimaq said.

He pushed past me, opened the door and bowed through, the darkness flecked with snow. Then he was gone, shutting the door and working the wooden lever. The door was small, to help keep out bears in the old days.

I did what Gwimaq had asked. As I sent the Lund puttering into fog, moonlight glancing off the aluminum, I heard shots spaced several seconds apart—*bap! bap! bap!*—from the HUD house Preston Robert shared with his friends. The porch light was on. I saw Gwimaq emerge and run toward the bridge—without me. I rushed inside our house, gathered my son in my arms and what I planned to take with us, and was at the door when it opened. Even before Preston Robert bowed through I knew what lesson life was meant to teach me.

That fathers and brothers are forever leaving us.

Preston Robert looked down at me, a line of blood across his temple and scalp. He moved his fingers along the blood as though straightening back his hair, and touched the fingertips to his tongue.

"Your brother never could shoot worth a shit," he said.


Now that you understand more than what your father and brother tried to teach you, and your aura has united with the aurora, you watch in fascination at the outpouring of numbers from the woman on the bridge, the woman you used to be. Birds peck at them like pebbles, gorge on them as they continue to tear off flesh to take home to youngling.

Thus do the numbers wend through the food chain, linking into sets, forming algorithms. Freed from minds that produced them, they seek justice for the girl, for all the damaged of the world, and for the world herself. There is little left of the ice caps, little of the ocean that has not been spoiled, little air that has not been defiled.

The aurora, linked to every aura, oversees the earth and gathers its intelligence as the numbers coalesce, becoming part of every biome. Your psyche flows inseparable from the numbers, inseparable from the earth, inseparable from the raped domain. You realize that physical causes do not send hurricanes, topple oil rigs, parch deserts, heat the sea. From the aurora, from its timeless moiling beneath the stars, you realize that the world warms not from humans or from sun cycles—but out of anger. She does not seek to heal herself but to kill herself. And all upon her.

You watch with grim satisfaction as water inexorably rises around the island you once called home.

# FARMEARTH

Paul Di Filippo

I couldn't wait until I turned thirteen, so I could play FarmEarth. I kept pestering all three of my parents every day to let me download the FarmEarth app into my memtax. What a little makulit I must have been! I see it now, from the grownup vantage of sixteen, and after all the trouble I eventually caused. Every minute with whines like "What difference does six months make?" And "But didn't I get high marks in all my omics classes?" And what I thought was the irrefutable clincher, "But Benno got to play when he was only eleven!"

"Look now, please, Crispian," my egg-Mom, Darla, would calmly answer, "six months makes a big difference when you're just twelve-point-five. That's four percent of your life up to this date. You can mature a lot in six months."

Darla worked as an osteo-engineer, hyper-tweaking fab files for living prosthetics, as if you couldn't tell.

"But Crispian," my mito-Mom, Kianna, would imperturbably answer, "you also came close to failing integral social plectics, and you know that's nearly as important for playing FarmEarth as your omics."

Kianna worked as a hostess for the local NASDAQ Casino. She had hustled more drinks than the next two hostesses combined, and been number one in tips for the past three years.

"But Crispian," my lone dad, Marcelo Tanjuatco, would irrefutably reply (I had taken "Tanjuatco," his last name, as mine, which is why I mention it here), "Benno has a different mito-Mom than you. And you know how special and respected Zoysia is, and how long and hard even she had to petition to get Benno early acceptance."

Dad didn't work, at least not for anyone but the polybond. He stayed home, cooking meals, optimizing the house dynamics, and of course playing FarmEarth, just like every other person over thirteen who wasn't a maximal grebnard.

The way Dad—and everyone else—pronounced Zoysia's name— all smug, reverential, and dreamy—just denatured my proteome, and I had to protest.

"But Benno and I still share your genes and Darla's! That's ninety percent right there! Zoysia's only ten percent."

"And you share ninety-five percent of your genes with any random chimp," said Darla. "And they can't play FarmEarth either. At least not maybe until that new generation of kymes come online."

I knew when I was beaten, so I mumbled and grumbled and retreated to the room I shared with Benno.

Of course, at an hour before suppertime he just had to be there. . . playing FarmEarth.

My big brother Benno was a default-amp kid. His resting brain state had been permanently overclocked in the womb, so even when he wasn't consciously "thinking" he was processing information faster than you or me. And when he really focused on something, you could smell the neurons burning.

But no good fairy ever gave a gift without a catch. Benno's outward affect was, well, "interiorized." He always seemed to be listening to some silent voice, even when he was having a conversation with someone. And I'm not talking about the way all of us sometimes pay more attention to our auricular implants and the scenes displayed on our memtax than we do to the person facing us.

Needless to say, puffy-faced Benno didn't have much of social life, even at age sixteen. Not that he seemed to care.

Lying on his back on the lower bunk of our sleeping pod, Benno stared at some unknown landscape in his memtax, working his haptic finger bling faster than the Mandarin's grandson trying to take down Tony Stark's clone in *Iron Man 10*.

I tried to tap into his FarmEarth feed with my own memtax, even though I knew the dataflow was encrypted. But all that happened was that I got bounced to Benno's public CitizenSpace.

I sat down on the edge of the mattress beside him, and poked him in the ribs. He didn't flinch.

"Hey, B-man, whatcha doing?"

Benno's voice was a monotone even when he was excited about something, and dealing with his noodgy little brother was low on his list of thrills.

"I'm grooming the desert-treeline ecotone in Mali. Now go away."

"Wow! That is so stellar! Are you planting new trees?"

"No, I'm upgrading rhizome production on the existing ones."

"What kind of effectuators are you using?"

"ST5000 Micromites. Now. Go. Away!"

I shoved Benno hard. "Jerk! Why don't you ever share with me! I just wanna play too!"

I jumped up and stalked off before he could retaliate, but he didn't bother to respond.

So there you have typical day in the latter half of my thirteenth year. Desperate pleas on my part to graduate to adulthood, followed by admonitions from my parents to be patient, then by jealousy and inattention from my big brother.

As you can well imagine, the six similar months till I turned thirteen passed by like a Plutonian year (just checked via memtax: 248 Earth years). But finally—finally!—I turned thirteen and got my very own log-on to FarmEarth.

And that's when the real frustration started!

Kicking a living hacky sack is a lot more fun in meatspace than it is via memtax. You can feel muscles other than those in your fingers getting a workout. Your bare toes dig into the grass. You smell sweat and soil. You get sprayed with saltwater on a hot day. You even get to congratulatorily hug warm girls afterwards if any are in the circle with you. So while all the kids gripe about having to leave their houses every day for two whole shared hours of meatspace schooling at the nearest Greenpatch, I guess that, underneath all our complaints, we really like being face to face with our peers now and then.

That fateful day when we first decided to hack FarmEarth, there were six of us kicking around the sack. Me, Mallory, Cheo, Vernice, Anuta, and Williedell—my best friends.

The sack was an old one and didn't have much life left in it. A splice of ctenophore, siphonophore, and a few other marine creatures, including bladder kelp, the soft warty green globe could barely jet enough salt water to change its midair course erratically as intended. Kicking it got too predictable pretty fast.

Sensing what we were all feeling and acting first, Cheo, tall and quick, grabbed the sack on one of its feeble arcs and tossed it like a basketball into the nearby aquarium—splash!—where it sank listlessly to the bottom of the tank. Poor old sponge.

"Two points!" said Vernice. Vernice loved basketball more than anything, and was convinced she was going to play for the Havana Ocelotes someday. She hugged Cheo, and that triggered a round of mutual embraces. I squeezed Anuta's slim brown body—she wore just short-shorts and a belly shirt—a little extra, trying to convey some of the special feelings I had for her, but I couldn't tell if any of my emotions got communicated. Girls are hard to figure sometimes.

Williedell ambled slow and easy in his usual way over to the solar-butane fridge and snagged six Cokes. We dropped to the grass under the shade of the big tulip-banyan at the edge of the Greenpatch and sucked down the cold soda greedily. Life was good.

And then our FarmEarth teacher had to show up.

Now, I know you're saying, "Huh? I thought Crispian Tanjuatco was that guy who could hardly wait to turn thirteen so he could play FarmEarth. Isn't that parity?"

Well, that was how I felt before I actually got FarmEarth beginner privileges, and came up against all the rules and restrictions and duties that went with our lowly ranking. True to form, the adults had managed to suck the excitement and fun and thrills out of what should have been sweet as planoforming—at least at the entry level for thirteen-year-olds, who were always getting the dirty end of the control rod.

"Hi, kids! Who's ready to shoulder-surf some pseudomonads?"

The minutely flexing, faintly flickering OLED circuitry of my memtax, powered off my bioelectricity, painted my retinas with the grinning translucent face of Purvis Mumphrey. Past his ghost-like augie-real appearance, I could still see all my friends and their reactions.

Round as a moonpie, framed by wispy blond hair, Mumphrey's face revealed, we all agreed, a deep sadness beneath his bayou bonhomie. His sadness related, in fact, to the assignment before us.

Everyone groaned, and that made our teacher look even sadder.

"Aw, Mr. Mumphrey, do we hafta?" "We're too tired now from our game." "Can't we do it later?"

"Students, please. How will you ever get good enough at FarmEarth to move up to Master level, unless you practice now?"

Master level. That was the lure, the tease, the hook, the far-off pinnacle of freedom and responsibility that we all aspired to. Being in charge of a big mammal, or a whole forest, say. Who wouldn't want that? Acting to help Gaia in her crippled condition, to make up for the shitty way our species had treated the planet, stewarding important things actually large enough to see.

But for now, six months into our novice status, all we had in front of us was riding herd on a zillion hungry bacteria. That was all the adults trusted us to handle. The prospect was about as exciting as watching your navel lint accumulate.

At this moment, Mr. Mumphrey looked about ready to cry. This assignment meant a lot to him.

Our teacher had been born in Louisiana, prior to the Deepwater Horizon blowout. He had been just our age, son of a shrimper, when that drilling rig went down and the big spew filled the Gulf with oil for too many months. Now, twenty years later, we were still cleaning up that mess.

So rather than see our teacher break down and weep, which would have been yotta-yucky, we groaned some more just to show we weren't utterly buying his sales pitch, got into comfortable positions around the shade tree (I wished I could have put my head into Anuta's lap, but I didn't dare), and booted up our FarmEarth apps.

Mr. Mumphrey had access to our feeds, so he could monitor what we did. That just added an extra layer of insult to the way we were treated like babies.

Instantly, we were out of augie overlays and into full virt.

I was point-of-view embedded deep in the dark waters of the Gulf, in the middle of a swarm of oil-eating bacteria, thanks to the audiovideo feed from a host of macro-effectuators that hovered on their impellors, awaiting our orders. The cloud of otherwise invisible bugs around us glowed with fabricated luminescence. Fish swam into and out of the radiance, which was supplemented by spotlights onboard the effectuators.

Many of the fish showed yotta-yucky birth defects.

The scene in my memtax also displayed a bunch of useful supplementary data: our GPS location, thumbnails of other people running FarmEarth in our neighborhood, a window showing a view of the surface above our location, weather reports—common stuff like that. If I wanted to, I could bring up the individual unique ID numbers on the fish, and even for each single bacteria.

I got a hold of the effectuator assigned to me, feeling its controls through my haptic finger bling, and made it swerve at the machine being run by Anuta.

"Hey, Crispy Critter, watch it!" she said with that sexy Bollywood accent of hers.

Mumphs was not pleased. "Mr. Tanjuatco, you will please concentrate on the task at hand. Now, students, last week's Hurricane Norbert churned up a swath of relatively shallow sediment north of our present site, revealing a lode of undigested hydrocarbons. It's up to us to clean them up. Let's drive these hungry bugs to the site."

Williedell and Cheo and I made cowboy whoops, while the girls just clucked their tongues and got busy. Pretty soon, using water jets and shaped sonics aboard the effectuators, we had created a big invisible water bubble full of bugs that we could move at will. We headed north, over anemones and octopi, coral and brittle stars. Things looked pretty good, I had to say, considering all the crap the Gulf had been through. That's what made FarmEarth so rewarding and addictive, seeing how you could improve on these old tragedies.

But herding bugs underwater was hardly high-profile or awesome, no matter how real the resulting upgrades were. It was basically like spinning the composter at your home: a useful duty that stunk.

We soon got the bugs to the site and mooshed them into the tarry glop where they could start remediating.

"Nom, nom, nom," said Mallory. Mallory had the best sense of humor for a girl I had ever seen.

"Nom, nom, nom," I answered back. Then all six of us were nom-nom-noming away, while Mumphs pretended not to find it funny.

But even that joke wore out after a while, and our task of keeping the bugs centered on their meal, rotating fresh stock in to replace sated ones, got so boring I was practically falling asleep.

Eventually, Mumphs said, "Okay, we have a quorum of replacement Farmers lined up, so you can all log out."

I came out of FarmEarth a little disoriented, like people always do, especially when you've been stewarding in a really unusual environment. I didn't know how my brother Benno kept any sense of reality after he spent so much time in so many exotic FarmEarth settings. The familiar Greenpatch itself looked odd to me, like my friends should have been fishes or something, instead of people. I could tell the others were feeling the same way, and so we broke up for the day with some quiet goodbyes.

By the time I got home, to find my fave supper of goat empanadas and cassava-leaf stew laid on by Dad, with both Moms there, too, I had already forgotten how bored and disappointed playing FarmEarth had left me.

But apparently, Cheo had not.

The vertical playsurface at Gecko Guy's Climbzone was made out of MEMs, just like a pair of memtax. To the naked eye, the climbing surface looked like a gray plastic wall studded with permanent handholds and footholds, little grippable irregular nubbins. But the composition of near-nanoscopic addressable scales meant that the wall was instantly and infinitely configurable.

Which is why, halfway up the six-meter climb, I suddenly felt the hold under my right hand, which was supporting all my weight, evaporate, sending me scrabbling wildly for another.

But every square centimeter within my reach was flat.

The floor, though padded, was a long way off, and of course I had no safety line.

So even though I was reluctant to grebnard out, I activated the artificial setae in my gloves and booties, and slammed them against the wall.

One glove and one bootie stuck, slowing me enough to position my second hand and foot. I clung flat to the wall, catching my breath, then began to scuttle like a crab to the nearest projecting holds, the setae making ripping sounds as they pulled away each time.

A few meters to my left, Williedell laughed and called out, "Ha-ha, Crispy had to go gecko!"

"Yeah, like you never did three times last week! Race you to the top!"

Starting to scramble upward as fast as I could, I risked a glance at Anuta to see if she was laughing at my lameness. But she wasn't even looking my way, just hanging in place and gossiping with Mallory and Vernice.

Sometimes I think girls have no real sense of competition.

But then I remember how much attention they pay to their stupid clothes.

Williedell and I reached the top of the wall at roughly the same time, and gave each other a fist bump.

Down on the floor, Cheo hailed us. "Hey, Crispian, almost got you that time, didn't I!"

Cheo's parents owned the Climbzone, and so the five of us got to play for free in the slowest hours—like now, 8:00 AM on a Sunday. Cheo had to work a few hours on the weekends—mainly just handing out gloves and booties and instructing newbies—so he couldn't climb with us. Of course, he had access via his memtax to the wall controls, and had disappeared my handhold on purpose.

I yelled back, "Next time we're eating underwater goo, you're getting a faceful!"

For some reason, my silly remark made Cheo look sober and thoughtful. "Hey, guys, c'mon down! I want to talk about something with you."

The girls must have been paying some attention to our antics, because they responded to Cheo's request and began lowering themselves to the floor. Pretty soon, all five of us were gathered around Cheo.

There were no other paying customers at the moment.

"Let me just close up the place for a few minutes."

Cheo locked the entrance doors and posted a public augie sign saying BACK IN FIFTEEN MINUTES. Then we all went and sat at the snack bar. As usual, Williedell made sure we were all supplied with drinks. We joked that he was going to grow up to be a flight attendant on an Amazonian aerostat—but we didn't make the joke too often, since he flared up sensitive about always instinctively acting the host. (I think he got those hospitality habits because he was the oldest in his semi-dysfunctional family and always taking care of his sibs.)

Cheo looked us up and down and then said, "Who's happy with our sludge-eating FarmEarth assignments? Anyone?"

"Nope." "Not me." "I swear I can taste oil and sardines after every run."

That last from Mallory.

"And you know we've got at least another six months of this kind of drudgery until we ramp up maybe half a level, right?"

Groans all around.

"Well, what would you say if I could get us playing at a higher level right away? Maybe even at Master status!"

Vernice said, "Oh, sure, and how're you gonna do that? I could see if Crispy here maybe said he had a way to bribe his Aunt Zoysia. She's got real enchufe."

"Yeah, well, I know someone with real enchufe too. My brother."

Everyone fell silent. Then Anuta said quietly, "But Cheo, your brother is in prison."

As far as we knew, this was true. Cheo's big brother Adán had gotten five years for subverting FarmEarth. He had misused effectuators to cultivate a few hectares of chiba in the middle of the Pantanal reserve. The charges against him, however, had nothing to do with the actual dope, because of course chiba was legal as chewing gum. But he had misappropriated public resources, avoided excise taxes on his crop, and indirectly caused the death of a colony of protected capybaras by diverting the effectuators that might have been used to save them from some bushmeat poachers. Net punishment: five years hospitality from the federales.

Cheo looked a bit ashamed at his brother's misdeeds. "He's not in prison anymore. He got out a year early. He racked up some good time for helping administer FarmEarth among the jail population. You think we got shitty assignments! How would you like to steward gigundo manure lagoons! Anyhow, he's a free man now, and he's looking for some help with a certain project. In return, the people he takes on get Master status. It may not be strictly aboveboard, but it's really just a kind of shortcut to where we're heading already."

I instantly had my doubts about Adán and his schemes. If only I had listened to my gut, we could have avoided a lot of grief. But I asked, "What is this mysterious project?"

"In jail, Adán hooked up with Los Braceros Últimos. You know about them, right?"

"No. What's their story?"

"They think FarmEarth is being run too conservatively. The planet is still at the tipping point. We need to do bigger things faster. No more tiptoeing around with little fixes. No more being overcautious. Get everybody working on making Gaia completely self-sustaining again. And the Braceros want to free up humanity from being Earth's thermostat and immune system and liver."

"Yeah!" said Williedell, pumping his fist in the air. Mallory and Vernice were nodding their heads in agreement. Anuta looked with calm concern to me, as if to see what I thought.

Four to two.

I didn't want to drag everyone else down. And I *was* pretty sick of the boring, trivial assignments we were limited to in FarmEarth. All I could suddenly picture was all the fun that Benno had every day. My own brother! Ninety percent my own brother anyhow. I felt a wave of jealousy and greed that swept away any doubts. The feelings made me bold enough to take Anuta's hand and say, "Count us in too!"

And after that, it was way too late to back out.


We met Adán in the flesh just once. The seven of us foursquared a rendezvous at the NASDAQ Casino where my Mom Kianna worked. The venue was cheap and handy. Because we weren't adults, we couldn't go out onto the gaming floor, where the Bundled Mortgages Craps Table and Junk Bond Roulette Wheels and all the other games of investa-chance were. But the exclusion was good, because that was where Mom hustled drinks, so we wouldn't bump into her.

But the Casino also featured an all-ages café with live music, and I said, "We shouldn't try to sneak around with this scheme. That'll just attract suspicion. We've hung out at the Casino before, so no one will think twice to see us there."

Everyone instantly agreed, and I felt a glow of pride.

So one Friday night, while we listened to some neo-Baithak Gana by Limekiller and the Manatees (the woman playing dholak was yotta-sexy) and sipped delicious melano-rambutan smoothies, we got the lowdown from Cheo's brother.

Adán resembled Cheo in a brotherly way, except with more muscles, a scraggly mustache, and a bad fashion sense that encouraged a sparkly vest of unicorn hair over a bare chest painted with an e-ink display screen showing cycling porn snippets. Grebnard! Did he imagine this place was some kind of craigslist meat market?

The porn scenes on Adán's chest—soundless, thank god—were very distracting, and I felt embarrassed for the girls—although they really didn't seem too hassled. Now, in hindsight, I figure maybe Adán was trying to unfocus our thinking on purpose.

Luckily the café was fairly dark, and the e-ink display wasn't backlit, so most of the scenes were just squirming blobs that I could ignore while Adán talked.

After he sized us up with some casual chat, he said, "You kids are getting in on the ground floor of something truly great. In the future, you'll be remembered as the greatest generation, the people who had the foresight to take bold moves to bring the planet back from the brink. All this tentative shit FarmEarth authorizes now, half-measures and fallback options and minor tweaks, is gonna take forever to put

Gaia back on her feet. But Los Braceros Últimos is all about kickass rejuvenation treatment, big results fast!"

"What exactly would we have to do?" Anuta asked.

"Just steward some effectuators where and how we tell you. Nothing more than you're doing now at school. You won't necessarily get to know the ultimate goal of your work right from the start—we have to keep some things secret—but when it's over, I can guarantee you'll be mega-stoked."

We all snickered at Adán's archaic slang.

"And what do we get in return?" I said.

Adán practically leered. "FarmEarth Master status, under untraceable proxies, to use however you want—in your spare time."

Williedell said, "I don't know. We'll have to keep up our regular FarmEarth assignments, plus yours. . . When will we ever *have* any spare time?"

Adán shrugged. "Not my problem. If you really want Master status, you'll give up something else and manage to carve out some time. If not—well, I've got plenty of other potential stewards lined up. I'm only doing this as a favor to my little bro after all. . ."

"No, no, we want to sign up!" "Yeah, I'm in!" "Me too!"

Adán smiled. "All right. In the next day or two, you'll find a FarmEarth key in your CitizenSpace. When you use it, you'll get instructions on your assignment. Good luck. I gotta go now."

After Adán left, we all looked at each other a little sheepishly, wondering what we had gotten ourselves into. But then Mallory raised her glass and said, "To the Secret Masters of FarmEarth!"

We clinked rims, sipped, and imagined what we could do with our new powers.


The mystery project the six of us were given was called "Angry Sister," and it proved to be just as boring as our regular FarmEarth tasks.

Three years later, I think this qualifies as some kind of yotta-ironic joke. But none of us found it too funny at the time.

We were tasked with running rugged subterranean effectuators—John Deere molebots—somewhere in the world, carving out a largish tubular tunnel from Point A to Point B. We didn't know where we were, because the GPS feed from the molebots had been deactivated. We guided our cutting route instead by triangulation via encrypted signals from some surface radio beacons and reference to an engineering schematic. The molebots were small and slow: The six of us barely managed to chew up two cubic meters of stone in a three-hour shift. A lot of time was spent ferrying the detritus back to the surface and disposing of it in the nearby anonymous ocean.

The mental strain of stewarding the machines grew very tiresome.

"Why can't these stupid machines run themselves?" Vernice complained over our secure communications channel. "Isn't that why weak AI was invented?"

Cheo answered, "You know that AI is forbidden in FarmEarth. Don't you remember the lesson Mumphs gave us about Detroit?"

"Oh, right."

A flock of macro-effectuators had been set loose demolishing smart-tagged derelict buildings in that city. But then Detroit's Highwaymen motorcycle outlaws, having a grudge against the mayor, had cracked the tags and affixed them to Manoogian Mansion, the official mayoral residence.

Once the pajama-clad mayor and his half-naked shrieking family were removed from their perch on a teetering fragment of Manoogian Mansion roof, it took only twenty-four hours for both houses of Congress to forbid use of AI in FarmEarth.

"Besides," Mallory chimed in, "with nine billion people on the planet, human intelligence is the cheapest commodity."

"And," said Anuta, "having people steward the effectuators encourages responsible behavior, social bonding, repentance, and contrition for mankind's sins."

Williedell made a rude noise at this bit of righteous FarmEarth catechism, and I felt compelled to stand up for Anuta by banging my drill bit into Williedell's machine.

Vernice said, "All right, all right, I give up! We're stuck here, so let's just do it. And you two, quit your pissing contest!"

The six of us went back to moodily chewing up strata.

After a month of this, our little set had begun to unravel a tad. Each day, when our secret shift of moonlighting was over, none of us wanted to hang together. We were all sick of each other, and just wanted to get away to play with our Master status.

And that supreme privilege did indeed almost make up for all the boredom and tedium of the scut work.

Maybe you've played FarmEarth as a Master yourself. (But I bet you didn't have to worry, like us six fakes did, about giving yourself away to the real Masters with some misplaced comment. The paranoia was mild but constant.) If so, you know what I'm talking about.

You've guided a flock of aerostatic effectuators through gaudy polar stratospheric clouds, sequestering CFCs.

You've guarded nesting mama Kemp's Ridley turtles from feral dogs.

You've quarried the Great Pacific Garbage Patch for materials that artists riding ships have turned on the spot into found sculptures that sell for muy plata.

You've draped skyscrapers with vertical farms.

You've channeled freshets into the nearly dead Aral Sea, and restocked those reborn waters.

You've midwifed at the birth of a hundred species of animals: tranked mamas in the wild whose embryos were mispositioned for easy birth, and would have otherwise died.

That last item reminds me of something kinda embarrassing.

Playing FarmEarth with big mammals can be tricky, as I found out one day. They're too much like humans.

I was out in Winnemucca, Nevada, among a herd of wild horses. The FarmEarth assignment I had picked off a duty roster was to provide the herd with its annual encephalomyelitis vaccinations. That always happened in the spring, and now it was time.

My effectuator was a little rolligon that barreled across the desert disguised as tumbleweed. When I got near a horse, I would spring up with my onboard folded legs, grab its mane, give the injection, then drop off quickly.

But after a while, I got bored a little, and so I hung on to this one horse to enjoy the ride. The stallion got real freaky, dashing this way and that, but then it settled down a bit, still galloping. I was having some real thrills.

And that was when my ride encountered a mare.

I hadn't realized that spring was breeding time for the mustangs.

Before I could disengage amidst the excitement and confusion, the stallion was sporting a boner the size of Rhode Island, and was covering the mare.

I noticed now that the mare wore a vaccinating effectuator too.

The haptic feedback, even though it didn't go direct to my crotch, was still having its effect on my own dick. It felt weird and creepy—but too good to give up.

Before I could quite climax in my pants, the titanic horsey sex was over, and the male and female broke apart.

Very cautiously, I pinged the other FarmEarth player. They could always refuse to respond.

Anuta answered.

Back home in my bedroom, my face burned a thousand degrees hot. I was sure hers was burning too. We couldn't even say a word to each other. In another minute, she had broken the communications link.

When we next met in the flesh, we didn't refer to the incident in so many words. But we felt compelled to get away from the others and make out a little.

After a while, by mutual consent, we just sort of dribbled to a stop, without having done much more than snog and grope.

"I guess," said Anuta, "that unless we mean to go all the way, we won't get to where we were the other day."

"Yeah, I suppose. And even then. . ."

She nodded her head in silent agreement. Regular people sex was going to have to be pretty special to live up to the equine sex we had vicariously experienced in FarmEarth.

I felt at that moment that maybe FarmEarth Master privileges were kept away from us kids for a reason.

And a few weeks later, when everything came crashing down, I was certain of it.


My Moms and Dad were all out of the house that fateful late afternoon. I was lying in bed at home, bored and chewing up subsoils with my pals and their effectuators, eking out a conduit which we had been told, by Adán, represented the last few yards of tunnel, in accordance with our schematics, when I felt a poke in my ribs. I disengaged from FarmEarth, coming out of augie space, and saw my dull-faced brother Benno hovering over me.

"Crispian," he said, "do you know where you are?"

"Yeah, sure, I'm eating up hydrocarbons in the Gulf. Nom, nom, nom, good little Crispy Critter."

"Your statement exists in noncompliance with reality."

"Oh, just go away, Benno, and leave me alone."

I dived back into augie space, eager to get this boring "Angry Sister" assignment over with. We were all hoping that the next task Adán gave us would be more glamorous and exciting. We all wanted to feel that we were big, bold cyber-cowboys of the planet, riding Gaia's range, on the lookout for eco-rustlers, repairing broken fences. But of course, even without star-quality assignments, we still had the illicit Master privileges to amuse—and scare—us.

"Hey," said Mallory when I returned to our subterranean workspace, "where'd you go?"

"Yeah," chimed in Vernice, "no slacking off!"

"Oh, it was just my stupid grebnard brother. He wanted to harass me about something."

Cheo said, "That's Benno, right? Isn't his mom Zoysia van Vollenhoven? I heard he's hot stuff in FarmEarth. Inherited all his Mom's chops, plus more. Maybe he had something useful to tell you."

"I doubt it. He's probably just jealous of me now."

Anuta sounded worried. "You don't think he knows anything about what we're doing?"

"No way. I just mean that he sees me playing FarmEarth eagerly all the time now, so he must have some idea I'm enjoying myself, and that pisses him off. He's always been jealous of me."

At that moment, I felt a hand clamp onto my ankle in meatspace, and I was dragged out of bed with a *thump*! I vacated my John Deere and confronted Benno from my humiliating position on the floor.

"What exactly is the matter with you, Ben? Do you have a short circuit in your strap-on brain?"

Benno's normally impassive face showed as much emotion as it ever did, like, say, at Christmas, when he got some grebnard present he had always wanted. The massive agitation amounted to some squinted eyes and trembling lower lip.

"If you do not want to admit your ignorance, Crispian, I will simply tell you where you are. You are at these coordinates: sixty-three degrees, thirty-eight minutes north, and nineteen degrees, three minutes west."

I didn't bother using my memtax to look up that latitude and longitude, because I didn't want to give Benno's accusations any weight. So I just sarcastically asked, "And where exactly is that?"

"You and your crew of naïve miscreants are almost directly

underneath the Katla volcano in Iceland. How far down you are, I have not yet ascertained. But I would imagine that you are quite close to the magma reservoirs, and in imminent danger of tapping them with your tunnel. Other criminal crews spaced all around the volcano are in similar positions. May I remind you that whenever Katla has gone off in the past—the last time was in 1918—it discharged as much toxic substance per second as the combined fluid discharges of the Amazon, Mississippi, Nile, and Yangtze rivers."

Holy shit! Could he be right? My voice quivered a little, even though I tried to control it. "And why would we be in such a place?"

"Because Los Braceros Últimos plan to unleash the Pinatubo Option."

Now I started to *really* get scared.

Every schoolkid from first grade on knew about the Pinatubo Option, named after a famous volcanic incident of the last century. It was a geoengineering scheme of the highest magnitude, intended to flood the atmosphere with ash and other aerosols so as to cut global temperatures by a considerable fraction. Consensus wisdom had always figured it was too risky and uncontrollable a proposition

"I cannot let you and your friends proceed with this. You must tell them to halt immediately."

For a minute, I had almost felt myself on Benno's side. But when he gave me that order in his know-it-all way, I instantly rebelled. All the years of growing up together, with him always the favored one, stuck in my throat.

"Like hell! We're just doing what's good for the planet in the fastest way possible. Los Braceros must have studied everything better than you. You're just a kid like me!"

Benno looked at me calmly with his stony face. "I am a Master Class Steward, and you are not."

"Well, Mr. Master Class Steward, try and stop me!"

I started to climb to my feet when Benno tackled me and knocked me back down!

We began to wrestle. I expected to pin Benno in a couple of seconds. But that wasn't how things went.

I had always believed my brother was a total lardass from all his FarmEarth physical inactivity. How the heck was I supposed to know that he spent two hours every weekend in some kind of martial arts training? Was I in charge of his frigging schedule? We didn't even share the same mito-Mom!

I found myself snaffled up in about half a minute, with Benno clamping both my wrists together behind my back with just one big strong hand.

And then, with the other hand, he rawly popped out my memtax, being none too gentle.

I felt blinded! Awake, yet separated from augie space for more than the short interval it takes to swap in fresh memtax, I couldn't access the world's knowledge, talk to my friends, or even recall what I had had for breakfast that morning.

Next Benno stripped me of my haptic bling. Then he said, "You wait right here."

He left, locking the bedroom door behind him.

I sat on the bed, feeling empty and broken. I couldn't even tell you now how much time passed.

The door opened and in walked Benno, followed by his mito-Mom, Zoysia van Vollenhoven.

Aunt Zoysia always inspired instant guilt in me. Not because of anything she said or did, or any overbearing, sneering attitude, but only because of the way she looked.

Aunt Zoysia was the sexiest female I knew—and not in any kind of bulimic high-fashion designer-label manner either, like those thoroughbreds the Brazilians engineer for the runways of the world. I always thought that if Gaia could have chosen to incarnate herself, she would have looked just like Aunt Zoysia, all overflowing breasts and hips and wild mane of hair, lush wide mouth, proud nose and piercing eyes. She practically radiated exuberant joy and heartiness and sensuality. In her presence, I always got an incipient stiffy, and since she was family—even though she and I shared no genes—the stiffy was instantly accompanied by guilt.

But this was the one time I didn't react in the usual manner, I felt so miserable.

Aunt Zoysia came over and sat on the mattress beside me and hugged me. Even those intimate circumstances did not stir up any horniness.

"Crispian, dear, Benno has described to me the trouble you've gotten into. It's all right, I completely understand. You just wanted to play with the big boys. But now, I think you'll admit, things have gone too far, and must be brought to a screeching halt. Benno?"

"Yes, Mother?"

"Please find a fresh pair of memtax for your brother. We will slave Crispian's to ours, and bring him along for the shutdown of Los Braceros Últimos. It will be highly instructional."

Benno went out and came back with new memtax in their organic blister pack, I wetted them and inserted them, and put on my restored haptic bling. I booted up all my apps, but still found myself a volition-less spectator to the shared augie space feed from Zoysia and Benno.

"All right, son, let's take these sneaky bastards down."

"Ready when you are, Mom."

You know, I thought I was pretty slick with my Master Class privileges, could handle effectuators and the flora and fauna of various biomes pretty deftly. But riding Zoysia's feed, I realized I knew squat.

The first thing she and Benno did was to go into God Mode, with Noclip Option, Maphack, Duping, and Smurfing thrown in. That much I could follow—barely.

But after that, I was just along for the dizzying ride.

Zoysia and Benno took down Los Braceros Últimos like a military sonic cannon disabling a pack of kittens. Racing around the globe in augie space, they undercut all the many plans of the Pinatubo-heads, disabling rogue effectuators and even using legal machines in off-label ways, such as to immobilize people in meatspace. I think the wildest maneuver, though, was when they stampeded a herd of springboks through the remote Windhoek encampment where some of the conspirators were operating from. The eco-agitators never knew what hit them.

The whole roundup lasted barely an hour. I found myself back in my familiar and yet somehow strange-seeming bedroom, actually short of breath and sweaty. Zoysia and brother Benno were unruffled.

"Now, Crispian," said my aunt sweetly, no sign of the moderate outlaw blood she had spilled evident on her perfect teeth or nails, "I hope you've learned that privileges only come to those who have earned them, and know how to use them."

"Yes'm."

"Perhaps if you hung out a little more with your brother, and consented to allow him to mentor you. . ."

I turned to glare at Benno, but his homely, unaggressive expression defused my usual impatience and dislike. Plus, I was frankly a little frightened of him now.

"Yes'm."

"Very well. I think then, in a few years, given the rare initiative and skills you've shown—even though you chose to follow an illegal path with them—you should be quite ready to join us in ensuring that people do not abuse FarmEarth."

And of course, as I've often said to Anuta, wise and sexy Aunt Zoysia predicted everything just right.

Which is why I have to say goodbye now.

Something somewhere on FarmEarth is *wrong*!

# SUNDOWN

Chris Lawson

You never met her, child, so don't drop Riki's name like she would have taken your side. She would have wanted me to go. Sure, she would have cried about it, but she still would have wanted me to go. You need to understand.

Riki owned a small holding of land in a place called the Kaimai Mamaku Forest, not far from here. Her land would have looked huge to you, but to people of the time it was small: just an acre or two of cleared land surrounded by a national park. She ran animals called alpacas. They walked on four legs, had shaggy fur and long, long necks and they spat on people they didn't like. Riki's property was too small to make a living as a working farm, but she liked having animals and she liked the forest.

## First Phase: Sundown

Riki used to get up every day before dawn to feed the alpacas. She was up as usual, tossing hay to her five alpacas, when she noticed the sky was darker than it should be and the morning birdsong was mysteriously quiet. She looked up at the sky and saw her namesake, Matariki:

what we call the Pleiades. They shone brightly, like it was midnight. Riki knew that something was wrong.

The sound of her telephone began to ring from her cottage, and that was wrong, too. Nobody called her that early. She ran to the cottage and answered the phone. It was Max Cammen, and he said to her, "I'm calling from Mauna Loa. You need to go outside and tell me what you see."

So Riki went outside. She told Max about the dark sky, the quiet birds, and the bright stars.

He said, "Tell me about the sun."

"It's not sunrise here for another few minutes."

"Well when the sun comes up, I need you to describe it for me."

She asked, "What's going on, Max?"

"The solar constant just dropped thirty percent in an hour," he said. Max, you see, was a scientist who studied the sun. There were satellites—there still are, actually, but most of them don't work any-more—and Max's job was to read satellites that measured the light put out by the sun.

"That's not possible," said Riki.

"That's what I thought," said Max. At first Max had assumed that the readings were in error. He checked feeds from several sources. The data were consistent. He had even checked the internet for infor-mation from South Pacific nations to see if there were any eyewitness reports, but nothing was coming through. "I need to know exactly what the sun looks like, from an observer who can tell me what I need to know."

So Riki gave him a running commentary.

Looking to the east, over the Pacific Ocean, a faint blue glow pre-ceded the dawn, with a dim umber light nearer the water. Then the sun cracked the horizon. At first it looked no different from any other morning sun. As the sun crept higher, though, Riki could see that it had changed. Before that day, the sun burnt bright and yellow and you could not glance at it for more than a blink without hurting your eyes. What Riki saw was the sun we see today: dull and orange and cold. There was no warmth in the light.

She described the sun to Max, giving him every detail she could think of and answering his questions.

"When is the sun going to come back to normal?" she asked.

"Riki," he said, "the solar constant is still dropping. I don't even know where it's going to bottom out."

At first Riki refused to accept what was happening. There was no physical explanation and there was no precedent.

Max, though, had become aware earlier and had longer to adjust to the new information. He told Riki, as he told many others that day, that we don't know everything about the universe. We can't even identify all the lines in the sun's spectrum. There are physical processes inside the sun that we don't even recognize, let alone understand. Max had seen Fraunhofer lines changing in his satellite data. Something was happening inside the sun.

However absurd it might seem, it was happening. A man about to be gored by a minotaur should not waste his breath complaining to the minotaur about its biological implausibility.

As for the lack of precedent: Max said that we notice big events like exploding stars even though they are very rare, because they can be seen halfway across the universe. In comparison, a G-class star losing some magnitude would be near impossible to notice, even among our stellar neighbors. The night sky is lit with great infernos while our sun is just one ember-fleck that lost a little of its glow.

"So what now?" asked Riki.

"That's the other reason I called you," said Max. "We have work to do."

## Second Phase: The Frost

And so Riki set to work. She loaded up emergency supplies in her four-wheel drive and left the farm. That was the last time she ever saw her land.

She worked in a little research station just east of a city called Hamilton, and that was where she headed. It was around an hour's drive back when the roads were still usable, and she used that time to phone as many workmates as she could. I was one of them.

I remember swearing at her for calling me so early. After Riki talked, I woke up plenty fast. The first thing I did was go out and look for myself. I know it's hard to understand because the sun has always looked like this to you, but for us old-timers the new sun was a giant sign in the sky saying the world is doomed. Which it is and always was, but we used to think we had a few billion years to spare.

We each loaded our cars with whatever vital supplies we had at hand and we met at the lab.

Kiri's experimental work was what saved us. She had created vats full of a special algae that was intended to feed astronauts on long missions to Mars. The algae grew under a wide range of conditions and had been engineered to produce vitamins and essential nutrients. We spooned the algae into as many buckets and tanks as we could load into our cars and utes.

Kiri had another experiment running besides. It was a micro-ecosystem rather than a single organism, and it was designed to test the possibility of terraforming cold planets and moons. These vats we took outside and emptied onto the ground. If the organisms were going to survive, they would have to manage by themselves.

Then we packed up and drove down to Rotorua, where the thermal springs are. As we drove, the air began to chill. Even though it was late summer, a light snow was falling. In open fields and meadows, the ground had frosted over and small streams started to freeze. We had to stop to put chains on our tires.

All the while we drove, we were phoning people we knew with skills we needed: carpenters, plumbers, seamstresses, engineers, mechanics, doctors, nurses, organizers, and told them to meet us at Rotorua.

### Third Phase: The Ice Forest

By the time we got to Rotorua, the trees were dripping with ice.

We set up generators and tents and began building shelters. Belinda Larsson, who used to manage a hospital auxiliary group, ran the storage and distribution of food. Brad Longine, a carpenter who had built movie sets, and a bunch of helpers threw together our first hall, complete with scavenged insulation, in about five hours. It didn't last, of course, but it was enough to keep a lot of people alive long enough to build a better shelter. Ngaire Butler installed a septic system, and Harry Viczak wired up a generator and an electrical system. It was amazing. There was very little I could do. My skill set as a biochemist would become vital, but at that time I could only give little bits of help here and there. Belinda Larsson knocked up a roster for people at a loose end and even those of us who couldn't build a paper hat made ourselves busy helping those who could.

It was an extraordinary time for us. The community you see here now, diminished as it is, was founded in those hours. We worked together, for one and for all, and some of us paid with our lives, and each of us paid in one way or another with grief for distant loves who could not make it here.

That evening, we all went out to watch the sunset. As it went down in the west, the sun gave a feeble red cast over a stand of huge kauri trees that were now encased in rivulets of ice. But there, standing between us and the trees, was our little bit of hope. We stood on the shore of a small pond of liquid water in the surrounding ice. Steam rose from the surface, lit red by the dying light. And the only reason this pond had not frozen over was that its warmth did not rely on the sun. Our savior was the heat inside the earth itself.


### Fourth Phase: The South Pacific Ice Sheet

There are only a few thousand of us left at Rotorua, but at least we've survived the winter. The sun is still cold, but even a cold spring gives us some hope. There are other communities like ours scattered over New Zealand. If it hadn't been for Riki and her algae, none of us would be here at all. Through shortwave radio we know there are other communities out there around the world, mostly clustered around natural geothermal regions like us. We listened to the last days of people who had burrowed down into mines, where the temperature was fine but there was no way to make food. We heard from a distance the dying of the great power stations, which had become refuges for the desperate people all over the world. But even those stations eventually ran out of energy. Coal stations went offline as they ran out of coal to burn. The nuclear stations could have run almost forever on the planet's natural resources, but nobody was able to dig uranium out of the ground anymore. Renewable power stations, hydroelectric, and wave-power came to a halt when lakes and rivers and eventually oceans froze solid. Even wind power, of which there is no natural shortage, collapsed because the generators were not engineered for the new conditions. All that remains is geothermal power and, paradoxically perhaps, a few communities that rely on solar panels for their energy.

It has been a terrible time, but we still live. As do others. Heat is no longer the crucial concern for our survival. The problem now is nutrition. We evolved in a food chain that no longer exists. Most survivors had managed by raiding supermarkets for protein and vitamin supplements, but the raids are becoming riskier as each source becomes exhausted and more distant targets are needed. And vitamins decay. Eventually we need a renewable source of food. That's where we come in. Thanks to Riki, we have that, and we have managed to deliver it to the other communities in New Zealand. Those missions alone cost us dozens of lives, but they were essential not just for the communities we saved, but for ourselves as well.

I went back to the lab at Hamilton last week with the salvage team. There were a few green stains on the rocks around the buildings. We scraped a tiny bit off and tasted it. It may be nutritious, but it tasted damn bitter. Kiri's cold organisms are growing, and one day they might colonize much of the planet. Growth will be slow, however, as the microbes can only reproduce on those few days when the sunlight is warm enough to create a meniscus of liquid water. This green revolution will take far too long to save anyone alive today.

The distant communities will die without Riki's manna—and for those in the northern hemisphere, their first true winter is coming. That is why I must go. We have built a vehicle capable of crossing the Pacific ice sheet on diesel. I won't lie to you. It will be very dangerous, more hazardous by far than our previous missions. We have to cross seven thousand kilometers of untested ice.

We'll take Riki's manna. We'll also take some of her cold organisms and seed the Pacific as we crawl our way to Hawaii. From Hawaii, we'll send missions to the west of the Americas and eastern Asia. If we had tried to live safe in Rotorua, we would have doomed ourselves from the start. Even with the other New Zealand communities, we need as much genetic and intellectual diversity as possible. If the communities across the ocean die, then eventually so will we. Besides, I'd like to meet Max Cammen face to face.

Riki did more than just provide our food. She was one of the people who molded our community, and although she was adamant that we not take unnecessary risks, she would have given her blessing to this.

You know that I love you and that, if I live long enough, I will come back across the ocean one day. I know it's hard for you, and I know you think I would stay if I was your biological parent, but I must join the mission team and you're not old enough to come with me.

Just before Riki died, she told me that the one thing that she regretted was leaving her alpacas behind. At first I thought she meant that they would have been useful for food, or maybe she missed their company. What she really meant, though, was that she still felt awful that she had left them to freeze. She wished that she had taken a few minutes to shoot them. After all that she had done for us, and all that she had been through, it seemed a strange thing for her to lament. After a time, though, I came to understand what she meant. One day I think you will understand too.

# FISH CAKES

Ray Vukcevich

## 1

Sometimes getting out of the house means actually getting up and putting on old clothes and checking and double-checking your things before leaving. Yes, the wallpaper screens are sleeping, the coffee maker is unplugged, the window is locked.

Don't forget to turn off the cats!

Walk out the door and along the long quiet hallway. Hurry down the flights of stairs from the top floor to the ground floor and dip into the shopping mall. Do some random zigzagging through maybe a dozen people buying things they don't want to have delivered.

Get on a bus.

Go to the airport.

Be a hero.

Ilse hadn't actually asked Tyler to come to Phoenix, but he could read between the lines. Her grandmother had died. None of her friends around the world knew what to say. They posted nice comments on her blog and gave her virtual hugs wherever they ran into her.

Tyler didn't know what to say either, but then it hit him that the thing to do was to just show up in the flesh and be there for whatever use she might make of him. It was a huge gesture. Their friends were all abuzz over it.

"Grams left me her recipe and the Secret Ingredient for her fish cakes," Ilse told them.

Tyler knew the story. Ilse's grandmother had liked to think she was famous for her fish cakes. She made them on very special occasions. Ilse had only tasted them a few times, the last time being ten years ago at her wedding. Neither the marriage nor the taste of the fish cakes had lasted long. She remembered the big deal her grandmother had made of them and the way everyone was very polite about it. There was always an undercurrent of resentment toward seniors, but Grams had been able to rise above that. She simply didn't allow Ancestor Resentment to exist in her world. I am no Ancestor, she'd say, I'm alive.

But now she wasn't, and Tyler was both in Phoenix and on his way to Phoenix. The Phoenix he was in was the city in the game *Still Burning*. The Phoenix he was approaching was in Arizona. He supposed both places were really about the people who had stayed behind in Arizona or who had returned after the Great Migration north. The average temperature in the Southwest had only risen about eight degrees in the last fifty years, but that was enough to make a huge, sprawling, water-hungry city in the desert unworkable.

They had met when Tyler first logged into *Still Burning*. Ilse had been an old hand. She had killed him. He had killed her. One thing had led to another. Now three years later, they were best friends—pals, lovers, comrades in arms who rode the deserted freeways on jet skateboards and evaded evil Sheriffs and fought giant Scorpions together.

"You don't have to do this," she said.

"Yes, I do," he said.

Both cities of Phoenix were quite real, but the emphasis changed as Tyler moved from his apartment in Eugene, Oregon, toward the desert city where he would rescue Ilse from grief and heat and carry her away to cool safety.

Eugene was organized around a dozen small shopping malls. Tyler's apartment was on the fourth and top floor of a building on the north side of the Jefferson Street Mall. His window looked out on greenery he seldom visited. He had just over five hundred square feet of space. There was a main room where he slept on a deep foam futon and supplemented his energy allowance on the exercise/generator bike, a kitchenette, a bathroom, and a smaller room where he had installed 3-D monitor wallpaper on all four walls. Motion sensors tracked his slightest movements.

Inside that room, Tyler was like a brain in a skull—his little you, the classic homunculus, never mind that that was not really how brains worked, in his head, the mind, the soul of the bigger, wider, far-ranging Tyler who looked out into worlds from his wallpaper screens and heard things from many speakers and felt them through vibrating devices that were only getting better every day. Taste and smell were still weak, not because they couldn't be done but because they were not really worth it. You could eat things while you were in the room, and you could smell things if you brought things with you to smell, but that was largely a waste of time, he thought, and a mess. It was difficult to switch among smells, so to hell with it. He worked and socialized and goofed off in that room. It was his portal to the rest of the Multiverse. Tyler was a man of his times, a multiperson. Modern people were packages made up of all the people they were in all the worlds they inhabited. Most people worked and shopped near the places they lived. A large percentage seldom left their homes. As the warm seasons got longer and longer, people came to understand that almost everything could be done in electronic worlds. "Meatings" were vaguely distasteful to most. The more you stayed inside, the more the planet liked you.

But now Tyler had impulsively run off into the world of meat which was a very dangerous place since there were few do-overs and no ultimate reset. His mobile devices sucked in comparison to his room of wallpaper screens, but he was trying not to be a jerk about it by grumbling too much. Ilse was doing her best to encourage him as he moved toward her. They were having dinner at her favorite

Mexican restaurant in *Still Burning*. Ilse was obviously trying to distract him from the grim reality of the airport since a Mexican restaurant was prime territory to attract a Sheriff and provoke a running gun battle over your Papers.

Tyler also faced an Airport Official, a woman who seemed amazed anyone would want to go anywhere, much less Arizona. Her desk was a restaurant table on the left side where Ilse sat. Scattered throughout the restaurant were friends from around the planet who had popped in to see what was what with Ilse and Tyler and the Secret Ingredient. Tyler dipped into their comments almost without noticing he was doing it.

Someone thought the Secret Ingredient had to be hoarded cans of edible tuna.

Or even salmon!

"She made me promise to keep making those famous fish cakes," Ilse told everyone.

"Purpose of your trip?" the airport woman asked.

"A death in the family," Tyler said.

"She would have liked it that you considered her family," Ilse said.

The airport woman said, "I don't see that you have family in Arizona."

"In another world," Tyler said.

The airport woman gave him a sharp look like he was trying to make her life more difficult. "You should have entered that fact in your profile. Are you allergic to any medications?"

"Not that I know of," Tyler said. She was asking just to point out his laziness in not maintaining his profile since his entire medical history was right there in front of her.

She quickly finished confirming his travel information. "Walk that way." She pointed at a sign that said SECURITY CHECKPOINT.

A guy dressed as an old prospector, a Lost Dutchman, a few tables over was talking about how Ilse should sell all of that canned fish, pay off the house, and retire with a nice piece of change.

His dinner date thought Tyler was a gold digger. "Why would he move the meat all the way to Arizona if he doesn't expect to strike it rich?"

"Will she wait until he gets there to see what the Secret Ingredient is?"

"She certainly should, since he's killing windmills for her."

Tyler undressed and threw his clothes in a recycle barrel.

People in the Mexican restaurant whistled and hooted and threw money at him. The money winked out in flames or turned to butterflies before it reached him.

Tyler followed painted arrows through another door to a small room where he was met by a man in white and a security guard with an automatic weapon. Tyler assessed the gun critically. He had used such a weapon on giant bugs more than once.

The man in white gave him a very thorough body search. When he got to the top he made an exasperated sound and asked, "Didn't you read all the instructions?"

"What?"

"Remove your augs," the man said.

Tyler's mobile consisted of molded ear buds with a thin wire running from ear to ear behind his head. Images were projected to contact lenses. He hadn't realized that he would have to remove them. "You can't mean I'll be cut off for the trip."

"Of course you'll be cut off," the man said. "Hurry up, we haven't got all day."

Maybe he should just go home. This grand gesture was stupid. What a buffoon he was. Ilse could work out her grief on her own. What could he do for her anyway? Oh, step up and grab the bull by the balls, you pussy, this is where the sheep and the goats eat with different forks, where the metal meets the road or the pedal or whatever, where you could be a naked man or a mouse with automatic weapons and a jet skateboard.

Ilse smiled at him and turned her eyes down and busied herself with her tacos.

The Princess, the Dragon, the Rescue.

Everyone was watching. What would Sir Tyler do now? Was he all talk? When a real obstacle arose did he simply fold?

"Bye, Ilse," he said.

He entered the sequence to clear local memory and kill his cloud connection, and then pulled the mobile out of his ears and from behind his head and popped the contacts.

A single sharp and chilly aspect of the Multiverse seized him as if he'd been tossed into a cell and someone had slammed the door behind him.

"See you soon," he said, a pointless follow up remark since she was now truly more than a thousand miles away.

He was a naked man in this one place at this one time. The world was so quiet! Death must be like this, he thought. One place, one time, just you, and then nothing at all.

The airport guy held out his hand for Tyler's mobile equipment and said, "You can go back and start over, pay to ship this, probably miss your flight. Or you can recycle and replace at your destination."

Tyler knew if he didn't go now, he probably never would. "Recycle," he said.

The man took his stuff. "Get up on the gurney."

Tyler climbed up and stretched out on the gurney. The man shackled his left ankle to a bar at the bottom end.

"You'll feel a small poke." He gave Tyler a shot in his upper arm almost before he finished the sentence.

The guard stepped forward and walked along ahead of them as the man pushed Tyler toward the loading dock. Tyler could feel the sedative dragging him down. So much for the hope of getting a day's work done on the way to Phoenix.

They slid his gurney sideways into a slot with a metallic bang, leaving the legs and wheels behind. There was the whir and grind of gears, and he felt himself move up and into a tight dark space. Making room for the next passenger to be slid in under him, he realized. He could smell metal and oil and himself. He closed his eyes and ran for the light at the end of the tunnel.

## 2

**Her Grandmother's Fish Cakes**

> 3 cups instant mashed potatoes
> 1 teaspoon salt
> 3 drops seafood flavor
> As much of the Secret Ingredient as the occasion merits
>
> Prepare the potatoes as per the instructions on the box.
> Mix in salt, seafood flavor, and the Secret Ingredient.
> Form as many little cakes as possible and fry them in a neutral oil.

At the other end, Tyler was unshackled, given a thin paper robe and temp ID, and pointed toward the exit of the secure area of Phoenix Sky Harbor Airport. He thought Ilse would be there when he came out into the public spaces, but he didn't see her. She might be somewhere in the crowd, but he figured she'd be watching for him if she had really come to meet him—maybe bouncing up and down and waving to get his attention. Most of the people not in paper robes wore shorts and T-shirts and sandals. Even at only a fifth of its pre-migration size, Phoenix was much bigger than Eugene. Most of the many terminals had been closed down, but what was left was a little overwhelming. Dim hallways extended like spokes from the hub of a wheel. Long narrow black treadmills, moving sidewalks, he thought, ran in double rows down the hallways. When he got closer, he discovered the sidewalks weren't actually moving.

He spotted a purple and green glow to one side of the huge room and set off in that direction guessing correctly that it was a bank of vending machines.

He was in a strange city wearing nothing but a paper robe that didn't even reach his knees, and his feet were bare, but nonetheless, his first priority was to replace his mobile augs and get back to the real worlds.

He keyed in his financial info and put his face into the machine that would fit his new contacts. He took several minutes pushing buttons for the features he wanted. Nothing fancy since he'd probably recycle them on the way home.

He switched on and was swept back into the Multiverse.

"Hi there," Ilse said. "Welcome to Phoenix."

Tyler leaped to his left arming his shields and activating his jet skateboard. He landed fully locked and loaded and made a quick circle scanning for incoming enemies to shoot.

"No, no!" she laughed. "I mean welcome to Phoenix, Arizona."

She'd been teasing him with the phrase you always heard when you first came into the Phoenix of *Still Burning*. She had come to meet him, after all, but not in the flesh. Who could blame her?

She was wearing her tall, slender, curvy look with the shocking cloud of red hair and sparkling green eyes. Long black boots with high heels. Short skirt. Crossed bandoliers of bullets.

"Hi," he said. "It's wonderful to see you again."

"You should dress."

He would still be projecting the default of his new augs which was Any Man. He switched on his rugged desert warrior look and moved to a pants machine for light canvas shorts. Then he got a white T-shirt and flip-flops.

"You better get a hat, too," Ilse said.

"An actual hat? Cool."

She pointed at a machine that said "Punctuation Caps."

"All the rage."

Tyler bought a white cap with a red question mark for a logo.

"And a water bottle!" she said.

He bought a reusable bottle of water with the "full" option and stepped behind the changing screen and got dressed.

Sky Harbor was not so dreary with the overlays Ilse projected for him. There were big yellow flowers on the walls. The travelers now wore business suits and bright tourist outfits. There was music.

When they came out of the terminal, the famous heat banged down on Tyler like falling rocks. "Good god!" he yelled.

"Oh, come on. Don't be such a baby. We only just had our first one hundred degrees day. Just wait until April!"

Tyler brought up a thermometer and saw that it was a hundred and nine.

"In a few months you wouldn't be able to be out here at all," Ilse said. "Still people come in the summertime. Heat tourists. Who can understand them?"

When the bus came, Tyler discovered the fare got higher and higher as the temperature rose and more cooling was needed to make the interior habitable. Habitable, but nothing more, he thought. His temperature readout told him it was an even hundred degrees inside the bus. And it was more crowded than he had ever seen a bus be. It was a little past two in the afternoon. Where were all the people going? He was lucky to find two empty seats together so Ilse could appear to sit beside him. She looked pretty cool and collected.

He minimized his overlays and saw that some of this Phoenix was familiar to him. It was the foundation that *Still Burning* had been based on. The city was very flat with clusters of tall buildings scattered about. There were no jet skateboarders on deserted freeways. The freeways were not, in fact, deserted. There were many buses and cargo vehicles, but more amazing there were quite a few cars in the dedicated auto lane. There were cars in Eugene, but they were strictly status symbols and mostly only brought out for the parade during the annual Eugene Day. Here people seemed to be using them to move the meat around.

"Almost there!" Ilse said at every stop.

They were on the bus for a long time, and Tyler was glad to have his water bottle.

Finally, she said, "This is it!"

He got off the bus.

"Now it's a short ride up to my place." She led him to a bank of bicycles that you could rent for a few dollars.

"I'm afraid I don't know how to ride a bicycle," Tyler said.

"What?" Ilse sounded astonished. "You're from Oregon!"

He worked at home. He shopped in the mall downstairs. Where in the world would he go on a bicycle?

"Okay, okay," she said. "We'll walk."

He followed her down a street that snaked around houses the color of dried mud with orange tile roofs. They all had solar panels. They all seemed very quiet and dark.

There were quite a few of the big saguaro cacti scattered about like giants holding up their hands at a bank robbery. "Really more green than I expected," he said.

"All stuff that doesn't need to be watered." She went on to point out ocotillo cacti and prickly pear with pale purple fruit.

At last they came to Ilse's house, and she disappeared from his side before he reached the door.

It was much cooler under the extension of the roof. The door itself was made of heavy wire screen, and he could see a shadowy figure approaching from the dim interior.

Then she opened the door and there she was smiling at him—a woman in her early fifties with short brown hair and pale blue eyes. She wore a loose smock with no sleeves. It was bright blue with green leaves. No shoes. Her toenails were pink. She was very tan and what was the word? Weathered, maybe. She was around five-five.

"Tyler," she said and put out her hands, and he took them. Her hands were soft and warm and a little moist. She pulled at him. "Come in! Come in!"

He wanted to give her a big hug, but he felt suddenly shy with her which was silly after all they had been through together. She let go of his hands and latched the screen door behind him.

"More to drink first," she said.

She took him to the kitchen and poured him a glass of cool tea.

"Let me show you the house."

The small house she had shared with her grandmother was full of shadows and dim spaces. There was a front room, a kitchen, a bathroom, and two bedrooms. It was all very open and there was always a breeze coming from somewhere. It was eighty-five degrees inside, he saw, and after the extreme heat outside, it felt pretty comfortable.

Ilse's room reminded him of his own except hers had only three walls of screens. The fourth wall was open to a shady area outside.

"My garden," she said. "I don't have to close this room down and run the cooler until almost May."

He had imagined she would be struggling in sweltering misery and eager for him to rescue her and take her away, but she seemed to be trying to impress him with how well she lived.

"I didn't really wait to see what the Secret Ingredient was until you got here," she admitted.

"I wouldn't have expected it," he said, but he had sort of expected it. All their friends certainly expected her not to look until he got to Phoenix. Thinking of their friends made him realize that they were alone. She must be closing out the others. She must want him all to herself.

"But I do think your coming all this way is a special occasion that demands Grams's fish cakes," she said.

She led him back to the kitchen and told him to take a seat. There was a dark wooden box on the table. It was about the size of a shoebox, and the lid was nicely carved with angels playing harps and horns.

Ilse put a pot of water on to boil and said, "Step one. Prepare instant mashed potatoes as per instructions on the box."

She poured instant mashed potatoes into a measuring cup and then stood there looking down at the pot of water on the stove. Would she stand there until it boiled?

No. She turned away and came over to the table and put a clear glass mixing bowl, a teaspoon, and the recipe down next to the carved box. Then she sat down across from Tyler.

"One teaspoon salt," she said. "And three drops of seafood flavor."

"Is that the Secret Ingredient?" Tyler asked.

"Nope," she said.

"What is seafood flavor, anyway?"

"No idea." She pulled the wooden box across the table and opened it.

She took out an old letter and put it to one side. She took out a string of black pearls and held them up to the light.

"Pretty," Tyler said.

She put the pearls down on the letter and took out an old coin purse and opened it and handed coins to him one at a time—a quarter from 1923, a half-dollar from 1960, a dime from 2006, and a penny from 1959.

"You'll have to look them up," Tyler said.

"Just junk. Horrible condition. But I will look them up anyway."

She put a small bright yellow can down on the table and closed the box. "This is it. The Secret Ingredient."

He waited a moment then picked up the can.

*New!*

*Tropical Flakes!*

*Net weight 1.0 oz.*

He turned the can around and read the label on the back.

"You do realize 'fish food' is not like 'cheese food?'" he asked.

"Of course I do." She took the can from him. "It's food for fish."

She opened the can and smelled what was inside. "The recipe says to use 'as much of the Secret Ingredient as the Occasion merits.' So, how much do you suppose this occasion merits?"

She held out the can for him to smell. He leaned forward and saw that there was a little less than half left. The Tropical Flakes were orange and several shades of green. They smelled like he imagined fish would smell or maybe fishy water.

She put the can down on the table and got up and walked back to the stove. She took the pot off the burner and dumped the instant mashed potatoes into it. But then she put the pot on the counter and came back to the table and sat down again.

"There's this famous video," she said, "of a guy eating bluefin tuna sushi. Do you know it?"

"I don't think so," Tyler said.

"Probably from a cooking or travel show. Close-up of the chef cutting a thin slice of pink fish and putting it on a wad of rice and sliding it in front of this bald guy in a flowery shirt. He picks it up and puts the whole thing in his mouth. And the look on his face! You'd think he died and gone to heaven. Then he talked about how you needed to get the fish in touch with the roof of your mouth to really appreciate it. Then he had another slice!"

"Ancestors," Tyler muttered. "He could have left a slice or two for us. They didn't have to use up every last good thing they had."

"It wasn't Grams's fault," Ilse said. "She could have run off during the Great Migration but she stayed here and helped make the place livable for the rest of us."

"She must have been amazing," he said.

"She was." She lifted the can of Tropical Flakes again. "But her fish cakes were awful, if you want the truth."

She picked up the teaspoon and dipped it into the can. Her hand shook a little and a few flakes fell to the table. She put the spoon in her mouth and closed her lips around it.

Good? Bad? Tyler couldn't tell from her expression. He was sure she was not on her way to heaven.

She pulled the spoon out of her mouth and dipped it back into the can and held it out to him.

He hesitated a moment then leaned forward and opened his mouth, and she fed him the spoonful of tropical flakes.

The sea, the sea.

He pushed the flakes against the roof of his mouth like the guy with his sushi.

A little repulsive really. The flakes clung to the back of his teeth and he had some trouble getting them off with his tongue.

Ilse ate another spoonful and then fed him one.

"I'm done with the fish cakes," she said.

By the time they finished the tropical flakes, she looked a little green. He was not feeling so hot himself.

"Will the children hate us now?" she asked. "The way we sat here and polished off the Secret Ingredient?"

"You're not coming back to Oregon with me, are you?"

"No," she said, "but thanks for almost asking."

# TRUE NORTH

M. J. Locke

On the last day of March 2099, on the rocky, parched slopes west of
Rexford, Montana, Lewis Behrend Jessen met Patricia de la Montaña
Vargas.

Jessen was sixty-seven years old. Everybody who mattered called
him Bear. He had been American by birth, back when that sort of
thing mattered, and Danish by ancestry. He was so pale his skin had
peeled and burned in successive layers over the years, always revealing deeper, ruddier ones. Each layer also added freckles and age spots,
too, till now he looked like a ruined patchwork man. His eyes were
blue, like a cloudless sky. His hair, when he'd had any, had been red
as rubies. His belly, when he'd had one, had hung over his big sterling
silver horseshoe belt buckle. (Tacky? Damn straight. It had belonged
to his father, as had the Colt .45 revolver with ivory grips. The Brown-
ing 9mm, and the shotgun for scaring away the megafauna, he had
bought for himself.)

Bear was seven feet tall, broad-shouldered and big-boned. These
days he looked more like a giant human walking-stick, ninety percent
bones and one hundred percent wrinkles. He lived in an aging ranch-
style house he and Orla had built in Rexford back when they moved
up here. That was in the late sixties, maybe twenty years before the
collapse was officially acknowledged, but by then everybody who had
a lick of sense had seen it coming.

Rexford was just south of the Canadian border. A lot of people had moved through over the years, trying to make it across into Canada. Bear and Orla had talked about trying for it themselves. But at first they thought they wouldn't need to, this far north, and later it just seemed as if it were too late to try.

Bear had just celebrated his forty-second anniversary the night before, over a trout he had caught that very evening, at a fire he built in his back lot, on the banks of the stream. Maybe it had been the fire that attracted the girl.

It was a miracle anyway that that seasonal wash could house a living fish, choked as it was with algae and weeds. The fish was certainly an endangered species. But hell; who wasn't, these days?

Here's a curious thing: when Bear cut the fish's belly open he found an aluminum ring, a soda can pop-top. They didn't make soda cans anymore—never mind the kind of pop-tops you can wear. Bear washed the blood off the ring in the stream, kissed it, and put it on his pinkie finger. As he did so he had to shake his head at his foolishness. Orla would have been amused. They had had to barter the real ring away long ago, along with Orla's. The reason had seemed important at the time, and it wasn't as if their marriage had suffered for want of a wedding band or two. Now that she was dead he rather wished he hadn't.

With her gone, truth to tell, Bear didn't mind much whether he lived or died. He'd had his share of living, and was ready to be done with it all.

Orla had not approved of his thoughts of suicide.

"Why?" he had asked. Seeing her on her deathbed (it had been late last fall; lung cancer, Orla believed, though they weren't sure - anyway, it didn't matter, since they had no way to treat it), he had made up his mind. Bear did not want to outlive his wife. He had gotten out his Colt .45 and thumbed cartridges into the cylinder, one by one. "I figure it's better to go out together. Don't you?"

She had wheezed, "Lewis. . ." A pause for air. "Behrend Jessen. Put that. . . thing away." She was glaring at him as fierce as the day they'd wed. "Don't you. . . *fucking* dare."

He eyed the gun with a sigh. Where did she get the energy to pick a fight at a time like this? Damned woman. "Now, Orla, for cry-eye—"

She clutched her mother's blue cross-stitched coverlet that she loved so much. "Don't. . . bullshit me, fool. Put it. . . away."

He started to argue; she coughed up blood. You can't trump bloody gobbets for settling an argument. He put the gun away, intending to get it out later. He was baffled by her obstinacy.

The next night, he held her hand and said again, "Why not?"

She did not answer right away, and he thought maybe that was it, that she was gone. But she squeezed the words out between inhalations. "There's. . . a. . . reason."

He did not reply right away. He felt her implacable gaze, felt her grip on his hand.

"Promise. . . me."

He scowled. "Orla Jessen, you have never believed in God. If you are going to tell me the Lord Almighty has a plan for me, I swear I'll put a bullet in my brain right this minute."

"Reason," she said again. It was quite literally a gasp. And it was her last word. Perhaps an hour later, perhaps two, her breathing ceased.

When he thought about it afterward he figured Orla would have been glad that was her last word. She was an atheist from way back. The reason she spoke of would be logical. Not metaphysical.

Bear still believed in the Protestant God of his youth (he'd been brought up Methodist), but it was not a worshipful relationship. Oh my, no. He was furious with God, who had promised salvation and had delivered hell on earth. Refugees passing through had spoken of the die-offs. Faithful or no, people were dying—had died—by the billions. By the *billions*. God was a big fat eternal asshole, and Bear had stopped caring long before who heard him say so. His pastor,

Desmond Marcus, had kicked him out of the church, ten years back, and had said some hurtful things about Orla. That was hard; they had been close friends. Des and Gloria had moved on a few years ago, headed to Seattle, Bear had heard, to apply for entry there, or perhaps north to Victoria, where the summers were still tolerable.

He fingered his Colt, thinking about Des's opinion of suicide. There had been waves of them over the years, and Des had been quite vocal about how we mustn't succumb to despair. The man knew how to inspire you, for sure. How to keep you hanging onto hope. But in the end, Des had given up, too, in his own way. Bear had seen it in his eyes.

*This isn't despair*, Bear thought. *I'm just done, is all. I'm done.*

Bear could have gone ahead and offed himself then, as Orla lay cooling in their bed. But in the face of her earlier implacability, it seemed too violent. Disrespectful. And after Bear had buried her he lost whatever spark of initiative he had had. That had been four months ago, now.

Truth was, Orla was wrong. There was simply no reason he was still living, when so many had died. Billions meant *thousands of millions*. A hundred New Yorks. Loads of Londons, a plethora of Parises, trainloads of Tokyos, whole basketsful of Beijings, Torontos, Jakartas, Mumbais. If you stacked the bodies, Orla had told him once, they'd reach to the moon and back *four times over*. (She'd always been the one with the head for figures.) All gone. In two short generations human civilization had collapsed under its own weight, the way Ponzi schemes do. Now even the greatest cities were in their death throes. The people out in the big empty middle of the U.S. had been on their own for decades. Last he heard, scientists were saying human population would stabilize at somewhere under a hundred million, worldwide, once the resource wars and genocides died down: most of them within the Arctic and Antarctic circles.

A hundred million starving, miserable people. Of every hundred people, ninety-nine dead, within a hundred years of humanity's apex.

Might as well call it extinction and be done with it. No reason *he* should still be hanging around.

Bear fingered the ring. He felt as though he had made his wife a promise, though he had never spoken the words. *Happy goddamn anniversary.*

Orla would only have laughed and kissed him. Eventually, he figured, he'd either get over being mad at her for dying first, or die too, and end the argument that way.

Thanks to the fish with the ring in its belly, hunger didn't wake him early the next morning. And that changed everything.

The morning after the fish dinner he awoke to a cool breeze blowing through the window. The sun was up. The window screen was gone, and a girl was exiting Orla's closet. Bear lay still and observed her through slitted eyes. She had dark, tangled, dirty hair that went down well past her skinny butt. She had pulled on some clothes of Orla's: a shirt, a pair of jeans. They hung off her. She was struggling into a pair of Orla's walking shoes, biting her lip and grimacing. Bear could see the crusted sores on her feet from where he lay. She couldn't have been more than thirteen years old.

Next she moved over to his chest of drawers, not three feet away from the bed. He breathed through his mouth, shallow and quiet.

She must have climbed the dead aspen. He had left the window open to let the breezes in. These days you didn't say no to a cool breeze, not even at night in winter. It was a screened, second-story window on the slope of a steep hill, and the aspen was dead: brittle and as skinny as she was. A difficult climb. Anyone bigger wouldn't have been able to pull it off.

He was not sure why he had awakened. She was quiet as a whisper as she emptied his drawers and pocketed the few items she seemed to find useful. It may have been the stink: she reeked of feces and body odor.

He spoke finally. "You won't find much in there, I'm afraid."

She spun to face him. She had a petite face with big eyes as dark and clear as obsidian. Sunlight glinted on the knife blade in her hand. It was a long blade, a serrated one. A fine hunting knife. It would gut him as easily as he had gutted that trout last night.

"Stay where you are," she said. She stood just beyond arm's length. From her accent he could tell her native language was Spanish. Orla would have known what country she was from. She had been in Central America back in the sixties. *Medecins sans Frontieres.* But the girl's English was sharp and clear as broken glass. "Try anything and I'll kill you."

"Fair enough."

A tense silence ensued. He felt a twinge—it wouldn't be breaking his promise to Orla if someone else did him in. But his intruder, she was just a kid. She did not want to harm him, or she would have killed him at the outset. He didn't want to make a murderer out of her for his own convenience. Besides, she might muff it, and sepsis was an awful, lingering way to go.

"I have provisions downstairs," he said. "I'll show you where I keep them. You look like you could use some, young lady."

She eyed him suspiciously, but the left corner of her mouth twitched at the "young lady." After another long pause, she shrugged. "All right. Get up. Don't get cute."

He swung his legs out of bed and stood. His joints were always stiff in the mornings.

She stared as he stood, and stepped back. "*Usted es un gigante!*" He remembered a little of his college Spanish: *You are a. . .* what? Oh. Of course. *A giant.*

It was true. Even in his current state he could easily have overpowered her. But he did not. He felt a deep pity. A dreadful fate, to be alive so young at the end of the world.

He led her into the kitchen and showed her the hidden door in his pantry. It led down into the cellar. As she stepped over the threshold and headed down the complaining stairs, he shone his flashlight in across the shelves onto Orla's hand-labeled Mason jars.

The entire underside of their ranch house was filled with food. Jars of pickled turnips, potatoes, peppers, carrots, green tomatoes, and a hundred or more different kinds of jams. Sealed carboys, filled with beans, rice, and corn.

It'd been at least two decades since they had had access to groceries shipped from elsewhere, and maybe twelve years since the local open-air market that replaced the grocery store petered out. Since then, he and Orla had lived off wild game, water hand-pumped from their private well, and supplies they had stored up before the collapse. Orla had spent years preparing. All the years of their marriage. She had dedicated herself to their survival—even before it was clear to most that collapse was imminent; well after everyone else had died or moved on. Cured hams and chickens and turkeys hung from the rafters, and a rack held jalapeño jerked beef. Bear figured he had a good three or four years' supplies left, if he continued the way he had. After that it was the bullet, dammit, whether Orla liked it or not.

What caught the girl's eye, he could tell, was the medical supplies. Orla had been an ER doctor till the town had shut down ten years back, and had stocked up on bandages, antibiotics, medicines, and whatnot. All kinds of whatnot. There were vitamins and supplements, cold remedies, and the like. Most of these were post-date by now. After the last and biggest Deflation in '84, even the mercy shipments had stopped coming in.

The girl stood on the bottom step, silhouetted by the light he shone—fists tight little balls, shoulders stiff. Then she turned and darted up the stairs, past him into the kitchen, where she pulled the tablecloth off the table. One of Orla's handmade vases shattered on the floor. Bear looked at it. His vision went red. He roared—grabbed the girl's arm, wrenching it—yanked her off her feet. Her eyes went wide.

"You little shit!" he yelled in her face.

Then he felt the sharp bite of her knife blade in his gut and dropped her. She backed away, knife at the ready, eyes wide, breathing fast. Mentally, he revised her age upward. She was more like eighteen. He lifted his torn, bloodied shirt and checked his belly. Just a scratch. The folds of skin there had protected him.

He ignored the girl—maybe he'd get lucky and she'd slit his throat while his back was turned—and knelt to pick up the pieces of broken vase. These he carried gingerly into the study. He laid the pieces out on the hearth. *Maybe I can glue them back together.* But pain squeezed at his heart and he knew he never would. He just didn't have it in him.

He heard the girl clattering around, and after a few moments he sensed her watching him. He turned. She stood in the kitchen doorway. Orla's tablecloth was slung over her shoulder like a hobo bag. Medical supplies and jars and bags of food stuck out between the hastily tied knots. The burden of living had never been heavier on his shoulders than it was in that instant.

"Sorry," she said finally.

Bear passed a hand over his eyes. "Just go."

She stood there silent for another moment. When he looked back next she was gone.

Two mornings later when he went downstairs, he found the vase glued back together, its cracks all but invisible. It sat on the kitchen table next to his now-empty, second-to-last bottle of Super-Glue, with the now-slightly-soiled tablecloth beneath it.

That week fire season started. The winds came up and lightning storms rolled across the sky. Smoke hung in the air. It clung to the low areas and snaked through the valley below his house. Charred wood smell stank up Bear's clothes and hair and made his eyes burn. Bear spent the two days hiking through the back twenty, scanning the horizons from every angle, checking for fires. From the ridge that stretched along the southern edge of his property, he saw what he had been dreading. A line of smoke and flame snaked along the ridge next door.

He trudged back home. His house perched on a ridge that adjoined the one now aflame, the ridge about a mile or two to the west. Uncleared brush and dying trees filled the valley between the two. If the wind got much stronger, it would carry sparks into the valley and up toward his ridge. Time to chop down the last two trees in range of the house: the dead aspen next to his bedroom window and the big ponderosa by the front porch.

The aspen he didn't care about. But the ponderosa. . . Orla had loved that damn pine, with its widespread branches and needles green and vibrant; its slats of rust-colored bark and the black vertical fissures that separated them.

"She'll outlast both of us," Orla had told Bear once. She called the tree Old Lady, or Old Woman Pine. When it dropped its cones on their roof, they would bounce down on the shingles with a frightful clatter, and drop around the eaves onto a cushion of pine needles so soft you never heard them land. Orla would look up from whatever it was she was doing and smile. "Old Lady's heard from."

He looked up through the branches that morning. "Nothing lasts," he said.

First he brought down the aspen. He used a comealong and an axe. Once he had it down, he was dirty and sweating, and doused himself in the icy well water. Then he chopped the wood into sections, dragged it over near the workshop, and cut it down into firewood. Next day it was time to deal with the ponderosa. He got out his axe and his comealong. He went so far as to lift the axe and give the old lady a whack. The bark shattered where the blade struck, and the wet white living wood beneath splintered. He rested the bit of the blade against the tree's root, rubbed his face, and looked up through the branches.

He couldn't do it. Old Lady Pine had been too much a part of their lives, for too many years. He ran his hand over the gouge he'd made. *If this tree is to be the death of me, so be it.* He put his tools away.

That night Bear woke to find his bedroom on fire. Flames crawled in through the window and across the ceiling. Acrid smoke clawed his sinuses and lungs.

He rolled onto the floor, choking and gagging. Somehow he made it down the stairs. No conscious thought was involved. He returned to himself on the lawn in front of his home, watching flames devour his home. Painful welts bubbled up along his left forearm but he had no memory of how he had gotten them.

The winds were up. The ponderosa whipped to and fro in the grip of the flames devouring it. The roof had already started to cave in. Orange light shone from the upper-story windows. Even from here, the heat scorched his face and the light hurt his eyes. Through the open front door he saw that the staircase banister was alight. And now flames attacked the ceiling beams in the living room.

He looked at the blazing door frame and a powerful urge gripped him. *I'm going to perdition anyway, for loving Orla more than I ever loved God.* It was as good an end as any.

But in that instant before action followed thought, a yank on his arm threw him off balance. Something—someone—was dragging him away from the flames. The young woman who had broken in before pulled at him now.

"Come on!" she yelled above the noise. "*Venga!* We have to go!"

He looked down at her. She was covered in soot and her gaze was wild with fear.

He looked back at the house. *Orla. Orla.*

Then he saw a troupe of children at the far edge of the lawn. They were skinny as this young woman was, dirty and stiff with terror. The fire hadn't jumped to that copse where they stood, but soon it would. Old Woman Pine was cracking—splitting—about to go down. When it did, it would tip down the hill toward them. He couldn't run into a fire and leave them with that memory. God knew what else they had already seen. With a grunt of anguish, he ran after the young woman, amid falling branches and billowing smoke. He snatched up a couple of the littlest ones. So did the young woman. The rest fell in around them. Down the hill they went.

They ran far and hard, following the muddy creek. He noticed a youth—the next oldest after the young woman. He carried a younger boy on his back. Others carried toddlers. He glimpsed an infant. Babies saving babies. The young woman yelled at them, dragged them back to their feet when they stumbled, forced them on, away from the burning trees. At least three times she circled back and returned with someone who had stumbled or fallen behind.

They found a mine-tailing pile against a hillside. It was poisoned—lifeless. No brush to betray them by catching fire while they slept. They all huddled on the rocky ground in the predawn chill. Even the littlest ones were too spent to weep.

The fire moved on around them. Bear eventually dozed.


When he awoke, he found himself surrounded by a silent, ragged army of sleeping children. He sat up in the predawn gray, gazing around in wonder. They ranged in age from infants to preteens. Most of them looked to be maybe between five and eight years old. There must have been twenty or so: girls and boys, about evenly mixed, best he could tell. Some of the older ones had weapons: knives, clubs, sticks. All had sticklike arms and legs; several had distended bellies, including the one infant, who hung limp in the arms of one of the five-year-olds, clearly too weak to cry.

It was a boy—he had no diaper—and lay limp in a foul, brown-stained blanket in the lap of one of the younger girls. The corners of his eyes crawled with flies.

The young woman soon came into view dragging a heap wrapped

in a filthy blanket. Bear recognized the blanket: it had come from the house. She was covered in soot and had swaddled her head in an old torn T-shirt. She had a military-issue rifle on her shoulder. She dumped the bundle at the feet of the youth, and gave him a good, hard shove with her foot.

"Tomás," she said. Her tone was sharp. "Get them up."

The boy groaned, gave her a sullen look, and sat up rubbing his arm. "All right."

"Get them fed. Get Vanessa to help you. I need everyone to meet me at this man's house *tan rápido que posible. Bueno?*" As quickly as possible. The boy blinked and nodded. He shook the girl next to her, who stirred. They two began waking the others.

"You." The young woman gestured at Bear. "Come with me."

He raised his eyebrows and leaned his elbows on his knees. "Try again," he said.

She grimaced. He spotted impatience and regret. "I need your help," she said. "We need supplies. Your—*¿como se dice?—su bodega.*" She wiped at her eyes and he could see her exhaustion. "I'm sorry. Usually my English is better. Under your house—the food. *La medicina.* It is still there. We need it. The children need it." A pause. "Please."

He stood. He couldn't help it; he towered over her. She stepped back and half-raised her rifle. But Bear simply extended his hand. "Lewis Behrend Jessen. Pleased to meet you."

She looked at his hand as if she had forgotten what the gesture meant. Then she blinked, lowered her weapon, and took his hand in a brief, strong grip. "Patricia de la Montaña Vargas," she replied. "Call me Patty."

"I'm Bear."

While they hiked back along the stream bed, he asked, "Where are you from?"

"Mexico City. My parents were *profesores.* Professors. At the university."

She said nothing else. He didn"t pry, but clearly there was a lot more to tell. How had she made it so far, across the thousands of war-torn miles between there and here? Where did the children come from? Where were they all headed? And why?

As they came up over the rise, he saw the smoking ruins of his home. The fires appeared to have burned themselves out. The air was still and cool.

Old Lady Pine rose above the rubble: a blackened, ruined post. Everything but the barn had burned to the ground. His hundred-acre wood was now nothing but ash and char. The sun rose, swollen and red as a warning, over the eastern ridge.

As Patty had said, the larder was mostly intact. In another stroke of luck, though the barn roof had caved in on one side thanks to a fallen tree, the walls still stood. So they had shelter.

It took them three full days to extract the supplies. Bear insisted on doing it right, pulling out the debris and shoring up the cellar infrastructure as they went. He had been a mine worker in his college days, before he got his engineering degree.

Patty paced across the ridge with the crook of her rifle in her arm, watching the horizons, while Bear organized his tools, built the supporting structures, and directed the children to carry the timber and debris out of the way.

By the first evening they had extracted enough rations for a decent meal. They camped out in the shell of the barn, exhausted. A soft rain started and the temperature dropped sharply. They huddled, shivering, under the portions that had a roof. Still, Bear was grateful for the rain. He persuaded Patty that it would be safe to have a fire in a barrel for cooking, light, and warmth.

"No one will see the flames behind these walls," he said. "And with all the fires right now, the smoke means nothing."

"A fire would be nice," she replied, and sent the children to the unburned areas below to gather firewood.

By the end of the second day they had most of the supplies out of the cellar. He found the gun safe. The children cheered when he brought out his Colt and shotgun, and all the boxes of ammo. He felt better for having his Colt—not least because of what the children had told him the night before.

There were twenty-three, including Patty. Bear set about trying to learn all their names. He kept asking over dinner that first night, and they kept telling him, but their names rolled off his old brain. They were all so dirty and bony and so quicksilver fast he couldn't tell them apart. For now, he settled for remembering Tommy (Patty called him Tomás, but he was of Asian ancestry and told Bear his name was Tommy Chang) and Vanessa (a freckled girl of Northern European ancestry, with curly red hair and a lisp, who didn't know her last name). They were the next oldest after Patty. Tommy didn't know how old he was but thought he might be thirteen. Vanessa said she was twelve. They told her that Patty had rescued them from a work camp down in Denver, two months before.

"There's a man chasing us," Tommy said. "The man who ran the camp in Denver. The colonel, they called him."

"That's why she's so worried," Vanessa added in a whisper, glancing over her shoulder at Patty, who was pacing at the edge of the camp. "She's scared he's going to catch us."

Bear laid a hand on the butt of his shotgun and wondered how real the danger was.

The first and second days they worked till there was no more light. But when the sun was low in the sky on the third day, Patty called a halt to the preparations and clapped her hands. "Time for school!"

*School?*

Patty chose a slope facing the sun. The children jostled each other as they sat down in a rough semicircle on the hillside. She used a stick to draw letters, pronounce them, and had the children repeat the work with a stick at their own feet. Then she spelled some simple words. After this she drew numbers and tried to teach the older ones how to add.

She walked around checking their work: encouraging, cajoling, and scolding. She had a hard time keeping their attention, though. The older kids spent most of their time taking turns with the infant, who whimpered incessantly, or chasing toddlers and keeping them from putting things in their mouths that they shouldn't. The toddlers ran around, naked from the waist down, giggling, scuffing up the students' work.

Tom and Vanessa paced behind the students while Patty talked, and occasionally gave the rowdier students a whack across the shoulders to make them be quiet. It was Keystone Elementary. Bear rubbed his face, unsure whether to laugh or cry. *Well*, he thought, *points for trying.*

He sat a short ways up the hillside at the class's back; now he stood up and walked over to Tom, who had raised his stick to strike seven-year-old Jonas. The younger boy had not seen Tom coming. He was giggling after kicking dirt over little Hannah's work and she cried and rubbed her eyes with her knuckles. Bear caught the stick and gave Tom a warning head shake. He pressed a finger to his lips, then caught hold of Jonas and lifted him back over to his own spot, as easily as someone else might lift a doll.

"That'll be quite enough of that," he told Jonas. "Do your numbers like your teacher says."

He said it rather mildly, he thought, but with a look that brooked no back talk. The little boy's reaction shocked him: he stared at Bear in sheer terror, sat right down, and started sketching in the dirt with a shaking hand. His sketch came out looking more like a tree than the numeral 9. Urine spread on the ground behind the boy's seat.

Bear understood, and felt sick.

He sat next to Jonas. "It's all right, son," Bear said. "It's all right. I won't hurt you."

The boy leaned away from Bear, trembling like an aspen leaf.

*Nothing I say or do will make this better.* Bear stood up, brushed the dirt off, and went over to Patty to put in a quiet word about what had happened. She gazed at him and gave a nod.

"Class is over," Patty announced. "Now Bear is going to tell a story."

While Bear distracted the other kids with "The Three Little Pigs," Patty led Jonas over to get washed up and changed, before the other children noticed and teased him.


By that third evening he had learned the names of most of the children, but couldn't put them to the right faces with one hundred percent accuracy. (As an engineer, accuracy was very important to him.) They were all so somber. He'd never seen children so silent. To cheer them up he told them the story of "Jack and the Beanstalk," and acted out all the parts. They listened raptly, even the two Patty had told to take the first night shift, standing guard. They went still when he stomped about, acting out the part of the giant: *Fee! Fi! Fo! Fum!* When Jack chopped down the beanstalk and the giant fell to his death, they all cheered.

Later Patty sat beside Bear, next to the fire. She handed him a picture, half burned, of him and Orla. "I found it in the debris."

"Thank you." He rubbed a thumb over it, rubbing the charring off Orla's face. He tucked it into his wallet.

"*Fee, fi, fo, fum.* . ." She wore a smile. "I like the magic beans, and the golden eggs."

"Do you know the story?"

She shook her head. "But my mother used to tell me a different story about a giant. *El Secréto del Gigante.* The giant's secret. Do you know it?"

It was Bear's turn to shake his head.

"This giant too had a magical egg. It held his soul, and so the giant could not be killed. The hero had to find and destroy the egg. There was a maiden, of course, and a happily-ever-after." She pulled her knees to her chest and her gaze grew distant and sad.

To distract her, Bear asked, "Where did you find all these kids?" He gestured at the children now setting down to sleep around them.

She shook her head. "The past doesn't matter. Only the future does."

Bear had to smile. "Okay, so. . . where are you taking them?"

She hesitated for a long time and her eyes glinted in the flames' light as she studied him. "North," she said finally. "As far north as we can go."

She fell silent, but Bear saw how she bunched her blanket between her fists. She was holding onto something big. He sat quiet, watching the flames dance through the holes they had cut in the barrel. If she trusted him enough, she would tell him. Finally she got up and threw another log onto the fire. Then she sat next to him and leaned over her rifle, lowering her voice. He had to strain to hear.

"My parents were part of—how do you say, *una expedicíon*?" she asked.

"An expedition?"

"*Sí.* It was a secret. A group of thinkers. Academics? Is that the word? And others who saw. They gathered all books, all data, *todo el conocimiento*—literature, art, science, and technical books. Like you with your food, only knowledge instead. They gathered from all over the world. They worked for many years, since the twenty-twenties, my father told me. No one knew, not even heads of government. They didn't trust them. Instead they took money from their grants, their salaries. Just little bits, here, there. You understand?" Bear nodded. "They hid it away, combined it, and bought land up there. Up north." She gestured vaguely northward. "They built a secret network. Peer-to-peer, my father told me. *Escondido*—concealed, you call it?

"It happened over so many years. You can't imagine. My grandfather, Papa Chu, was a founder. Thousands of people all over the world collected and stored the knowledge. When the collapse came, they would take their families and start anew. It's on the shores of the Arctic Ocean. It's called Hoku Pa'a. That means the North Star in Hawaiian."

Bear eyed her, a queasy feeling in his belly. *Stuff and nonsense.* More folk tales—fantasies—to keep a child from being afraid to sleep at night. But when all you have is fairy tales, it's a cruel man who steals those from you. So he said nothing.

She read it in his expression anyway, and shrugged. "You can believe me or not. But I know it is there. My mother told me how to find it, before she and my father left for the last time." She tapped her head. "I'm taking the children to Hoku Pa'a."

"How will you cross the border?" he asked. "Canada has guards at all the major roads, and the warlords cover the land in between."

"We will find a way."

The campfire was dying down; only the dullest glow issued from the old cut-down barrel. "Tomorrow we will prepare," she said softly, "The next day we leave. We will head up Highway 93. You must help us get across the border."

Bear had known this moment would come but his heart leapt like a frightened jackrabbit. He had watched them this afternoon: They had rigged harnesses for themselves out of some rope, and had attached them to the flatbed. He shuddered to think of those kids tied to that trailer, straining to pull it along. They'd be easy targets for the warlords, who kept watch in the hills approaching the border. Yet there was no way they could afford to abandon such a cache of food, water, goods, and ammunition.

He said, "It'd be better to hole up somewhere nearby, you know, find a well-defended place to put down roots. It gets hot as blazes in the summer here now, but it's dry enough you can survive it. Not like the Wet-Bulb Die-Offs in the southeast."

She shook her head. "And do what? This food won't last us all through next winter and the land is too dry and rocky for crops. No, Bear. No. We have to go somewhere else, where we can grow food, raise livestock. Where we have a chance to survive and make a better life. We must find Hoku Pa'a. You have to help us."

Bear sighed. "Patty, this is madness. It's over two thousand miles to the Arctic Ocean from here. What are you going to do, *walk* all the way?"

A smile curved her lips. "Why not? I've walked over two thousand miles here from *La Ciudad de México*."

"I don't think you understand. Canada has been inundated with refugees; they have a full deportation policy now. And even they have lost control of their unpopulated territory. They don't have the resources to keep the warlords under control."

"And I don't think *you* understand," she said. "Nothing has stopped us yet and nothing will."

Bear eyed her with deep reluctance.

Truth was, for these kids, the chances were not so good no matter which way you cut it. Sometime soon they'd starve, or be cut down by a warlord's snipers. Or get murdered, thrown into a work camp, or made into sex slaves. Bear and Orla had survived so long because they had kept low—stayed out of sight. That suited him much better than a journey off into the unknown, where you didn't know the terrain or who was patrolling it. Patty might have an unstoppable will, but even she couldn't fend off with her bare hands the bullets and hatchets, that barehanded violence that would befall these kids once they stepped onto the roads.

But Patty was right that there was not much point in staying here. And their chances of making it someplace safe were even worse without him. He knew the area; he was a decent shot and a good hunter. His many years of life experience could come in handy. And Canada was the only nation in this hemisphere whose lands had remained partially arable, and whose cities were mostly still viable. If they could get the kids across the border, maybe someone in authority somewhere would have pity on them. It was their best chance to survive. Edmonton, perhaps, or Calgary.

And if they were going to try for Canada, Highway 93 was better than I-15 or U.S. 287. Refugees who traveled those two roads were not long for the world.

*Anyway,* he thought, *death by Good Samaritanism isn't such a bad way to go.*

"All righty, then," he said, and slapped his thighs. "I'm in."


As they were preparing their bedrolls, Sarah, the girl whose turn it was to care for the baby, came to Patty. She held the infant out. He hung limp in her hands. The little girl said, "He won't wake up."

Patty took the baby in her lap and examined him. Her expression told Bear everything he needed to know. "Thank you, Sarah. Go get ready for bed now."

"Gone?" Bear asked softly.

She nodded, lips thin. "He had diarrhea. Day after day. We tried. Nothing worked." Her eyes glittered in the dim light of the fire and she passed her hands over them. After a silence she said, "The day he was born, it was the day his mother died. I promised her. I said I would take him, that I would protect him. But I knew even then. I knew it would be too much. No food. No water for days, till we got here. And the food was not right for him. I had hope, when we found *la medicina. Pero no le ayudó.*"

She stroked the infant's head, looking at Bear. "If I had cared for him only, and a few others, he might have survived. I hoped the children could do it. . ."

"Sounds like you had to make a tough call," he said.

She nodded and wiped tears away. Then she swaddled the infant's body in a clean blanket and set it on the floor away from the others. She grabbed a shovel but Bear took it. "Let me." Tom and Vanessa jumped up to help, too.

She took it back, and yelled at all of them, "Go to bed! You need your rest," and strode out into the dark.

"Mind the little ones," Bear told them. He grabbed his pickaxe and went outside. The moon had just risen, a pale lopsided knob beyond distant veils of smoke. Patty was nowhere to be seen. He made his way to the grove where he had buried Orla.

"You see?" he told the stone that covered her grave. "You see? This is exactly why I should not have listened to you."

He took out his anger on the unforgiving ground: He pummeled it with his pickaxe, blow after jarring blow. After a while, he noticed Patty standing at the hole. She picked up the shovel and dug out the soil and rocks he had loosened. Neither of them said anything. They worked hard and long, till Bear's back ached and his lungs screamed for mercy. When they finished, the moon was touching the western peaks of the Grand Tetons, and the stars in the east were starting to fade. They returned to the barn trembling with exhaustion, and pumped well water for each other to rinse off the dirt.

Patty finally said, "Thank you."

"No trouble," he mumbled. Damn stubborn woman.


Bear did not wake till well after sunup. Not even the children's noisy morning preparations fully awakened him. Finally Vanessa shook him and called his name. She handed him a cup of bitter black coffee and a handful of dried apples. The barn was empty but for the two of them. The infant's wrapped body was gone.

"Patty says you need to wake up now. It's time to bury Pablo."

He gulped down the tepid coffee and ate the apples. Then he followed Vanessa along the hillside to Orla's grove. Everyone else had gathered there, around the deep hole Bear and Patty had dug. Patty stood at the head of the grave. They all held little handfuls of wildflowers and grasses and twigs. Bear and Vanessa took their places among the mourners. Bear saw that the infant's body had been laid in the hole.

"Pablito," Patty said, "You were very brave." Her voice quavered. "We will always remember you." She threw a flower into the grave and the others followed suit. "I know Pablo is with his mother now," she told the others, and said the Lord's Prayer in Spanish.

"Amen," Bear said, out of courtesy, though the days were long gone when he could take comfort from prayer.


They rested that afternoon, and went to bed early that night. The children were all subdued. For a change they didn't beg him for a story. But Bear sensed that this was not the first death they had seen. They had shown a quiet competence today. They knew how to say goodbye to the dead.


After breakfast the next morning, Patty insisted that everyone take a bath. Bear said, "I thought you were in a hurry." Tom and Vanessa thought it was a waste of water. "We're just going to get dirty again," the younger girl pointed out.

"I don't care!" Patty said. "It's not healthy to be dirty all the time. When we can, we wash. So don't argue." To Bear she pointed out, "We'll have a better chance at the border if we don't look dirty."

The kids lined up and took turns bathing and washing their clothes, using water from Bear's well, and soap and shampoo from Bear's supplies. They ran a bucket brigade and set up a tarp near the well, so the kids could have a little privacy. Bubbles slowly spread from under the tarp, and shrieks, laughter, and splashing sounds issued forth. Patty went last. The relief on her face as she exited, combing her soaked hair with her fingers, spoke louder than a shout. The littlest ones, of course, were already dirty again, and Patty scolded them, and made them clean up again. She made them all brush their teeth, too. Everyone groaned and complained.

"You want all your teeth to fall out? You'll look like this!" She made gumming faces at them with her lips.

Next they checked the kids' wounds and sores, and treated them with Betadine and bandages. It was mostly their feet that needed attention. Bear used his hunting knife to rig sandals from the tires of his old Ford and leather bridle straps from the days they had kept horses. It took them all day. Patty didn't want to lose another day, but when she got a look at the first pair he made, she agreed it was a good tradeoff.

Vanessa, Patty, and Tom helped. Bear taught them how to measure and cut the rubber, how to weave in the leather straps and lace them up. They were all hot and sweaty again by the time they finished, and the kids were scattered about the meadow, running about and admiring their new shoes.

"Time to go," Patty said. Everyone lined up. The fourteen kids who were big enough (the kids who looked to be between six and nine) would pull the tarped load. The eldest four would walk alongside with their weapons. The six littlest ones would ride in the front of the trailer. Of these, four were perhaps four or five years old. Patty put them in charge of the two toddlers. Patty told the elder four, "You mind those babies! If they get hurt and it's your fault, I'll leave you by the roadside!"

They stared at her and sucked their fists. They knew she meant it.

Bear had argued with her over his own role. He had insisted on taking the front position at the harness but she said no; she needed him to keep watch. "You have to trust me, Bear. They are strong! They can do it."

"How are we different than the slavers, then?" he asked.

She gasped in outrage. "Because we *feed* them every day, and teach them their letters, and make sure they bathe. We are trying to save them—not rape them, not make them kill their mothers and fathers, their sisters and brothers!"

She turned away, fists clenched, breathing hard.

"I'm sorry," he said.

She turned back. "Bear, you hurt me very badly with your words. I wish they could have had the years I had and you had, of being a child without so many worries and so much hurt. But those times are gone.

"*Mira.*" She shook her rifle. "We have this. Now a shotgun, thanks to you. And two *pistoles*, and plenty of bullets. That's good, yes? We need all the weapons we can against *los caudillos.*" The warlords. "Now look around and tell me. Besides you, me, Tomás, and Vanessa, who should handle such a weapon?"

He looked across at the children's faces and sighed. *Babies*, he thought. *An army of babies, Orla.*

They set off shortly before sunset, down the rough gravel road of Bear's driveway toward a farm-to-market road that fed onto Highway 93 about a mile and a half to the west.

Everyone pushed, to start out. Once the wheels were rolling, the oldest four took their positions: Bear in front, Patty in the rear, and Tom and Vanessa flanking them.

Privately Bear had thought that Patty's plans were far too ambitious. The children would surely give up and she would have to stop. But he was wrong. The children strained and hurled themselves against the harness, time and again, till he thought his heart would burst with pride and anguish. They pulled the trailer over the bumpy road, up and down the hills, but no one uttered a sound, other than grunts as they struggled over the cracks and potholes in the asphalt. Even the infant and toddlers were silent (perhaps they slept).

They'd reach 93 by twilight. Bear knew the road so well he could walk it with his eyes closed. And it was a good thing: Tonight would be a dark night. The moon, half full, would not be up till well after midnight.

They paused for a rest. Sunlight's last vestiges made a mauve smudge above the western peaks and a night breeze cooled their sweat. Patty gave Tommy Bear's night-vision binoculars and sent him and Vanessa ahead into the hills, to scout for criminals and warlords. Then they got moving again. Bear walked ahead with Jonah and Margaritte, who led the team pulling the wagon. Despite Patty's instructions, he helped haul. It was a clear, cool night, and the starlight gave them just enough light once their eyes had adapted to avoid the worst of the cracks and potholes.

They reached 93, maybe three miles from the border. There they paused for dinner and a rest. The aurora borealis put on quite a show while they ate. Luminous purple and green veils of light rippled across the Milky Way's pale white band of stars. The children gasped and Patty grabbed Bear's arm. "What is that? It's so beautiful." Bear explained about the Earth's magnetic field and how it created these lights. She said, "I've heard of these. But I think also it is a sign. We are very close!"

They got going again. Soon, Tommy and Vanessa emerged from the trees and joined Bear and Patty, out of breath.

"We found bandits," Vanessa said. "Two men." Tommy added, "On the hills above the highway. About a mile north of here."

Bear stood. "I'll take care of it." He handed Patty his shotgun. He stuck his Colt into the belt at his back and his hunting knife into his left boot, and then pulled a bottle of Jack Daniel's Black Label out of the trailer. "Stay here till you hear from me or until you hear gunfire. If you hear weapons, hide the kids and the trailer. Gunfire echoes far among these hills, and lots of unsavory sorts might come around to investigate. Okay?"

"Be careful," she said. "Tomás, you show Bear where."

Bear had to give Tommy credit: He knew how to move quietly. They walked along the hill's shoulder a good long ways, then crept up a slope at an angle. Soon they observed two men squatting on an outcropping that overlooked Highway 93.

Bear recognized them. They were Lona and Gene's sons, Arden and Zach. The Hallorhans had left Rexford ten years ago. Apparently they hadn't gone far. Or at least, the boys hadn't. They were in their twenties now: big strapping men who weren't hurting for a meal. A two-way radio Zach wore spat occasional chatter.

Bear and Tommy listened for a while. Most of their talk was about people they both knew, including a man they called the colonel, and grumbling about their rations and duties. Bear wondered if he was the same as Patty's *el coronel*. He feared it was. They both had automatic weapons and belts heavy with ammo.

Arden said with a heavy sigh, "Man, *nobody's* ever going to come by."

"Yeah, I bet Marco and Jay got I-15 watch. They get all the big hauls."

They started joking about things they had seen and done to refugee convoys that made Bear feel ill. *Enough of this.* He looked at Tommy and pressed a finger to his lips. Tommy nodded. Bear pried the cork out of the whiskey bottle with his teeth. He swished a mouthful of liquor around to foul his breath, and sprinkled more on his clothes. Then he staggered noisily into their campsite. They came half to their feet, then saw his face.

"I know you. . ." Arden said, and Zach said, "It's Bear Jessen."

"Hey, Ardie—hey, Zach," he said, slurring his words a bit. "Thought I heard somebody in the woods out here." He sat down next to them and took a fake gulp of whiskey. "Didn't even know you boys were still around! How are your parents?"

The two young men looked at each other. Zach was the elder brother, and Bear guessed, the tougher. He was gazing at Bear with a puzzled expression that could quickly pivot to suspicion. "I didn't know you were still around these parts."

"Oh, yeah. Hell, yeah. Orla and me, we didn't really have any place to go. Figured we'd stock up and do for ourselves, once everybody left."

At *stock up*, he sensed both young men's attention sharpen.

"Back at your place?" Arden asked.

"Yup. Thass right."

"Orla there now?" Zach asked.

"Yup. Bet she'd make you boys a proper meal. Wanna pay a visit?"

The two young men exchanged a glance. "I'm up for it," Zach said.

"Me, too," Arden said. They stood, and started down toward the road.

Bear said, "Nah, it's quicker to take the trail over the ridge. Come on."

He led them up to the trail, and on the way he pretended to drink. The young men had military-issue flashlights. Bear walked in front and avoided looking at the lights, to keep his night vision. To deaden theirs, he offered them the bottle, and both young men partook heavily. Soon their own steps on the trail grew uncertain and their words grew slurred.

By this point Bear's house stood out against the ridge, a faint black shape in the distance. The house's shape was wrong. He doubted Zach and Arden would notice.

Bear ducked off the trail at a turn and moved behind a boulder. He pulled the knife from his boot and flanked them silently. The flashlight beams bounced around as the two brothers stumbled on, boots scraping against stone. Then they slowed to an uncertain halt.

He thought, *I'm nowhere near as agile as them, and not as strong as I used to be. Need to make this quick.*

"Bear?" they called. "Hey, old man!—Hello!"

"We lost him," Zach said softly. "Probably fell onto his drunk old ass."

"Shit," Arden replied. "He's onto us."

"Shut up, you idiot," Zach said, but apparently decided the same thing. "Listen here, you old fucker! Come out now or I'll cap your ass! Or I'll do your old lady and then cap *her*."

Bear moved up from behind a boulder, pulled Zach backward off his feet, and slit his throat. Sticky, warm fluid washed over his face, neck, and arms. He got a mouthful of blood.

Arden came around the rock and shone the light in Bear's face. "What the—?"

He opened his mouth in a scream of rage and raised his automatic. Then he toppled and fell over his brother's corpse with a hatchet jutting from his upper spine. He twitched. Little Tommy stood behind him, a silhouette against the stars.

Bear suppressed his gorge, looking down at his neighbor's sons. When they were little, they'd climbed Old Lady Pine and picked wild strawberries on the back twenty.

*War makes us all monsters*, he thought, and slapped Tommy's back. "Quick thinking. Let's strip them of their weapons and supplies. We'll get cleaned up in the stream and catch up with the others."


It was all for naught. They crossed the border unharmed but were stopped by the Mounties the next morning, about five miles in. The Canadians were not cruel, but they said little. They confiscated the trailer—all their food and water and medicines. Bear complained and the soldiers only shrugged. They locked them in a windowless warehouse at their border station, along with dozens of other refugees: people of all nationalities, all religions, all races. The world's detritus, tossed up against a nation's borders. Bear tried to doze on the hard concrete. His tailbone ached and the burn on his arm hurt like hell.

They were there for about six days. They were fed, but the cramped and uncomfortable quarters and their own low spirits made time drag. Late one afternoon—or so Bear guessed from the slant of the sun's rays on the wall—he heard noises outside. After a while, the guards brought them out into the sunlight, where a convoy of big military trucks waited. A Canadian officer turned them over to a group of men in a hodgepodge of American uniforms. Patty gripped Bear's arm so tight she nearly broke the skin.

"You know them?" Bear asked.

She nodded. "I recognize that one." She gestured with her chin at the officer who spoke to the Canadians. "He is *el coronel's* number-three man." Her skin had gone pallid. "The man whose camp we escaped in Denver."

She faded back among the others and kept her head down as the first lieutenant walked past. He wore Air Force insignia. The man stopped and looked Bear over.

"Name?" he asked.

"Bear Jessen. Lately of Rexford."

The lieutenant shouted over his shoulder, "Load them up!"

They were hustled toward the trucks. They tried to stay together, but the trucks only held twelve or so. This did not bode well.

Bear towered above the rest. He caught Patty's gaze, and then Tommy's and Vanessa's. Somehow, they all understood what needed to happen—they each gathered the children nearest them, whispering, passing the word. Bear took the youngest six, the five-and-under set. Bear and his kids sat near the back of the open transport, across from a young soldier with a rifle across his knees. Land passed by; Bear recognized the road, and the miles and miles of wind power generators. They were headed over the Grand Tetons, toward Spokane.

Penelope and Paul, the toddler twins, cried inconsolably. Bear pulled them onto his lap and bounced them on his knee making shushing sounds. The other little ones sat looking out at the scenery, to all appearances unafraid.

That night they reached a military base. The sign by the road said FAIRCHILD AIR FORCE BASE. They passed a munitions dump and an enormous hangar, and rows and rows of military barracks. The trucks came to a halt at a roundabout in the middle of the camp. Soldiers unloaded them all from the trucks. Floodlights lit the concrete pad they stood on. They gathered the refugees in a circle. Two officers came out of the nearby barracks. One of them spoke to the lieutenant. Bear knew instantly he was the colonel.

The colonel was a big man, perhaps six-foot-four. He wore a gun at his belt and Air Force insignia. He was no true military man, though: His hair was long and unkempt and he wore a bushy beard.

"We need to resolve some questions," the colonel said. He looked them all over, then walked up to Bear. "I understand that it was your group that had these. . ." He had one of his men spread out on the ground the weapons and supplies Bear and Tommy had taken from Zach and Arden. "I think you must be the leader. I want to know who the members of your group are, and what happened to my two men."

Bear merely looked at him. The colonel pulled out his gun and shot one of the other refugees in the head, a young man Patty's age. Bear cried out. He couldn't help himself. *Not one of ours*, he thought, heart pounding. *Not one of ours*. He felt shame that that mattered.

"What kind of sick bastard are you?"

"I do my duty," the colonel replied. "And I look after my men. Anyone who harms them has to account for it. You people"—he gestured at Bear and the rest of the refugees—"may be useful to me. But only up to a point."

Bear opened his mouth to tell the man exactly where he could stuff his duty. That would no doubt have been the end of him. But Patty stepped out and spoke up.

"He is not the leader," she said. "I am."

Recognition bloomed on the colonel's face.

"Patricia," he said. "Is it really you? Somehow I'm not surprised to find you mixed up with the disappearance of my men. Lieutenant, get her cleaned up and take her to my quarters. I want to question her personally. Take the rest of the refugees to be processed."

Another man strode up, saying "Excuse me, Colonel. Colonel!"

Bear recognized that voice. He turned to stare. His old pastor! Des had aged. He looked as healthy as ever, though; even rotund. He wore his reverend's collar and a cross. The military man watched Des greet Bear. Then Des turned to the colonel. "Colonel O'Neal, I can personally vouch for this man. He was part of my congregation for years. He doesn't belong with them." Des waved a hand at the rest of the refugees. He said more quietly, "He's an engineer."

The colonel gave Bear a penetrating look, then shrugged.

"Very well. If he's of use. . . But I believe he is mixed up with the disappearance of some of my men. I'll want to question him. Meanwhile, I'll hold you responsible for him, Reverend." He waved them away. Bear felt Patty's gaze burning into the back of his neck, as he let himself be led away by his old friend.

"Thank the Lord you are still alive," Des said as he showed him through the darkened camp. "I've wondered about you over the years. Gloria will be so happy to see you. Orla?"

Bear shook his head. "Lost her," he said. "Lung disease. Cancer, we think."

Des looked up at Bear and laid a hand on his arm. "She's with God now."

Bear's molars ground together. But he tried to take the words as Des intended: as comfort.

"Don't worry about the colonel," Des said. "Just keep your head down. You'll do fine."

"Hard for me to do," Bear replied, "keeping my head down." Des seemed to think he was joking, and chuckled. "How did you end up here?"

"Gloria and I never made it to Seattle. Fortunately we found this refuge. We joined Colonel O'Neal's company a long time since, and we have been here doing the Lord's work, helping to comfort the soldiers and succor the refugees."

*Succor?* Was that what they were calling it now?

"Colonel O'Neal is building an army," Des went on. "He is working with others across the U.S. to rebuild and reclaim our country. It's a great endeavor! You must join us. We need you." He showed Bear the barracks, the "soldiers" doing drills, the fuel and military vehicles. Obviously O'Neal had big plans.

"The man doesn't look very military."

"Well. . . technically, he's not." In fact, the remaining few U.S. military battalions had been disbanded twelve years ago. There might be a few companies here and there, in the major cities, but they reported up no chain of command. "But that's going to change soon. He wants to reconstitute the U.S: reunite the entire northern portion of the country."

He went on like this for a while. Bear fell silent. Des eventually seemed to notice. He stopped and turned. "I know we parted on less-than-friendly terms, Bear, but that's all behind us. I hope you know that. It's a sign from God that you are here. I'm so thankful to see you."

Bear said, "Pastor, we were friends once, and I'm grateful for your help just now. But I have no intention of joining Colonel O'Neal in these escapades. I simply want to take my kids and go."

"Kids?" Pastor Des seemed confused. "You and Orla never had kids."

"I mean the kids I came in with. The refugees. I made a promise. I mean to keep it."

Des got a horrified look. "Oh, no, no, no. You have to let that go,

326  WELCOME TO THE GREENHOUSE

Bear. There's nothing you can do for them now. They're destined for a munitions factory in Denver. We need all the hands we can get, to help us prepare for war."

"*What?*"

"This is God's plan! To make America great. We're going to invade Canada."

Now it was Bear's turn to stare, horrified. "Des. . . that's insane."

"I thought so too, at first. But it's a good plan. Let me show you."

He had brought Bear to a giant hangar. The hangar had big radioactivity warning signs on it, and AUTHORIZED PERSONNEL ONLY. A guard stood outside. He glowered at them, but Desmond gave him a stern look and he let them through. Des must be in good with the colonel. Or he had something on him.

Inside the hangar was a blimp—the largest airship Bear had ever seen. It was lit by floodlights. People, ant-size against its flanks, swarmed around working on it. Beneath its belly was a cabin the size of a 757, and numerous missiles. Nuclear weapons.

"It's nearly ready," Des said. "It's one of five military blimps that were built in the thirties and forties. Four are still in good repair. They've been moved to our northern border and are being outfitted for battle. The colonel is coordinating with other military commanders west of the Great Lakes." You mean warlords, Bear thought. "We've uncovered this cache of nuclear warheads, and are going to use our blimp to deliver them to the other airships soon. I'm told they are even getting orders from *Washington*," he said in a hushed voice tinged with awe. Unlikely, Bear thought, unless a tin pot dictator had set up shop in the White House. Which since Washington, D.C., was uninhabitable in the summer, like most of the U.S. south of about forty degrees north latitude, did not make sense.

Des went on, "We're shorthanded. We need engineers who can help keep equipment in repair. Here's a chance for you to show your worth. The colonel will reward you."

Bear stared at his old friend. They stood beneath one of the few lights in the camp that was not burned out. Words wouldn't come. Nuke Canada? The sheer delusional magnitude of the plan overwhelmed thought.

Des misinterpreted his silence. "Impressive, isn't it? Our glory days are ahead."

Bear rubbed his mouth. "I'm a railroad engineer, Des. I know nothing about aeronautics. Never mind airship technology. Or nuclear weapons."

"A machine is a machine. You'll figure it out."

Des took Bear to his place, where Gloria made him a late dinner. They served a meal the likes of which he had not had in years: bread with real butter, roast chicken, yams, and asparagus, with a glass of '82 Merlot.

"Impressive provisions," he remarked. Des beamed. "Yes. The colonel has his connections."

"I'll get the cheesecake," Gloria said, laying her napkin on the chair. She shared a look with Bear that told him a great deal about Des, Gloria, and the choices they had made.

Des swirled his wine in his glass. "Too bad you didn't find us earlier, Bear. Maybe they could have treated Orla's cancer."

Really, he shouldn't have mentioned Orla. "You never much cared for her, did you, though?" Bear asked.

"Aw, Bear. That's water under the bridge."

But something about deciding he was ready to die made all this a lot easier for Bear. The church held no more power over him. And he found he had a lot of things to say. "I seem to recall you hated her for her defiance of the church."

Des's face grew stiff. "It was not for me to judge her. That's God's job."

A knock came at the door. Gloria answered, looking anxious. An enlisted man stood there. "The colonel wants to talk to Mr. Jessen."

Bear shook his head. "You still spin such amazing bullshit out of your own hot air."

Des's lips went thin. He stood and threw his napkin on his chair. "You want to know what I think? God punished your wife for her defiance. It's too late for her. But *you* have a chance to repent. Jesus welcomes you with open arms. Come to me when you are ready."

"I don't think so." Bear stood. *Orla, he shouldn't have implied that, about your cancer being God's punishment.* At the door, he turned. "I'm done with your God and I don't think we have anything more to say to each other."

The airman took Bear to a room at the command barracks, where Colonel O'Neal and his second-in-command waited. Two armed men stood outside the door. They made him sit in the room's only chair.

"Now it's time for you to tell us what happened to my men out on Highway 93," the colonel said.

*What the hell*, Bear thought. "All right. I killed your men myself. I'd do it again if I had the chance. They were about to slaughter a group of innocent children."

They stared at him as if he had grown two heads. The colonel said, "I didn't think we'd have it out of you so quickly."

Bear shrugged. Death by firing squad seemed an okay way to go. Death by torture, not so much.

"They weren't necessarily going to kill them," the colonel said. "We need strong arms and backs for our war effort. Of course I give my troops broad discretion. We have an agreement with the Canadians. We help protect their borders and they give us any refugees who make it across."

"Ironic, that, since you are using those refugees to build ammunition to attack the Canadians."

The colonel looked at him thoughtfully. "Yes." He paced for a moment. The major stood by the door, silent. "Ordinarily I would have you executed, Mr. Jessen. But we are in sore need of engineers. So Major Stedtler and I"—he gestured at the other officer—"have decided to give you a reprieve. If we can count on your cooperation, we will keep the children you traveled with here, and not send them off to the factory."

*Hostages*, Bear thought. "How do I know I can trust you?"

"I'm a man of my word, Mr. Jessen."

*The hell you are.* "What about Patty?"

"No, you can't have Patricia. I have other plans for her."

At that, Bear caught a fleeting shadow in the major's eyes. Disgust? Anger? Or envy?

"I want to see the children now."

The colonel studied Bear. "All right. Fair enough. But I have my limits. For every stunt you pull, one of your kids gets a bullet. Clear?"

"As crystal."

Bear might be old. He might not be as massive as he once was, and his joints in the morning were stiff. But he was still plenty big and plenty strong. And he wasn't afraid of dying anymore. He surged at the colonel and picked him up by the neck. His hand encircled the colonel's neck as easily as a normal-sized adult's hand might encircle a child's. He plucked the gun from the colonel's holster with his other hand. To Bear's joy, it turned out to be his own Colt .45.

The colonel flailed in his grip, pinned with his back against Bear's massive chest. Bear put the colonel between himself and the major and eased his grip on the colonel's throat, just enough to let air through. As he did so, the two armed men burst in and aimed their weapons at him. Colonel O'Neal made wheezing noises but couldn't speak. Bear said, "Drop your guns on the floor. Kick them over to me. Then lie on the floor with your hands on your heads."

The men did so. The major said, "You'll never make it out of here."

"You let me worry about that part," Bear said.

He got the information he needed from the major, and left him trussed up and gagged in the interrogation room, secured to a pipe. Each of the colonel's two guards he left in their own little rooms, also securely tied and gagged. He wasn't a big fan of shooting people out of turn, but couldn't have them alerting the camp. He tied and gagged the colonel, too, and carried him out over his shoulder, like a sack of grain. He crossed the camp in darkness to the building Des had pointed out to him as the colonel's quarters. He knocked several times before Patty's face appeared at the window.

Her eyes widened. She gestured and shouted. He could barely hear her.

"It's locked! I can't get out!" So Bear kicked the door in.

He came inside and dumped the colonel on the carpet. The room was dark other than the light streaming in through the door. Patty gazed at the colonel with contempt. She was wearing a flimsy nightgown. She gave him a good, hard kick in the testicles. Colonel O'Neal curled up with a moan.

"Let me get dressed," she said.

"Hurry."

When she came back in, she was wearing her clothes from before, Orla's jeans and sneakers and a T-shirt, and was tying her long hair into a bun. "What are we going to do with him?" she asked, gesturing at the colonel.

Bear hadn't wanted to kill the colonel. But after seeing Patty in the nightgown, he had changed his mind. He raised his gun but Patty put her hand on the barrel. "No. We may need him." She pulled Bear out of the colonel's earshot. "We can rescue the children and steal a vehicle."

"And I know *exactly* which vehicle to steal," Bear said, thinking of the airship. "Do you know where the kids are?"

"I do. They are in a big building," Patty said. "A room with benches where people watch sports. What do you call it?"

"A gymnasium?" Bear asked.

"Yes. A gymnasium." She pronounced it *hymn-nauseum.*

"All right, then. We're getting out of here. We're headed to Hoku Pa'a."

Amusement glinted in her gaze. "I thought you didn't believe in Hoku Pa'a."

"If it doesn't exist yet, it will when we get there."

She smiled.

The best-guarded place in camp was the hangar with the nuke-encrusted blimp. He glanced at his watch. It was midnight. They needed to be out of here before dawn and there was too much to do before then. He looked at Patty, so fierce a woman, so tiny—barely more than a child herself. He grimaced. *Dammit, Orla; she's given me something to care about.* He handed her an automatic weapon. "Can you rescue the children on your own?"

"I can."

"You sure? It's important, Patty. Don't say yes if you don't mean it."

"I saw only two guards guarding the gymnasium as we passed by, and they were both drunk." She glowered. "You have to trust me, Bear. I know what I am doing."

"All right. I'm going to need time to rig a diversion. It'll take most of the night." He took her to the kitchen, and gestured at Des and Gloria's place. A light shone in their window. "I want you to take the kids *there.*" He pointed. "Hide the kids. Take Desmond—the man— hostage. Tell him you need to talk to his wife. When she comes out, you bring out the kids out. Her name's Gloria. You tell her Bear said they needed a good meal and a decent night's sleep. She'll make sure they are taken care of.

"But you have to watch Des, the pastor. The man. You understand? He's afraid of *him*"—he gestured at O'Neal, who glared at them from the carpeting—"and he'll turn you in or raise the alarm, if he gets a chance. Also, don't let Desmond get Gloria alone, or he will bully her into doing what he wants. Got that?"

"Yes, I understand."

"At six AM, bring the children and meet me near the airship hangar. You can't miss it—it's the giant building at the base of the hills. That way." He pointed out the window, at the black hills that blotted out the starlight to the southeast. "Don't be late."

Two guards were at the munitions shack. They were both asleep when he found them, and stank of booze. He took their flashlights and other equipment, tied them up with electrical cord, and left them a safe distance from the shed. In the munitions shack he found everything he needed. Bear might not know nukes, but as a former railroad man, he knew explosives. He spent the next several hours prepping charges and setting up a radio detonator.

Then Bear went back for O'Neal. The warlord (Bear refused to think of him as true military) had managed to worm his way from the middle of his living room carpet to the kitchen and was on his knees by the kitchen counter. . . presumably trying to get a knife out of the drawer. Bear slung him over his shoulder and headed out toward the blimp hangar. It was almost six AM.

The sky was still dark as pitch. Patty was waiting for him, and so were the rest of the kids. The children swarmed around Bear and greeted him. They were all there, miraculously, in one piece, along with a few other people Bear didn't recognize. "They needed help too," Patty said.

Bear dumped O'Neal on the ground and cut the bonds on his ankles. He ungagged him. O'Neal spat, and gazed at Bear with the requisite fear and loathing.

"Don't much like being on the receiving end, do you, son?" Bear asked.

"There's no way you can escape."

Bear put his Colt under the man's chin, finger on the trigger. "You're only alive because *she*"—he gestured in Patty's direction— "reminded me you might be useful. Mind your manners."

Patty edged over. "What now?" she asked in a low voice.

"Fireworks," Bear said. "Make sure the kids are behind the dumpsters."

Patty did so, and gave him the OK signal. He blew the munitions dump. The response was gratifying. It made a very big boom. Everyone in the entire camp, it seemed like, went running to help put out the fire.

"Follow me," Bear told Patty. "Bring the kids." He carried O'Neal over and set the man down between himself and the soldier standing guard at the hangar door.

"Don't make me hurt you, son," Bear said. The soldier stood there for a moment staring first at the gun and then up at Bear. Then he threw down his own weapon and ran.

And so did they all run—Bear and Patty and Vanessa and Tommy, and Nabil and Margaritte and Phyllis and Angelique and Jonah and Katie and Earl and Janette and Frankie and George and Bill and Jess, and Teresa and Mimi and Sandra and Lin—except of course, the three littlest ones, Penelope and Paul and Latoya, who were carried— for the blimp.

O'Neal's second-in-command, Stedtler, stepped out from behind the airship as they neared it. He had with him a handful of large, well-armed men. He gestured at the rafters, where more soldiers crouched, aiming weapons at them. Desmond stood there, too, hands clasped before him and a grim, worried look on his face. Bear realized Des must have found and freed the major.

*Des,* Bear thought, sad. *At least you could have stayed home.*

"I should have shot you when I had the chance," Bear told Stedtler, who gave him a gallows grin. Bear looked around for Patty. She and the children had all moved to a spot between the containers and the airship cabin, mostly out of range of snipers. Bear put his weapon against the joint of O'Neal's jaw. "Tell your men to put down their weapons."

Stedtler stared hard at O'Neal. "Do it," O'Neal said. Stedtler gestured to his men and they lowered their guns. Bear waved Patty and the children into the airship cabin.

"I want all the weapons on the floor," Bear said. None complied. By now the last of the refugees were scrambling up the ramp. Bear did a quick calculation, and started edging toward the ramp himself. The soldiers began raising their weapons' points again. Bear stopped moving. He felt the ramp's rim against his right heel.

O'Neal tried to look over his shoulder at Bear. "We can't let you take our nukes."

"Nobody needs nukes," Bear replied. He kept his grip around O'Neal's chest as firmly as he could, but it had been a long night without sleep, and weariness was creeping in around the edges.

"Give up this foolishness," Des said. "Be a patriot, Bear. Let go of the colonel and I can guarantee you no one will be hurt."

Bear gave his old friend an incredulous look. Did he really believe that? "The U.S. is *gone*, Des. Long gone. These men are nothing but bullies and warlords, who use fairy tales to get people to listen to their ravings. The last thing our Canuck neighbors need is crazy people like O'Neal dropping nuclear weapons on their heads."

O'Neal gave a sudden lurch while Bear was talking and managed to break Bear's grip. The two men wrestled for Bear's Colt. Bear tripped on the edge of the ramp and went down on his tailbone. O'Neal pointed the gun at him, but a shot struck him in the forehead and he fell backward, looking surprised. Bear's Colt skittered across the hangar floor. Bear bade it goodbye. Bullets started to fly—he scrambled up the ramp with hands and feet.

Patty dragged him into the blimp and hit the switch to close the cabin door. He lay down. "You shot the colonel, didn't you?" he asked. "Good work."

She was pressing her hands against his diaphragm. Blood was leaking out of him from somewhere and he realized he was going into shock. "He's been hit," Patty said to someone Bear couldn't see, as she faded away.

*Damn shame,* Bear thought. *Just when I'd about decided to live.*

Orla came to him in a dream. There was nothing consequential— nothing he remembered later. Just that she was standing with him, smiling. Somehow their love outlived her, and he thought it might even outlive him as well, as something he passed along to Patty and the little ones. It pleased him to think so, anyway.

He woke up in the airship infirmary. A woman there identified herself as Dr. Maribeth Zedrosky. "You missed a bit of excitement," she said, fiddling with his bandages.

"How long have I been out?"

"Four days, just about." He gaped. It didn't seem possible.

"How do you feel?"

He felt like a crap sandwich with a side of crap. "I'll live." He sat up with a grunt. His midriff and neck were swathed in bandages, and his calf was in a cast.

"What happened?"

"You were shot. Three times. We had to operate to remove a bullet in your lung. Another struck your ankle, fracturing it, and a third one grazed your carotid. Luckily for you, we are well stocked with medical supplies. This airship was designed to be a field hospital, among other things."

"No. I mean, what happened to my friends? Are we safe? Did we escape O'Neal and his crew?"

The woman gave him a big smile. "We are safe."

He blinked. He felt groggy and couldn't think clearly. "How?"

"Once your young friend Patty dragged you inside and sealed the cabin, O'Neal's men tried to scale the blimp and steal the warheads. We blew a hole in the hangar door and floated away on a breeze."

"You're not with them, I take it," he said. The warlords, he meant.

She made a rude noise. "Not by a long shot. They've held five of us here for months. They've been forcing us to work on the airship. When we didn't cooperate, they would start killing the other prisoners. Right now," she said, "we are about three miles up, heading northwest toward the Arctic Ocean. We're nearly there. You should come see."

She helped Bear along the corridor and down a spiral stair to a lounge that hung at the bottom of the airship, below the pilot's bridge.

The lounge was big enough for a whole platoon, Bear thought. Near the rear were the tables and the mess. Some of the children were there. Three adults Bear did not know were teaching some of the older children how to play cards. The little ones were tottering around in makeshift diapers. Near the front sat Patty on the floor, legs curled under her, looking at maps and out at the terrain. She wore a worried look and looked out the floor-to-ceiling windows that lined the front and sides of the lounge.

Beyond the glass, the air was a dark, intense blue strung with piles of cumulus. The early spring sun shone behind them, casting their shadow ahead of them onto a nearby cloud. Far below lay a swatch of brilliant green. Livestock and herds of wild caribou dotted the landscape, and rivers snaked through sodden marshes that had once been tundra. The sun shone over across the Arctic Sea to the north. Islands jutted up from the sea, and their peaks cast long shadows across the choppy water.

When Patty spotted Bear, she gave a happy shriek, bounced over the couch, and hugged him. It sent shooting pains down his side and he groaned.

"I'm so sorry!" she said, and released him.

The children came up too, nine or ten of them. They jumped up and down and all wanted a hug.

"Careful, please—careful!" Patty scolded. She grabbed his hand in a tight grip. "Bear, thank God you are all right. You nearly died! Your lung collapsed and they had to do an emergency surgery—what do you call it?" she asked Dr. Zedrosky, who stood at the stair up to the main deck, arms folded, looking amused. "Oh, never mind. You are here now," she said to Bear. "That is what matters."

He looked over her head toward the others. Tom was there, and Jonah, and perhaps another six of the children. "Vanessa?" he asked. "Where is she? Where are the others?" A spasm of fear gripped him.

"No, no—don't worry. She is fine. They are all fine. No one was hurt. Vanessa is learning to fly the blimp."

"It's not fair!" Tom told Patty. "I have to watch the twins and Latoya," he said, turning to Bear. "I wanted to go first."

Patty said, "Be patient, Tomás. You always nag!"

Bear laid a hand on Tom's shoulder. "You'll have your turn soon."

Patty introduced Bear to the other scientists at the table near the back.

"Thank you," Bear told them. "Thanks for rescuing us."

A man about his age replied, "You're the ones who rescued *us*." They shook hands all around.

"Excuse me," Patty said, "but I need to talk to Bear." She pulled him over to the front of the lounge. "I'm very worried. Come see." She set him up in a cushioned seat with pillows propping up his ankle, and laid a set of maps across his lap. It'd been a long time since he'd seen working smartpaper. He wondered whom O'Neal had stolen it from.

"I've plugged in my parents' coordinates," she said. "But they aren't right. I just don't understand." She pointed out features below and before them on a mountain range. "Those peaks are right, but look out there. Where we are going, it is not supposed to be an island. My parents made me memorize, and this is wrong. What happened?"

"The seas have risen," he told her, "since the maps were made."


At the location where Patty's coordinates said they should land, they began their descent, slow as a soap bubble, into a mountain valley lush and green. Bear should not have been surprised, but he was, when they peered at the ground through their instruments and what appeared to be ground cover was revealed to be camo netting.

Patty could hardly stand still. She paced like a cat in the lounge, and glanced over at him with an expression that said, *See? What did I tell you?*

The "fifteen minutes to touchdown" alert sounded. Patty dropped into a seat next to Bear's. "How has it come to this?" she asked.

She meant, *Why?* She meant, his generation, and all those before them. Why had nothing been done, while there had still been time to act?

Because of men like O'Neal, he wanted to say, and the people who are afraid, and want him to tell them what to do.

There was perhaps truth in that. But it was also a lie.

*We carry the past with us*, he thought. *The living and the dead, and all our past choices.* No one person, no one nation, even, could have saved the planet alone. And we were incapable of working together. We were too greedy—too hungry, too afraid. Too distracted. Orla would have pointed out that there had been numerous extinctions before. *We're just clever monkeys, after all.* Smart mammals, social chimps. Just not. . . quite. . . social enough.

In the end, he just shrugged and gave her a hug.


The entire population of the blimp crowded around the hatch when the airship alighted. The door went up and light streamed in. Bear was among the last to exit. Patty helped him down the ramp but she was wound as taut as a coiled spring.

"Go!" he said grumpily. "I'm not a child." With a grateful glance, she raced ahead.

The ground was spongy and the morning air was chilly. Bear found himself wanting a jacket during daytime, for the first time in, oh, forty years.

A group of people came out of long, low buildings. Patty cried out. A man and woman who resembled her picked her up and hugged her close. They spoke together in rapid-fire Spanish. Patty sobbed. The woman cradled her and made crooning noises. Bear had never seen Patty cry till this moment.

The man came over to Bear. "Jesus de la Montaña."

"Bear Jessen." Bear shook his hand.

"You have returned our daughter to us. The *soldados* attacked and when we came back for her she was gone. We feared the worse. *Gracias. Mil gracias.* How can we ever repay you?"

"Your daughter," Bear replied, "is a remarkable young woman." He looked around. "This is Hoku Pa'a?"

"It is. Welcome. Make yourself at home."

"Is it true what Patty said? You've stored the world's knowledge?"

"We have tried. Much is lost. But not all. And we have ideas for how to remove carbon from the atmosphere, how to restore and rebuild. It will be the work of many lifetimes. Perhaps next time we will do a better job of caring for the world."

"And each other," Bear said.

"*De verdad*," Patty's father said.

Bear watched the Hoku Pa'ans welcome the travelers. They viewed the children with surprise and delight. He watched the little ones spread out across the green valley—running, skipping, shrieking—giddy with joy.

"Fee! Fi! Fo! Fum!" Jonah yelled. "I'm a giant!"

"No you're not," Angelique said. "You're a midget. Bear is the giant!" "Am too a giant!" "Are not!" "Tag, you're it!" Off they went.

Bear thought at Orla, *Oh, fine. You win. There was a reason. I'll carry on for the young ones' sake. But I'm still not ready to let you off the hook for dying first. Damn you.* He glared at his pop-top ring. Then he kissed it. Of course, Orla would laugh and kiss him and call him a fool.

# ACKNOWLEDGMENTS

In assembling this book, almost all of the contributors went out of their way to offer helpful suggestions for other writers and stories. In addition to them, I'd also like to thank the following people: Fernanda Diaz, Joshua Garrett-Davis, John Joseph Adams, Paolo Bacigalupi, Anatoly Belilovsky, Roberto de Sousa Causo, Bradley Denton, Cory Doctorow, Gardner Dozois, David Hartwell, John-Henri Holmberg, Yoshio Kobayashi, Stephen Mazur, Jean-Pierre Moumon, Barbara Norton, Al Reynolds, Kim Stanley Robinson, Lisa Rogers, Alexander Shalganov, Lewis Shiner, Martin Sust, Harry Turtledove, Rachel Van Gelder, Vernor Vinge, and Jim Young. The biggest thanks of all go to John Oakes, without whom this book would not be.

# ABOUT THE CONTRIBUTORS

Brian W. Aldiss, OBE, is the author of classics such as *Hothouse* (a 1962 novel about climate change, also known as *The Long Afternoon of Earth*), *Greybeard*, and *The Malacia Tapestry*. The three novels in his Helliconia trilogy depict an Earthlike planet where seasons last for centuries. He lives in Oxford, England.

Michael Alexander lives in western Oregon and holds degrees in chemistry and pharmacology. He considers the current yelling about climate change this century's equivalent to the reception of Darwinian evolution one hundred fifty years ago, and fully expects the debate to be continuing one hundred fifty years from now, with both sides pointing and yelling while standing up to their waists in warm water.

Gregory Benford is a professor of physics at UC-Irvine who has published more than thirty books, mostly novels. His award-winning novel *Timescape* occurs against a background of climate change, as do many of his short stories. He has published scientific papers on the capture of carbon dioxide and on the methods described in his story here. He has also consulted with several government agencies on responses to the climate change problem and the coming energy crisis.

Jeff Carlson is the international bestselling author of the *Plague Year* trilogy. To date, his work has been translated into fourteen languages.

He is currently at work on a new standalone thriller. Readers can find free fiction, videos, contests, and more on his website at www.jverse. com.

Paul Di Filippo has sold nearly two hundred short stories and several novels in his thirty-year career to date. His story "Life in the Anthropocene," appearing in the anthology *The Mammoth Book of the End of the World*, considers a Greenhouse Earth scenario in which the planet nonetheless manages to support nine billion people.

Alan Dean Foster's first stories appeared in *The Arkham Collector* and *Analog* in the late 1960s. His first novel, *The Tar-Aiym Krang*, was published in 1972. It is still in print. His short fiction has appeared in all the major magazines and numerous anthologies. Six collections of his short form work have been published. Foster has written more than 100 books (science fiction, fantasy, mystery, western, historical, contemporary fiction, and also nonfiction) and his work has been translated into more than fifty languages. He is the author of screenplays, radio plays, talking records, and the story for the first *Star Trek* movie.

Joseph Green worked for thirty-seven years in the American space program, six military and thirty-one civilian. At NASA he specialized in preparing fact sheets, brochures, and other semitechnical publications for the general public, explaining complex scientific and engineering concepts in layman's language. As a part-time freelancer he published five science fiction novels and about seventy-five shorter works. One of his novels, *Star Probe*, examined environmental change from a different perspective, that of fanatics trying to sabotage the American space program in the belief that it wasted resources better devoted to saving Earth. Green has a BA from the University of Alabama, and worked as mill hand, construction worker, and shop supervisor for Boeing before moving to the Kennedy Space Center. He retired as deputy chief of the education office.

George Guthridge has lived in rural Alaska for twenty-eight years, including six in an Eskimo village on a Bering Sea island. He has been nationally honored five times for his work with Alaska Native youth and for having co-created the nation's most successful college preparatory program for Native Americans. He has sold sixty stories, mostly to such magazines as *The Magazine of Fantasy & Science Fiction, Analog,* and *Asimov's,* and has been a Nebula and Hugo Award finalist. In 1997 he and co-author Janet Berliner won the Bram Stoker Award for Best Horror Novel, for *Children of the Dusk.*

Matthew Hughes writes science-fantasy in a Jack Vance mode. His latest novels are: *Hespira: A Tale of Henghis Hapthorn, Template,* and *The Damned Buster).* His short fiction has appeared in *Asimov's, The Magazine of Fantasy & Science Fiction, Postscripts, Storyteller,* and *Interzone.* He has won the Canadian equivalent of the Edgar, and been shortlisted for the Aurora, Nebula, and Derringer Awards. For thirty years, he was a freelance speechwriter for Canadian corporate executives and political leaders. At present, he augments a fiction writer's income by housesitting and has no fixed address. His web page is www.archonate.com.

Chris Lawson is a doctor, teacher, and writer who lives on the Sunshine Coast, Queensland, Australia.

M. J. Locke is an engineer and writer eking out an existence in the urban wilds of New Mexico. Locke's novel *Up Against It* is due out in March 2011. *Up Against It* is the first book of WAVE, a science fiction series about a group of souls struggling to survive on the treacherous frontiers of interplanetary space, the infosphere, and human nature.

Pat MacEwen has a B.S. in marine biology. She is a physical anthropologist who worked as a CSI in California for a decade. Currently, her research is focused on a detailed comparison of the genocidal campaigns carried out in Kosovo and Rwanda. Her short fiction has appeared in *Aeon*, *The Magazine of Fantasy & Science Fiction*, and *Full Spectrum 5*.

Judith Moffett is the author of eleven books in five genres. Her science fiction novels include the *Holy Ground Trilogy*—*The Ragged World* (Vol. 1), *Time, Like an Ever-Rolling Stream* (II), and *The Bird Shaman* (III) —as well as *Pennterra*, a standalone. All four focus on ecological themes, including climate change. She has been honored with the Theodore Sturgeon Award (1987) and the John W. Campbell Award for Best New Writer (1988), and has been nominated for a number of others.

David Prill is the author of the cult novels *The Unnatural, Serial Killer Days*, and *Second Coming Attractions*, and the collection *Dating Secrets of the Dead*. His short fiction has appeared in *The Magazine of Fantasy & Science Fiction*, *Subterranean*, *SCIFICTION*, *Cemetery Dance*, and the original anthologies *Salon Fantastique*, *Poe*, and *Logorrhea: Good Words Make Good Stories*. He lives in a small town in the Minnesota north woods, where he is working on an offbeat baseball novel.

Bruce Sterling is the author of a dozen novels, including *Islands in the Net, Distraction, Zeitgeist, The Difference Engine* (written with William Gibson), and most recently, *The Caryatids*. His 1996 novel *Heavy Weather* depicts stormchasers in the American Midwest in a future where global warming has made tornadoes more active. Bruce Sterling writes frequently for *Wired* and for many online publications. Originally from Texas, he currently lives in Europe and travels a lot.

Ray Vukcevich's new book is *Boarding Instructions*. His other books are *Meet Me in the Moon Room* and *The Man of Maybe Half-a-Dozen Faces*. He lives Oregon. Read more about him at www.rayvuk.com.

# ADDITIONAL READING

Most of the contributors to this anthology have written novels on this subject, ranging from Brian W. Aldiss's novels of environment and season to Judith Moffett's alien invasion novels to Jeff Carlson's eco-disaster books. For readers interested in more stories about climate change, here's a list of other books that might be of interest. These suggestions are neither comprehensive nor wholly recommended; instead, they are meant to point you in a few directions if you're interested in reading more speculations about climate.

*Always Coming Home* by Ursula K. Le Guin (1985)
*Antarctica* by Kim Stanley Robinson (1997)
*Arctic Drift* by Clive Cussler and Dirk Cussler (2008)
*The Child Garden* by Geoff Ryman (1990)
*Climate of Change* by Piers Anthony (2010)
*The Drought* by J. G. Ballard (1968)
*The Drowned World* by J. G. Ballard (1968)
*The Drylands* by Mary Rosenblum (1993)
*Earth* by David Brin (1990)
*Eruption* by Harry Turtledove (forthcoming 2011)
*Exodus* by Julie Bertagna (2005)

*Far North* by Marcel Theroux (2009)

*The Flood* by Maggie Gee (2005)

*Forty Signs of Rain* (2004), *Fifty Degrees Below* (2005), and *Sixty Days and Counting* (2007) by Kim Stanley Robinson

*Future Primitive: The New Ecotopias* edited by Kim Stanley Robinson (1994)

*The Great Bay: Chronicles of the Collapse* by Dale Pendell (2010)

*Greenhouse Summer* by Norman Spinrad (1999)

*Greensword by Donald J. Bingle (2009)*

*Greenwar* by Steven Gould and Laura J. Mixon (1997)

*The Ice People* by Maggie Gee (2005)

*In Flight Entertainment* by Helen Simpson (2010)

*Mother of Storms* by John Barnes (1994)

*The Other Side of the Island* by Allegra Goodman (2008)

*Oryx and Crake* by Margaret Atwood (2004)

*Primitive* by Mark Nykanen (2009)

*Pump Six and Other Stories* by Paolo Bacigalupi (2008)

*The Road to Corlay* by Richard Cowper (1978)

*River of Gods* by Ian McDonald (2004)

*The Sea and Summer* (aka *The Drowning Towers*) by George Turner (1987)

*The Snow* by Adam Roberts (2004)

*Solar* by Ian McEwan (2010)

*State of Fear* by Michael Crichton (2004)

*Sunshine State* by James Miller (2010)

*Ultimatum* by Matthew Glass (2009)

*Water Rites* by Mary Rosenblum (2007)

*The Windup Girl* by Paolo Bacigalupi (2009)

*World made by hand by James Howard Kuntsler (2008)*

*The Year of the Flood* by Margaret Atwood (2009)